Ed McBain is one of the most illustrious names in crime fiction. In 1998, he was the first non-British author to be awarded the Crime Writers' Association/Cartier Diamond Dagger Award and he is also holder of the Mystery Writers of America's coveted Grand Master Award. His latest novel in Orion paperback is *The Frumious Bandersnatch*, and his latest novel in hardback, *Hark!*, is also available from Orion. Visit his website at www.edmcbain.com.

THE HECKLER

SEE THEM DIE

Ed McBAIN

The city in these pages is imaginary. The people, the places are all fictitious. Only the police routine is based on established investigatory technique.

The Heckler
First published in Great Britain by T. V. Boardman in 1962

See Them Die
First published in Great Britain by T. V. Boardman in 1963

This omnibus edition published in 2008
by Orion Books Ltd
Orion House, 5 Upper St Martin's Lane
London WC2H 9EA

A CIP catalogue record for this book is available from the British Library.

ISBN 978-1-4072-1513-6

Printed and bound in Great Britain by
Clays Ltd, St Ives plc

The Orion Publishing Group's policy is to use papers that are natural, renewable and recyclable products and made from wood grown in sustainable forests. The logging and manufacturing processes are expected to conform to the environmental regulations of the country of origin.

www.orionbooks.co.uk

THE HECKLER

Ed McBAIN

This is for my father-in-law Harry Melnick –
who inspired it

1.

SHE CAME IN like a lady, that April.

The poet may have been right, but there really wasn't a trace of cruelty about her this year. She was a delicate thing who walked into the city with the wide-eyed innocence of a maiden, and you wanted to hold her in your arms because she seemed alone and frightened in this geometric maze of strangers, intimidated by the streets and the buildings, shyly touching you with the pale gray eyes of a lady who'd materialized somehow from the cold marrow of March.

She wandered mist-shrouded through the city, a city that had become suddenly green in exuberant welcome. She wandered alone, reaching into people the way she always does, but not with cruelty. She touched well-springs deep inside, so that people for a little while, sensing her approach, feeling her come close again, turned a soft vulnerable pulsing interior to her, turned it outward to face the harsh angles of the city's streets and buildings, held out tenderness to be touched by tenderness, but only for a little while.

And for that little while, April would linger on the walks of Grover Park, linger like white mist on a mountain meadow, linger on the paths and in the budding trees, spreading a delicate perfume on the air. And along the lake and near the statue of Daniel Webster below Twelfth Street, the cornelian cherry shrubs would burst into early bloom. And further west, uptown, facing Grover Avenue and the building which housed the men of the 87th Precinct, the bright yellow blossoms of forsythias would spread along the park's retaining wall in golden-banked fury while the Japanese quince waited for a warmer spring, waited for April's true and warm and rare and lovely smile.

For Detective Meyer Meyer, April was a Gentile.

Sue him; she was a Gentile. Perhaps for Detective Steve Carella April was a Jewess.

Which is to say that, for both of them, April was a strange and exotic creature, tempting, a bit unreal, warm, seductive, shrouded with mystery. She crossed the avenue from Grover Park with the delicate step of a lady racing across a field in yellow taffeta, and she entered the squadroom in her insinuating perfume and rustling petticoats, and she turned the minds of men to mush.

Steve Carella looked up from the filing cabinets and remembered a time when he was thirteen and experiencing his first kiss. It had been an April night, long, long ago.

Meyer Meyer glanced through the grilled windows at the new leaves in the park across the street and tried to listen patiently to the man who sat in the hard-backed chair alongside his desk, but he lost the battle to spring, and he sat idly wondering how it felt to be seventeen.

The man who sat opposite Meyer Meyer was named Dave Raskin, and he owned a dress business. He also owned about two hundred and ten pounds of flesh which was loosely distributed over a six-foot-two-inch frame garbed at the moment in a pale blue tropical suit. He was a good-looking man in a rough-hewn way, with a high forehead and graying hair which was receding above the temples, a nose with the blunt chopping edge of a machete, an orator's mouth, and a chin which would have been completely at home on a Roman balcony in

2

1933. He was smoking a foul-smelling cigar and blowing the smoke in Meyer's direction. Every now and then Meyer waved his hand in front of his face, clearing the air, but Raskin didn't quite appreciate the subtlety. He kept sucking on the soggy end of his cigar and blowing smoke in Meyer's direction. It was hard to appreciate April and feel like seventeen while swallowing all that smoke and listening to Raskin at the same time.

'So Marcia said to me, you work right in his own precinct, Meyer's,' Raskin said. 'So what are you afraid of? You grew up with his father, he was a boyhood friend of yours, so you should be afraid to go see him? What is he now, a detective? This is to be afraid of?' Raskin shrugged. 'That's what Marcia said to me.'

'I see,' Meyer said, and he waved his hand to clear the air of smoke.

'You want a cigar?' Raskin asked.

'No. No, thank you.'

'Good cigars. My son-in-law sent them to me from Nassau. He took my daughter there on their honeymoon. A good boy. A periodontist. You know what that is?'

'Yes,' Meyer said, and again he waved his hand.

'So it's true what Marcia said. I did grow up with your father, Max, God rest his soul. So why should I be afraid to come here to see his son, Meyer? I was at the *briss*, would you believe it? When you were circumcised, *you*, I was there, *me*. So I should be afraid now to come to you with a little problem, when I knew your father we were kids together? I should be afraid? You sure you don't want a cigar?'

'I'm sure.'

'Very good cigars. My son-in-law sent them to me from Nassau.'

'Thank you, no, Mr Raskin.'

'Dave, Dave. Please. Dave.'

'Dave, what seems to be the trouble? I mean, why *did* you come here? To the squadroom.'

'I got a heckler.'

'What?'

'A heckler.'

'What do you mean?'

'A pest.'

'I don't think I understand.'

'I've been getting phone calls,' Raskin said. 'Two, three times a week. I pick up the phone and a voice asks, "Mr Raskin?" and I say, "Yes?" and the voice yells. *"If you're not out of that loft by April thirtieth, I'm going to kill you!"* And then whoever it is hangs up.'

'Is this a man or a woman?' Meyer asked.

'A man.'

'And that's all he says?'

'That's all he says.'

'What's so important about this loft?'

'Who knows? It's a crumbly little loft on Culver Avenue, it's got rats the size of crocodiles, you should see them. I use it to store dresses there. Also I got some girls there, they do pressing for me.'

'Then you wouldn't say it was a desirable location?'

'Desirable for other rats, maybe. But not so you should call a man and threaten him.'

'I see. Well, do you know anyone who might want you dead?'

'Me? Don't be ridiculous,' Raskin said. 'I'm well liked by everybody.'

'I understand that,' Meyer said, 'but is there perhaps a crank or a nut among any of your friends who might just possibly have the foolish notion that it might be nice to see you dead?'

'Impossible.'

'I see.'

'I'm a respected man. I go to temple every week. I got a good wife and a pretty daughter and a son-in-law he's a periodontist. I got two retail stores here in the city, and I got three stores in farmers' markets out in Pennsylvania, and I got the loft right here in this neighborhood, on Culver Avenue. I'm a respected man, Meyer.'

'Of course,' Meyer said understandingly. 'Well, tell me, Dave, could one of your friends be playing a little joke on you, maybe?'

'A joke? I don't think so. My friends, you should pardon the expression, are all pretty solemn bastards. I'll tell you the truth, Meyer, no attempt to butter you up. When your dear father Max Meyer died, God rest his soul, when your dear father and my dear friend Max Meyer passed away, this world lost a very great funny man. That is the truth, Meyer. This was a hilarious person, always with a laugh on his lips, always with a little joke. This was a very funny man.'

'Yes, oh yes,' Meyer said, and he hoped his lack of enthusiasm did not show. It had been his dear father, that very funny man Max Meyer who – in retaliation for being presented with a change-of-life baby – had decided to name his new son Meyer Meyer, the given name to match the surname. This was very funny indeed, the gasser of all time. When Max announced the name at the *briss* those thirty-seven years ago, perhaps all the guests, including Dave Raskin, had split a gut or two laughing. For Meyer Meyer, who had to grow up with the name, the humor wasn't quite that convulsive. Patiently he carried the name like an albatross. Patiently he suffered the gibes and the jokes, suffered the assaults of people who decided they didn't like his face simply because they didn't like his name. He wore patience as his armor and carried it as his standard. *Omnia Meyer in tres partes divisa est*: Meyer and Meyer and Patience. Add them all

5

together, and you got a Detective 2nd/Grade who worked out of the 87th Squad, a tenacious cop who never let go of anything, who doggedly and patiently worried a case to its conclusion, who used patience the way some men used glibness or good looks.

So the odd name hadn't injured him after all. Oh yes, it hadn't been too pleasant, but he'd survived and he was a good cop and a good man. He had grown to adult size and was apparently unscarred. Unless one chose to make the intellectual observation that Meyer Meyer was completely bald and that the baldness could have been the result of thirty-seven years of sublimation. But who the hell wants to get intellectual in a detective squadroom?

Patiently now, having learned over the years that hating his father wasn't going to change his name, having in fact felt a definite loss when his father died, the loss all sons feel when they are finally presented with the shoes they've wanted to fill for so long, forgetting the malice he had borne, patiently reconstructing a new image of the father as a kind and gentle man, but eliminating all humor from that image, patiently Meyer listened to Raskin tell about the comedian who'd been his father, but he did not believe a word of it.

'So it isn't a man trying to be funny, believe me,' Raskin said. 'If it was that, do you think I'd have come up here? I got nothing better to do with my time, maybe?'

'Then what *do* you think, Dave? That this man is really going to kill you if you don't get out of the loft?'

'Kill me? Who said that?' It seemed to Meyer in that moment that Dave Raskin turned a shade paler. '*Kill* me? *Me?*'

'Didn't he say he was going to kill you?'

'Well yes, but—'

'And didn't you just tell me you didn't think this was a joke?'

'Well yes, but—'

'Then apparently you believe he *is* going to kill you unless you vacate the loft. Otherwise you wouldn't be here. Isn't that correct?'

'No, that's not correct!' Raskin said with some indignation. 'By you, maybe, that is correct, but not by me. By me, it is not correct at all. Dave Raskin didn't come up here he thinks somebody's going to kill him.'

'Then why did you come up, Dave?'

'Because this heckler, this pest, this shmuck who's calling me up two, three times a week, he's scaring the girls who work for me. I got three Puerto Rican girls they do pressing for me in the Culver Avenue loft. So every time this bedbug calls, if I don't happen to be there, he yells at the girls, *"Tell that son of a bitch Raskin I'm going to kill him unless he gets out of that loft!"* Crazy, huh? But he's got the girls scared stiff, they can't do any work!'

'Well, what do you want me to do?' Meyer asked.

'Find out who he is. Get him to stop calling me. He's threatening me, can't you see that?'

'I see it, all right. But I don't think there's enough here to add up to extortion, and I can't— This guy hasn't made any *real* attempts on your life, has he?'

'What are you gonna do?' Raskin asked. 'Wait until he kills me? Is that what? And then you'll make a nice funeral for me?'

'But you said you didn't think he was serious.'

'To kill me, I don't think so. But *suppose*, Meyer. Just suppose. Listen, there are crazy people all over, you know that, don't you?'

'Yes, certainly.'

'So suppose this crazy nut comes after me with a shotgun or a butcher knife or something? I get to be one of those cases in the newspaper where I went to the police and they told me to go home and don't worry.'

'Dave—'

' "Dave, Dave!" Don't "Dave" me. I remember you when you was in diapers. I come here and tell you a man said he's going to kill me. Over and over again, he's said it. So this is attempted murder, no?'

'No, this is not attempted murder.'

'And not extortion, either? Then what is it?'

'Disorderly conduct,' Meyer said. 'He's used offensive, disorderly, threatening, abusive, or insulting language.' Meyer paused and thought for a moment. 'Gee, I don't know, maybe we have got extortion. He *is* trying to get you out of that loft by threatening you.'

'Sure. So go pick him up,' Raskin said.

'Who?' Meyer asked.

'The person who's making the calls.'

'Well, we don't know who he is, do we?'

'That's simple,' Raskin said. 'Just trace the next call.'

'Impossible to do in this city,' Meyer said. 'All our telephone equipment is automatic.'

'So what do we do?'

'I don't know,' Meyer said. 'Does he call at any specific time?'

'So far, all the calls have come in the afternoon, late. Just about closing time, between four and five.'

'Well, look,' Meyer said, 'maybe I'll stop by, this afternoon or tomorrow. To listen in on the calls, if any come. Where's the loft?'

'Twelve thirteen Culver Avenue,' Raskin said. 'You can't miss it. It's right upstairs over the bank.'

In the streets, the kids were yelling 'April Fool!' as the punch line to their first-of-April jokes. And they chased each other into Grover Park the way kids will always chase each other, leaping the stone walls and cavorting along the path and ducking behind trees and bushes.

8

'Watch out, Frankie! There's a tiger on that rock!' and then the shouted 'April Fool!'

And then dashing off again to duck behind another rock or another tree, the punch line old and clichéd by this time, but delighting them nonetheless each time it was shouted.

'Over your head, Johnny! An eagle! *April Fool!*'

Running over the close-cropped grass and then one of the boys ducking into the trees again, and his voice coming from somewhere in the woods, a voice tinged with shock and awe, reaching out for the path.

'Frankie! There's a dead guy in here!'

And this time no one shouted 'April Fool!'

2.

THE GENTLEMAN THEY found in Grover Park had been dressed for the approaching summer. Or perhaps *undressed* for it, depending on how you chose to view the situation. No matter how you chose to view it, he was wearing only a pair of black shoes and a pair of white socks, and that's about as close to being naked as you can come in the streets of any big city. Not that this gentleman was overly worried about arousing the ire of the law. This gentleman was dead.

He had, in fact, if a summary glance at the wounds in his chest meant anything, been killed by a shotgun at fairly close range. He lay on his back under the trees and a small knot of experts in death surrounded the body and made faces indicative of disgust and empathy and boredom and indifference, but mostly of pain. Steve Carella was one of the policemen who looked down at the body of the naked man. Carella's eyes were squinted almost shut even though there was no sunshine under the canopy of the trees. There was a sour look on Carella's face, a look of disapproval and anger laced with discomfort. He looked at the man and he thought *Nobody should die in April*, and he noted automatically the shotgun wounds on the man's chest and, just as automatically, he noticed that there was a single large entrance wound and several zones of small satellite perforations produced by pellets which scattered from the main charge. The large entrance wound told him that the gun had been fired anywhere from one to three yards away from the victim. Up to a yard's distance, the shotgun would have produced a wound with a lot of tattooing, burning, and blackening. And beyond three yards, the shot would have dispersed, and formed constellation-like patterns on the victim's skin. Knowing this, and not knowing much more than this at the moment, Carella's mind made the accusations unconsciously and unemotionally while another part of him looked down at this person who had once been a man and who was now a ludicrously naked, loosely jointed pile of fleshy, angular rubbish – no longer a man; simply something soft and spongy, but not a man. Life had been robbed from this mass of flesh, and now there was nothing but death housed in the skin case. Carella wiped a hand across his mouth even though he was not sweating.

It was cool in the copse of trees where the policemen worked. Flashbulbs popped around the dead man. A powdered chalk line was sprayed onto the ground, outlining the body. The laboratory technicians searched the bushes for footprints. The men stood about in uneasy clusters, discussing the world's heavyweight champion fight, the pennant race, the nice weather they'd had this past week, anything but death which stared up at them from the ground. And then they finished their work, all the work they could do for the time being. They hoisted the corpse onto a stretcher and carried it to the path, and then out of the park and over to the curb where an ambulance was waiting. They slid the corpse into the back of the meat wagon, and took it to General Hospital where the autopsy would be performed. Carella thought for a moment about the stainless-steel autopsy table which was laced with troughs like a carving board's, troughs to catch the blood – the table slightly tilted – and channel it toward the basin at the far end, he thought of that goddam unemotionally sterile stainless-steel table, and he thought of scalpels and he tightened

11

his fists in anger and again he thought *Nobody should die in April*, and he walked out to the police sedan parked at the curb and drove back to the precinct house. He could not find a parking space closer than two blocks away. He parked the car on Grover Avenue and walked back to the building facing the park.

Somehow the mottled stone front of the ancient building seemed to blend with April. The gray assumed a softer tone when juxtaposed to the vibrant blue sky beyond it. The hanging green globes captured something of the blue, and the white numerals '87' on each globe picked up a touch of the clouds that hung fat and lazy in the early spring sky. The similarity ended the moment Carella climbed the low flat steps of the front stoop and passed into the muster room. High-ceilinged, bare except for the muster desk and Sergeant Dave Murchison who sat behind it, the room resembled nothing more than the cheerless, featureless face of an iceberg. Carella nodded to the sergeant and followed the pointing white wooden hand which told him – in case he didn't know after all these years – where to find the DETECTIVE DIVISION. Where to find it was upstairs. He mounted the iron-runged steps, noticing for the first time what a clatter his shoes made against the metal, turned left into the upstairs corridor, passed the two benches flanking the hallway, and was passing the men's lavatory when he almost collided with Miscolo who came out of the room zipping up his fly.

'Hey, you're just the man I want to see,' Miscolo said.

'Uh-oh,' Carella answered.

'Come on, come on, stop making faces. Come into the office a minute, will you?'

The office he referred to was the Clerical Office, labeled with a hand-lettered sign in the corridor, a cubbyhole just outside the slatted, wooden railing which divided

12

the corridor from the detective squadroom. Alf Miscolo was in charge of the Clerical Office, and he ran it with all the hard-fisted, clearheaded mercilessness of an Arabian stablekeeper. His horses, unfortunately, were usually a handful of patrolmen who had pulled twenty-fours, duty as records clerks. But if Miscolo had been given, let us say, a hundred men with whom to run his clerical office, all crime in that fair city would have been eliminated in the space of two days. In conjunction with the police laboratory downtown on High Street, and the Bureau of Criminal Identification, Miscolo's dossier on criminals would have made it absolutely impossible to commit a crime without risking immediate capture and incarceration. Or so Miscolo fantasied.

The Clerical Office, at the moment, was empty. Its green filing cabinets lined the right-hand wall of the room, facing the two desks opposite it. At the far end of the room, a single huge window, covered on the outside with wire mesh and the grime of a decade, was opened to the fragrance of April.

'What a day, hah?' Miscolo said. He wagged his head in appreciation.

'All right, what's on your mind?' Carella said.

'Two things.'

'Shoot.'

'First, May Reardon.'

'What about her?'

'Well, you know, Stevie, Mike Reardon worked here for a long time before he got killed. And I liked Mike. I mean, everybody did. You did, too.'

'I did,' Carella admitted.

'And he left May and two kids. That ain't no picnic, Stevie. So she makes the precinct beds, but what the hell does that give her? Enough to feed two kids? Stevie, this is a tough pull. You got a wife, you got kids. God forbid,

13

suppose something should happen to you, you want Teddy living on what precinct beds get her? Do you?'

'No,' Carella said. 'What do you want?'

'I thought we could all chip in. The guys on the squad, and the patrolmen, too. Just a little something more each week to boost that bed money. What do you say, Stevie?'

'Count me in.'

'Will you talk to the other bulls?'

'Now, listen—'

'I'll talk to the patrolmen. What do you say?'

'I'm a lousy salesman, Miscolo.'

'Aw, this ain't like selling nothing, Stevie. This is giving that little girl a break. Did you ever see that little girl, Stevie? She's so goddam Irish, you want to cry.'

'Why?'

'I don't know. Irish girls make me want to cry.' He shrugged. He was not a handsome man. His nose was massive, and his eyebrows were bushy, and there was a thickness about his neck which created the impression of head sitting directly on shoulders. He was not a hand-some man. And yet, in that moment, as he said what he had to say about Irish girls, as he shrugged boyishly afterwards, there was an enormous appeal to the man. He realized in an instant that Carella was staring at him, and he turned away in embarrassment and said, 'What the hell do I know why? Maybe the first girl I laid was Irish – how do I know?'

'Maybe,' Carella said.

'So, will you talk to the other bulls or not?'

'I'll talk to them,' Carella said.

'Okay. Jesus, to get something done around here, you got to go around pulling teeth.'

'What was the second thing?'

'Huh?'

'The second thing. You said there were two—'

'Yeah, that's right, I did.' Miscolo frowned. 'I can't think of the other thing right now. It'll come to me.'

'That's it, then?'

'Yeah. You just come up from the street?'

Carella nodded.

'How's it look out there?'

'Same as always,' Carella said. He sat for just a moment longer and then waved at Miscolo and went out of the office into the corridor. He pushed through the gate in the railing, threw his Panama at the hat rack, missed, and was heading to pick it up when Bert Kling stooped for it.

'Thanks,' Carella said. He began taking off his jacket as he walked to Meyer's desk.

'What was it?' Meyer asked.

'Looks like a homicide,' Carella answered.

'Man or woman?'

'Man.'

'Who?'

'No identification,' Carella said. 'He got shot at close range with a shotgun, that's my guess. All he was wearing was shoes and socks.' Carella shrugged. 'I better make out a report. I didn't see anybody from Homicide there, Meyer. Suppose they've given up on us?'

'Who knows? They only like to make noise, anyway. They know the stiff officially belongs to whichever precinct is lucky enough to find it.'

'Well, this one belongs to us,' Carella said, wheeling over a typing cart.

'They doing an autopsy?' Meyer asked.

'Yeah.'

'When do you suppose we'll have the report?'

'I don't know. What's today?'

Meyer shrugged. 'Bert! What's today?'

'April first,' Kling said. 'Steve, some dame phoned about—'

'Yeah, but what *day*?' Meyer asked.

'Wednesday,' Kling said. 'Steve, this dame called about an hour ago, something about a dry-cleaning store and a counterfeit bill. You know anything about it?'

'Yeah, I'll call her back later,' Carella said.

'So when do you think we'll have the report?' Meyer asked again.

'Tomorrow, I suppose. Unless the M.E.'s office got an unusually large number of stiffs today.'

Andy Parker, who was sitting by the water cooler with his feet up on the desk, threw down a movie magazine and said, 'You know who I'd like to get in the hay?'

'Anybody,' Carella answered, and he began typing up his report.

'Wise guy,' Parker said. 'I been looking over these movie stars, and there is only one girl in this whole magazine who'd be worth my time.' He turned to Kling who was reading a paper-backed book. 'You know who, Bert?'

'Quiet, I'm trying to read,' Kling said.

'I wish some of you guys would try to *work*,' Meyer said. 'This goddam squadroom is beginning to resemble a country club.'

'I *am* working,' Kling said.

'Yeah, I can see that.'

'These are stories about the deductive method.'

'The what?'

'Of detection. Haven't you ever heard of Sherlock Holmes?'

'Everybody's heard of Sherlock Holmes,' Parker said. 'You want to know which of these broads—'

'I'm reading a very good story,' Kling said. 'You ever read it, Meyer?'

'What's it called?'

' "The Red-headed League," ' Kling said.

'No,' Meyer answered. 'I don't read mysteries. They only make me feel stupid.'

The autopsy report did not arrive at the squadroom until Friday afternoon, April 3. And, as if by black magic, a call from the assistant medical examiner came at the exact moment the Manila envelope bearing the report was placed on Carella's desk.

'Eighty-seventh Squad, Carella,' he said.

'Steve, Paul Blaney.'

'Hello, Paul,' Carella said.

'Did that necropsy report get there yet?'

'I'm not sure. A man with hospital pallor just dumped an envelope on my desk. It may be it. Want to hang on a second?'

'Sure,' Blaney said.

Carella opened the envelope and pulled out the report. 'Yeah, this is it,' he said into the phone.

'Good. I'm calling to apologize. We just had a full house, Steve, and first things came first. Yours was the shotgun murder, wasn't it?'

'Yeah.'

'I hate shotgun wounds,' Blaney said. 'Shotgun wounds really look like gun wounds, have you ever noticed that? Especially when they're fired at close range.'

'Well, a forty-five doesn't leave a very pretty hole, either,' Carella said.

'Or a thirty-eight, for that matter. But there's something more lethal about a shotgun, I don't know. Did you see the size of the hole in your customer?'

'I did,' Carella said.

'It's worse in contact wounds, of course. Jesus, I've

17

seen cases where guys have stuck the barrel of a shotgun into their mouths and then pulled the trigger. Man, that is not nice to look at. Believe me.'

'I believe you.'

'All the goddam explosive force of the gases, you know. In contact wounds.' Blaney paused, and for a moment Carella could visualize the man's violet eyes, eyes which seemed somehow suited to the dispassionate dismemberment of corpses, neuter eyes that performed tasks requiring neuter emotions. 'Well, this wasn't a contact wound, but whoever did the shooting was standing pretty close. You know how a shotgun cartridge works, don't you? I mean, about the wad of coarse felt that holds the powder charge at the base of the cartridge?'

'Yes.'

'Well, the goddam cartridge wad was driven into the track together with the pellets.'

'What track? What do you mean, track?'

'Of the cartridge,' Blaney said. 'The track. The path of the pellets. Into the guy's chest. Into his body. The track.'

'Oh.'

'Yeah,' Blaney said, 'and the goddam felt wad had followed the pellets into the guy's chest. So you can imagine the force of the blast, and how close the killer was standing.'

'Any idea what gauge shotgun was used?'

'You'll have to get that from the lab,' Blaney said. 'I sent over everything I dug out of the guy, and I also sent over the shoes and socks. I'm sorry about being so late on the report, Steve. I'll make it up to you next time.'

'Okay, thanks, Paul.'

'Looks like another nice day, doesn't it?'

'Yeah.'

'Okay, Steve, I won't keep you. So long.'

'So long,' Carella said. He put the phone back into its cradle, and then picked up the report from the Medical Examiner's office. It did not make very pleasant reading.

3.

THREE OF THE men in the poker game were getting slightly p.o.'d. It wasn't so much that they minded losing – the *hell* they didn't mind! – it was simply that losing to the fourth man, the man with the hearing aid, was somehow degrading. Perhaps it was the cheerlessness with which he played. Or perhaps it was the air of inevitability he wore on his handsome features, a look which told them he would ultimately triumph, no matter what skill they brought to the game, no matter how often fortune smiled upon them.

Chuck, the burliest of the four men, looked at his cards sourly and then glanced across the table to where the deaf man sat. The deaf man was wearing gray flannel slacks and a navy-blue blazer over a white dress shirt open at the throat. He looked as if he had just got off a yacht someplace. He looked as if he were waiting for a butler to serve him a goddam Martini. He also looked like a man who was sitting with four cards to a high straight.

The game was five-card stud. Two of the players had dropped out on the third card, leaving only the deaf man and Chuck in the game. Looking across at the deaf man's hand, Chuck saw the three exposed cards: a jack of spades, a queen of clubs and a king of diamonds. He was reasonably certain that the hole card was either a ten or an ace, more probably a ten.

Chuck's reasoning, to himself, seemed sound. He was sitting with a pair of aces and a six of clubs exposed. His hole card was a third ace. His three-of-a-kind had the deaf man's possible straight beat. If the deaf man's hole card was a ten, he was sitting with a four-card straight, both ends of which were open. The chances of filling it seemed pretty slim. If his hole card was the ace, his straight was open on only one end, and the chances of filling it were narrower. Besides, there was always the possibility that Chuck would catch either a full house or four-of-a-kind on that last card. His bet seemed like a safe one.

'Aces bet a hundred,' he said.

'Raise a hundred,' the deaf man answered, and Chuck had his first tremor of anxiety.

'On what?' he asked. 'All I see is three cards to a straight.'

'If you looked more closely, you'd see a winning hand.'

Chuck nodded briefly, not in agreement with the deaf man, but with an inner conviction of his own. 'Raise *you* a hundred,' he said.

'That's fair,' the deaf man said. 'And once again.'

Chuck studied the deaf man's hand once more. Three cards to a straight showing. The fourth card to the straight obviously in the hole. Whether it was open on one end or both, it still needed a fifth card.

'*And* a hundred,' Chuck said.

'Be careful now,' the deaf man advised. 'I'll just call.'

He put his chips into the pot. Chuck dealt the next card. It was the ten of hearts.

'There's your goddam straight,' he said.

He dealt his own card. The four of diamonds.

'Aces still bet,' the deaf man said.

'I check,' Chuck said.

'I'll bet a hundred,' the deaf man said, and Chuck's face fell.

'Yeah,' he answered. 'I'll see you.'

The deaf man turned over his hole card. Sure enough, it was the ace.

'Straight to the ace,' he said. 'I think that beats your three aces.'

'How'd you know I had three aces?' Chuck asked, watching the deaf man pull in his winnings.

'Only from the force of your betting. I don't think you'd have bet so heavily with two pair. So I assumed you already had your third ace.'

'And you raised three aces? On the strength of a *possible* straight?'

'On the strength of percentages, Chuck,' the deaf man said, stacking his chips into a neat pile. 'On the strength of percentages.'

'Some percentages,' Chuck said. 'Luck, that's all. Dumb luck.'

'No, not quite. I was sitting with four cards to a one-ended straight: the jack, queen, king and ace. In order to make my straight, I needed a ten – any ten. And this was the only possible way of improving my hand to beat your three aces. I had to catch that ten. If *not*, if for example I simply paired one of my cards, I couldn't possibly beat you. Am I right? So what were my chances of completing the straight? My chances against making it were nine to one, Chuck.'

'Well, those seem like pretty damn steep odds to me.'

'Do they? Consider the fact that no tens had appeared at any time during the game. Of course, either you – or our friends before they dropped out – could have been holding tens in the hole. But I knew you had an ace in the hole, and I took a chance on our friends.'

'The odds were still too steep. You should have dropped out.'

'But then I'd have lost, wouldn't I? And your own odds against improving your hand were even steeper.'

'How could they be? I had you beat to begin with! I had three aces!'

'Yes, but how could you improve them? In one of two ways. Either by catching a fourth ace or by catching another six to give you a full house. I knew you *couldn't* catch the fourth ace because I was sitting with it in the hole. In any case, the odds on catching it, even if I *hadn't* been holding it, would have been thirty-nine to one. Considerably higher than nine to one, don't you think?'

'What about the possibility of a full house? I could have caught that other six.'

'True, you could have. The odds against it, though, were fourteen and two-thirds to one. Which, again, is higher than the nine to one odds I was bucking. And, weighted against this was the fact that our two friends were both showing sixes when they dropped out. This means there was only one six left in the deck, and it further means that the odds on catching that last six were essentially the same as they'd be for catching the fourth ace – thirty-nine to one. Get it, Chuck? My odds were nine to one. Yours were thirty-nine to one.'

'You're forgetting something, aren't you?'

'I never forget anything,' the deaf man said.

'You're forgetting that *neither* of us could have improved our hands. And if neither of us improved, I'd have won. Three aces beat an incompleted straight.'

'That's true. But it's not something I forgot. It was simply a calculated risk. Remember, Chuck, that your pair of aces didn't turn up until the fourth card had been dealt. If your first two exposed cards had been aces, I'd have dropped out immediately. Up to that point, we were both on equal footing more or less. You had an ace and a six showing on the board. I had an ace in the hole, and a king and queen showing on the board. My hand seemed just about as strong as yours. I suspected you had a pair of aces but, considering my own ace in the hole, I thought you might be bluffing a strong bet on a pair of

23

sixes. And *any* pair I caught would have beat those. I think I played the hand correctly.'

'I think it was luck,' Chuck maintained.

'Perhaps.' The deaf man smiled. 'But *I* won, didn't I?'

'Sure. And since you won, you can come on real strong about how you figured it all out beforehand.'

'But I did, Chuck.'

'You only *say* you did. If you'd have lost, it'd be a different story. You'd have been making excuses all over the lot to explain away your mistakes.'

'Hardly,' the deaf man said. 'I am not a person who admits to mistakes. The work *mistake* isn't even in my vocabulary.'

'No? Then what do you call it?'

'Deviation. Truth is a constant, Chuck. It is only the observation of truth which is a variable. The magnitude of error depends on the difference between the unchanging truth and the faithfulness of the observation. And so error can only be defined as deviation, not mistake.'

'Bullshit,' Chuck said, and the other men around the table laughed.

'Precisely,' the deaf man said, laughing along with them. 'Bullshit. Error is simply the amount of bullshit attached to any true observation. Do you want to deal, Rafe?'

The tall thin man on Chuck's left raised his gold-rimmed spectacles and wiped the tears from his eyes. He took the cards and began shuffling them.

'One thing I've got to say is that this is gonna be the goddammedest caper there ever was.' He shoved the deck at Chuck. 'You want to cut?'

'What's the use?' Chuck said petulantly. 'Run them.'

The man sitting opposite Rafe said, 'What's the game?' He put the question tentatively because he was a newcomer to the group, and not yet too sure of his standing. Nor was he yet too certain as to exactly who his predecessor had been or why he'd been dropped from the quartet. He possessed only one quality which could be considered useful to the group, and he had stopped considering that a quality some ten years ago. This quality was the making of bombs. Bombs, that is. You know, bombs. The old man sitting at the table with the other three had been quite adept at fashioning lethal exploding devices. He had lent his talents at one time to a certain foreign power and had spent a good many years in prison regretting this peccadillo, but his early political affiliations had not been questioned by the deaf man when he'd been hired. The deaf man was content to know he could still put together a bomb if called upon to do so. He was particularly interested in learning that the old man could put together incendiary bombs as well as the exploding garden variety. His versatility seemed to please the deaf man immensely. Pop couldn't have cared less either way. All he knew was that he was being hired to do a job – and as far as he could tell, the only qualification he possessed for that job was his ability to make bombs.

He could not have known, not at this stage of the game, that his second qualification was his age. Pop was sixty-three years old, and that was just young enough, just old enough; that was perfect.

'This is seven-card stud,' Rafe told him. 'Deuces wild.'

'I don't like these bastardized versions of poker,' the deaf man said. 'They throw off the percentages.'

'Good,' Chuck said. 'Maybe we'll stand a chance of winning. You play poker as if you're out to slit your mother's throat.'

'I play poker as if I'm out to win,' the deaf man said. 'Isn't that the right way to play?'

Rafe began laughing again, his blue eyes misting

behind their gold-rimmed eyeglasses. He dealt the cards, said, 'King bets,' and put the deck down on the table.

'Twenty-five,' the old man said hesitantly.

'Call,' Chuck said.

'I'll see you,' Rafe said.

The deaf man studied his cards. He was holding a six in the hole, together with a jack. His exposed card was a five. He glanced around the table quickly, and just as quickly pulled his cards together.

'I fold,' he said.

He sat just a moment longer and then rose suddenly, a tall good-looking man in his late thirties who moved with the economy and grace of a natural athlete. His hair was blond and cut close to his skull. His eyes were a dark blue. They flicked now to the street outside, through the plate-glass window of the store front and the inverted legend:

CHELSEA POPS, INC.

The street side of the store was quiet. An old woman struggled past with a full shopping bag and then moved out of sight. Behind the store, at the back of it, all was chaos. Bulldozers, steam shovels, construction crews swarmed over the vast leveled lot.

'You'd better make this the last hand,' the deaf man said. 'We've got lots of work to do.'

Rafe nodded. Chuck raised the pot, and the old man dropped out.

'Want to come with me a minute?' the deaf man asked him.

'Sure,' he said.

He pushed back his chair and followed the deaf man to the door leading down to the cellar. The cellar was cool and moist. The smell of fresh earth clung to the walls. The deaf man walked to a long table and opened a box there. He pulled out a gray garment and said, 'You'll be wearing this tonight, Pop. While we work. Want to try it on?'

Pop took the garment and fingered it as if he were making a purchase in a men's clothing store. His fingers stopped suddenly, and his eyes widened.

'I can't wear that,' he said.

'Why not?' the deaf man asked.

'I won't put it on. Not me.'

'Why not?'

'There's blood on it,' Pop said.

For a moment, for a brief moment in the still, earth-smelling coolness of the basement, it seemed as if the deaf man would lose his temper, as if he would flare into sudden undisciplined anger at the old man's rebellion. And then he smiled suddenly, radiantly.

'All right,' he said. 'I'll get a new one for you.'

He took the gray garment from the old man and put it back into the box.

4.

A PICTURE OF the unidentified dead man ran in three of the afternoon tabloids on Thursday, April 9. The papers hit the stands at about twelve noon, one of them carrying it on the front page, the others relegating it to page four, but all of them running the shrieking headline DO YOU KNOW THIS MAN? The man in the photo seemed to have his eyes closed, and a police artist had sketched a pair of swimming trunks over his exposed genitalia. If anything, the black shoes and white socks looked even more ludicrous now that they were accompanied by the trunks.

'DO YOU KNOW THIS MAN?' the reader read and then looked at this picture of an old duffer who'd undoubtedly been snapped sleeping at a public beach, one of those fellows whose soles are tender and who wears shoes while traversing the sand, some sort of publicity stunt probably, and then the reader saw the copy under the picture, and the copy under the picture informed one and all that this old duffer was not asleep, that he was deader than a mackerel and that the smear on his chest was not a printer's smudge but a bona fide shotgun wound which has been carelessly left there by a man with urticaria of the trigger finger.

The papers hit the stands at about twelve noon.

At twelve-fifteen, Cliff Savage showed up in the muster room of the 87th Precinct. Spotlessly dressed, a tan Panama shoved onto the back of his head, a white handkerchief peeking from the breast pocket of a brown Dupioni silk suit, Savage sauntered up to the desk and said, 'My name's Savage. I'm a reporter.' He threw the picture of the unidentified dead man onto the desk. 'Who's handling this case?'

Sergeant Dave Murchison looked at the photo, grunted, looked at Savage, grunted again, and then said, 'What did you say your name was?'

'Cliff Savage.'

'And what newspaper are you from?'

Savage sighed and pulled a press card from his wallet. He put the card into the desk top, alongside the newspaper photo of the dead man. Murchison looked at it, grunted, and said, 'Steve Carella's on the case. How come your name sounds familiar, Mac?'

'Beats me,' Savage said. 'I'd like to see Carella. He in?'

'I'll check.'

'Don't bother. I'll just go straight up,' Savage said.

'The hell you will, mister. You just hold your horses. That press card don't give you the run of the station house.' Murchison picked up one of the wires protruding from the switchboard and plugged it in. He waited a moment, and then said, 'Steve, this is Dave downstairs. A guy named Cliff Savage is here, says he's a reporter, wants to— What? Okay.' Murchison pulled out the wire. 'Says you should go drop dead, Mr Savage.'

'He said that?'

'Word for word.'

'What the hell kind of an attitude is that?' Savage wanted to know.

'I gather he don't like you too much, is what I gather,' Murchison said.

'Can you plug in and let me talk to him?'

'Steve wouldn't like that, Mr Savage.'

'Then get me Lieutenant Byrnes.'

'The lieutenant ain't in today.'

'Who's catching up there?'

'Steve.'

Savage frowned, picked up the press card and, without another word, walked out of the muster room. He walked down the low flat steps onto the sidewalk and then he turned right and walked two blocks in the April sunshine to a candy store on Grover Avenue. He made change at the counter, walked to the telephone booth at the rear of the shop, dug a small black address book from his back pocket, and searched for an 87TH PRECINCT listing. There was none. He looked up BYRNES, PETER, and found a number for the precinct, FRederick 7-8024. He put his dime into the slot and dialed it.

'Eighty-seventh Precinct, Sergeant Murchison,' a voice on the other end said.

'You ran a picture of a dead man in the newspaper today,' Savage said.

'Yeah? What about it?'

'I know who he is. I'd like to talk to the detective handling the case.'

'One moment, sir,' Murchison said.

Savage nodded, grinned, and then waited. In a moment, another voice came onto the line.

'Eighty-seventh Squad, Detective Carella.'

'Are you the cop in charge of the case involving the man they found in the park?'

'That's right,' Carella said. 'Who's this, please?'

'Are you the cop who sent the pictures out to the newspapers?'

'That's right. Sir, the desk sergeant tells me—'

'Why didn't you send one to my paper, Carella?'

'Wha—' There was a long pause on the line. 'Is that you, Savage?'

'Yeah, this is me.'

'Didn't you get my message?'

30

'It would be inconvenient for me to drop dead at the moment.'

'Look, Savage, I'm not a polite feuder. I'm not interested in mixing clever talk with you. You almost got my wife killed once, you son of a bitch, and if you ever show your face around here I'll throw you out the window. Does that make it clear?'

'The Commissioner might like to know why every other paper in the city—'

'The hell with you and the Commissioner both! Goodbye, Savage,' Carella said, and he hung up.

Savage held the dead receiver in his hand for just a moment, then he slammed it onto the hook and stormed out of the booth.

The Puerto Rican girl's name was Margarita. She had been in the city for only six months, and she didn't speak English too well. She enjoyed working for Mr Raskin because he was a nice cheerful man who did not shout too much. It was important to Margarita that the person for whom she worked did not shout. Margarita reported for work at nine o'clock each morning. The Culver Avenue loft was only five blocks from her house, and she enjoyed the walk to and from work each day. Once she got to the loft, she went into the bathroom and changed from her street clothes to a smock which she wore while pressing. Since she lived so close to the loft, someone had once suggested to her that she wear the smock to work rather than changing after she got there. But Margarita felt that the smock was not suitable attire for the street. And so every morning she put on a sweater and a skirt and then changed to the smock after she got to the loft. She never wore anything under the smock. She pressed dresses all day long, and it got very hot in that loft and she didn't want the bother of panties and brassiere.

She was a very well-formed girl, Margarita, and as she hefted that steam iron her breasts frolicked beneath the loose smock in time to the accompanying jiggle of her buttocks. Which was another thing she liked about Mr Raskin. Mr Raskin never came up behind her and pinched her. She had worked for another man before him, and he was always pinching her. Mr Raskin was a very cheerful man who kept his hands to himself and who didn't mind the girls telling jokes in Spanish every now and then. So long as they got the work done.

There were two other girls besides Margarita, but Margarita was the unofficial foreman of the group. Each morning, when all the girls had had their second cup of coffee and changed into their smocks and fixed their makeup, Margarita would roll over the dollies with the cartons of dresses which Mr Raskin had bought in wholesale lots, and she would turn them over to the girls who would press out all the wrinkles. Margarita would work right alongside them, that iron flashing over the creased skirts and bodices, those breasts jutting and bouncing. Then she would have a consultation with Mr Raskin about pricing the dresses, and then she and the girls would mark each of the dresses and that evening Mr Raskin would take them to the retail stores or to the farmers' markets, depending on which outlets needed merchandise. It was a very smooth-running operation. Sometimes, when she discussed prices with Mr Raskin, he would try to see into the low front of her dress because he knew she wore nothing underneath, but she didn't mind him looking because he never touched. He was a gentleman, and she liked working for him. As far as Margarita was concerned, David Raskin was the nicest man in the world.

Which is why she couldn't understand the threatening calls.

Why would anyone in the world want to threaten Mr Raskin? And especially over so stupid a thing as a dirty loft? No, Margarita could not understand it, and each time the caller phoned again, she would feel frightened for her boss, and she would say a silent prayer in Spanish.

She was not frightened on the afternoon of Thursday, April 9 when the delivery man entered the loft.

'Anybody here?' he called from the door at the opposite end.

'Jus' a mini',' Margarita said, and she put down her steam iron and then ran the length of the loft to the entrance doorway, forgetting that she was wearing nothing beneath the smock, and puzzled by the goggle-eyed expression on the delivery man's face when she reached him.

The delivery man took a handkerchief from his back pocket and wiped his forehead with it.

'You know something?' he said breathlessly.

Margarita smiled. 'What?'

'You ought to be in burlesque, sister. I mean it. Burlesque is crying for you.'

'What eees thees bul-esk?'

'Oh, sister. Oh, sister.' The delivery man sighed and rolled his eyes. 'Look, where do you want these cartons?' he asked, his eyes swinging back to the low-cut front of the smock. 'I've got about fourteen cartons of stuff downstairs, so tell me where you want it, and it's yours.'

'Oh, I don' know,' Margarita said. 'My boss, he is no' here ri' now.'

'I only want to know where you want it dumped, sister.'

'What ees it, anyways?' Margarita asked.

'Don't know, sister, I only work for the trucking company. Come on, choose a spot. Go down to the other end of the loft again, and then run down this way and choose a spot as you come, okay?'

Margarita giggled. 'Why I got to run for?' she asked, knowing full well what he was referring to. 'You put them inside here, near the door, okay?'

'Okay, sister.' The delivery man winked. 'Sssssss,' he said, as if he were a steam radiator. He wiggled his eyebrows, rolled his eyes and then went downstairs. He came up a few moments later with another man, carrying a heavy carton between them. Together they began setting it down just inside the door. The first man gestured with his eyebrows toward Margarita who was stooping to pick up a hanger. The second man almost crushed his fingers as they put down the carton. It took them an hour and a half, what with the various distractions provided by Margarita, to carry thirteen of the cartons upstairs. They were carrying the fourteenth and final carton into the loft when Dave Raskin arrived.

'So what's all this?' he asked.

'Who are you?' the delivery man said. 'Mr Minsky?' He winked at Raskin. Raskin didn't get the joke, so he didn't wink back. Margarita had gone back to her pressing and was throwing herself into her work with wild abandon. The second delivery man was leaning against one of the cartons and wishing he had a better seat and a box of popcorn.

'Who is Mr Minsky?' Raskin said. 'Who, in fact, are *you*? And what is all these boxes, would you mind telling me?'

'Are you David Raskin?'

'I am he.'

'Darask Frocks, Inc.?'

'Yes?'

'Then these are yours, mister.'

'*What* is mine?'

'Search me. We're only truckers, mister. What does it say on the cartons?'

Raskin studied the bold black lettering on the side of one of the cartons. 'It says "Sandhurst Paper Company, New Bedford, Massachusetts"!' Raskin scratched his head. 'I don't know any Sandhurst Paper Company in New Bedford, Massachusetts. What is this?'

The delivery men were in no hurry to leave. Margarita at the table was pressing up a storm, and it was a delightful storm indeed.

'Why don't you open one of the cartons?' the first man suggested.

The second man nodded in vague abstraction and said, 'Sure, why don't you?'

'Will that be all right?' Raskin asked.

'Sure. It's addressed to you, so open it.'

'Sure,' the second man said.

Raskin began struggling with the carton. The two delivery men sat on the edge of his desk and watched Margarita's monumental bout with the steam iron. Finally, Raskin managed to pry loose two of the staples holding the carton closed. He tore the cardboard flap open, ripped the opening still larger and reached into the carton where he found a horde of smaller boxes resembling shoe boxes. He pulled one of these out, placed it on his desk top, and then lifted the lid.

The box was full of envelopes.

'Envelopes?' Raskin said.

'That's what they are,' the first man said.

'That's what they are, all right,' the second man said.

'Envelopes? But who ordered . . . ?' and Raskin suddenly stopped talking. He pulled one of the envelopes from the box and turned it over so that he could read the printing on the flap. It read:

David Raskin
The Vacant Loft, Inc.
30 April Avenue
Isola

'Is that a new store you're opening?' the first man asked.

'Take these back,' Raskin said. 'I didn't order them.'

'Hey, we can't do that, mister. You already opened—'

'Take them back,' Raskin said, and he pulled the telephone to him.

'Who you calling?' the second man said. 'The manufacturer?'

'No,' Raskin answered. 'The police.'

Teddy Carella was in a robe when her husband came home from work that night. He kissed her as he crossed the threshold of the big monstrous house they lived in, and didn't truly realize she was so attired until they'd gone into the kitchen together. Then, surprised because the house was so still at six-thirty in the evening, surprised that Teddy was wearing high-heeled bedroom slippers with the robe – her *silk* robe, at that – he asked first, 'Where are the children?'

Teddy's hands moved in silent answer. *Asleep.*

'And Fanny?' he asked.

Her fingers moved again. *Thursday.*

'Oh yeah, her day off,' and suddenly it was all very clear to him. He did not acknowledge that he'd tipped to her plans or her preparations. He pretended he did not see the bottle of white wine resting on its side in the refrigerator when she opened the door to take out the melon. He pretended that he didn't notice the exaggeratedly female way in which Teddy moved this evening, or the fact that she was wearing a subtly penetrating

36

perfume, or that she had made up her eyes, startlingly wide and brown in her oval face, but that her lips carried not a trace of lipstick, her lips seemed more than anxious to be kissed – he pretended he noticed none of these things.

He went into the bathroom to wash, and then he took off his holster and gun and put them into the top drawer of their dresser, and then he put on a tee shirt and threw his soiled white shirt into the hamper, and then he came downstairs. Teddy had set the table outdoors on the patio. A cool breeze rustled through the grape arbor, crossed the patio, lifted the skirt of her robe to reveal the long lissome curve of her leg. She did not move to flatten the skirt.

'Guess who I ran into today?' Carella said, and then realized that Teddy's back was to him, and that she could not hear him. He tapped her gently and she turned, her eyes moving instantly to his lips.

'Guess who I ran into today,' he repeated, and her eyes followed each muscular contraction and relaxation of his mouth so that – though she was born a deaf mute – she could almost hear each separate word as it rolled from his tongue. She raised her eyebrows in question. There were times when she used sign language to convey her thoughts to her husband; other times, when there was no real necessity for a formal language between them, when the simple cocking of an eye or nuance of mouth, sometimes a glint, sometimes the rarest of subtle expressions served to tell him what she was thinking. He loved her most during those times, he supposed. Her face was a beautiful thing, oval and pale, with large brown eyes and a full sensuous mouth. Black hair curled wildly about her head, echoing the color of her eyes, setting the theme for the rest of the woman who was Teddy Carella, a theme of savagery which sprang through the blatant curve of her breast and the ripe swelling of hip and thigh and splendid calf, narrow ankles, narrow waist, a woman with the body of a barbarian and the gentle tenderness of a slave. And never was she more lovely than when her face explained something to him, never more lovely than when her eyes 'spoke.' She raised her eyebrows in question now, and fastened her eyes to his mouth again, waiting.

'Cliff Savage,' he said.

She tilted her head to one side, puzzled. She shrugged. Then she shook her head.

'Savage. The reporter. Remember?'

And then she remembered all at once, and the light broke over her face and her hands moved quickly, bursting with questions. *What did he want? My God, how many years has it been? Do you remember what that fool did? We weren't even married then, Steve. Do you remember? We were so young.*

'One at a time, will you?' Carella said. 'He was beefing because I'd sent that I.D. photo to every newspaper but his.' Carella chuckled. 'I thought that'd get a rise out of the bastard. And it did. Man, was he steaming! Do you know something honey? I don't think he even realizes what he did. He doesn't even know he could have got you killed.'

Carella shook his head.

What Savage had done, actually, was run a story in his newspaper several years back, a story which had strongly hinted that a detective named Steve Carella had confided to his fiancée, a girl named Theodora Franklin, some suspicions he had about a series of cop killings. In addition, Savage had also listed Teddy's address in the newspaper, and he could not have fingered her more effectively than if he'd led the killer to her apartment in person. The news story had indeed smoked out the killer. It had also damn near got Teddy killed.

38

Do you remember? she said with her hands again, and an expression of total sadness crossed her face and Carella remembered what she had said to him not a moment ago, *We were so young*, and he wondered what she'd really meant and suddenly he took her into his arms.

She came to him desperately, as if she had been waiting for his arms all day long. She clung to him, and he was not surprised to find her hot tears on the side of his neck.

'Hey, what's the matter?' he said. Weeping, she kept her face buried against the side of his neck so that she could not 'hear' him. He twisted his right hand in her hair and pulled back her head. 'What's the matter?'

She shook her head.

'Tired of your humdrum existence?' he asked.

She did not answer.

'Bored by the four walls?'

Still she would not answer.

'Long for a life of romantic adventure?' Carella paused. 'What's the matter, honey? Look, your eyes are running all over your face, and after you spent so much time making them up.'

Teddy sat bolt upright in his lap, an expression of shocked outrage on her face. Her black brows swooped down. Her right hand darted up in front of his face. Rapidly the fingers spelled out their message.

My eyes!

'Well, honey—'

Then you did notice! And you probably noticed everything else, too! The—

'Honey, what are you getting all—?'

Shut up! Get away from me!

She tried to get off his lap, but his hands slid up under the robe, and though she struggled to free herself, his hands were strong upon her and at last she relaxed in his

39

arms, and his hands roamed beneath the loose gown, touching her belly and her smooth flanks, stroking her gently as he spoke, his lips moving beneath her listening fingers.

'So sometimes you feel like an old matron,' he said. 'Sometimes you roam this big shell of a house in your dirty dungarees and you wipe runny noses all day long and keep cigarette butts out of the twins' mouths, and wonder when the hell your adventuresome husband is coming home. And sometimes you long for it to be the way it used to be, Teddy, before we were married, when every time was like the first time and the last time rolled into one, when my eyes went up like butane every time I saw you, when it was young, Teddy, when it was new and shining and young.'

She stared at her husband in solemn wonder because there were times when he seemed to be such an insensitive lout, times when he seemed to be only the uncouth slob who told dirty jokes in a detective squadroom and who brought all of his grubbiness home with him, times when she felt alone in her silent world without even the comfort of the person who had been to her the one shining spark in her life, and then suddenly – suddenly there he was again, the person she had known all along, her Steve, the person who knew the things she was feeling, who had felt them himself, and who could talk about them until, until . . .

'And you want it to be that way again, honey, that wild crazy young flying way that was for kids, Teddy, but we're not kids, anymore. So you dressed yourself up for me tonight. It's Fanny's day off, so you rushed the kids into their beds, and you put on your black shorty nightgown – I saw it when the wind caught your robe – and your good silk robe and your fancy high-heeled slippers, and you put that shadow all round your eyes, and you left your lips naked and Teddy, Teddy baby, I love you anywhich way you are, in a potato sack, or digging in the back yard, or right after you had the babies and they rolled you in all sweaty and stinking on the maternity table, or taking a bath, or cooking, or swimming, dressed, naked, reading, weeping, baby, baby I love you and it only gets better all the time and I'll be goddammed if I'm going to cater to your silly back-to-seventeen movement and get all excited because you're in a nightgown and high-heeled pumps, especially, especially when I've been planning on *exactly* this all day long, all goddam day long! Take your fingers off my mouth, I want to kiss you.'

He kissed her, and he didn't ask her afterward whether or not there was any of that flying jazz they had known as kids, or whether or not the world went up in neon, and whether or not Mongolian gongs and bugles went off – he didn't ask her. Instead he slipped the robe from her shoulders, lowered it to her waist, kissed the full rich globes of her breasts, felt her trembling beneath his fingers, and carried her to the new grass lining the patio. And then he held her to him naked, and he didn't ask her anything, and she didn't say anything, and whereas neither of them flew and whereas there was no flash of neon and no crashing of gongs or bleating of bugles, he had the distinct impression that the sky was crumbling and that he was about to fall off the edge of the earth. And, from the way she clung to him so desperately, he knew she was experiencing the same odd sensation.

5.

THE SQUADROOM WAS jammed to capacity on that Friday, April 10. Sometimes it just happened that way. There were days when the man who was catching barely had anyone to talk to. Everybody else on the team was out preventing crime or collecting graft or some damn thing. But on that Friday, April 10, that old squadroom was just the most bustling old place on Grover Avenue. Detectives, patrolmen, the lieutenant, the captain, messengers from downtown, citizens making complaints — everybody seemed to be in the room that morning. Telephones rang and typewriters clattered and the place had the air of a thriving, if small, business concern.

At the desk closest to the grilled windows that faced the street, Meyer Meyer was on the telephone talking to Dave Murchison, the desk sergeant.

'That's right, Dave,' he said. 'Sandhurst Paper Company in New Bedford, Massachusetts. What? How the hell do I know where New Bedford is? Right next to Old Bedford and Middle Bedford, I guess. That's the way it usually works, isn't it?' he paused. 'Right. Buzz me when you've got them.' He hung up to find Andy Parker standing alongside the desk.

'There's also,' Parker said, 'East Bedford and West Bedford.'

'And Bedford Center,' Kling put in.

'You guys got nothing to do but clown around?' Meyer asked. 'Come on, look alert. Suppose the Chief of Detectives should walk in here?'

'He can't,' Parker said. 'He's downtown running the

lineup. He wouldn't come visit no grubby squadroom like this. Downtown, they give him a microphone and a bunch of bulls who have to laugh at his crumby jokes every morning.'

'Except Fridays, Saturdays and Sundays,' Kling said. 'Today is Friday.'

'That's right,' Meyer said. 'So you see, he just *might* walk in here and find you with your thumb up your behind.'

'The fact is,' Parker said, 'I only come in here to see if there was any messages for me. Because maybe you didn't notice it, but I'm dressed for a plant, and in exactly' – he shoved back his cuff and looked at his wrist watch – 'in exactly forty-five minutes, I'll be leaving you gentlemen to take up my position in the candy store.'

'What are you supposed—'

'So don't make no cracks about my working or not working. I go on at ten-thirty, and that's that.'

'Yeah, but what are you supposed to be dressed *as*?' Meyer asked.

In truth, the question was not put in jest. For whereas Andy Parker may have felt he'd donned a costume for his candy store plant, the fact was that he looked much the same as he always looked. Which was to say, he looked like a slob. There are people, you know, who always look like slobs. There's simply nothing to be done about it. This tendency toward sloppiness first exhibits itself when the subject is still a child. Dress him for a birthday party and five minutes later he will look as if he'd been run over by a steamroller. Nor will he look that way because he's run through a mud puddle or anything. Oh, no. He will simply look that way because he has within him, inside his beating little heart, the makings of a true slob. It is not good to discourage slobs. They will become slobs anyway.

Andy Parker was a true slob. Five minutes after he'd

43

shaved, he looked as if he needed a shave again. Ten minutes after he'd tucked his shirttail into his trousers, the shirttail was hanging out again. Fifteen minutes after he'd shined his shoes, his shoes were scuffed again. Listen, that was the way he was. Did this necessarily make him a bad cop? Absolutely not. His being a bad cop had nothing whatever to do with his being a slob. He *was* a slob, and he *was* a bad cop – but the two phenomena were not at all related.

In any case, Lieutenant Byrnes had planted Andy Parker in a candy store on North Eleventh with the idea of getting him to smell out the alleged pushers who were peddling their lovely little packets of junk in that spot. Andy Parker was supposed to look like a junkie. It hardly seems necessary to explain, in this communications-enlightened day and age, that a junkie is not a man who buys and sells scrap iron. A junkie is a person who buys junk. Junk is dope. A junkie, in short, is a drug addict – as if you didn't know. Now, Parker had seen a great many junkies throughout his career and it could be assumed that he knew what a junkie looked like. But if the casual observer took his 'costume' as an indication, that observer would be forced to conclude that a junkie looked like Andy Parker. For although Meyer Meyer was studying him quite closely, Andy Parker seemed to be dressed the way he always dressed. Which was like a slob.

'Don't tell me what you're supposed to be,' Meyer said. 'Let me guess.' Meyer wrinkled his brow. 'A floor-walker in a department store. Am I right?'

'That's what he's supposed to be,' Kling said. 'Only, Andy, you forgot a carnation in your lapel.'

'Come on, don't kid me,' Parker said seriously.

'Then what could he be?' Meyer said. 'Just a minute, I've got it! An usher at a fancy wedding!'

'Come on, come on,' Parker said, just as Lieutenant

Byrnes pushed his way through the slatted-rail divider and into the office.

'Mark my words,' he said, 'this precinct is going to have the biggest traffic problem in the city as soon as that damn shopping center is finished. I just drove through there and even the *workmen's* cars are causing a bottleneck. You can imagine what it's going to be like when all those stores are finished.' Byrnes shook his head and said to Parker, 'I thought you were supposed to be in that candy store.'

'Ten-thirty,' Parker said.

'Won't kill you to get there a little early,' Byrnes said.

'I already established that I'm a late sleeper.'

'You established that the minute you began working for this squad,' Byrnes said.

'Huh?'

'I'm telling you, Frick's gonna have to detail six squad cars to that shopping center,' Byrnes said, dismissing Parker's puzzled look. 'Did you see the big sign they've got up, listing all the stores? There's gonna be a bakery, and a movie house, and a supermarket, and a bank, and a delicatessen, and a department store, and—'

'That's why he's the lieutenant around here,' Meyer said. 'Because he's so observant.'

'The hell with you,' Byrnes said, grinning, and he went into his office to the left of the divider. He paused at the door and said, 'Steve in yet?'

'Not yet,' Meyer said.

'Who's catching?'

'I am,' Kling answered.

'Let me know when Steve gets in, will you?'

'Yes, sir.'

The telephone on Meyer's desk rang. He picked up the receiver quickly. 'Eighty-seventh Squad, Meyer. Oh yes, Dave, put it right through.' He covered the mouthpiece

45

and said to Kling, 'My New Bedford call,' and then waited.

'Detective Meyer?' a voice asked.

'Yes?'

'I have your party on the line. One moment, please.'

Meyer waited.

'Go ahead, please,' the operator said.

'Hello?' Meyer said.

A static-filled voice on the other end said, 'Sandhurst Paper Company, good morning.'

'Good morning,' Meyer said. 'This is Detective Meyer of the Eighty-seventh Detective Squad down in—'

'Good morning, Detective Meyer.'

'Good morning, I'm trying to trace an order that was placed for—'

'One moment please, I'll give you our Order Department.'

Meyer waited. In the promised moment, a man's voice came onto the line.

'Order Department, good morning.'

'Good morning, this is Detective Meyer of the Eighty-seventh Squad, in—'

'Good morning, Detective Meyer.'

'Good morning. I wonder if you can help me. A man named David Raskin here in Isola received several cartons of envelopes and stationery from your company, but he did not place an order for this material. I wonder if you could tell me who *did*.'

'What was his name again, sir?'

'David Raskin.'

'And the address?'

'Darask Frocks, Inc., Twelve thirteen Culver Avenue here in the city.'

'And when was the order delivered, sir?'

'Just yesterday.'

46

'One moment, please.'

Meyer waited. While he waited, Steve Carella came into the squadroom. Meyer covered the mouthpiece and said, 'Steve, the loot wants to see you.'

'Right. Did the lab call?'

'Nope.'

'Any luck on the photo so far?'

'Not a peep. Give it time. It only ran yester— Hello?'

'Detective Breyer?' the voice on the phone said.

'Yes?'

'That order *was* placed by Mr Raskin.'

'When was this, please?'

'Ten days ago. It usually takes us a week to ten days to fill an order.'

'Then that would be on April first, is that right?'

'March thirty-first, to be exact, sir.'

'Was it a mail order?'

'No, sir. Mr Raskin called personally.'

'He called and ordered the material, is that right?'

'Yes, sir, he did.'

'What did he sound like?'

'Sir?'

'What kind of a voice did he have?'

'A very nice voice, I think. It's difficult to remember.'

'Is there anything you *do* remember about him?'

'Well, not really. We handle a great many orders each day, you understand, and—'

'I understand. Well, thank you very much for—'

'There *was* one thing.'

'What was that, sir?'

'He asked me to talk a little louder, Mr Raskin did. During the conversation. He said, "Excuse me, but would you talk a little louder? I'm slightly deaf, you know."'

'I see,' Meyer said, shrugging. 'Well, thanks again.'

The telephone on the desk nearest Meyer's rang. Andy

Parker, who was doing nothing but killing time, picked up the receiver.

'Eighty-seventh Squad, Detective Parker,' he said.

'Carella there?' the voice on the other end asked.

'Yeah, just a second. Who's this?'

'Peter Kronig at the lab.'

'Just a second, Kronig.' Parker put down the phone and bellowed, 'Steve, for you!' He looked around the squadroom.

'Where the hell's Carella? He was here a minute ago.'

'He went in to see the loot,' Kling said.

Parker picked up the phone again. 'Kronig, he's in with the lieutenant. You want him to call back, or you want to give it to me?'

'This is just a report on those shoes and socks the mortuary sent over. You got a pencil?'

'Yeah, just a second,' Parker said sourly. He hadn't hoped to become involved in any work this morning before heading for his candy store, and he silently vowed never to pick up a ringing telephone again unless it was absolutely necessary. He sat on the edge of the desk and reached over for a pad and pencil. He wiped one finger across his nose, said, 'Okay, Kronig, shoot,' into the telephone and leaned over the desk with the pencil poised over the pad and the receiver propped against his ear.

'The socks can be had anywhere, Parker. Just a blend of sixty per cent dacron and forty per cent cotton. We could have narrowed it down to four or five trade names, but there didn't seem much sense to doing that. You can pick the damn things up in the five and ten, if you like.'

'Okay,' Parker said. 'That it?' On the pad he wrote simply, 'Socks – No make.'

'No, there's the shoes,' Kronig said. 'We may have run into a bit of luck there, though we can't figure out how it ties with the morgue's description of the body.'

'Let me have it,' Parker said.

'The shoes are simple black shoes, no perforation on the top, quarter or heel. No decorations anywhere. We checked them through and found out they're manufactured by the American T. H. Shoe Company in Pittsburgh. This is a pretty big outfit, Parker, and they put out a huge line of men's shoes and women's play shoes, casual stuff, you know?'

'Yeah,' Parker said, and still he wrote nothing on the pad. 'So what about this particular pair of shoes?'

'Well, this outfit makes shoes for the US Navy. Just a single model. A plain black shoe.'

'Yeah,' Parker said.

'You got it?'

'I got it. This is the shoe, right?'

'Right. So how does that check out against the morgue's description?'

'What do you mean?'

'They said the guy was sixty-five years old! You know any sixty-five-year-old sailors?'

Parker thought for a minute. 'I'll bet there are some sixty-five-year-old admirals,' he said. 'They're sailors, ain't they?'

'I never thought of that,' Kronig said. 'Well, anyway, that's it. They make the shoe for the Navy, and it can only be purchased from Navy ship's services. Eight ninety-five the pair. Think an admiral would wear such a cheap shoe?'

'I don't know any admirals,' Parker said. 'Also, this is Carella's headache, not mine. I'll pass it on to him. Thanks for calling.'

'Don't mention it,' Kronig said, and he hung up.

'Do admirals wear shoes that cost only eight ninety-five?' Parker asked no one.

'*I* wear shoes that cost more than that,' Meyer said, 'and I'm only a cop.'

'I read someplace that J. Edgar Hoover doesn't like cops to be called cops,' Kling said.

'Yeah? I wonder why that is?' Parker scratched his head. 'We're cops, ain't we? If we ain't cops, what are we then?'

Captain Frick pushed his way through the gate in the railing and said, 'Frankie Hernandez here?'

'He's in the john, Captain,' Meyer said. 'You want him?'

'Yeah, yeah,' Frick said. There was a pained and harried expression on his face, as if something dreadful had happened and he didn't quite know how to cope with it. If the truth were known, of course, there weren't very many things that Captain Frick could cope with. He was technically in charge of the entire precinct, although his actual command very rarely extended beyond the uniformed force. In any case, he hardly ever offered any advice to Lieutenant Byrnes who ran the detective squad quite capably and effectively. Frick was not a very bright man, and his approach to police work was perhaps comparable to the approach of an old woman toward a will to be settled. He allowed the actual settling to be handled by those better qualified to handle it, and then he reaped the rewards. And yet, all the while it was being handled for him, he fretted and fussed like a hen sitting on a laggard egg.

He fretted and fussed now while he waited for Frankie Hernandez to come out of the men's room. He would have followed him into the room but Frick firmly believed that police business should be conducted in dignified surroundings. So he paced back and forth just inside the railing, one eye on the closed men's room door, waiting for the appearance of the detective. When

Hernandez did come out of the room, he went to him immediately.

'Frankie, I've got a problem,' he said.

'What is it, Captain Frick?' Hernandez asked. He was drying his hands on his handkerchief. He had, in fact, been heading for the Clerical Office to tell Miscolo there were no more paper towels in the bathroom when Frick intercepted him.

'There's a boy who keeps getting into trouble, a nice kid, but he keeps swiping things from the fruit carts, little things, nothing to get upset about, except he's done it maybe seven, eight times already, he's a Puerto Rican kid, Frankie, and I think you know him, and I think we can save both him and the law a lot of headaches if somebody talks to him right now, which is why I'm coming to you, I'm sure you know the kid, his name is Juan Boridoz, would you talk to him please, Frankie, before he gets himself in trouble? His mother was in here yesterday afternoon and she seems like a nice hardworking lady, and she doesn't deserve a kid who'll wind up in the courts. He's only twelve, Frankie, so we can still catch him. Will you talk to him?'

'Sure, I will,' Hernandez said.

'You know the kid?'

Hernandez smiled. 'No,' he said, 'but I'll find him.' It was a common assumption among the men of the 87th that Frankie Hernandez knew every single person of Spanish or Puerto Rican descent in the precinct territory. He had, it was true, been born and raised in the precinct, and he *did* know a great many of the residents therein. But there was more to the assumption of the other men than a simple recognition of his birthplace. Frankie Hernandez was a sort of liaison between the cops and the Puerto Ricans in the precinct. The other cops came to him when they wanted advice or information. Similarly, the people came to him whenever they needed protection, either from criminal elements or from the law. There were people on both sides of the fence who hated Frankie Hernandez. Some men in the department hated him because he was Puerto Rican and, despite department edicts about the prevalence of brotherhood among the men in blue, these men simply felt a Puerto Rican had no right being a cop and certainly no right being a detective. Some people in the streets hated him because he had flatly refused to square any raps for them, raps ranging from speeding tickets to disorderly conduct, or sometimes assault, and on several occasions burglary. Hernandez wanted no part of it. He let it be known quickly and plainly that, old neighborhood ties be damned, he was a cop and his job was enforcing the law.

For the most part, Frankie Hernandez was a highly respected man. He had come out of the streets in one of the city's hottest delinquency areas, carrying the albatross of 'cultural conflict' about his youthful neck, breaking through the 'language barrier' (only Spanish was spoken in his home when he was a child) and emerging from the squalor of the slums to become a Marine hero during the Second World War, and later a patrolman ironically assigned to the streets which had bred him. He was now a Detective 3rd/Grade. It had been a long hard pull, and the battle still hadn't been won – not for Frankie Hernandez, it hadn't. Frankie Hernandez, you see, was fighting for a cause. Frankie Hernandez was trying to prove to the world at large that the Puerto Rican guy could also be the *good* guy.

'So will you talk to him, Frankie?' Frick asked again.

'Sure I will. This afternoon some time. Okay?'

Frick's mouth widened into a grateful smile. 'Thanks, Frankie,' he said, and he clapped him on the shoulder and went hurrying off down the corridor to his office downstairs. Hernandez opened the door to the Clerical Office and said, 'Miscolo, we're out of towels in the bathroom.'

'Okay, I'll get some,' Miscolo said, without looking up from his typing. Then, as an afterthought, he wheeled from the machine and said, 'Hey, Frankie, did Steve mention about May Reardon.'

'Yeah.'

'You in?'

'I'm in.'

'Good, good. I'll get a fresh roll of towels later.'

Hernandez went into the squadroom. He was just about to sit at his desk when the telephone rang. He sighed and picked it up.

Behind the closed door marked LT. PETER BYRNES, Steve Carella watched his superior officer and wished this were not quite as painful for Byrnes as it seemed to be. The lieutenant clearly had no stomach for what he was doing or saying, and his reluctance to carry out an obviously unpleasant task showed in his face and in the set of his body and also in the clenching and unclenching of his hands.

'Look,' Byrnes said, 'don't you think I hate that son of a bitch as much as you do?'

'I know, Peter,' Carella said. 'I'll do whatever—'

'You think I enjoyed that call I got from Detective Lieutenant Abernathy yesterday afternoon? Right after you left, Steve, the phone buzzes and it's a patrolman in the Public Relations Office downtown on High Street, and he asks me to hold on a moment for a call from Lieutenant Abernathy. So Abernathy gets on the phone and he wants to know if a man named Steve Carella works for me, and did I know that this man had sent out photos to all the newspapers except one and that if the police department was to expect co-operation from the press in the future, it would have to show equal consideration to *all* of the city's newspapers. So he demanded that I give this Carella a reprimand and that a copy of the photo go out to Cliff Savage's paper immediately, together with a note from Carella apologizing for his oversight. Abernathy wants to see a copy of the note, Steve.'

'Okay,' Carella said.

'You know I hate that son of a bitch Savage.'

'I know,' Carella said. 'I should have sent him the picture. Kid stuff never gets anybody anyplace.'

'You sore at me?'

'What the hell for? The order came from upstairs, didn't it?'

'Yeah.' Byrnes shook his bullet-shaped head and pulled a sour face. 'Just write a little note, Steve. Sorry I overlooked your paper, something like that. The day we have to kiss Savage's ass is the day I turn in my buzzer.'

'Okay,' Carella said. 'I'll get on it right away.'

'Yeah,' Brynes said. 'You get any make on that picture yet?'

'Not yet,' Carella said, and he opened the door. 'Anything else, Pete?'

'No, no, go ahead. Get back to work. Go ahead.'

Carella went out into the squadroom. Hernandez came over to him and said, 'There was a call for you while you were with the loot, Steve.'

'Oh?' Carella said.

'Yeah. Some guy saw the picture of the stiff in the papers. Said he recognized him.'

6.

THE MAN WHO had phoned the 87th to identify the photograph of the stiff was named Christopher Random. He was a man in his early sixties, and he had only four teeth in his mouth, two upper front and two lower front. He had told Detective Hernandez that he could be found in a bar called Journey's End, and it was there indeed that Carella and Hernandez found him at eleven-thirty that morning.

Journey's End may have been just that for a good many of the bar's customers. They were all wearing wrinkled and soiled gray suits. They were all wearing caps. They were all past fifty, and they all had the veined noses and fogged eyes of the habitual drinker.

Christopher Random had that nose and those eyes, and in addition he had only those four teeth, so that he looked like a remarkable specimen of something preserved in alcohol. Carella asked the bartender which of the men in the gray wrinkled suits was Random, and the bartender pointed him out and he and Hernandez went to the end of the bar and Carella flashed the tin at Random, who blinked, nodded and casually threw off the shot of whiskey which rested on the bar before him.

He burped and the fumes damn near killed Carella and Hernandez.

'Mr Random?' Carella said.

'That's me,' Random said. 'Christopher Random, scourge of the Orient.'

'What makes you say that?' Carella asked.

'I beg your pardon? Say what?'

'Scourge of the Orient.'

'Oh.' Random thought for a few moments. 'No reason,' he said, shrugging. 'Just an expression.'

'You called the precinct, sir, to say you knew who that dead man was, is that right?'

'That is right, sir,' Random said. 'What is your name, sir?'

'Carella. And this is Detective Hernandez.'

'Nice to meet you two gentlemen,' Random said. 'Would either of you care for a little refreshment, or are you not allowed to imbibe while wearing the blue?' He paused. 'That's just an expression,' he said.

'We're not allowed to drink on duty,' Carella said.

'That is a shame,' Random said. 'Sir, that is a crying shame. Barkeep, I would like another whiskey, please. Now then, about that photograph?'

'Yes, sir, what about it?' Carella said. 'Who was he?'

'I don't know.'

'But I thought—'

'That is to say, I don't know what his name is. Or, to be more precise, I don't know what his full name is. I do know his first name.'

'And what's that?' Hernandez asked.

'Johnny.'

'But Johnny what, you don't know?'

'That is correct, sir. Johnny what, I do not know. Or even Johnny Who.' Random smiled. 'That's just an expression,' he said. 'Ahh, here's my whiskey now. Drink hearty lads, this stuff here puts hair on your clavicle it does, arghhhhh!' He smacked his lips, set the glass down again and asked, 'Where were we?'

'Johnny.'

'Yes, sir. Johnny.'

'What about him? How do you happen to know him?'

'I met him in a bar, sir.'

56

'Where?'

'On The Stem, I believe.'

'The Stem and where?'

'North Eighteenth?'

'Are you asking us or telling us?' Carella said.

'I don't know the street exactly,' Random said, 'but I do know the name of the bar, it is called, sir, the Two Circles, does that help you?'

'Maybe,' Carella said. 'When did this meeting take place?'

'Let me think,' Random said. His brow wrinkled. He sucked spit in around his four teeth and made horrible noises with his mouth. 'I think better with a bit of refreshment before me,' he said subtly.

'Bartender, another whiskey,' Carella said.

'Why, thank you, sir, that's good of you,' Random said. 'I think I met him a few nights before the beginning of the month. March twenty-ninth or thirtieth, something like that. It was a Saturday night, I remember.'

Carella flipped open his wallet and pulled a small celluloid calendar from one of the compartments. 'Saturday was the twenty-eighth,' he said. 'Was that the date?'

'If it was the last Saturday in March, yes sir.'

'There were no Saturdays in March after that one,' Carella said, smiling.

'Then that, sir, was the date, yes, sir. Ahhh, here's my whiskey now. Drink hearty, lads, this stuff here puts hair on your clavicle it does, arghhhhh!' he smacked his lips, set the glass down again and asked, 'Where were we?'

'Johnny,' Hernandez said. 'Met him in a bar called the Two Circles up on The Stem on Saturday night, March twenty-eighth. Go on.'

'Did you write all that down, sir?' Random asked.

'I did.'

'Remarkable.'

'How old would you say the man was?' Carella asked. 'This fellow Johnny.'

'In his sixties, I would say.'

'In good health, would you say?'

Random shrugged. 'I don't know. I'm not a physician, you understand.'

'I know. But was he coughing or anything? Did he look pale or run-down? Did he have any tics or nervous mannerisms? Did he—'

'He seemed to be in perfectly good health,' Random said, 'as far as I could tell. You understand, I didn't ask him to take off his clothes so I could give him a physical examination, you understand, sir. I am saying only that, on the surface, looking at him with my naked eye, and without the benefit of a medical education, I would say this fellow Johnny was as fit as a fiddle.' Random paused. 'That's just an expression,' he said.

'Okay,' Carella said, 'he told you his first name was Johnny. Did he mention his last name?'

'No, sir, he did not. Sir, with all due respect to the Police Department, any extended conversation makes me exceedingly thirsty. I do wish I could . . .'

'Bartender, another whiskey,' Hernandez said. 'He didn't give you his last name, correct?'

'Correct.'

'What did he say?'

'He said he was on his way to work.'

'Work? What kind of work?'

'He didn't say.'

'But this was the nighttime, wasn't it?'

'That is correct, sir. It was a Saturday night.'

'And he said he was going to work?'

'Yes, sir, that is exactly what he said.'

'But he didn't say what kind of work?'

'No, sir,' Random said. 'Of course, he was wearing the uniform.'

'Uniform?' Carella said.

'Uniform?' Hernandez echoed.

'Was it a sailor's uniform?' Carella asked. 'Was he a sailor, Mr Random?'

'Ahhhh,' Random said, 'here's my whiskey now. Drink hearty, lads, this stuff here puts hair on your clavicle, it does, arghhhhh!' He smacked his lips, set the glass down again and asked, 'Where were we?'

'The uniform. Was it a sailor's uniform?'

'A sailor's uniform? On a man well into his sixties? Now, sirs, that's pretty silly, if you ask me.'

'Well what kind of a uniform was it?'

'It was gray,' Random said.

'Go on.'

'It could have been a postman's uniform,' Random said.

'*Was* it?'

'I don't know. Or a bus driver's?'

'Well, which was it? A postman's or a bus driver's?'

'I don't know. To tell you the truth, I wasn't feeling too well that night, you understand. I was having a little trouble with my eyes, you understand. Focusing, you understand. So all I can remember is that it was a gray uniform, with a uniform cap and all.'

'It wasn't a chauffeur's uniform, was it?'

'No, sir, it was gray. *Gray*. Not black. No, not a chauffeur's uniform.' Random paused. 'But he *was* working for somebody. I remember that. So I guess that would let out the post office, wouldn't it? Unless he was talking about his foreman, that's a possibility, isn't it?'

'He mentioned his employer's name?' Carella asked.

'Well, no, not exactly,' Random said. 'Only indirectly.'

'What did he say?'

'He said he had to get to work or the deaf man would be angry. That's what he said.'

'The who?' Carella asked. 'The *dead* man?'

'No, no, the *deaf* man. Deaf. You know. Hard of hearing. Deaf. Of course, that may have been just an expression.'

'You're sure that's what he said?' Carella asked.

'Yes, sir.'

'Anything else about this deaf man?'

'No, sir.'

'Or about where he was going to work?'

'No, sir. Not a word.'

'You're sure you're remembering this correctly, Mr Random?' Hernandez asked.

'Of course I remember it,' Random said. 'Why shouldn't I?'

'Well, you said you were a little out of focus.'

'Yes, but—'

'What you meant was that you'd had a little too much to drink, isn't that right?' Hernandez asked.

'Well, yes, but—'

'What you meant was that you had a couple of sheets to the wind, isn't that right?' Hernandez asked.

'That's just an expression,' Carella said quickly. '*Were* you kind of loaded, Mr Random?'

'I suppose so,' Random said philosophically.

'But in spite of that, you do remember what happened?'

'I do, sir,' Random said.

'What do you think?' Hernandez asked.

Carella nodded. 'I believe him.'

The man was wearing a chauffeur's uniform. He stood in the doorway of the haberdashery, and he looked around at the fedoras and derbies and caps and Homburgs, and he held his own hat in his hands and stared into the shop, waiting. One of the salesmen spotted him and walked over instantly.

'Yes, sir,' he said. 'May I help you?'

'Mr Lombardo, please?' the chauffeur said.

'Just a moment. He's in the back. I'll get him for you.'

The salesman went into the back of the store and returned a moment later with Mr Lombardo, the owner. Lombardo wore a dark gray suit and a beautiful white shirt with a gray foulard necktie. A cat's-eye ring glistened on his pinky.

'Yes, sir?' he said to the chauffeur. 'May I help you?'

'Mr Lombardo?' the chauffeur said.

'Yes?' Mr Lombardo frowned. Perhaps he already knew what was coming.

'The car's waiting, sir,' the chauffeur said.

'You don't say?'

'Yes, sir.'

'*What* car, may I ask?'

'The car you ordered, sir.' The chauffeur looked puzzled. 'I'm from Carey Cadillac, sir.' He nodded his head, as if that simple statement explained everything.

'Carey Cadillac?' The chauffeur kept nodding. 'The car? It's outside? Waiting?'

He nodded again, studied Lombardo's scowl, and desperately plunged ahead. 'You said twelve noon, sir, and it's twelve noon now. So I'm ready and waiting, sir.' He tried a grin which evaporated the moment he saw Lombardo's scowl deepen. Finally, completely routed, he returned to his original statement, delivering it with cold hauteur. 'The car's waiting, sir.'

'I didn't order any car,' Lombardo said calmly.

'But you did, sir. James Lombardo, Lombardo's haber-dashery, eight thirty-seven—'

61

'I did not order any automobile!' Lombardo said, his voice rising.

'It's that lunatic again, Mr Lombardo,' the salesman said.

'I know it!'

'Call the police, Mr Lombardo,' the salesman advised. 'This has gone too far. Those telephone threats and all these—'

'You're right,' Lombardo said. 'This has gone far enough.' And he started for the telephone.

'Hey, what about the car?' the chauffeur wanted to know.

'I didn't order it,' Lombardo said, dialing. 'Some madman has been trying to get me to vacate my store. This is just another one of his stunts.'

'Well, look—'

'I did not order it!' Lombardo shouted. Into the telephone, he said, 'Operator? Get me the police.'

The chauffeur shrugged, stared at Lombardo for a moment, and then put on his cap and went out of the haberdashery. The black Cadillac was parked at the curb, but he didn't go directly to it. Instead, he went to the plate-glass front of the store next door to the haberdashery. And, longingly, he studied the sapphires and rubies and emeralds and diamonds which were spread on black velvet in the window.

Sighing, he went back to the car and drove away.

THE DEAF MAN and Rafe had been sitting in the ferry-house waiting room for close to a half-hour, watching the people who came and went, watching especially the number of policemen patrolling the docks or hanging around the waiting room, or coming on and off the ferry itself. A huge clock was at one end of the pale green room, and the deaf man looked up at the clock occasionally, and occasionally he studied the ferry schedule in his hands. The inside of the schedule looked like this:

ISOLA TO MAJESTA Daylight Saving Time Schedule symbols should be checked carefully against "REFERENCES" in center of tables.		REFERENCES	MAJESTA TO ISOLA Daylight Saving Time Schedule symbols should be checked carefully against "REFERENCES" in center of tables.	
Lve Isola	Arr Majesta	A—Will run on Saturdays only.	Lve Majesta	Arr Isola
12:15AM	12:45AM	B—Will run on Sundays only.	1:00AM	1:30AM
A12:45	1:15		A 1:45	2:15
1:45	2:15		2:30	3:00
A 2:15	2:45	C—Will run on Saturdays and Sundays only.	A 3:15	3:45
2:45	3:15		B 4:45	5:15
B 3:45	4:15		C 5:00	5:30
C 4:15	4:45	D—Will run on weekdays only.	6:45	7:15
6:05	6:35		8:15	8:45
D 7:30	8:00		D 8:30	9:00
D 8:00	8:30	E—Will run only on May 30, July 4, and September 7.	D 8:45	9:15
9:05	9:35		. 10:00	10:30
11:00	11:30		11:45	12:15PM
12:30PM	1:00PM		1:30PM	2:00
2:15	2:45	Authorized and distributed by the River Harb Ferry Company, not responsible for errors, all times subject to change without notice, all fares ten cents additional if tickets are purchased on boat.	3:00	3:30
4:05	4:35		5:00	5:30
5:45	6:15		D 5:30	6:00
6:05	6:35		6:30	7:00
E 7:15	7:45		8:00	8:30
8:45	9:15		9:30	10:00
9:15	9:45		10:00	10:30
9:45	10:15		10:20	10:50
11:00	11:30		11:35	12:05AM

The deaf man studied the timetable, made a mental note and then walked to the nearest ticket booth.

'Good morning,' he said to the ticket seller in his gentle voice, smiling.

'Morning,' the ticket seller said, not looking up. The ticket seller seemed to be counting something. All ticket sellers always seem to be counting something no matter when you approach their windows. They are either counting money, or new tickets, or cancelled tickets, or stamps, or schedules, or sometimes they are counting their big toes, but they are always counting something, and they are always too busy with what they are counting to look up at you. This one was no exception. The deaf man was smiling his most powerful smile and talking in his most persuasively gentle voice, but the ticket seller went right on counting whatever it was he was counting, and he didn't look up once during the entire conversation.

'Does your ferry carry trucks?' the deaf man asked.

'Depends on how big.'

'Well, I wasn't thinking of a trailer truck,' the deaf man said, gently, his blue eyes twinkling.

'Well, what kind of a truck *were* you thinking of?'

'An ice-cream truck.'

'Ice-cream truck, huh? You mean like Good Humor? Like that?'

'Yes. Not Good Humor, but a truck of that size. That's exactly what I meant.'

'We carry 'em.'

'What was that? I'm sorry, I'm a little deaf.'

'I said we carry 'em. Ice-cream trucks.'

'Do I need a ticket in advance, or can I buy it on the ferry?'

'You buy it on the ferry.'

'Would you mind looking at this ferry schedule, please?' the deaf man said, and he shoved the schedule under the barred window. The ticket seller did not look up. His eyes shifted toward the schedule, but he continued counting, and he would not look up at the deaf man.

'What about it?'

'It says it's effective April 13. That's next Monday.'

'That's right. What about it? We still got some old schedules over there, if you want them.'

'No, no, this is just what I want. But will these arrivals and departures be in effect for a while?'

'Absolutely. Don't put out a new schedule until June sometime. And even that'll be the same, actually, except it makes people feel better when they see new dates on a timetable.'

'Then these times will be in effect throughout April and May, is that right?'

'June, too,' the ticket seller said. '*And* July, for that matter. *And* August. Schedule don't change again until we go off daylight-saving time. That's in September sometime.'

'I see, thank you. And I can buy a ticket for the truck after I have boarded the ferry with it, is that also correct?'

'Yes, that's right.'

'Should I get here very far in advance, or can you usually accommodate all the vehicles that want passage?'

'We got room for twenty-five cars. Seldom get more'n a dozen. Plenty of room aboard the old tub. Not many people want to go to Majesta. Sure, it's nice and quiet there, but it ain't exactly anybody's idea of city life, if you know what I mean.'

'Well, thank you very much,' the deaf man said. 'What time does the next ferry leave?'

The ticket seller did not stop counting, nor did he look up at the clock or down at his wrist watch. He simply said, 'Eleven o'clock.'

'Thank you,' the deaf man said. He walked away from

the window, nodded pleasantly at a uniformed cop standing near the newspaper stand, and strode rapidly to where Rafe was sitting on the bench. He sat beside him unobtrusively.

'I'll be going over to Majesta,' he said. 'You have some phone calls to make, don't you?'

'Yes, I do,' Rafe said, nodding. The sight of the uniformed cop made him somewhat anxious. He did not like policemen. He had spent five years in prison because of policemen.

'I just checked the schedule,' the deaf man told him. 'We'll plan on catching the 5:45 P.M. boat on the evening of the caper. The one after that is at 6:05. That gives us a twenty-minute leeway, should anything go wrong.'

'Do you think anything will go wrong?' Rafe asked. He was a tall thin man with a wild manner, a manner accentuated by the gold-rimmed eyeglasses and sandy-blond hair.

'No,' the deaf man said confidently. 'Nothing will go wrong.'

'How can you be sure?'

'I can be sure because I have studied the probabilities. And I can be sure because I know exactly what we are dealing with.'

'And what's that?'

'An outmoded police force,' the deaf man said.

'They weren't so outmoded when they sent me to jail,' Rafe said quietly, glumly.

'Examine the Police Department, if you will,' the deaf man said. 'There are approximately thirty thousand cops in this sprawling metropolis. And this figure includes all of them, inspectors, deputy inspectors, detectives, patrolmen, veterinarians, policewomen, everything. The total police force numbers thirty thousand. That's it.'

'So?'

'So there are approximately ten million people in this city. And it is the task of those thirty thousand policemen to see that those ten million people do not commit various criminal acts against each other. If we divide the number of potential lawbreakers by the number of policemen, we can say – roughly – that each cop is responsible for the conduct of about three hundred thirty-three people, am I right?'

Rafe did some laborious long division. 'Yes, that's about right.'

'Now, obviously, one cop – even assuming he is armed with the most modern weapons – couldn't possibly control three hundred thirty-three people should they, for example, decide to commit three hundred thirty-three crimes in three hundred thirty-three places at the same time. It would be physically impossible for one cop to prevent all of those crimes because he couldn't possibly be in two places at the same time, one of the basic laws of physics. But, of course, there are a vast number of policemen who, in combination, can be brought into action against a multitude of simultaneous criminal explosions. But even these men, in combination, could not cope with, if you will, ten million people committing ten million crimes simultaneously. Despite the permutations.'

'I don't understand you,' Rafe said.

'Permutations,' the deaf man said. 'The number of possible ways – well, let's take a deck of cards. You'll be more at ease with cards than with policemen. There are fifty-two cards in the deck. If we want to know how many possible ways there are of arranging those fifty-two cards, we start with the simple permutation, written this way.' He took a slip of paper from his pocket and quickly jotted:

'I still don't understand,' Rafe said.

'That's simply the mathematical way of writing the permutations of 52. We call *all* the arrangements we can make by selecting all the numbers of a group "simple permutations." The equation becomes . . .' And he wrote:

$$52p52=52!$$

'That tells us how many possible ways there are of arranging a deck of 52 cards.'

'What's the exclamation point for?' Rafe asked.

'It's not an exclamation point. There are no interjections in mathematics. It simply indicates that the number must be multiplied by every whole number below it until we get to 1. For example, the number four followed by that symbol simply means 4 times 3 times 2 times 1.'

'So how many ways *can* you arrange a deck of cards?'

'52! ways – or 52 times 51 times 50 times 49 times – well, all the way down until you reach the figure 1. It would take all day to multiply it out. But at the risk of making you nervous again, let's get back to something of more concern to us, policemen. And, specifically, the detectives of the Eighty-seventh Squad. There are normally sixteen men on the squad. But when we pull our job, two will be on vacation and two will be in Washington taking an FBI course.'

'That leaves twelve,' Rafe said.

'Right. Let's try to figure how many possible combinations those twelve men can arrange themselves into, shall we? The equation would be this.' He wrote:

$$12p12=12!$$

'Which means,' he went on, '12 times 11 times 10, and so on. Let's see what that comes to.' Quickly, he began multiplying figures on his sheet of paper. 'Well, here you are,' he said. 'All the possible combinations for twelve men, 12 times 11 times 10 down through 1, is 479,001,600. it sounds staggering, doesn't it?'

'It sure does. Even *one* cop sounds staggering to me,' Rafe said.

'Of course, detectives usually work in pairs, and not in teams of twelve or eight or six or what have you. And this would automatically limit the number of possible combinations. Besides, we need not concern ourselves with the permutations of those twelve men. We need only to abstract a theory about law enforcement and crime prevention. It seems to me, Rafe, that the police operate on their own limited theory of probability. Obviously, with their inadequate force of thirty thousand, they cannot possibly hope to be everywhere at once. This is a damned big city and a great many people in it are practicing criminals. So the police operate against percentages. They figure in this fashion, more or less: A certain number of criminals must escape detection *for the moment* because we can't possibly hope to be where they are when a crime is being committed or because we can't successfully investigate every crime even after it's been committed; however, *in the long run*, we will one day catch a previously undetected criminal because we will be in the right place at the right time or because the situation for a successful investigation will present itself. "*In the long run*" – those are the key words in probability.'

'I think I'd better go make my phone calls,' Rafe said. 'Besides, your ferry's coming in.'

'Just a moment, Rafe. "*In the long run*." Remember those words. If you flipped a penny five times in succession, the first five flips might come up tails. If you stopped flipping right there, you might come to the conclusion that a penny will come up tails one hundred per cent of the times it is flipped. Deviation, remember?

The difference between observation and reality. Actually, the longer you kept flipping that penny, the closer you would come to the truth. Which is, of course, that it will turn up heads fifty per cent of the time and tails the remaining fifty per cent. So the cops are playing the long run. They've got this rather cute, quaint, antiquated, friendly, bumbling law enforcement machine and *in the long run*, through a combination of choice and chance, they will make their arrests and maintain order – primarily because the percentages are on their side. Most citizens, you see, are law-abiding. But tell me something, Rafe.'

'What?' Rafe asked.

'What happens when someone comes along and screws up the percentages? What happens when the police are forced to cope with something the likes of which they've never encountered before? What happens when they're pushed into dealing with the *short* run?'

'I don't know,' Rafe said. 'What happens?'

'We'll walk off with two and a half million bucks,' the deaf man said. 'That's what.'

The real estate agent in Majesta was quite taken with his caller. The man was tall and good-looking, with pleasant blue eyes and a manner reminiscent of the Old South. At the same time, the man knew what he wanted and he wasted no time in stating his needs.

'A small house with a garage,' the deaf man said. 'It needn't be close to the ferry, and I shall only need it for a few weeks. The garage must be large enough to hold two cars; a sedan and a small truck.'

'I see, sir,' the agent said. 'And the house? How large a house need it be?'

'It should accommodate four adults,' the deaf man said. He grinned pleasantly. 'My colleagues and I are working on a screenplay which will be shot in the city streets this summer. We want two weeks of uninterrupted work, no telephones, no visitors. That's why we thought of Majesta.'

'I see,' the agent said. 'You're a screen writer then, is that right?'

'That's right.'

'Well, I knew you were *something* right off the bat. I could tell.'

'Well, thank you,' the deaf man said.

'Sure. And I think I've got just the house for you.' He paused. 'What movie company do you work for?'

'An independent outfit,' the deaf man said quickly.

'You write anything else besides movie scripts?'

'Oh yes, a great many things.'

'Would I know your name?' the agent asked.

'Perhaps.'

'Well, what is it? I'll need it for our records, anyway.'

'Thomas Wolfe,' the deaf man said.

'Oh, sure,' the agent said, smiling. 'Sure. I think I even read a few of your books. Sure.'

Sitting in the phone booth, Rafe put a small tick mark alongside the tenth number on his list. There were fifteen numbers after that one, and all of the exchanges were for locations on the south side of the city, or – to be more precise – on the south side of the territory under the command of the Eighty-seventh Precinct. David Raskin's phone number was among those on the list. So was James Lombardo's. Dave Raskin ran a dress loft. Jim Lombardo ran a haberdashery. The two men had nothing at all in common. Unless one wished to comment on the fact that Dave's loft was over a bank and Jim's hat store was next door to a jewelry concern. Otherwise, there was no similarity.

71

Of the twenty-five numbers on the list, six belonged to clothing stores, eight belonged to restaurants, one belonged to Raskin, one belonged to Lombardo, three belonged to candy shops, two belonged to leather goods stores, one belonged to a travel agency, two belonged to shoe stores, and the last belonged to a tie shop.

Very innocent-looking concerns.

But Dave Raskin's loft was over a bank. And Jim Lombardo's hat shop was next door to a jewelry concern. Thirteen more of the stores on that list were next door to banks. Six were next door to rather fancy jewelry shops. One was next door to a firm which made money loans. Another was next door to a firm which sold silverware. The twenty-fourth store on the list was a Chinese restaurant which was located on the second floor of a building which housed a quaint little shop on the ground floor; the shop had close to five hundred thousand dollars' worth of Oriental jade in the window. And the twenty-fifth store was next door to a company which dealt in foreign exchange and which kept huge sums of cold cash in its safe.

Rafe dialed the eleventh number on his list and waited for the phone to be picked up on the other end. When the voice came on, he asked, 'Mr Carmichael?'

'Yes?' the man said.

'Get out of that store, Mr Carmichael!' Rafe shouted. 'Get out before the thirtieth, or I'll kill you!'

8.

'CAR TWENTY-THREE, car twenty-three, signal thirteen, signal thirteen.'

'This is twenty-three.'

'Signal thirteen, seven three five Gramercy Street, repeat seven three five Gramercy Street, complainant Sergei Rosnakoff, stink bomb in incinerator, signal thirteen. Car thirty-six, car thirty-six, signal eleven, signal—'

'This is thirty-six. Go ahead.'

'This is twenty-three, what was that address again?'

'Hold it, thirty-six. I gave it to you twice, twenty-three. What the—'

'This is thirty-six, thirty-six, over.'

'That's seven three five Gramercy. You got that, twenty-three?'

'Seven three five Gramercy, Roger.'

'Car thirty-six, car thirty-six, come in car . . .'

CENTRAL COMPLAINT DESK REPORT

TIME	DATE	RECEIVED BY
9:12 AM	APR 13	PTL. JACOBS
CITY SECTION	**PRECINCT**	**DESK OFFICER**
BETHTOWN	HQ COMMAND	SGT EDWARDS

ADDRESS _735 GRAMERCY STREET_ FLOOR _GROUND_

NAME OF COMPLAINANT _SERGEI ROSNAKOFF_

CRIME REPORTED _DISORDERLY CONDUCT (?)_

DETAILS _STINK BOMB IN INCINERATOR. BUILDING SUPER SMELT
SOMETHING STRANGE, SAYS SOMEBODY THREW A STINK BOMB
DOWN THE INCINERATOR. DISPATCHED TO BETHTOWN MOTOR PATROL._

DISPATCHER NO. _12_ TIME _9:15 AM_

C.R.D. 16

POLICE DEPARTMENT

Case Report

For _Captain Charles Hendricks_

CLASSIFICATION _Investigation of Complaint_

Officer Assigned _Patrolman Ralph Allan_ Shield No. _35-416_

Place of Occurrence _735 Gramercy Street_

Date of Occurrence _April 13_   Time of Occurrence _9:00 AM_

Date Reported _April 13_   Time Reported _9:12 AM_

BRIEF OUTLINE OF CRIME

Super of the building said somebody threw a stink bomb into the garbage incinerator. Investigated claim, found what caused smell, but it was no stink bomb. Removed same from incinerator room.

WITNESSES (Name, Address, and Nature of Testimony)

Sergei Ronakoff
735 Gramercy Street

Super of the bldg, man who made the complaint

EVIDENCE (Quantity, Form, and Relationship to Crime)

Burnt clothing and tobacco pouch.

75

EVIDENCE TAG

NAME OF DEFENDANT	—
ADDRESS OF DEFENDANT	—

PRECINCT 102nd   **ARREST NO.** —

DATE 4/13   **AIDED NO.** —

CHARGE

NAME OF COMPLAINANT
Sergei Romakoff

ADDRESS OF COMPLAINANT
735 Gramercy St

NAME: INJURED DECEASED

ADDRESS

PR. CLK. VOUCHER NO
3412

PCT. VOUCHER NO.
102-451

NATURE AND DESCRIPTION OF EVIDENCE

Burnt material found in incinerator

ARRESTING OFFICER
Ptl. Ralph Allona

TIME AND PLACE COURT EXAMINATION

Pr Clk 2a

76

IF DELIVERY URGENT BUT PICKUP & HOLD CONTACT
RIVERHEAD PCT (*(*(* 98TH PCT 98TH XXXXXXXX
XXXXXXXXXX
INFORMATION REQUEST HQ COMMAND GENERAL REQUEST
ALL PCTS ALL PCTS ALL PCTS XXXXXXXXX PRECINCTS
GEN RQUEST INFORMATION XXXXXXX MAN'S UNIFORM
GREY BRASS BUTTONS TOBACCO POUCH FOUND REMAINS
BURNT CHARRED BETHTOWN APT BLDG INCINERATOR XXX
SUSPECT POSS POWDER BURNS ON CLOTH XXXXX INFO OR
ASSIST UNSOLVED SHOOTING CASES CONTACT HQ XXX
HQ COMMAND DET LT DOUGHETY DOUGHERTY DOUGHERTY
XXXXXXXXX
          X   XXXXXX   XXXXX   XXX
APRIL 13 GENERAL ALARM ALL PCTS BE ON LOCKOUT
WOMAN BLONDE AGE 24   5 FEET 4 INCHES 110 LBS
EXTREMELY ATTRACTIVE LAST SEEN WEARING BLUE S

POLICE DEPARTMENT

Police Headquarters Command

89 High Street, Isola

BY MESSENGER

BY MESSENGER

TO:

Detective Stephen Louis Carella
87th Detective Squad
87th Precinct
711 Grover Avenue
Isola

Enclosed herewith is laboratory report received on the charred scraps
of uniform garment taken from Bethtown incinerator, and forwarded as
per your request received at 3:07 P.M. this afternoon.

Please note that report is preliminary and incomplete concerning matchbook discovered in pocket of uniform coat, but laboratory tests should
be complete by tomorrow Tuesday April 14 and suggest you contact Lieutenant Samuel Grossman at that time should you desire further information your case.

Sincerely,

Albert N. Dougherty

Det/Lt. Albert N. Dougherty
Headquarters Command

AD/rl
cc: Lt. Samuel Grossman

78

LABORATORY REPORT;

PR. CLK. VOUCHER NO. _____ 3412 _____ PCT. VOUCHER NO. ___ 102-451 ___

LABORATORY REPORT NO. ___ L-9034 ___ TECHNICIAN ___ Peter Kronig ___

DATE RECEIVED _____ 4/13 _____ DATE THIS REPORT ___ 4/13 ___

NATURE OF EVIDENCE. Burnt material and tobacco pouch found in
incinerator of apratment building.

CONCLUSIONS:

1) Material is 60% nylon, 40% wool, apparently a man's garment, grey in color, with brass buttons, no labels or ident tag, no mfg name on buttons. Suggest that garment is uniform of some type.

2) For most part, garment burnt and charred by incinerator fire but indication fm powder burn and are too similar shotgun markings portion below last pocket. Metal staple in pocket ash ashes indicates possible presence of matchbook tests to be concluded.

2) Tobacco pouch remaining ashes leather and rubber, smoldering rubber caused small precipitating complaint. Tobacco scraps present in untouched portion of pouch mixture tradename Smoker's Pipe, Noralco Noralco Tobacco, North Carolina, nationally distributed, soft pack and in

4) Hair oil or other grease stain portion of garment which seems to be lapel, but being run prove negative for compo or make.

REMARKS;

Should staple prove to have come from match folder, report on same will follow.

9.

LIEUTENANT SAM GROSSMAN was one of those rare and vanishing individuals who take extreme pride in their work. As one of these, he was not the type of man who would wait for someone to call for information once that information was available. He had worked all day Monday on the matchbook remains which had been found with the charred uniform material in the incinerator. He was in receipt of a carbon copy of Dougherty's letter, and so he knew that Steve Carella was interested in the case. But even if the interested party hadn't been someone Grossman knew and liked, even if it had been an obscure patrolman pounding a beat on Majesta, Grossman's attitude would have remained the same. He was now in possession of information which could prove extremely valuable to the man investigating the case. He'd be damned if he was going to wait for that man to call him.

Nor had Grossman come into possession of this possibly valuable information through a stroke of luck, or even through the performance of a few simple laboratory tests. There are, you know, some laboratory tests which are extremely simple and which require no patience or perseverance. The reconstruction of burnt paper, unfortunately, does not fall into this category.

To begin with, the matchbook found with the material was contained by what the lab assumed to be the breast pocket of the jacket. The presence of the matchbook would not have been suspected at all had not one of Grossman's capable assistants noticed the glint of metal among the commingled ashes. Upon study, the metal turned out to be a tiny staple of the kind that holds matches to an outside cover. And once the presence of the remains of a matchbook had been determined, the real work lay just around the corner.

There were possibly four or five methods which could have been used to reconstruct the burnt matchbook, all of which required the patience of Job, the steadiness of Gibraltar, and the perseverance of Senator McCarthy. The method best suited to this particular document was discussed by Grossman and his assistants and, when they'd agreed on the proper approach, they rolled up their sleeves and got to work.

The first thing they did was to prepare a hot solution of one per cent gelatin in water. They then placed this solution in a flat developing pan. Then, with his assistant holding a glass plate as close to the ash as he could get, Grossman delicately and gingerly fanned the ash out onto the plate. No one breathed. Inching the plate toward the gelatin solution, the men slowly submerged it so that the solution just covered the surface of the plate. The ash had now been moistened, and the difficult and painstaking job of flattening it without destroying it remained to be done. Finally another glass plate was pressed into place above the first one, and both were squeezed together to dispel any air bubbles. The plates sandwiching the ash were then put into a printing frame and the suspect matchbook was photographed on an orthochromatic plate and printed on compression paper.

Simple.

It took five hours.

At the end of that time, the men went home.

On Tuesday morning, Sam Grossman called Steve Carella.

'Hello, Steve,' he said. 'I hate to barge in, but I've got a report on that match folder, and I couldn't see any good reason for waiting for you to call me. You don't mind, do you?'

'Not at all, Sam. How've you been?'

'Fine, thanks. I'm sorry that report on the uniform wasn't more helpful, Steve.'

'It was a pretty good one.'

'Not really. What the hell good is a report on a uniform if we can't tell you what kind of a uniform it was? Who cares whether it was nylon or wool or horse manure? You want to know whether it belonged to a bus driver or a mailman or whatever, am I right?'

'That's right, Sam. But some of that other stuff in the report—'

'Side effects and not really important. The folder may be something else again, though.'

'Something good?'

'Considering what we had to work with, I think we did an amazing job.'

'What have you got, Sam?'

'Well, to begin with, your suspect is twenty-three years old and probably a college graduate.'

'Huh?'

'He has, at some time during the past year, smoked a marijuana cigarette and gone to bed with a blonde between the ages of nineteen and twenty-two.'

'What!' Carella said, astonished.

'Yes,' Grossman said. 'And from this match folder ash, we were able to determine that our suspect served in the US Cavalry as a gunner in a tank during the Korean War. In addition to that—'

'You got all this from the burnt matchbook?' Carella asked, and Grossman began laughing. The dawn broke slowly. Carella, holding the phone close to his violated ear, began to grin. 'You bastard,' he said. 'I believed you for a minute there. What *did* you get from the matchbook?'

'The name of a hotel,' Grossman said.

'Here? This city?'

'Yep.'

'Shoot.'

'The Hotel Albion. It's on Jefferson and South Third.'

'Thank you, Sam.'

'Don't thank me yet. You can probably pick up these matches in any cigar store in the city.'

'Or maybe not, Sam. Maybe they're private hotel stock. The Albion, the Albion. That's not one of those big chain jobs like Hilton runs, is it?'

'No. It's a small quiet place right on Jefferson.'

'That's what I thought. So maybe this *is* a break. In any case, I'll check it out. Thanks again, Sam.'

'Right. How's Teddy?'

'Fine.'

'And the twins?'

'Growing.'

'Good. I'll be talking to you,' Grossman said, and he hung up.

Carella looked at the hotel name he'd jotted onto the pad on his desk. He nodded, pulled the phone to him, and dialed the number of his home in Riverhead.

'Hello?' a sprightly voice answered.

'Fanny, this is Steve,' he said. 'Is Teddy still there, or did I miss her?'

'She's upstairs taking a bath. What is it, Steve? I was just feeding the twins.'

'Fanny, I'm supposed to meet Teddy at three o'clock outside Bannerman's and I thought I'd be able to make it, but it doesn't look that way now. Would you just tell her I'll meet her for dinner at six at the Green Door? Have you got that? Six o'clock at—'

'I heard it the first time. Your son is screaming his head off at me, would you mind if I – Oh, holy mother of God!'

'What's the matter?'

'He's just thrown his spoon at April and hit her right in the eye with it! I don't know why I stay on in this madhouse. It seems to me—'

'Aw, you love us, you old bag,' Carella said.

'An old bag is what I'll be before the year is out. Me who used to provoke street whistles not two months ago.'

'Will you give her my message, dearie?' Carella asked, imitating her thick Irish brogue.

'Yes, I'll give her your message, dearie. And will you take a message from me, dearie?'

'What is it, dearie?'

'In the future, don't be calling at twelve noon because that is the time your darling little twins are being fed. And I've got my hands full enough with *two* Carellas not to have a third come bothering me. Is that clear, sir?'

'Yes, dearie.'

'All right, I'll give your wife the message. Poor darling, she's been rushing about like a mad fool so that she'd meet you on time, and now you call with—'

'Goodbye, dearie,' Carella said. 'Go take the spoon out of April's eye.'

He hung up, smiling, wondering how he and Teddy had ever managed to run a household without Fanny. Of course, he told himself, before Fanny there hadn't been the twins, either. In fact, had the twins not been born, Fanny would not have been hired as a two-weeks, post-natal nurse. And then when they'd moved into the new house, the monster which was on the market for back taxes, and Fanny's two weeks were up – well, it was difficult to say exactly what had prompted her to stay on at practically no salary, unless it was the fact that she had come to think of the Carellas as her own. Whatever her motive, and Carella never thought too much about motive except when he was working on a case, he was damned grateful for her existence. He sometimes had qualms that his children would grow up speaking with an Irish brogue since, by necessity, it was her speech they imitated and not the nonexistent speech of their mother. And only last week, he was nearly shocked out of his skin when young Mark said, 'Dammit, dearie, I don't want to go to bed yet.' But all in all, things were working out fine.

Carella stood up, opened the top drawer of his desk, took his gun and holster from it, and clipped it to the right side of his belt. He took his jacket from where it was draped over the back of his chair, put it on, and then tore the top page from the pad and stuck the sheet into his pocket.

'I probably won't be back for the rest of the day,' he told Parker.

'Where you going?' Parker asked. 'A movie?'

'No, a burlesque,' Carella said. 'I dig naked broads.'

'Ha!' Parker said.

They're tearing down the whole damn city, Meyer thought as he passed the building site of the new shopping center on Grover Avenue and the huge sign announcing that the work was being done by the Uhrbinger Construction Company. In truth, his observation was slightly in error since what they were doing was not tearing down the whole damn city but building up a major portion of it. As Lieutenant Byrnes had reported so accurately, the new shopping center would be a self-contained commercial operation with a large parking lot and with a conglomeration of services designed to lure housewives from everywhere in the city. The new stores were set in a low modern building which clashed violently with the surrounding grimy fingers of the slum tenements but which nonetheless presented an open area of clean space where the city dweller felt as if he could once again breathe while picking up his package of Wheaties or while cashing a twenty-dollar bill at the bank. Of course, entering the bank or the supermarket was still some weeks away from reality. The sites of these enterprises still crawled with workmen in overalls and sweat-stained shirts, so that perhaps Meyer's observation was not too far from the truth after all. The men rushing about with wooden beams and copper pipes *did* seem to be a demolition crew rather than a construction gang.

He sighed heavily, wondering how he would ever adjust to this new image of a neighborhood he had come to know quite well over the years. It was odd, he thought, but a person very rarely looked at the neighborhood where he spent his entire working day, until they began to make changes there. And then, quite suddenly, the old way, the old buildings, the old streets seemed to become very dear and the new way seemed to be an encroachment upon something private and familiar.

What the hell's the matter with you? he thought. *You like slums?*

'Yeah, I like slums.'

Besides, the 87th Precinct isn't a slum. Part of it is a slum, yes. But you couldn't call the apartment houses lining Silvermine Road a slum. And some of the shops on The Stem were actually pretty fancy. And Smoke Rise, along the river, was as elegant as anything you were likely to find anywhere. So, all right, I'm rationalizing. For the most part, this is probably the crumbiest neighborhood in the city, and we've undoubtedly got the highest crime rate and our fire department is probably the busiest in the world, but I guess I like it here. I've never asked for a transfer and God knows there have been times when I was pretty damned disgusted, and yet I've never asked for a transfer, so I guess I really like it here.

Which, again, answers your question.

Yeah, I like slums.

I like slums because they are alive. I hate them because they breed crime and violence and filth – but I like them because they are alive.

It was twelve noon, and Meyer Meyer walked the streets of this slum that was alive, passing the construction site on Grover Avenue and then cutting up Thirteenth and walking north. The neighborhood was a rich amalgam of color, the color of flesh tones ranging from the purest white through the myriad shades of tan and brown and into the deepest brown, a brown bordering on black. Color, too, in the April finery of the precinct citizens, and color in the shop windows, bolts of blue silk and pink taffeta, and color on the sidewalk stands, the rich scarlet of ripe apples, and the subtle sunshine of bananas, and the purple bruise of grapes. And color, too, in the language of the streets, the profanity interlaced with the pseudo-musical jargon, the English of the underprivileged, and the bastardized Spanish, the Jewish peddler shouting his wares with a heavy Yiddish accent, the woman on the street corner wailing psalms to the indifferent blue sky of April. And all of it alive, all of it bursting with the juice of life, all of it raw and primitive somehow, stripped of all the nonsense of twentieth century ritual, that is what he meant by alive, this is what Meyer Meyer meant. For perhaps it was uncouth and uncivilized, but there was no question here of which fork to pick up first at the dinner table, and no question here of the proper way to introduce a duchess to a marquis, no question here of the little civilities, the little courtesies that separate us from the barbarians and at the same time steal from us our humanity. The precinct was as basic as life itself – and as rich.

And so he walked the streets there without fear even

though he knew that violence could erupt around him at any moment. And he walked with a spring to his step, and he breathed deeply of air which stank of exhaust fumes but which was, nonetheless, the heady air of April, and he felt very glad to be alive.

The loft which David Raskin occupied was directly over a bank.

Mercantile Trust was the name of the bank. The name was engraved onto two bronze plaques, one of which decorated either side of the huge bronze bank doors which were open to admit the noonday traffic. A sign stuck to one of the open doors advised any interested party that the bank was changing quarters on April thirtieth and would be ready for business at its new location on May first. Meyer passed the bank, and the sign, and then climbed the steps to David Raskin's loft. A thumb-smeared sign hanging to the left of a huge fireproof door advised Meyer Meyer that he had located

DARASK FROCKS, INC.
Women's Garments Of
Distinction

Meyer did not knock. He went into the loft, stared down at the front of Margarita's low-cut smock for a second or two, asked for Dave Raskin and was ushered to the back of the loft where Raskin himself, standing in his undershirt and sweating profusely, was working with the girls pressing dresses. Raskin seemed to be in excellent high spirits.

'Hallo, hallo, Meyer!' he shouted. 'What a day for pressing dresses, hah? A beautiful April day, what a day! It's nice out, hah, Meyer?'

'Beautiful,' Meyer replied.

'April, that's the only time of the year. April is just right for everything, and I mean *everything*, Meyer, even an old man like me could say it, *everything*, Meyer!'

'You seem very happy today,' Meyer said.

'Yes, yes, I'm happy like a little lark. You know why? I'll tell you why. To begin with, my crazyman hasn't called since Friday. Already this is Tuesday, and thank God nothing has come for me, no stationery, nothing, and no telephone calls, either.' Raskin beamed. 'So I'm happy. My girls aren't frightened, and I'm not pestered by this *meshugenuh* heckler. Also, I'm making money like a crazy thief.'

'Good,' Meyer said. 'Maybe he's given up the game, huh? Figured he wasn't getting enough of a rise out of you, maybe.' Meyer shrugged. 'I'm glad to hear there've been no incidents since Friday, Dave. And of course I'm glad to hear your business is going so well.'

'It couldn't be better. I got six dozen summer dresses yesterday for – guess what? Guess how much?'

'I don't know. How much?'

'A dollar each dress! Can you imagine something like that? These beautiful little summer things, sleeveless you know, and a little tight across the backside, I'll sell them like hot cakes, they'll come running all the way from Bethtown to buy these, I can sell them for four dollars each and they'll snap them up! I'm telling you, Meyer, I'll make a fortune. You saw the bank downstairs when you were coming in?'

'Yes,' Meyer said, grinning.

'Okay. Right under where we're standing, right here under my feet, they got their vault. And into this vault, Meyer, I'm going to place thousands and thousands of dollars!'

'You'd better do it in a hurry,' Meyer said, 'because the bank is moving at the end of the month.'

'Slow or in a hurry,' Raskin said, chuckling, 'I'll do it. I'll be known as the sultan of sexy garments, the lama of ladies' coats and dresses, the monarch of maternity clothes, the king of Culver Avenue! Me, David Raskin! If I keep buying dresses at a dollar each – *oi gevalt*, what a steal! – a dollar apiece and selling them for four dollars, Meyer, I could build my *own* bank! I won't need already the vault downstairs! Meyer, I'll be a millionaire! Can't you see me now? I'll only—'

The telephone rang. Raskin walked to it, still talking to Meyer, not breaking his conversational stride—

'— drive a Cadillac car, nothing else, and I'll wear silk underwear and in Miami Beach I'll be known as—'

He picked up the receiver.

'Hello – the biggest tipper on Collins Aven—'

'You son of a bitch!' the voice said. 'Get out of that loft before the thirtieth, or I'll kill you!'

10.

THE HOTEL ALBION was on Jefferson Avenue near South Third Street. A narrow green canopy stretched from the hotel entrance to the street, and a doorman wearing a green uniform and watching the girls strut by in their April cottons, sprang to attention as Carella approached, promptly pulled open one of the brass-bound doors for him, and damn near threw a salute.

'Thank you,' Carella said.

'You're-welcome-sir!' the doorman shouted smartly.

Carella raised his eyebrows appreciatively, went into the lobby, and felt immediately that he had left the city somewhere far behind him. The lobby was small and quiet. Rich dark woods dominated the ceilings and the walls. A thick Persian carpet covered the floor. The furniture was upholstered in vibrant red-and-green velvet, and a huge cut-glass chandelier dominated the ceiling. He felt that he was no longer in the United States, felt somehow that Venice must look like this, rich and vibrant and somehow decadent, somehow out of place with the bustling twentieth century, a city misplaced in time. He had never been to Venice, never indeed been outside of America except during the war, and yet he knew instinctively that this hotel would have fit into that waterlogged city with uninhibited ease. He took off his hat and walked to the main desk. There was no one behind it. The hotel, in fact, seemed to be deserted, as if news of an impending atom bomb blast had sent everyone creaking downstairs to the wine cellar. A bell rested on the counter. He reached out with one hand and tapped it. The bell tinkled in the small lobby, cushioned by the velvet chairs and the Persian rug and the thick draperies on the windows, muffled by the overwhelming soddenness of the surrounding materials.

Carella heard the shuffle of soft-soled slippers sliding over steps. He looked up. A small thin man was coming down from the first floor. He walked with a slight stoop, a man in his sixties wearing a green eye shade and a brown cardigan sweater which had been knitted for him by a maternal aunt in New Hampshire. He looked like that Yankee-type fellow who plays the small-town hotel clerk in all the movies or the small-town postmaster, or the one the convertible pulls alongside to ask directions of, that guy, you know the one. He looked exactly like him. For a moment, listening to his creaky tread on the steps, watching him come into the cloistered silence of the lobby, Carella had the feeling that he was in a movie himself, that he would speak a line which had been written for him by some Hollywood mastermind and would be answered in turn with another scripted line.

'Hello, young feller,' the Yankee-type said. 'Can I be of some assistance?'

'I'm from the police,' Carella said. He reached into his back pocket, pulled out his wallet, and opened it to where his shield was pinned to the leather.

'Um-hum,' the Yankee said, nodding. 'What can I do for you?'

'I don't believe I caught your name, sir,' Carella said and knew instantly that the man would reply, 'Didn't throw it, young feller,' and almost winced before the words left the old-timer's mouth.

'Didn't throw it, young feller,' the Yankee said. 'But it's Pitt. Roger Pitt.'

'How do you do, Mr Pitt. My name is Detective Carella. We found the remains of a—'

'Carella, did you say?'

'Yes.'

'Carella?'

'Yes.'

'How d'do?' Pitt said.

'Fine, thank you. We found the remains of a uniform in an incinerator, sir, and we also found a matchbook from your hotel, the Hotel Albion, and there's the possibility that this uniform might tie in with a case we are investigating, and so I wondered—'

'*You* investigating the case?'

'Yes, sir.'

'You a detective?'

'Yes, sir.'

'Well, what was it you wanted to know?'

'To begin with, do you know anyone named Johnny?'

'Johnny what?'

'We don't know. But he might have been the person who was wearing this uniform.'

'Johnny, huh?'

'Yes. Johnny.'

'Sure.'

The lobby was silent.

'You know him?' Carella asked.

'Sure.'

'What's his last name?'

'Don't know.'

'But . . .'

'Lotte's feller,' Pitt said.

'Lotte?'

'Lotte Constantine. Lives right upstairs. He's been by here a lot, Johnny.'

'I see. And this Lotte Constantine is his girl friend, is that right?'

'That's right,' Pitt said.

'How old a man would you say this Johnny was?'

'Was?' Pitt asked quickly, his eyes narrowing. 'In his sixties, I guess.'

Carella reached into his inside jacket pocket. He pulled out a photograph encased in lucite. He put it face up on the counter. It was the photo of the dead man which had run in the metropolitan dailies.

'Is that the man you're thinking of?' Carella asked.

Pitt studied the photo. 'Course,' he said, 'I never seen him in a bathing suit. Or asleep.'

'But is that him?'

'It could be. This ain't a very good picture, is it?'

'Perhaps not.'

'I mean, it looks like Johnny, and yet it don't. There seems to be something missing.'

'There is,' Carella said.

'What's that?'

'Life. The man in that picture is dead.'

'Oh.' Pitt seemed to wash his hands of the matter quite suddenly. 'Look, maybe you better ask Lotte. I mean, she'd know better than me.'

'Where can I reach her?'

'She's right upstairs. I'll give her a ring, and maybe she'll come on down to the lobby.'

'No, that's all right, I'll go up. I wouldn't want—'

'Won't take a second to buzz her,' Pitt said. He went to the switchboard and plugged in one of the rubber snakes there. Holding the earpiece to his right ear, he waited a moment and then said, 'Lotte? This is Roger downstairs. There's a feller here asking questions about Johnny. Yes, that's right, *your* Johnny. Well I thought maybe you wouldn't mind talking to him. Well, he's from the police, Lotte. Now, Lotte, there's no need to go getting upset. No, he seems to be a very nice young feller. Okay, I'll tell him.'

Pitt put down the headset, pulled out the plug, and said, 'She'll be right down. She got a little upset when she heard you was a cop.'

'Everybody gets upset when they hear that,' Carella said, smiling.

He leaned against the counter and waited for the arrival of Miss Lotte Constantine. If there was one thing he disliked, he supposed it was interrogating old people. Actually, there was a great many things he disliked, and a great many people who would testify to the fact that Steve Carella was, on occasion, a goddammed crab. So it was an understatement to say, 'If there was *one* thing he disliked.' But, among his other dislikes, interrogating oldsters took high priority, and interrogating old *women* particularly annoyed him. He had no idea why he disliked old women unless it had something to do with the fact that they were no longer young. In any case, he found talking to them trying to his patience, and he was not now looking forward to meeting Miss Lotte Constantine, the girl friend of a man who had been in his sixties.

He watched a luscious redhead in a very tight skirt as she navigated her way down the carpet-covered steps from the first floor. Because the skirt was so tight, the girl had lifted it above her knees, and she walked downstairs with her head slightly bent, watching the steps, a hank of red hair falling over one eye.

'Here she is now,' Pitt said, and Carella turned to look into the lobby, saw no one there, and then looked up the steps beyond the redhead, still seeing no one, and then the redhead was swiveling over to the desk with a lubricated hip and thigh movement that made him seasick, and she extended a hand tipped with scarlet claws and she said in the sexiest voice since Mae West was a girl, 'Hello, I'm Lotte Constantine.'

Carella swallowed hard and said, 'You? Are? Miss Constantine?'

The girl smiled. Her lips moved back from her teeth like tinted clouds pulling aside to let the sunshine through. A dimple appeared in either cheek. Her green eyes flashed. 'Yes,' she said. 'And you are . . . ?'

'Detective Carella,' he said, struggling to regain some of his composure. He had expected a woman in her late fifties and when he'd been confronted with a *zaftig* redhead who'd seemed at a distance, to be in her early thirties, he'd been flabbergasted, to say the least. At close range, however, he realized this girl was no older than twenty-three, bursting all over the place with youth and vitality and abundant flesh that threatened every stitch of clothing she wore. So he automatically thought of the old man who had been Johnny Something-or-other, and then he automatically thought of *Middle of the Night*, and Oh my, he thought, oh my, oh my.

'Could we sit down and talk a little, Miss Constantine?' he asked.

'Certainly,' she said. She smiled shyly, as if she were unused to sitting with strange men. Her lashes fluttered. She sucked in a deep breath and Carella turned away, pretending to look for a chair.

'We can sit over there,' Lotte said, and she began leading the way. Carella walked behind her. Married man and all, he had to admit this girl had the plumpest, most inviting bottom he had seen in a dog's age. He was tempted to pinch her, but he restrained himself. I'm much too young for her, he thought, and he grinned.

'Why are you smiling?' the girl asked, sitting and crossing her legs.

'I was only thinking you're a lot younger than I imagined you would be.'

'What did you imagine?'

'Truthfully?'

'Of course,' Lotte said.

'A woman in her fifties.'

'Why?'

'Well . . .' Carella shrugged. He took the picture from his pocket again. 'Know this man?'

She glanced at the picture and nodded immediately. 'Yes,' she said. 'What's happened to him?' She did not blench or gasp or wince or blush or grimace. She simply said, 'Yes,' and then, matter-of-factly and just as quickly, said, 'What's happened to him?'

'He's dead,' Carella said.

She nodded. She said nothing. Then she gave a tiny shrug of her shoulders, and then she nodded again.

'Who was he?' Carella asked.

'Johnny.'

'Johnny who?'

'Smith.'

Carella stared at her.

'Yes, Smith,' she said. 'John Smith.'

'And who are you? Pocahontas?'

'I don't think that's funny. He told me his name was John Smith. Why shouldn't I believe him?'

'Why shouldn't you indeed? How long had you known him, Miss Constantine?'

'Since January.'

'When did you see him last?'

'Last month sometime.'

'Can you remember when last month?'

'The end of the month.'

'Were you and he very serious?'

Lotte shrugged. 'I don't know,' she said wistfully. 'What's serious?'

'Were you . . . more than just friends, Miss Constantine?'

97

'Yes,' she said abruptly. She nodded, as if lost in thought, as if alone in the silent lobby that reminded Carella of Venice. 'Yes.' She nodded again. 'Yes, we were more than just friends.' She lifted her eyes and then tossed her head and brushed a long strand of red hair away from her forehead. Defiantly she said, 'We were lovers.'

'All right,' Carella said. 'Any idea who'd want him dead, Miss Constantine?'

'No.' She paused. 'How – how did he die?'

'I was wondering when you'd get to that.'

Lotte Constantine looked Carella straight in the eye. 'What the hell are you?' she asked. 'A tough cop?'

Carella did not answer.

'Do I *have* to want to know how he died?' she said. 'Isn't it enough that he's dead?'

'Most people would be curious,' Carella said.

'I'm not *most* people,' she answered. 'I'm me. Lotte Constantine. You're a great one, aren't you? A regular little IBM machine, aren't you? Punch-punch, put in the card and out comes the right answer. You come here telling me Johnny is dead, and then you start asking a lot of fool questions and then you tell me what the reaction of *most* people would be, well the hell with you, Detective Whatever-your-name-is, *most* twenty-two-year-old girls wouldn't fall in love with a man who's sixty-six years old, yes, sixty-six, don't look so goddammed surprised, that's how old Johnny was, so don't go telling me what *most* people would do, you can take *most* people and drown them, for all I care.'

'He was shot at close range with a shotgun,' Carella said, and he did not take his eyes from her face. Nothing crossed that face. No expression, not the slightest nuance of emotion.

'All right,' she said, 'he was shot at close range with a shotgun. Who did it?'

'We don't know.'

'*I* didn't.'

'Nobody said you did.'

'Then what the hell are you doing here?'

'We're only trying to make a positive identification, Miss Constantine.'

'Well, you've made it. Your dead man is John Smith.'

'Would you say that name was a great deal of help, Miss Constantine?'

'What the hell do you want from me? It was *his* name, not mine.'

'And he never told you his real name?'

'He said his name was John Smith.'

'And you believed him?'

'Yes.'

'Suppose he'd told you his name was John Doe?'

'Mister, I'd have believed him if he told me his name was Joseph Stalin. Now how about that?'

'That's how it was, huh?' Carella asked.

'That's how it was.'

'What'd he do for a living?' Carella asked.

'Retired. He was getting social security.'

'And the uniform?'

'What uniform?' Lotte Constantine asked with wide open eyes.

'The uniform. The one somebody stripped off of him and dumped into an incinerator.'

'I don't know what you're talking about.'

'You never saw him in a uniform?'

'Never.'

'Did he have any job? Besides the retirement money. Did he run an elevator or anything?'

'No. I gave him—' Lotte stopped suddenly.

'Yes?'

'Nothing.'

'You gave him money? Is that what you were about to say?'

'Yes.'

'Where did he live, Miss Constantine?'

'I . . . I don't know.'

'What do you mean, you—'

'I don't know where he lived. He . . . he came here a lot.'

'To stay?'

'Sometimes.'

'For how long?'

'The . . . the longest he ever stayed was . . . was for two weeks.'

'Pitt know about this?'

Lotte shrugged. 'I don't know. What difference does it make? I'm a good customer. I've been living in this hotel ever since I came to the city four years ago. What difference would it make if an old man—' She caught herself, stopped speaking, and returned Carella's level gaze. 'Stop staring at me as if I was Lolita or something. I loved him.'

'And he never mentioned a uniform, is that right? Or a job?'

'He mentioned a deal.'

'What kind of a deal?' Carella asked, leaning forward. The girl uncrossed her legs. 'He didn't say.'

'But he did mention a deal?'

'Yes.'

'When was this?'

'The last time I saw him.'

'What did he say?'

'Only that he had a deal cooking with the deaf man.'

They were sitting in velvet chairs around a small coffee table in an ornate lobby which suddenly went as still as death.

'The deaf man?' Carella said.

'Yes.'

He sucked in a deep breath.

'Who's the deaf man?'

'I don't know.'

'But Johnny had some kind of a deal with him, right?'

'Yes. That's what he said. He said he had a deal with the deaf man, and that he'd be very rich soon. He was going – We were going to get married.'

'The deaf man,' Carella said aloud. He sighed heavily. 'Where can I reach you if I need you, Miss Constantine?'

'Either here or at The Harem Club.'

'What do you do there?'

'I'm a cigarette girl. I sell cigarettes. That's where I met Johnny. At the club.'

'He bought cigarettes from you?'

'No. He smokes – he *smoked* – a pipe. I sold him pipe tobacco.'

'Smoker's Pipe?' Carella asked. 'Was that the brand?'

'Why . . . why, yes. How—'

'Here's my card, Miss Constantine,' Carella said. 'If you should think of anything else that might help me, give me call, won't you?'

'Like what?'

'What do you mean?'

'Like what do you want me to call you about? How do I know what'll help you?'

'Well, any further information about this deaf man would—'

'I don't know anything else about him.'

'Or anything Johnny might have said regarding this deal of hi—'

'I told you everything he said.'

Carella shrugged.

'You want your card back?' Lotte Constantine asked.

*

That night, the deaf man celebrated.

Perhaps things were going well at the ice-cream store behind the construction site. Or perhaps he was simply anticipating what would begin happening the next day. Perhaps, like a good general, he was drinking a symbolic toast on the eve of battle.

The symbolic toast, in this case, was the taking of a nineteen-year-old girl whose attributes were surely not mental.

But the deaf man, you see, was an economical man and a man who never lost sight of his goals. He was not interested, that evening, in a discussion of mathematics. Nor was he interested in learning about the ambitions or tribulations or strivings for independence or strugglings for realization of self of any member of the opposite sex. He was interested in making love, pure and simple. He had been casing his love partner in much the same way he'd have cased the site of a future robbery. He had been casing her for two weeks, attracted by her obvious beauty at first – the girl was a brunette with luminous brown eyes and a full pouting mouth; her breasts, even in the waitress uniform she wore, were large and inviting; her legs beneath the hem of the white garment were splendidly curved to a trim ankle – and attracted, too, by the smooth-skinned freshness of her youth.

But youth and beauty were not, to the deaf man, qualities which when taken alone would assure a good bed partner. He had explored the girl further.

He had noticed that her luminous eyes carried a challenge, and that the challenge was directed toward any man who walked into the restaurant. He was surprised to find such blatancy in the eyes of a nineteen-year-old, and he tried to evaluate it. He did not want a nymphomaniac. He knew that satisfaction could be multiplied to infinity when allowed to ricochet off the simultaneous pleasures of two, and he had no desire to become involved with an insatiable woman. At the same time, he did not want an uninitiated girl who would allow the evening to dissolve into a literal shower of blood, sweat and tears. The challenge in this girl's eyes boldly stated that she had been had, and that she could be had again, and that the taking might well be worth the efforts of whoever successfully met the challenge. Pleased with what he saw, he continued his surveillance.

The girl's breasts, while admittedly comfortable-looking, could have amounted to nothing more than so much excess fat imbued with a nonexistent sexuality by a culture with an obsessive mammary fetish – were it not for the way the girl carried them. She knew they were there. She never once took them for granted. Her every motion, her every step indicated an extreme awareness of the rich curve below her throat. He was sure that her awareness was sensual, an awareness so total could be nothing else. And, observing her secure knowledge, he never once doubted her potential passion.

Her legs, too, indicated a promising sensuality. They were well-shaped, with a full, curving calf that dropped with surprising grace and swiftness to a narrowness of ankle and a sharpness of arch. The girl was a waitress, and her expected footgear should have been flat-soled shoes. But she chose to emphasize the shape of her leg, and whereas she did not commit the folly of wearing a bona fide high-heeled spike she nonetheless wore a pump with a French heel that was both flattering and prom-ising. She used her legs in two ways. One was strictly utilitarian. They were strong legs, and they carried her from table to table with speed and directness. The other use was calculated and strictly decorative. She used her legs as pistons to manipulate her buttocks.

Casually, the deaf man struck up a conversation with her. The girl, as he'd suspected, would not qualify for a teaching position at Harvard. Their first conversation, as he later recalled it, went something like this. He had ordered a chocolate eclair for dessert.

The girl said, 'I see you have a sweet tooth.'

'Yes, indeed,' the deaf man said.

She had cocked one eyebrow coquettishly. 'Well, sweets for the sweet,' she answered, and swiveled away from the table.

Slowly, he had engaged her in further conversations, strengthening his opinion of her potential. When he finally asked her out, he was certain she would accept immediately – and she did.

That evening, the fourteenth of April, he had dazzled her with his brilliance at dinner. She sat in wide-eyed wonder, contributing little to the conversation, fascinated with his speech. They walked under a star-scattered sky later, guided imperceptibly by the deaf man to an apartment on Franklin Street. When the deaf man suggested that they go up for a drink, the girl demurred slightly, and he felt a quickening of passion; this would not be a pushover; there would be a struggle and a chase to whet his appetite.

They did not talk much in the apartment. They sat on the modern couch in the sunken living room and the girl took off her shoes and pulled her knees up under her, and the deaf man poured two large snifters of brandy, and they sat rolling the glasses in their hands, the girl peeking over the edge of her glass the way she had seen movie stars do, the deaf man drinking the brandy slowly, savoring the taste of the lip-tingling alcohol, anticipating what he would do to this girl, anticipating his pleasure with a slow cruelty that began mounting inside him, a carefully controlled cruelty – control, he reminded himself, control.

By midnight, the girl was totally witless.

Half naked, she did not know what was happening to her, nor did she care; she had no mind; she possessed only a body which was alive in his arms as he carried her down a long white corridor to the first of three bedrooms. Her stockings were off, she realized; he had taken off her stockings; firmly cradled in his arms, her skirt pulled back, she realized she was naked beneath the skirt, her blouse hung open; he had somehow removed her bra without taking off her blouse, she could see the white beating expanse below her neck and suddenly he was standing over her and she was looking up at him expectantly and seeing him and feeling sudden fear, the fear of true and total invasion, and then she knew nothing.

Nothing. She knew nothing. She was drawn toward a blazing sun, pulled away from it, he knew nothing inviolate, every secret place of her succumbed totally to his vicious onslaught, every aching pore of her was his to claim, she was drugged, she was not herself, she was not anyone she knew, she had been carried mindlessly to the edge of totality, violated and adored, cherished and possessed, worshiped and ravaged, there was no cessation, no beginning and no end, she would remember this night with longing and excitement, remember it too with shame and guilt as the night she surrendered privacy to a total stranger, with an abandon she had not known she'd possessed.

At three in the morning, he gave her a gift. He crossed the room and she was too weary to follow him even with her eyes, and suddenly he was beside her again, opening a long carton, pulling the filmy silk from within its tissue paper folds.

'Put this on,' he said.

She obeyed him. She would have obeyed whatever

command he'd given her. She rose and pulled the black gown over her head.

'And your shoes.'

She obeyed. She felt somewhat dizzy, and yet she longed to be in his arms again. The short nightgown ended abruptly above her thighs. She felt his eyes upon her, sweeping the curve of her leg, the long accentuated curve dropping to the high-heeled spike.

'Come here,' he said, and she went to him hungrily.

11.

WELL, THE FIFTEENTH was the middle of the month, and a hell of a month it was shaping up to be so far.

All things considered, and not even taking into account the petty little daily crimes which bugged every man working the squad, April so far – despite the lovely weather – was beginning to assume the characteristics of a persistent migraine. And no man on the squad had a bigger headache than Meyer Meyer.

Meyer, it seemed, had become the man officially assigned to the Heckler Case. That it was now a bona fide 'case,' there seemed to be no doubt. What had started with David Raskin as a simple series of threatening phone calls and foolish pranks had somehow mushroomed into something with the proportions of an epidemic. Slowly, bit by bit, the complaints had come in until the list of shop or restaurant owners reporting threatening calls and acts of harassment had grown to a total of twenty-two. Some of the complainants were truly terrified by the threats; others were simply annoyed by the disruption of their business. Meyer, taking the calls, became more and more convinced that one man, or group of men, was responsible for the heckling. In any case, the *modus operandi* seemed identical.

But what he couldn't understand was what the hell was so important about April thirtieth?

Or why these particular shops had been chosen? A haberdashery, a Chinese restaurant, a tie store, a leather goods shop, a candy shop – what was so important about these particular locations?

Meyer simply couldn't figure it.

Nor was Steve Carella much better off with his case, the case of the almost-naked dead man found in Grover Park. Why, he wondered, had anyone wanted old John Smith dead? Or, for that matter, why would the dead man have taken an assumed name? And such a phony one at that? John Smith! My God! How many hotel and motel registers in the United States carried that pseudonym daily? And who was this deaf guy? And why had twenty-two-year-old Lotte Constantine wanted to invest time and money in sixty-six-year-old John Smith? (The obvious alias rankled every time he thought of it.) The deaf man. Who? And he pulled a face at the ironies of fate. The one person who meant everything in the world to him was a deaf mute, his wife Teddy. And now his adversary was someone known only as the deaf man. The juxtaposition was irony with a knife-edge, but Carella was not amused. He was only puzzled. Truly and honestly puzzled.

And when it's going bad, you might expect the people who are causing you trouble to let up for a while, mightn't you? When two stalwart and intelligent detectives were struggling with two separate nuts which seemed uncrackable and which caused both men a considerable loss of sleep, when these two intrepid protectors of the innocent, these indefatigable investigators, these supporters of law and order, when these two darned nice fellows were trying their utmost to get out from under two miserable cases, wouldn't it have been decent and only cricket to leave them alone, to allow them a respite from their torments? Friends, wouldn't it have been the decent thing to do? Cop lovers of the world, wouldn't it have been the only nice way, the only good way, the only fair way?

Sure.

On April 15, which was a balmy spring day blowing fresh breezes off the River Harb to the north, the harassment began anew.

It began with a difference, however.

It seemed to be concentrated against Dave Raskin, as if all armies had suddenly massed on poor Raskin's frontiers and were pressing forward with their spring invasion. If you looked at this sudden offensive one way, you could assume the enemy was doing his best to plague Raskin and the cops. But if you looked at it another way, you could think of the concentrated attack as a guide, a signpost, a singling-out of the one store among twenty-five, a divine hand pointing, a divine voice saying, 'Look and ye shall see; knock and it shall be opened unto ye.'

Meyer Meyer looked, but he didn't see at first. Later on, when he knocked, it was truly opened unto him. And he didn't for a moment suspect that this was what was desired of him, that the sudden spring offensive against Dave Raskin's loft was designed to alert a police department which, with all due respect to those stalwarts, seemed to be somewhat asleep. You can play percentages only if your opponents are playing some sort of percentages themselves. Whatever the deaf man's plan, it wouldn't work if the cops didn't at least *suspect* what he was up to. And so the tanks rolled into high gear, churning through the spring mud, and the dive bombers warmed up on the airfields and took off into the chill early morning air and from across the city, the big guns began thundering against poor Dave Raskin's loft.

At ten o'clock on the morning of April 15, four hundred and thirty folding chairs were delivered to Raskin.

They were piled on the floor, and against the wall, and on the tables, and in the hallway, and down the steps, and some of them even overflowed onto the sidewalk.

David Raskin insisted that he had not ordered any folding chairs, but the truck driver was a persistent man who told Raskin he always delivered what he was supposed to deliver and if Raskin had a beef he could call the chair company and discuss it with them. David Raskin called both the chair company and the 87th Squad, and then he paced the floor of his loft waiting for the chair people to come pick up the chairs again and waiting for Meyer Meyer to do something. There was, naturally, nothing Meyer Meyer could do except call the chair company who confirmed the fact that David Raskin had ordered the chairs sometime last week for delivery that day which, again naturally, David Raskin had not done.

So Meyer Meyer ran his hand over his bald head and cursed in pig Latin, a trick he had learned as a boy because his mother had not allowed swearing in her house. And David Raskin paced the floor of his loft and cursed in very loud English which, fortunately, his Puerto Rican girls did not understand too well.

At twelve-thirty on the nose, the caterers arrived.

The caterers arrived and with them they brought enough food to feed the entire Russian Army together with a few Yugoslavian partisans, or so it seemed. Actually they brought only enough food to feed the four hundred and thirty lunch guests who were to occupy the four hundred and thirty folding chairs. They brought little bottles containing Martinis and Manhattans, and they brought celery and olives and carrot sticks, and they brought onion soup, and they brought roast beef and turkey and candied sweet potatoes and asparagus tips au gratin and coffee, tea or milk, and orange sherbet and chocolate layer cake and little mints and – man, David Raskin positively flipped! The caterers insisted that he had called them and ordered this veritable feast and Raskin told them he didn't know four hundred and thirty people in the entire world, let alone four hundred and thirty people he would care to invite for lunch, and the caterers said he had ordered the stuff, they had prepared all the food, what the hell were they supposed to do with it all, this wasn't folding chairs which you could return, this was food, food, FOOD, especially cooked and prepared for the occasion, who was going to pay the bill?'

'The man who ordered this *megillah!*' Raskin shouted.

'*You* ordered it!' the caterers shouted back.

'I ordered nothing! Get it out of here! Get it out! Out! Out! Out!'

And that was when the orchestra arrived.

There were fourteen musicians in the orchestra, and they were all carrying their instruments, instruments like trombones and saxophones, and a bass drum, and a bass fiddle, and trumpets, and even a French horn or two. And they were also carrying music stands and they wanted to know where they should set up, and Raskin told the leader – a small man with a Hitler mustache and a personality to match – that he could go set up in the River Dix, just get the hell out of his loft, he did not order any damned orchestra! To which the man with the Hitler mustache said, 'You came down to the union personally and left a twenty-dollar deposit when you hired the band!'

'*Me!*' Raskin shouted. '*I* came down to the *firshtunke-nuh* union? I don't even know where your dirty union *is*, *I* came down? Get out of here with those drums!' and that was when the men returned to pick up the chairs, and the way Raskin finally got everybody out of the place was by calling Meyer again, who rushed over and tried to settle things as best he could.

That was on the fourteenth, and a jolly Wednesday that was, by George.

111

On Monday the twentieth, only four items arrived, and they were obviously a mistake.

The four items were:

2 PICKS
2 SHOVELS

David Raskin mopped his feverish brow.

'I didn't order these,' he said.

The delivery boy shrugged and consulted the order slip. 'Two picks and two shovels. Says so right here.'

Patiently, Raskin said, 'I didn't order them. You see, there's a crazy man who—'

'Two picks and two shovels,' the delivery boy said firmly. 'Deliver to the loft at twelve thirteen Culver Avenue. See? Says so right here. Can you read that, mister?'

'I can read it, but I didn't order—'

'Deliver to the loft at twelve thirteen Culver Avenue after Darask Frocks, Inc. has vacated the premises. Oh.' The delivery boy's voice dropped as he continued reading. 'Call FRederick 7-3548 before delivery. Oh.'

'I got news for you,' Raskin said. 'That's my phone number, but I ain't never vacating these premises. So forget this delivery.'

'They've already been paid for,' the delivery boy said.

And suddenly, David Raskin felt extremely shrewd. Suddenly, David Raskin was confronted with the single clue which would split this mystery wide open, suddenly David Raskin was presented with that opportunity which comes to all men but once in a lifetime, the chance to solve something, the chance to be a hero.

'Tell me,' he said casually, though his heart was pounding, *'who ordered the picks and shovels?'*

The delivery boy looked at his slip. 'Here's the name of the man right here,' he said.

'What is it? What is it?' Raskin asked excitedly.

'L. Sordo,' the delivery boy replied.

Now, whereas Meyer Meyer, by his own admission, had *not* read 'The Red-headed League,' he *had* read a book by a gentleman known as Ernest Hemingway, and the title of that beautiful volume was *For Whom the Bell Tolls*, which is about a lovely guerrilla girl laid in Spain. There is a memorable character called El Sordo in the book and, as any half-wit knows, *el sordo* in Spanish means 'the deaf one' or, because of the masculine *o* ending, 'the deaf man.'

It seemed obvious to Meyer at this point that someone with a hearing deficiency was the person responsible for the various threats everyone had been receiving. The gentleman at the Sandhurst Paper Company in New Bedford, Massachusetts, had told Meyer not too long ago that the person who'd ordered the envelopes had said, 'Excuse me, but would you talk a little louder? I'm slightly deaf, you know.'

And now someone had ordered two picks and two shovels to be delivered *after* Darask Frocks, Inc. vacated the loft, but those picks and shovels had obviously been delivered by mistake *before* Raskin got out, and the man who'd ordered those tools was a man who called himself L. Sordo. So not only was there a strong possibility that this was the same man who'd ordered the Massachusetts envelopes but there was a sneaking suspicion on Meyer's part that this fellow wanted to be known, he wanted to be sure he was given credit for his handiwork, wanted to be certain his byline appeared on everything he created, El Sordo, The Deaf Man.

And sitting not three feet away from Meyer Meyer at his own desk was Detective Steve Carella who was fairly convinced that a person who'd used the alias of John

Smith had had something cooking with someone known only as the deaf man, and that if he could get some sort of a lead onto this deaf man fellow, he would be a lot closer toward solving the case.

The trouble was, of course, that Meyer Meyer was working on a series of threatening phone calls and harassments and Steve Carella was working on a shotgun homicide and neither man saw fit to discuss his respective case with his colleague. That was the way things were going that April. In a squadroom where everyone generally was willing to discuss anything and everything involving police work, toilet training, marital technique and pennant races, nobody seemed too talkative that April. Even Bert Kling, who managed to finish his volume of Sherlock Holmes stories between phone conversations with his fiancée, failed to discuss any of the yarns with Meyer Meyer. That's the way things were going that April.

Well, on Monday of the following week, the advertisement appeared in the two morning dailies which carried classified advertisements. The ad read:

WANTED

Redheads! Redheads! Redheads! To model women's dresses in swank Culver Avenue showroom. No experience necessary. Apply 12 noon. Darask Frocks, Inc. 1213 Culver Avenue, Mr Raskin. Redheads! Redheads! Redheads!

And, man, the redheads came out of the sewers that day! No one in the world would have believed there were so many redheads in the entire city. Rome is supposed to be the city of redheads, but at twelve noon on April 27 there were dozens, hundreds, thousands of redheads of every conceivable size, shape, and hue standing in a disorderly line in front of Dave Raskin's loft, trailing past the open doors of the bank and going around the corner. There were fat redheads and skinny redheads, tall ones and short ones, busty ones and flat-chested ones, hippy ones and straight ones, flaming redheads and auburn redheads, natural orange redheads and bleached scarlet redheads, and each and every one of them wanted to see Dave Raskin about this job of modeling women's dresses in the swank Culver Avenue showroom. The line sailed clear around the block and past the bank and into the open doorway alongside the bank and up the steps and into the loft where Dave Raskin frantically tried to explain he was not hiring any damn models that day.

And all of a sudden, the dawn broke.

All of a sudden, Meyer Meyer tipped to what was afoot.

Just the way he was supposed to.

115

12.

HE SLAMMED THE phone down angrily and said, 'Raskin again! The heckler sent him thousands of redheads! I'm telling you, Bert, this is driving me nuts. All of a sudden, he's concentrating on poor Dave. What does he want from the guy? What's he after?'

Kling, working hard at his desk, looked up and said, 'What's a four-letter word for walking sticks?'

'Huh?'

'The puzzle,' Kling said, tapping the newspaper on his desk.

'Is that all you've got to do with your time?'

'What's a four-letter—'

'There are no four-letter words in my vocabulary.'

'Come on. Walking sticks. A four-letter word.'

'Legs,' Meyer answered. 'So what could that crazy nut want from Raskin? Why does he want him out of that loft?'

'You think it *could* be?'

'Could be what? What are you talk—'

'Legs.'

'I don't know. Don't bother me. Why did he stop calling all the other guys? Twenty-three stores by the last count, and all of a sudden silence except for Raskin. What does he want from him? His money? But who keeps money in a loft? Where people keep money is in—'

Meyer stopped talking. A look of shocked recognition had crossed his face. His eyes had opened wide, and his mouth had dropped open in surprise. The word caught in is throat, refusing to budge.

116

'What's a four-letter word that means a slope or acclivity?' Kling asked.

'A bank,' Meyer said breathlessly, pushing the word out of his mouth.

'Yeah, that's right. Like the bank of a riv—'

'A bank,' Meyer said again, his mouth still hanging open, a dazed and glassy look in his eyes.

'I heard you the—'

'A bank!' he said. 'The bank! The bank under the loft! The bank, Bert! The goddammed bank!'

'Huh? What?'

'That's why he wants Raskin out! He wants to chop through that loft floor and come through the ceiling of the bank vault! That's what those picks and shovels were for! But they were delivered too early by mistake! He's going to rob that bank, but he's got to do it before the thirtieth of April because the bank is moving then! *That's* why all the pressure on Raskin! Oh man, how could I have—'

'Yeah, that was a good story,' Kling said, not looking up from his paper.

'*What* was a good story?' Meyer asked confused.

'The Red-headed League,' Kling said.

Meyer shrugged. 'Come on,' he said. 'I want to talk to the lieutenant.'

He grabbed Kling's wrist and dragged him across the room. He almost forgot to knock on Byrnes's door.

The squadroom was empty when Carella entered it not five minutes later. He looked around, yelled, 'Anybody home?' and went to his desk. 'Hey, where is everybody?' he yelled again.

The door to Byrnes's office opened briefly. Meyer's bald head appeared. 'In here, Steve,' he said, and then closed the door again instantly.

Carella took off his jacket, rolled up his sleeves, and frowned again. He had begun frowning a lot lately. He knew exactly why.

Ever since he had learned the dead man's alias – the patently transparent 'John Smith' – he had been going through the files of known criminals in an attempt to locate the man's real name. He had found nothing even resembling the dead man. It was now the twenty-eighth of April and he seemed no closer to identifying his man – much less solving his case – than he'd been on the day the body was discovered in the park. He supposed that set some sort of record for inept detection but, by Christ, he was really trying, and nothing seemed to jell. He had considered the possibility that the shapely Lotte Constantine had done in the old man herself, and he had assigned Bert Kling to a surveillance of the girl while he himself had tried to get a line on her. From what he could gather, the girl was perfectly clean. She had come to the city from Indiana some four years back. She had held a series of unrelated jobs before landing the job as cigarette girl in the Harem Club two years back. She had never been in trouble with the police. Her employer at the Harem described her as 'a lovely, quiet girl.' Her affection for the dead 'John Smith' had apparently been very real. Her co-workers at the club informed Kling that since she'd met the man who called himself 'Johnny,' she had not dated another man, even though men at the club were constantly asking her. Bert Kling, reporting on the girl's movements, stated that she generally slept late, went to dancing school on Mondays, Wednesdays and Fridays, dramatics classes on Tuesdays and Thursdays, and reported for work daily at the Harem at 8:00 P.M. where she donned her abbreviated costume and black net stockings, not removing them until three in the morning, at which time she went directly home.

Kling had been tailing her since April eighteenth and this was the twenty-eighth. In one of his reports, Bert Kling wrote, '*She has a lovely behind, this girl, and I don't mind tailing her. But Steve, I think she's clean. I think I'm wasting my time.*'

Carella was inclined to agree, but he decided to maintain the surveillance for at least a few more days.

But now, considering the seeming innocence of this girl, considering the fact that she and 'John Smith' really did seem to be in love with each other, it occurred to him that the man might possibly have been telling her the truth. In fact, Carella could find no really good reason for assuming the man had lied. And, in thinking about the situation, Carella realized that he had fallen into the trap of accepting the nearest and easiest conclusion without bothering to search for the more elusive but perhaps more rewarding answer. And, as frequently happened in such cases, the *real* truth was as close to hand as was the *apparent* truth. In this case, it was even closer.

John Smith was an obvious alias.

That was the apparent truth.

The girl Lotte Constantine had told Carella that John Smith was retired and living on his social security checks. Carella pulled the Isola telephone directory to him and looked up 'UNITED STATES GOVERN-MENT' and, under that, 'SOCIAL SECURITY ADMIN.' The small type advised Carella to 'See US Govt Health Educ&Welfare Dept of,' so he looked up 'HEALTH EDUC & WELFARE DEPT OF' on the same page but slightly to the left, under that he found:

Social Security Admin—
    Bur of Old Age & Survivors Ins—
        For Info Call The Office Nearest Your Home—
           Isola Dist Offices—

And beneath that were four listings for offices in Isola, none of which were near his home (which happened to be in Riverhead) but one of which was fairly close to the squadroom of the 87th Precinct, from whence he was making the phone call. Carella asked Murchison for an outside line, and he dialed the number. He identified himself, told the switchboard operator what information he was seeking, and was promptly connected to a woman with a kindly voice who said her name was Mary Goodery. Carella could not have invented a better name to have gone with that gentle voice. He told Mary Goodery what he wanted, and Mary Goodery asked him to wait.

When she came back onto the line, she said, 'Yes, indeed, we do have records for a Mr John Smith.'

'You do?' Carella said, amazed because he was certain the thing could not be as simple as all that.

'Yes, sir, we do.'

'This John Smith is how old, please?'

'Just one moment, sir,' Mary Goodery said, and she studied her record card, and then her voice came back to the telephone, 'Sixty-six in March. He has been receiving Federal social security benefits for more than a year now.'

'Would you know if he was also working? I mean, in addition to receiving his checks?'

'I wouldn't know, sir. You understand, don't you, that anyone who earns more than one hundred dollars a month – that's twelve hundred dollars for the year – is automatically disqualified for social security benefits?'

'No, I didn't know that.'

'Yes,' Miss Goodery said.

'I see. But you wouldn't know whether or not he was holding down a job which paid him less than a hundred a month, would you?'

'I have no record of that, sir, no.'

'Thank you, Miss Goodery.'

'Not at all,' she said, and she hung up.

Carella put the receiver back into the cradle and sat staring reflectively through the open window.

'Oh, my God!' he said suddenly, and he pulled the phone to him, got an outside line, and dialed rapidly.

'Social Security Administration,' a voice said.

'Would you get me Miss Goodery, please?' Carella said.

'Just a moment, sir.'

Carella waited, wondering how he'd ever got to be a detective, wondering how it happened that a *klutz* like him could manage to stay alive in a job which sometimes required quick thinking, wondering how . . .

'Miss Goodery,' that good woman said.

'This is Detective Carella again,' he admitted. 'I forgot to ask you something.'

'Yes?'

'Do you – do you have an address listed for John Smith?' Carella said, and he winced at his own stupidity.

'An address? Why, yes, I'm sure we do. If you'll just wait while I get his folder again.'

'Certainly,' Carella said, and he leaned back to wait.

In a few moments, Mary Goodery came back with the address for an apartment building on Franklin Street.

Fanny got her idea that afternoon at lunch, and she moved on it as soon as she had discussed it with Teddy. 'Discussed' is perhaps the wrong word. For, whereas Teddy was perfectly capable of having a discussion, the conversation which took place at the kitchen table that afternoon was not a discussion but a monologue.

The twins had already been fed and put in for their nap. Fanny had made a batch of scrambled eggs and onions for herself and Teddy, and the two women sat at the kitchen table now, eating in silence, the strong aroma of onions and eggs and hot coffee filling the large kitchen. Both women wore slacks, Teddy's form-fitting and trim over a youthful body, Fanny's form-fitting over a body which was thick and solid and which had served its mistress well for more than fifty years. Teddy was shoveling a forkful of eggs into her mouth when Fanny said, out of the blue, 'Why would they first strip the uniform off him and then throw it into an incinerator?'

Teddy looked up inquisitively.

'I'm talking about Steve's case,' Fanny said.

Teddy nodded.

'Obviously, that uniform is pretty damned important, wouldn't you say? Otherwise, why bother to take it off the man? Whoever killed him left his shoes and socks on, isn't that right? Navy shoes, mind you, but apparently the Navy part didn't mean a damn or they'd have taken the shoes off of him, too. But they did take the uniform off. That they did. Now why? I'll tell you why. Because that uniform probably had some kind of a marking on it, something that would have told any interested party something very important about the man who was wearing it. And maybe something about why he was killed. So what kind of a uniform could it be?'

Teddy shrugged and continued eating her eggs.

'Did you ever see a man in his sixties delivering mail, or driving a bus? I never did,' Fanny said. 'But I *have* seen men in their sixties working as bank guards, or night watchmen, or elevator operators. And didn't Steve say this John Smith was on his way to *work* the night Random met him in the bar? Isn't that what Steve said? Sure, it is. So why hasn't Steve thought of it before this? That man was a night watchman, or I'll eat my hat. And for some reason, that uniform would identify the place where he was a watchman, and whoever killed the man doesn't want that spot to be identified. Now that's what

I'm betting, Teddy, and I'm going to tell Steve the minute he gets here.' Fanny nodded emphatically. 'In fact, I'm going to call and tell him right now.'

She went to the telephone and dialed FRederick 7-8024.

'Eighty-seventh Precinct, Sergeant Murchison.'

'This is Fanny Knowles. May I talk to Steve, please?'

'Fanny *who?*' Murchison said.

'Fanny Knowles, you dumb Irishman!' Fanny shouted. 'Fanny Knowles who lives with the Carellas and who's only called that run-down station house a hundred times already in the past year and spoken to yourself, you big jerk sitting on your fat butt! Fanny Knowles, now get me Steve Carella, would you please, dearie?'

'One of these days, Fanny . . .'

'Yes, dearie?' she said sweetly.

'Never mind. I can't get you Steve because he's gone out, said he wouldn't be back until late this afternoon, if at all. Had an apartment on Franklin Street he wanted to check, and said it might take a bit of time.'

'That's too bad,' Fanny said. 'I had an idea for him, about the case he's working on.'

'Well,' Murchison said with saccharine solicitude, 'he'll just have to struggle along without your assistance, I guess. Was there any other cop you want to offer help to today? We got a whole squadroom of them upstairs.'

'Go to the devil,' Fanny said, and she hung up.

The whole squadroom of cops was really *none* of them at the moment. Carella had gone out to look up the address given him by Mary Goodery, Parker was still on his candy store plant, Hernandez was out interrogating a burglary victim, and Meyer and Kling were in the lieutenant's office. The squadroom was empty and stone silent. Anyone could have walked up there and marched out with all the typewriters and electric fans.

123

In Byrnes's office, Meyer was divulging his sudden brainstorm, his eyes aglow. Byrnes sat behind his desk, his fingers before him in a small cathedral. Kling leaned against the wall and listened skeptically.

'It's *obvious* that's what he's trying to pull,' Meyer said. 'I'm surprised I didn't see it before this.'

'It's too obvious,' Kling said dryly.

'What do you mean?' Meyer answered, annoyed. 'Don't start telling me—'

'Let him talk, Meyer,' Byrnes said.

'All I know is that a guy who's going to rob a bank isn't going to point a finger at it. He's not going to say, "This is it, fellas, so please be waiting for me when I bust in, okay?" It's just too damn obvious.'

'Then why were those shovels sent to the loft?'

'To let us *think* he was going to break into that bank,' Kling said. 'Aren't you forgetting something? He's been calling a bunch of *other* stores, too.'

'Restaurants, clothing stores, a tie—'

'So what's Raskin's place? The Taj Mahal?' Kling said. 'Raskin runs a wholesale dress business. What the hell does that matter? It's not Raskin's place he's calling attention to. It's the bank downstairs! Okay, how many of those other places are over banks, or next door to them?'

'I never thought of that,' Meyer said. 'Where's that list of stores?'

'On your desk,' Kling said.

Meyer ran out of the room. Kling shook his head and said, 'It looks like a smoke screen to me, sir. I may be wrong, but it smells to high heaven. The man couldn't be that stupid or that egotistical. He's pointed an obvious finger at Raskin's loft, right over the bank, and he's even had some picks and shovels delivered there, supposedly by accident. And the redheads today. It's just too obvious.'

'What about the redheads?' Meyer asked, coming back into the room with his list. He went directly to the phone, got an outside line and began dialing.

'The A. Conan Doyle story,' Kling said. ' "The Red-headed League." '

'Stop *hocking* me with your damn mysteries,' Meyer said. 'We're trying – Hello?' he said into the phone. 'Mr Lombardo? James Lombardo? This is Detective Meyer of the Eighty-seventh Squad. Listen, could you please tell me what's next door to you? What? Oh, a lingerie shop. Well, thank y— What? *What's* on the other side? Oh, I see. Thank you, Mr Lombardo. No, nothing yet. Thank you.' He replaced the phone on its cradle.

'Well?' Byrnes said.

'A lingerie shop on one side of him, and a jewelry shop on the other.'

'Jewelry,' Kling said.

'Yeah.' Meyer looked at his list again. 'Let me try another one of these.'

'Sure,' Kling said. ' "The Red-headed League." The son of a bitch is referring us to his source.'

'What do you mean, Bert?' Byrnes asked. Meyer, standing alongside him, was dialing again.

'You know the story, don't you? These men run an ad in a London paper, advertising for redheads to fill a vacancy in the League. The idea is that the League will pay this man I-forget-how-many pounds a week for copying words from the encyclopedia, but the copying job must be done in the League's offices. Well, this red-headed man applies for the position and gets it, and every day he trots out to the office and copies words.'

'It sounds implausible to me,' Meyer said. Into the phone, he said, 'Let me talk to Mr Chen, please.'

'Not implausible at all,' Kling said. Meyer suddenly began talking again, so he shifted his attention to

Byrnes. 'The reason they want the redhead out of his shop, you see, is because they're digging a tunnel to the bank across the way. Finally, when they're ready to rob the bank, the man loses his job. He contacts Holmes to see if he can't do something about his being fired, and of course Sherlock figures out exactly what's going on.'

'How the hell does he do that?' Meyer asked, hanging up. 'That was the Chinese restaurant. It's over an antique shop. Rare jade mostly. I'm gonna call one more place.' Rapidly, he began dialing again.

'So what's happened here?' Kling asked Byrnes. 'This guy called God knows how many stores which are alongside banks and jewelry shops and—'

'We're not sure on *all* of them yet,' Meyer said, waiting for someone to pick up the phone on the other end.

'We're pretty sure,' Kling said. 'He calls all these guys and he hopes one of them'll call the cops, or all of them. He wants them to call the cops. Why? Because there're twenty-three stores so far, and who knows how many others who didn't bother to call us. Then he directs attention to Raskin's loft because he wants us to think he's going to hit *that* bank. And today he takes out an ad for *redheads*, making sure we don't miss the significance of the Sherlock Holmes story. He draws a direct parallel. He wants us to tip, wants us to figure out he's going to rob the bank under Raskin's loft. Okay, why?'

Into the phone, Meyer said, 'Thank you very much, Mr Goldfarb. Yes, thank you.' He hung up. 'The travel agency,' he said. 'It's next door to a bank.'

'Sure,' Kling said. 'So you know why he's doing this?'

'Why?' Byrnes asked.

'Because he's not going to hit that bank under the loft at all. He's going to hit one of the other twenty-three. The rest are just his smoke screen.'

'Which one is he gonna hit?' Meyer asked.

Kling shrugged. 'That's the big question, Meyer.'

'What do we do, Pete?'

'What's today?' Byrnes asked.

'The twenty-eighth.'

'And his deadline is the thirtieth?'

'Yes.'

'That gives us two days. I imagine we can put some men on.'

'What do you mean?'

'We'll cover those shops. I'll have to get help from some of the other squads. One man to a shop. You say there are twenty-three of them?'

'So far.'

'That's a hell of a lot of men to be throwing out of action,' Byrnes said. He shook his head. 'I'd better call Headquarters on this. I'm going to need more help than the squads can give. We can't put so many detectives out of action.'

'Why not patrolmen?' Kling said.

'They'd never catch him. He'd spot the uniforms.'

'Put them on special duty. Plainclothes. It's only for two days.'

'That's a good idea,' Byrnes said. 'I'll talk to Captain Frick.' He reached for the phone. 'There's only one thing that puzzles me,' he said.

'What's that?'

'If none of these shopowners move – if none of them yield to his threat to get out by the thirtieth – how in hell will he pull his job?'

The men stared at each other blankly.

They had just asked the two-and-a-half-million-dollar question.

And none of them knew the answer.

13.

THE FOUR MEN sat on the hillside overlooking the ice-cream factory. The factory was surrounded by a cyclone fence and within that fence there were at least thirty white ice-cream trucks lined up in three identical rows. Two smokestacks jutted up into the April sky, and a huge sign straddled the stacks:

PICK-PAK ICE CREAM
The Big Lick on a Stick

The four men looked like a group of congenial buddies who had been out for a late afternoon stroll, who'd discovered this grassy hillock overlooking the ice-cream plant, and who'd decided to sit and rest their weary feet. There was certainly nothing sinister-looking about any of the men. If they'd showed up at Central Casting for parts in a grade-B gangster film, each and every one of them would have been turned down. And yet three of the four men had police records, and two of the men were, at that very moment, carrying guns. And even though their conversation was carried on in low and gentle tones, accompanied by sincere facial expressions, these men were discussing the future commission of a crime.

The deaf man was the tallest and handsomest of the four. He sat looking out over the rows of white trucks, a strand of grass between his teeth.

'That's where we get it,' he said.

Chuck, sitting next to him, fished for a cigarette in the pocket of his jacket, pulling out a single cigarette while leaving the package inside the pocket. He took out a book of matches, lifted the cover, bent one match over from the rest so that it was close to the striking surface, closed the cover, and then struck the match, all with one hand, the match flaming but still attached to the folder.

'Plenty trucks,' he said, and he blew out a stream of smoke.

'We only need one, Chuck,' the deaf man said.

'That's for sure. When do we grab it?'

'Tomorrow.'

'The day before, huh?'

'The *night* before,' the deaf man corrected.

'What time?'

'I figured along about midnight. Rafe's been casing the lot for a week. Rafe, do you want to fill us in?'

Rafe adjusted his gold-rimmed glasses, let out a sigh and ran a busy hand through his straw-blond hair. He seemed reluctant to speak. It almost seemed as if speaking pained him physically.

'There's a simple padlock on the gate,' he said, his voice very low, as if he had learned at an early age that people who speak softly are generally listened to. 'I can open it with a bobby pin.'

'He's speaking figuratively,' the deaf man said. He grinned. 'Aren't you, Rafe?'

'Sure, not a bobby pin, but this is a snap, believe me. Also, there's no watchman in the yard. So once we're in, we're in.'

'Are the ignition keys left in the trucks?' Chuck asked.

'No. We'll have to cross the wires.'

'No possibility of getting duplicates made?'

'I don't see how.'

'That might be worth thinking about,' Chuck said, turning to the deaf man. 'I mean, we can't keep the thing running all the time, can we? And if the law shows, who wants to be fooling around with wires under the dash?'

'Once we get the truck away from here, I can rig a switch that works without an ignition key,' Rafe said. 'Don't worry about that.'

'I'm not worried, I'm only thinking ahead. This isn't a penny-ante thing we're involved in here, Rafe.'

'Nobody said it was.'

'Okay. Is the fence wired?'

'No.'

'Are you sure?'

'Positive. Apparently they're not too concerned about the trucks. There's an alarm for the plant, and there's also a watchman who—'

'Uh-oh,' Chuck said.

'No, no, nothing to worry about,' the deaf man assured him quickly. 'He never comes out into the yard, and we won't make our play until he's up on the top floor of the building.'

'How do we know when that is?' Chuck asked.

'It's at eleven P.M.,' Rafe said. 'He begins making his rounds at that time. Takes the elevator up to the sixth floor and then starts down on foot. We'll start working on the fence at eleven. We'll grab the truck when he reaches the top floor.'

'And how will we know when he reaches the top floor?'

'You can see his flashlight as he walks around. It lights up the whole damn floor. Okay?'

'Sounds good so far. We grab the truck and we're out before he gets a chance to come all the way downstairs again, right?'

'Right.'

'Then what?' Chuck asked.

'We drive the truck to the store.'

'Think that's smart?'

'Why not? It says Chelsea Pops, Inc. right on our window, doesn't it?'

'Sure. But it says Pick-Pak Ice Cream on the side of the truck.'

'The truck'll be in the back yard. Nobody's going to go looking there. Besides, Pop can keep away any visitors while we work on it.'

Pop, who had not uttered a word thus far, cleared his throat and said, 'Sure, I can do that. It's Rafe and Chuck who'll be taking the truck, is that right?'

'That's right, Pop,' the deaf man said.

'And they'll drive it to the store where you and I'll be waiting, is that right?'

'That's right, Pop.'

'Will I be dressed, or what?'

'Yes, of course,' the deaf man said. 'Your job is to keep any unwanted visitors away.'

'Okay.' The old man put a hand up to shade his eyes and squinted at the rows of white trucks in the lot below. 'Is that tin covering the trucks?' he asked.

'It's a porcelainized metal of some sort,' Rafe answered. 'Why?'

'Will we have any trouble getting the new signs on it?'

'I don't think so. We've got an electric drill and carborundum bits. Those things can drill through *steel*.'

'Mmm, that's good,' the old man said, nodding.

'What about the license plate?' Chuck asked, sucking in on his cigarette.

'What about it?' the deaf man said.

'We're grabbing the truck the night before the job, aren't we?' he asked. He was truly an ugly man with the squat solidity of a gorilla, huge shoulders and long, dangling arms, massive hands, a square, short-snouted head. And yet he spoke quietly, almost gently.

131

'Yes, the night before the job,' the deaf man said.

'So they'll be looking for it, won't they? What I mean is, the watchman'll call the cops either as soon as he hears that truck taking off, or as soon as he realizes it's gone, depending on how much on the ball he is. Next thing you know a whole description is going out, you know how the cops work, don't you? So next thing you know, the license plate is being flashed to every squad car in the city. So where does that leave us? So that's what I meant when I asked about the plate.'

'Naturally, the plate will be changed.'

'But when? It's a long haul from here to the store. If that watchman is on the ball, the license plate number can be on the air in five minutes. I'll be driving this truck, you know.'

'So what's your idea?'

'I say we change the plate right here in the lot, even before we start the truck. That's what I say.'

'All right.'

'Fine. And it can't be an ordinary plate, you know. You look at those trucks down there, you'll see they're not carrying ordinary plates. That's a special kind of commercial plate. We'll have to scout around for some between now and the thirtieth.'

'We will,' the deaf man said.

'The other thing that bothers me is working in the open, in the back yard, when we get to the store. You know what I mean? Even if the license plate isn't flashed, every cop in the city'll be looking for a Pick-Pak Ice Cream truck. So there we are drilling holes into the side of one. That doesn't smell so hot to me.'

'What do you suggest?'

'Can't we build some kind of a temporary screen?'

'I'm afraid a screen would attract attention.'

'Well, I don't like working in the back yard. This is too big a thing to take a risk like that.'

'Could we take the truck to Majesta?' the old man asked. 'Work on it there?'

'That would really be dangerous. A half-hour ferry ride? No, that would be out of the question.'

'Why don't we rent a private garage somewhere near here?' Rafe asked. 'We can drive to it as soon as we have the truck, make our changes, and then go over to the store. Once the changes are made, we're safe.'

'I think that would be best,' the deaf man said. 'I'll contact some real estate agents tomorrow. This is a fairly rural section, so perhaps we'll have some luck. If not, we're simply going to have to chance working in the open.'

'If we can't get a garage near here, I'd rather drive it to some dark street and do the job there instead of in that back yard.'

'Let's not cross our bridges,' the deaf man said. 'It's agreed that I'll try to find a garage in this neighborhood tomorrow. Let's leave it at that for now.'

'Okay,' Chuck said.

'But we'll be taking the truck tomorrow, right?' the old man asked. He paused. 'I don't like to ask too many questions, but I did get in this sort of late, and . . .'

'That's all right. Yes. We take the truck tomorrow night.'

'And the big job?'

'The next day, of course. April thirtieth.'

The old man nodded. 'Who'll be driving on the day of the big job?'

'Rafe.'

'Who'll be with him?'

'I will,' the deaf man said.

'Have you got uniforms?'

133

'I've ordered them. I'm to pick them up tomorrow.'

'Where will Chuck and I be?' Pop asked.

'After you deliver your packages?' the deaf man said, and he grinned.

'Yes.'

'You'll go immediately to the house in Majesta. You should be finished by one o'clock or so. I expect you'll both catch the two-fifteen boat. Or, at worst, the four-oh-five.'

'And you and Rafe? Which boat will you be on with the truck?'

'We're trying for the five-forty-five. If not, we'll catch the six-oh-five.'

'And when's the one after that?'

'Seven-fifteen,' Rafe said.

'We don't have to worry about any boat beyond the six-oh-five,' the deaf man said. 'We're starting the job at five o'clock, and it shouldn't take more than ten minutes to do the remaining work. Another ten minutes to load the cartons, and another ten to get to the ferry slip.'

'With the loot,' Pop said.

'I should hope so,' the deaf man said, smiling.

'And when do we leave Majesta?'

'As soon as things begin to cool. We can work that out while we're there. We'll leave one at a time. Last man takes the car. The ice-cream truck stays behind, in the garage.'

'You think of everything, don't you?' Chuck said, and there was a tinge of bitterness to his voice.

'I try to,' the deaf man said flatly. 'I find it's just as simple to think of everything as *not* to. And a hell of a lot safer.'

'I hope you've thought of everything,' Chuck said.

'I have, believe me.' He looked at his watch. 'We'd

better get back to the store,' he said. 'I want to get to work again. We've got a lot to do before Thursday.'

'Look, I hate to sound too cautious,' the old man said.

'What is it?'

'I'm going to have to take another look at those maps you drew. I mean, I've got to know exactly where to plant those things.'

'Certainly,' the deaf man said, and he reached into his inside jacket pocket. 'I thought I had them with me,' he said. 'I guess I left them at the Franklin Street apartment. I'll stop by for them.'

'Think that's safe?' Chuck asked, a worried look on his ugly features. 'Going back to that apartment?'

'I think so, yes,' the deaf man said. 'As a matter of fact, I was there again last night, entertaining a lady friend.' He stared at Chuck defiantly. 'I'll meet you back at the store. You can begin working again as soon as it's dark. Pop, you take up your usual post. We have to be finished by Thursday, remember that.'

The building on Franklin Street was an elegant dwelling which, some twenty years ago, had been among the most aristocratic of apartment houses. Time and the vagaries of the taste makers, a fickleness which shifted the desirability of neighborhoods from the south side to the north side with the swiftness of summer lightning, had combined to render Franklin Street no longer as desirable as the buildings to the south. The local joke now was that no one went to the north side unless it was to take a steamer to Europe, and the bromide was not very far from the truth. But the buildings on Franklin Street had not succumbed to the shoddy encroachments of the slums as had some of the buildings within the territory of the 87th Precinct, buildings which had once been princely and which had slowly been strangled by the octopus of poverty. The buildings on Franklin Street still had doormen and elevator operators. There were no profanities scrawled on the walls of the entrance foyers. The rents in these now-unfashionable buildings were still very fashionably high.

Which led Carella to wonder how a man like John Smith, who had been existing on his social security checks, could afford to live in a joint like 457 Franklin Street. Carella stood on the sidewalk underneath the green canopy and looked into the entrance foyer. A doorman standing just inside the glass entrance doors stared out at him, opened one of the doors in anticipation, and came out onto the sidewalk.

'Help you, sir?' he asked.

'Yes. I'm trying to locate one of your tenants, a man named John Smith.'

'Yes, sir, he's one of our tenants,' the doorman said. 'But he ain't around right now. In fact, I ain't seen him for quite some time.'

'For how long?'

'Oh, since last month some time.'

'Mmm. How long has he been living here, would you know?'

'Just a few months, sir.'

'When did he move in, would you say?'

The doorman studied Carella narrowly. 'Are you a friend of his?' he asked.

'No, I'm a cop.' He flashed the buzzer.

'Oh.'

'Yes. When did he move in, can you tell me that?'

'The end of February, I think it was.'

'And the last time you saw him was in March, that right?'

'That's right.'

'Was he living alone?'

'I don't know. He was here quite a lot.'

'But alone?'

'What?'

'Alone? Was he here alone?'

'Well, I just told you—'

'There were visitors?'

'Yes.'

'Living with Smith?'

'Maybe. It don't matter to the building, you know. Long as a tenant don't disturb other tenants, it's his apartment, after all. So long as he don't play the radio late or make noise or do anything against—' The doorman's eyebrows went up quizzically. 'The *law?*' he asked. 'Is Mr Smith in some kind of trouble?'

'Well, I wouldn't worry about it, if I were you. I'd like to take a look at the apartment. Think you can let me in?'

'I'd have to check that with the building manager. And he won't be here until later this afternoon.'

'Call him,' Carella said.

'Well, I—'

'It's very important,' Carella said. He smiled. 'Call him, won't you?'

The doorman seemed dubious for a moment. Then he smiled back at Carella and said, 'Sure, I'll call him.'

Carella followed him into the building. The lobby had been redecorated recently, the furniture looking shining and new and unused. The doorman went into a small office, made his call and returned to Carella, still smiling. 'Miracles will never cease,' he said. 'The old bastard said okay. Only thing is we ain't got a pass key or anything. I mean, he said if you can get in, okay, he don't want any trouble with the police. But everybody buys their own locks, and we don't have keys to none of the apartments.'

'Well, just take me up, and I'll try some of my keys, okay?' Carella said.

'You carry skeleton keys, huh?' the doorman said, grinning knowingly.

Carella winked slyly. Together they took the elevator up to the sixth floor, and then walked down the corridor to apartment 6C.

'There it is,' the doorman said. 'Nice apartment. Seven rooms. Very nice. It has this sunken living room.'

Carella reached into his pocket and took out a ring of keys.

'Skeleton keys, how about that!' the doorman said, still grinning. The doorman watched him as he began trying the keys in the lock. There were, in addition to his own house keys, perhaps half a dozen skeleton keys hanging from the ring. He tried them all. Not one of them turned the lock.

'No good?' the doorman asked.

'Not very,' Carella said, shaking his head. 'How many floors to this building?'

'Nine.'

'Fire escapes?'

'Sure.'

'Think you can take me up to the roof?'

'You going to come down the fire escape?' the door-man asked.

'I'm going to try,' Carella said. 'Maybe Smith left his window open.'

'Man, you guys sure work for your money, don't you?' the doorman said admiringly.

Carella winked slyly and stepped into the elevator. He got off at the ninth floor and walked the flight to the roof, opening the fire door and stepping out onto the asphalt. He could see the city spread out around him as he crossed the roof, the sharp, vertical rectangles of the apartment buildings slit with open windows, the water tanks atop each roof nesting like shining dark birds, the blue sky beyond and the tracery of the bridges that connected Isola to the other parts of the city, the solid heavy lines of the old bridges, and the more delicate soaring lines of the newer bridges, and far below him the sound of street traffic and the hum of a city rushing with life, kids flying kites from neighboring rooftops, a man down the street swinging his long bamboo pole at his pigeons, the pigeons fluttering into the air in a sudden explosion of gray, beating wings, the April sun covering the asphalt of the roof with yellow warmth.

He walked to the edge of the roof and glanced down the nine stories to the interior courtyard below. Gripping the ladder tightly, he swung over the tiled parapet and began working his way down to the fire escape on the ninth floor. He did not glance into the windows. He didn't want any women screaming for a cop. He kept working his way downward, not looking to the right or the left, going down the ladder hand over hand, and then marching across the fire escape, and onto the next ladder until he reached the sixth floor. He squatted outside apartment 6C and looked through the window. The apartment was empty. He tried the window.

It was locked.

'Dammit,' he said, and he moved along the fire escape to the second window. He was beginning to feel like a burglar, and he wished he had a small hand drill with which to bore into the wood and a hunk of wire to slip into the hole to lift the window catch. He was beginning to feel like an ill-equipped thief until he tried the second window and lo and begorrah, the goddam window was unlocked. He looked into the apartment again, and then slowly slid the window up and climbed over the sill.

The place was silent.

He dropped onto the thick rug and hastily scanned an apartment done in expensive good taste, sleek modern furniture set low against muted wall tones. His eyes touched each piece of furniture, lighted on the Danish desk in one corner of the living room. He went to it instantly and pulled down the drop-leaf front. He hoped to find some letters or an address book or something which could give him a further lead onto the people Smith had known, and especially the identity of the deaf man. But there was nothing of value. He closed the desk and oriented himself, figuring the kitchen to be that way, off the dining room, and the bedrooms to be that way, at the other end of the living room. He walked through the living room, his shoes whispering against the thick rug, and through the open arch and into the first of three bedrooms flanking a Spartan white corridor.

There was a faint trace of perfume in the bedroom.

The bed was neatly made, a black nightgown folded at its foot. Carella picked up the gown and looked for a label. It had come from one of the most expensive stores in the city. He sniffed it, smelled the same perfume that was in the air, and then dropped it onto the bed again, wondering if the gown belonged to Lotte Constantine, wondering too if she'd been lying when she said she didn't know where John Smith had lived. He shrugged, snapped on a lamp resting on one of the night tables, and pulled open the top drawer of the table.

The first thing he saw was a series of crude drawings, either maps or floor plans, none of them labeled, all of them with several things in common. To begin with, each of the maps or floor plans, (it was difficult to tell exactly what they were supposed to represent) was marked with X's scattered onto the face of the drawing. There was no clue anywhere on any of the drawings as to just what the X's were supposed to represent. The maps

140

had something else in common. Each of them had a name scrawled onto the right-hand corner. There were six maps in all.

The name on three of the maps was: CHUCK.

The remaining three maps had first carried one name, and that name was: JOHNNY. But the name had been crossed off all three, and another name written in its place: POP.

Johnny, Carella thought, *John Smith?*

The second thing in the drawer was a portion of a blueprint, neat and professional. He unfolded it and studied it for a moment:

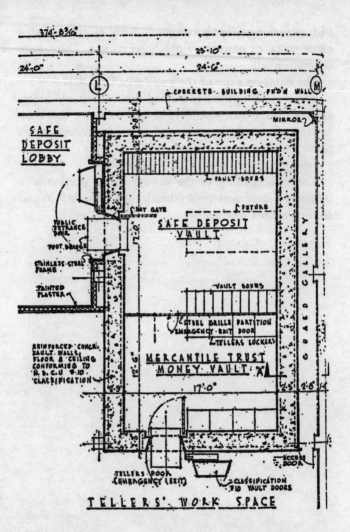

He was folding the blueprint again when the telephone rang, startling him. He hesitated a moment, debating whether or not he should answer it. He put the blueprint down on the night table, wiped his hand across his sweating upper lip, and then picked up the receiver.

'Hello,' he said.

'This is Joey,' the voice on the other end told him.

'Yes?'

'Joey, the doorman. The guy who took you upstairs.'

'Oh, yes,' Carella said.

'I see you got in.'

'Yes.'

'Listen, I didn't know what to do. So I figured I'd call and tell you.'

'Tell me what?'

'Mr Smith. John Smith, you know?'

'What about him?'

'He's on his way upstairs,' the doorman said.

'What?' Carella said, and at that instant he heard a key being turned in the front door.

14.

CARELLA STOOD IN the bedroom with the telephone receiver in one hand, the blueprint on the night table before him, the sound of the turning lock clicking into his mind. He put down the phone at once, turned off the light and moved to the right of the door, his hand going instantly to his service revolver. He flattened himself against the wall, the gun in his right hand, waiting. He heard the front door open, and then close again.

The apartment was silent for a moment.

Then he heard the cushioned sound of footsteps against the rug.

Did I leave that living-room window open? he wondered.

The footsteps hesitated, and then stopped.

Did I leave the desk open? he wondered.

He heard the footsteps again, heard a board squeak in the flooring, and then heard the sound of another door opening. A fine sheen of sweat covered his face now, clung to his chest beneath his shirt. The .38 Police Special was slippery in his fist. He could hear his own heart leaping in his chest with the erratic rhythm of an African bongo. He heard the door closing again, a closet he imagined, and then footsteps once more, and he wondered *Does he know I'm here? Does he know? DOES HE KNOW?* And then he heard a sound which was not familiar to him, a clicking metallic sound, as of metal grating against metal, an unfamiliar sound and yet a sound which was curiously familiar, and then the floor board squeaked again, and the cushioned footsteps came closer to the open arch at the end of the living room, and hesitated, and stopped.

Carella waited.

The footsteps retreated.

He heard another click, and then a twenty-second spell of dead silence; and then music erupted into the apartment, loud and raucous, and Carella instantly knew this man in the apartment was armed and would begin shooting within the next few moments, hoping to use the music as a cover. He did not intend to give his opponent the opportunity of being the one to start the festivities. He hefted the gun in his right hand, sucked in a deep breath, and stepped into the arch.

The man turned from the hi-fi unit alongside the wall.

In a split second, Carella saw the hearing aid in the man's right ear, and then the shotgun the man was holding, and suddenly it was too late, suddenly the shotgun exploded into sound.

Carella whirled away from the blast. He could hear the whistling pellets as they screamed across the confined space of the apartment, and then he felt them lash into his shoulder like a hundred angry wasps, and he thought only *Oh Jesus, not again!* and fired at the tall blond man who was already sprinting across the apartment. His shoulder felt suddenly numb. He tried to lift the hand with the gun and quickly found he couldn't and just as quickly shifted the gun to his left hand and triggered off another shot, high and wide, as the deaf man raised the shotgun and swung the stock at Carella's head. A single barrel, Carella thought in the split second before the stock collided with the side of his head, a single barrel, no time to reload, and a sudden flashing explosion of rocketing yellow pain, slam the stock again, suns revolving, a universe slam the stock, Oh Jesus, oh Jesus! And tears sprang into his eyes because the pain was so fierce, the pain of his shoulder and the awful pain of the heavy wooden stock of the shotgun crashing into crashing into – oh God oh mother oh God oh God

When Carella was carried to the hospital later that day, the doctors there knew that he was still alive, but most of them were unwilling to venture a guess as to how long he would remain that way. He had lost a lot of blood on the floor of that apartment. He had not been discovered lying there unconscious until some three hours after he'd been repeatedly clobbered with the rather unbending stock of the shotgun. It was the doorman of the building, Joey, who had discovered him at six o'clock that evening. Lieutenant Byrnes, interrogating the doorman in the presence of a police stenographer, got the following information:

BYRNES: What made you go up there, anyway?
JOEY: Well, like I told you, he'd been up there a very long time. And I had already seen Mr Smith come downstairs again. So I—
BYRNES: Can you describe this Mr Smith?
JOEY: Sure. He's around my height, maybe six-one, six-two, and I guess he weighs around a hun' eighty, a hun' ninety pounds. He's got blond hair and blue eyes, and he wears this hearing aid in his right ear. He's a little deaf. He come downstairs carrying something wrapped in newspaper.
BYRNES: Carrying what?
JOEY: I don't know. Something long. Maybe a fishing rod or something like that.
BYRNES: Maybe a rifle? Or a shotgun?
JOEY: Maybe. I didn't see what was under the paper.
BYRNES: What time did he come down?
JOEY: Around three, three-thirty, I guess.

BYRNES: And when did you remember that Detective Carella was still in the apartment?

JOEY: That's hard to say, exactly. I had gone over to the candy store where there's this very cute little blonde, she works behind the counter. And I was shooting the breeze with her while I had an egg cream, and then I guess I went back to the building, and I wondered if Car— What's his name?

BYRNES: Carella.

JOEY: He's Italian?

BYRNES: Yes.

JOEY: How about that? I'm Italian, too. A *paisan*, huh? How about that?

BYRNES: That's amazing.

JOEY: How about that? So I wondered if he was still up there, and I buzzed the apartment. No answer. Then – I don't know – I guess I was just curious, I mean, Mr Smith having come down already and all that, so I hopped in the elevator and went up to the sixth floor and knocked on the door. There was no answer and the door was locked.

BYRNES: What'd you do then?

JOEY: I remembered that Car— What's his name?

BYRNES: Carella, Carella.

JOEY: Yeah, Carella, how about that? I remembered he'd gone up on the roof, so I figured I'd go take a look up there, which I done. Then, while I was up there, I figured I might as well go down the fire escape and take a peek into 6C, which I also done. And that was when I seen him laying on the floor.

BYRNES: What'd you do?

JOEY: I opened the window, and I went into the apartment. Man, I never seen so much blood in my life. I thought he was dead. I thought the poor bast— Are you taking down *everything* I'm saying?

STENO: What?

BYRNES: Yes, he's taking down everything you say.

JOEY: Then cut out that word, huh? Bastard, I mean. That don't look nice.

BYRNES: What did you think when you found Carella?

JOEY: I thought he was dead. All that blood. Also, his head looked caved in.

BYRNES: What did you do?

(No answer)

I said what did you do then?

JOEY: I passed out cold.

As it turned out, not only had Joey passed out cold, but he had later revived and been sick all over the thick living-room rug, and had only then managed to pull himself to a telephone to call the police. The police had got to the apartment ten minutes after Joey had made the call. By this time, the living-room rug had sopped up a goodly amount of Carella's blood, and he looked dead. Lying there pale and unmoving, he looked dead. The first patrolman to see him almost tagged the body DOA. The second patrolman felt for a pulse, found a feeble one, and instantly called in for a meat wagon. The interne who admitted Carella to the Emergency Section of the Rhodes Clinic estimated that he would be dead within the hour. The other doctors refused to commit themselves in this day and age of scientific miracles. Instead, they began pumping plasma into him and treating him for multiple concussion and extreme shock. Somebody in the front office put his name on the critical list, and somebody else called his wife. Fanny Knowles took the call. She said, 'Oh, sweet loving mother of Jesus!' Both she and Teddy arrived at the hospital not a half-hour later. Lieutenant Byrnes was already there waiting. At 1 A.M. on April 29, Lieutenant Byrnes sent both Teddy and Fanny home. Steve Carella was still on the critical list. At 8 A.M., Lieutenant Byrnes called Frankie Hernandez at home.

'Frankie,' he said, 'did I wake you?'

'Huh? Wha'? Who's this?'

'This is me. Pete.'

'Pete who? Oh, oh, OH! Hello, Lieutenant. Whattsa matter? Something wrong?'

'You awake?'

'Is he dead?' Hernandez asked.

'What?'

'Steve. Is he all right?'

'He's still in coma. They won't know for a while yet.'

'Oh, man, I was just having a dream,' Hernandez said. 'I dreamt he was dead. I dreamt he was laying face down on the sidewalk in a puddle of blood, and I went over to him, crying for him, saying "Steve, Steve, Steve" again and again, and then I rolled him over, and Pete, it wasn't Steve's face looking up at me, it was my own. Oh man, that gave me the creeps. I hope he pulls through this.'

'Yeah.'

Both men were silent for several seconds. Then Byrnes said, 'You awake?'

'Yes. What is it?'

'I wouldn't cut in on what's supposed to be your day off, Frankie. I know you were up all last night . . .'

'What is it, Pete?'

'I want you to check out the apartment where Steve got it. I wouldn't ask you ordinarily, Frankie, but I'm in one hell of a bind here. You know, we've got these damn stores under surveillance because Meyer and Kling've got me convinced this nut's gonna hit one of them. Well, Captain Frick let me have the patrolmen I needed, but he reserved the right to pull them if he needs them anyplace else. So I had to work out some kind of a system where a team of detectives would be on the prowl ready to relieve any of these cops if something else came up. I couldn't pull Parker out of the candy store, and I couldn't get those two men back from Washington where they're taking that damn FBI course, so I had to pull two men off vacation, and I've got these two teams cruising around now, Meyer and Kling, and this other pair, ready to either relieve or assist, whichever is necessary. I'm practically running the squad singlehanded, Frankie. Steve's in the hospital, and I'm going out of my mind worrying about him, that guy is like a son to me, Frankie. I'd check this out myself, believe me, but I got to go down to City Hall this afternoon to make arrangements for that damn ball game tomorrow – of all times the Governor's got to come down to throw out the ball, and the damn ball park has to be in my precinct, so that'll mean – I don't know where I'm gonna get all the men, Frankie. I just don't know.'

He paused.

There was another long silence.

'His face is all smashed in,' Byrnes said at last. 'Did you see him, Frankie?'

'I didn't get a chance to go over there yet, Pete. I had—'

'All smashed in,' Byrnes said.

The silence came back. Byrnes sighed.

'You can see what a bind I'm in. I've got to ask you to do me the favor, Frankie.'

'Whatever you say, Pete.'

'Would you check that apartment? The lab's already been through it, but I want one of my own boys to go over it thoroughly. Will you?'

'Sure. What's the address?'

'Four fifty-seven Franklin Street.'

'I'll just have some breakfast and get dressed, Pete. Then I'll go right over.'

'Thanks. Will you phone in later?'

'I'll keep in touch.'

'Okay, fine. Frankie, you know, you've been on the case with Steve, you know what his thinking on it has been, so I thought . . .'

'I don't mind at all, Pete.'

'Good. Call me later.'

'Right,' Hernandez said, and he hung up.

Hernandez did not, in truth, mind being called on his day off. To begin with, he knew that all policemen are on duty twenty-four hours a day every day of the year, and he further knew that Lieutenant Byrnes knew this. And knowing this, Byrnes did not have to ask Hernandez for a favor, all he had to do was say, 'Get in here, I need you.' But he *had* asked Hernandez if he'd mind, he had put it to him as a matter of choice, and Hernandez appreciated this immensely. Too, he had never heard the lieutenant sound quite so upset in all the time he'd been working for him. He had seen Peter Byrnes on the edge of total collapse, after three days without sleep, the man's eyes shot with red, weariness in his mouth and his posture and his hands. He had heard his voice rapping out orders hoarsely, had seen his fingers trembling as he lifted a cup of coffee, had indeed known him at times when panic seemed but a hairsbreadth away. But he had never heard Byrnes the way he sounded this morning. Never.

There was something of weariness in his voice, yes, and something of panic, yes, and something of despair, but these elements did not combine to form the whole; the whole had been something else again, the whole had been something frightening which transmitted itself across the copper telephone wires and burst from the receiver on the other end with a bone-chilling sentience of its own. The whole had been as if – as if Byrnes were staring into the eyes of death, as if Byrnes were choking on the stench of death in his nostrils, as if Byrnes had a foreknowledge of what would happen to Steve Carella, a foreknowledge so strong that it leaped telephone wires and made the blood run suddenly cold.

In his tenement flat, with the sounds of the city coming alive outside his window, Frankie Hernandez suddenly felt the presence of death. He shuddered and went quickly into the bathroom to shower and shave.

Joey, the doorman, recognized him as a policeman instantly.

'You come about my *paisan*, huh?' Joey asked.

'Who's your *paisan*?' Hernandez asked.

'Carella. The cop who got his block knocked off upstairs.'

'Yes, that's who I've come about.'

'Hey, you ain't Italian, are you?' Joey asked.

'No.'

'What are you, Spanish or something?'

'Puerto Rican,' Hernandez answered, and he was instantly ready to take offense. His eyes met Joey's, searched them quickly and thoroughly. No, there would be no insult.

'You want to go up to the apartment? Hey, I don't even know your name,' Joey said.

'Detective Hernandez.'

'That's a pretty common Spanish name, ain't it?'

'Pretty common,' Hernandez said as they went into the building.

'The reason I know is I studied Spanish in high school,' Joey said. 'That was my language there. *Habla usted Espanol?*'

'*Si, un poquito,*' Hernandez answered, lying. He did not

152

speak Spanish only slightly. He spoke it as well as any native of Madrid – no, that was false. In Madrid, the Spanish were pure, and a *c* or a *z* before certain vowels took a *th* sound. In Puerto Rico, the sound became an *s*. The word for 'five,' for example – spelled *cinco* in both Spain and Latin America – was pronounced *theen-koh* in Spain and *seen-koh* in Puerto Rico. But he spoke the language like a native when he wanted to. He did not very often want to.

'I know Spanish proverbs.' Joey said. 'You know any Spanish proverbs?'

'Some,' Hernandez said as they walked toward the elevator.

'Three years of high-school Spanish, and all I can do is quote proverbs,' Joey said. 'What a drag, huh? Here, listen. *No hay rosas sin espinas.* How about that one? You know what that one means?'

'Yes,' Hernandez said, grinning.

'Sure. There ain't no roses without thorns. Here's another one, a very famous one. *No se ganó Zamora en una hora.* Is that right?'

'That's right,' Hernandez said. 'Your pronunciation is very good.'

'Rome was not built in a day,' Joey translated. 'Man, that one kills me. I'll bet I know more Spanish proverbs than half the people in Spain. Here's the elevators. So the guy who said he was John Smith wasn't John Smith, is that right?'

'That's right,' Hernandez said.

'So now the only real question is which of those two guys was John Smith? The blond guy with the hearing aid? Or the old duffer who used to come to the apartment and whose picture your lieutenant showed to me. That's the question, huh?'

'The old man *was* John Smith,' Hernandez said. 'And

whatever the blond's name is, he's wanted for criminal assault.'

'Or maybe murder if my *paisan* dies, huh?'

Hernandez did not answer.

'God forbid,' Joey said quickly. 'Come on, I'll take you up. The door's open. There was guys here all last night taking pictures and sprinkling powder all over the joint. When they cleared out, they left the door open. You think Carella's gonna be all right?'

'I hope so.'

'Me, too,' Joey said, and he sighed and set the elevator in motion.

'How often was the old man here?' Hernandez asked.

'That's hard to say. You'd see him on and off, you know.'

'Was he a hardy man?'

'Healthy, you mean?'

'Yes.'

'Yeah, he seemed pretty healthy to me,' Joey said. 'Here's the sixth floor.'

They stepped out into the corridor.

'But the apartment was rented by the blond one, is that right? The deaf man? He was the one who called himself John Smith?'

'Yeah, that's right.'

'Why the hell would he use the old man's name unless he was hiding from something? And even then . . .' Hernandez shook his head and walked down the hall to apartment 6C.

'You gonna need me?' Joey asked.

'No, go on.'

' 'Cause our elevator operator is sick, you know. So I got to run the elevator and also take care of the door. So if you don't mind . . .'

'No, go right ahead,' Hernandez answered. He went

154

into the apartment, impressed at once by the expensive modern furniture, overwhelmed at once by the total absence of sound, the silence that pervades every empty apartment like an old couple living in a back room. He walked swiftly to the arch between the living room and the bedroom corridor. The rug there was stained with dried blood. Carella's. Hernandez wet his lips and walked back into the living room. He tabulated the units in the room which would warrant a thorough search: the drop-leaf desk, the hi-fi and liquor cabinet, the bookcases, and – that was *it* for the living room.

He took off his jacket and threw it over one of the easy chairs. Then he pulled down his tie, rolled up his sleeves, crossed to the windows and opened them, and began working on the desk. He searched the desk from top to bottom and found nothing worth a second glance.

He shrugged, straightened up, and was walking toward the hi-fi unit when he noticed that something had fallen from his inside jacket pocket when he'd tossed it over the back of the chair. He walked across the room and stooped at the base of the chair, picking up the photograph encased in lucite, the photo of the dead man who had been identified as John Smith. He scooped his jacket from the back of the chair and was putting the picture into the pocket again when the front door opened suddenly.

Hernandez raised his eyes.

There, standing in the doorway, was the man whose picture he'd been looking at a moment before, the dead man named John Smith.

15.

'WHO ARE YOU?' the man in the doorway said. 'What do you want here?'

He was wearing a sailor's uniform, and he took a step into the room as Hernandez's hand dropped the photograph and reached for the Police Special holstered at his side. The sailor's eyes widened.

'What?' he started, and he turned toward the door again.

'Hold it!' Hernandez snapped.

The sailor stopped. Cautiously, he turned to face the .38.

'Wh – what's the gun for?' he asked.

'Who are you?' Hernandez asked.

'John Smith,' the sailor replied.

Hernandez moved closer to him. The voice had been young, and the man's body was trim and youthful in the tight-fitting Navy blues. Hernandez blinked, and then realized he was not looking at a reincarnation of the dead man they'd found in Grover Park, but he was damn well looking at a spitting image of him, some forty years younger.

'Where's my father?' Smith said.

'John Smith your father?'

'Yes. Where is he?'

Hernandez didn't want to answer that question, not just yet he didn't. 'What made you think you'd find him here?' he asked.

'This is the address he gave me,' the young John Smith said. 'Who are *you?*'

'When did he give you the address?'

'We've been writing to each other. I was down in Guantanamo Bay on a shakedown cruise,' Smith said. His eyes narrowed. 'You a cop or something?'

'That's what I am.'

'I knew it. I can smell fuzz a mile away. Is the old man in some trouble?'

'When did you hear from him last?'

'I don't know. Beginning of the month, I guess. What's he done?'

'He hasn't done anything.'

'Then what are you doing here?'

'Your father's dead,' Hernandez said flatly.

Smith backed up against the wall as if Hernandez had hit him. He simply recoiled from Hernandez's words, inching backward until he collided with the wall, and then he leaned against the wall, and he stared into the room, without seeing Hernandez, simply stared into the room blankly, and said, 'How?'

'Murdered,' Hernandez said.

'Who?'

'We don't know.'

The room was silent.

'Who'd want to kill him?' Smith asked the silence.

'Maybe you can tell us,' Hernandez said. 'What was his last letter about?'

'I don't know. I don't remember,' Smith said. He seemed dazed. He kept leaning against the wall, his head tilted back against the plaster, looking up at the ceiling.

'Try,' Hernandez said gently. He holstered the .38 and walked to the bar unit. He poured a stiff hooker of brandy and carried it to Smith. 'Here. Drink this.'

'I don't drink.'

'Take it.'

Smith took the glass, sniffed it, and tried to hand it back. Hernandez forced it to his mouth. Smith drank, almost gagging. He coughed and pushed the glass away from him.

'I'm all right,' he said.

'Sit down.'

'I'm all right.'

'*Sit down!*'

Smith nodded and went to one of the modern easy chairs, sinking into it. He stretched out his long legs. He did not look at Hernandez. He kept studying the tips of his highly polished shoes.

'The letter,' Hernandez said. 'What did it say?'

'I don't know. It was a long time ago.'

'Did he mention a girl named Lotte Constantine?'

'No. Who's she?'

'Did he mention anyone called the deaf man?'

'No.' Smith looked up. 'The *what?*'

'Never mind. What *did* he say in the letter?'

'I don't know. I think he started off by thanking me for the shoes. Yeah, that's right.'

'What shoes?'

'I got a pair of shoes for him from ship's service. I'm on a destroyer, we were just commissioned last month up in Boston. So my father sent me his shoe size and I picked up a pair for him in the ship's store. They're good shoes, and I get them for something like nine bucks, he couldn't come anywhere near that price on the outside.' Smith paused. 'There's nothing dishonest about that.'

'Nobody said there was.'

'Well, there ain't. I paid money for the shoes. It ain't as if I was cheating the government. Besides, it's all one and the same. Before he got this job, his only income came from the government, anyway. So it's six of one and half a dozen of—'

'What job?' Hernandez asked quickly.

'Huh? Oh, I don't know. In his last letter, he was telling me about some job he got.'

'What kind of job?'

'As a night watchman.'

Hernandez leaned closer to Smith. 'Where?'

'I don't know.'

'Didn't he say where?'

'No.'

'He *must* have said where!'

'He didn't. He said he was working as a night watchman, but that the job would be finished on May first, and after that he could afford to retire. That's all he said.'

'What did he mean?'

'I don't know. My father always had big ideas.' Smith paused. 'None of them ever paid off.'

'Afford to retire,' Hernandez said, almost to himself. 'On what? On a night watchman's salary?'

'He only just got the job,' Smith said. 'He couldn't have meant that. It was probably something else. One of his get-rich-quick schemes.'

'But he said he'd only be working until May first, is that right?'

'Yeah.'

'He didn't give the name of the firm? He didn't say where he was working?'

'No, I told you.' Smith paused. 'Why'd anyone want to kill him? He never hurt a soul in his life.'

And suddenly he began weeping.

The costume rental shop was in downtown Isola on Detavoner Avenue. There were three dummies in the front window. One was dressed as a clown, another was dressed as a pirate, and the third and last was dressed as a World War I pilot. The window was grimy, and the dummies were dusty, and the costumes looked moth-eaten. The inside of the shop looked grimy, dusty, and moth-eaten, too. The owner of the shop was a jovial man named Douglas McDouglas who'd once wanted to be an actor and who had settled for the next best thing to it. Now, rather than creating fantasies on stage, he helped others to create fantasies by renting the costumes they needed for amateur plays, masquerade parties and the like. He was no competition for the bigger, theater rental shops nor did he wish to be. He was simply a man who was happy doing the kind of work he did.

The deaf man entered the shop, and Douglas McDouglas recognized him at once.

'Hello there, Mr Smith,' he said. 'How's every little thing?'

'Just fine,' the deaf man answered. 'And how are things with you?'

'Couldn't be better,' McDouglas answered, and he burst into contagious laughter. He was a fat man, and the layers of flesh under his vest rippled when he laughed. He put his hands on his belly as if to control the pulsating flesh, and said, 'Are you here for the costumes?'

'I am,' the deaf man said.

'They're ready,' McDouglas said. 'Nice and clean. Just got them back from the cleaners day before yesterday. What kind of a play is this one, Mr Smith?'

'It's not a play,' the deaf man said. 'It's a movie.'

'With ice-cream men in it, huh?'

'Yes.'

'And night watchmen too, huh?'

'What do you mean?'

'The two night watchmen uniforms. The one you got 'way back, and the one you came in for near the beginning of the month. Ain't they for the movie, too?'

'Yes, I suppose so,' the deaf man said.

'Will you be returning them all together?'

'Yes,' he lied. He had no intention of returning any of the costumes.

'What's the movie called?' McDouglas asked.

The deaf man smiled. 'The Great Bank Robbery,' he answered.

McDouglas burst into laughter again. 'A comedy?'

'More like a tragedy,' the deaf man said.

'You filming it here in Isola?'

'Yes.'

'Soon?'

'We start shooting tomorrow.'

'Sounds exciting.'

'I think it will be. Would you get me the costumes, please? I don't want to rush you, but . . .'

'Sure thing,' McDouglas said, and he went into the back of the shop.

The Great Bank Robbery, the deaf man thought, and he grinned. I wonder what you would say, fat boy, if you really knew. I wonder what you will think when you hear the news over your radio. Will you feel like an accessory before the fact? And will you rush to the police with a description of 'John Smith,' the man who rented these costumes? But then, John Smith is dead, isn't he?

And you don't know that, Mr McDouglas, do you?

You don't know that John Smith, garrulous old John Smith, was shot to death while wearing a costume hired from this very shop, now do you? Garrulous old John Smith who, we discovered, was dropping just a few hints too many about what is going to take place tomorrow. A dangerous man to have about, that John Smith. And he remained talkative even after we'd warned him, and so Goodbye, Mr Smith, it was lovely having you in our friendly little group, but speech is silver, Mr Smith, and silence, ahhh, silence is golden, and so we commit you to eternal silence, BAM!

The deaf man grinned.

And then, of course, it was necessary to dispose of the costume. It would not have been necessary were you not such an organized man, Mr McDouglas. But stamped into the lining of each of your costumes is the name of your shop, and we couldn't have run the risk of the police stripping down a corpse and then coming here to ask you questions about it, now could we, Mr McDouglas? No, no, it was far better the way we did it. Strip the uniform from the body, cart it to Grover Park, and leave it there as naked as the jay-birds.

Again, the deaf man grinned.

I'm really terribly sorry to report, Mr McDouglas, that your lovely night watchman's uniform was burned to ashes in an incinerator. But that was the only way, you see. We shall do the same thing with these costumes. The police may get to you eventually, Mr McDouglas, but we certainly don't want them reaching you any sooner than they ordinarily might.

And when they get to you, you will of course describe me.

The deaf man grinned.

But is my hair really blond, Mr McDouglas? Or is it bleached especially for this jolly little caper? And am I *really* hard of hearing? Or is the button in my ear a further device to confuse identification? Those are the questions the police must ask themselves, Mr Mc-Douglas.

I somehow feel they'll have themselves a merry little chase.

'Here we are,' McDouglas said, coming from the back of the shop. 'How do you like them?'

The deaf man studied the white uniforms.

'Very nice, Mr McDouglas,' he said. 'How much is that?'

'Pay me when you bring them back,' McDouglas said.

The deaf man smiled graciously. 'Thank you.'

'I've been in this business twenty-five years,' McDouglas said, 'and I've never been stuck with a bum check, and I've never yet had anybody steal a costume from me. And in all that time, I never once took a deposit and the people always paid for the costumes when they brought them back.' McDouglas rapped his knuckles on the wooden counter. 'I've never been robbed yet.'

'Well,' the deaf man said, grinning, 'there's always a first time,' and McDouglas burst out laughing. The deaf man continued watching him, grinning.

When his laughter subsided, McDouglas said, 'Who's directing this movie of yours?'

'I am.'

'That must be hard. Directing a movie.'

'Not if you plan everything beforehand,' the deaf man answered.

That night, they put the first part of their plan into action.

At 11:01, a moment after the night watchman at the Pick-Pak Ice Cream Company entered the elevator which would take him to the top floor of the building, Rafe ran a bony hand through his straw-blond hair, adjusted his gold-rimmed eyeglasses and, without uttering a sound, promptly picked the lock on the front gate. Chuck, burly and apelike, pushed the gate back far enough for both men to enter. He rolled it closed again and they both walked to the nearest truck. Chuck got to work on the front license plate and Rafe got to work on the rear one.

At 11:03 they looked up to the top floor of the factory

and saw the night watchman's flashlight illuminating the blank windows like a flitting soul behind a dead man's eyes.

By 11:05 the transfer of plates had been effectively accomplished, Chuck opened the hood of the truck and climbed in behind the wheel. Rafe found the ignition wires and crossed them. Then he went to the gate and rolled it all the way open. Chuck backed the truck out. Rafe climbed in beside him. He did not bother to close the gate again. The time was 11:07.

It took them fifteen minutes to drive crosstown to the rented store near the new shopping center. Pop and the deaf man were waiting in the back yard when the truck pulled in. The deaf man was wearing dark gray slacks and a gray sports jacket. His black loafers were highly polished. They glowed even in the dim light from the street lamp.

Pop was wearing the uniform of a night watchman, the second uniform rented by the deaf man in Mc-Douglas's shop.

The time was 11:14.

'Everything go all right?' the deaf man asked.

'Fine,' Chuck said.

'Then let's get the signs on. Pop, you can take up your post now.'

The old man walked out to the sidewalk near the front of the shop. The other men went into the store and came out carrying a drill and a bit, an extension cord, a flashlight, two huge metal signs reading 'Chelsea Pops' and a box of nuts and bolts. Chuck began drilling holes into the side of the truck. Rafe and the deaf man began fastening on the first sign as soon as Chuck was finished.

The time was 11:23.

At 11:45, the patrolman appeared. His name was Dick

Genero, and he ambled along the sidewalk nonchalantly, not expecting trouble and not looking for it. He could see a light flashing behind the store rented by that ice-cream company, but the truck was effectively screened from the street by the building itself. On the sidewalk, he saw a man in uniform. At first, he thought it was another cop, then he realized it was only a night watchman.

'Hello,' he said to the man.

'Hello,' Pop replied.

'Nice night, huh?' Genero asked.

'Beautiful.'

Genero glanced toward the light in the back yard. 'Working back there?' he asked.

'Yeah,' Pop replied. 'The ice-cream people.'

'That's what I figured,' Genero said. 'Couldn't be the shopping-center people. They're all finished with their construction, aren't they?'

'Sure,' Pop said.

'You a new man?'

Pop hesitated. 'How do you mean?'

'Used to be another fellow here,' Genero said. 'When they were first building the center.'

'Oh, yeah,' Pop said.

'What was his name?' Genero asked.

For a moment, Pop felt as if he'd walked into a trap. He did not know the name of the man who'd preceded him. He wondered now if this cop knew the name and was testing him, or if he was just asking a simple question to make conversation.

'Freddie, wasn't it?' Pop said.

'I forget,' Genero replied. He glanced over at the center. 'They sure put these things up fast, don't they?'

'They sure do,' Pop answered, relieved. He did not look toward the back yard. He did not want this stupid

165

cop to think anything unusual was happening back there.

'The supermarket opened yesterday,' Genero said, 'and the drugstore, too. Bank's moving in tomorrow afternoon, be ready for business on the first. It's amazing the way they work things nowadays.'

'It sure is,' Pop said.

'A bank is all I need on my beat,' Genero said. 'Another headache to worry about.' He studied Pop for a moment, and then asked, 'You going to be here steady?'

'No,' Pop answered. 'I'm just on temporary.'

'Until all the stores are in, huh?'

'That's right.'

'Too bad,' Genero said, grinning. 'You'da made my job easier.'

The light behind the ice-cream store went out suddenly. Genero looked toward the back yard.

'Guess they're finished,' he said.

'I wish *I* was,' Pop answered. 'I'll be here all night long.'

Genero chuckled. 'Well, keep an eye on the bank for me, will you?' he said. He clapped the old man on the shoulder. 'I'll be seeing you.'

Whistling, he walked up the street past the ice-cream store, turned the corner, and moved out of sight.

The time was 12:00 midnight.

The truck behind the store now belonged to Chelsea Pops, Inc.

The three men who'd fastened the new signs into place went back into the store, and down into the basement, and then into the tunnel they'd dug across the back yard.

The tunnel was no makeshift job. They had, after all, been working on it for a very long time. It was high and wide, and shored up with thick wooden beams which braced the ceiling and the walls. It had been necessary to make a sturdy tunnel because men and equipment had been working aboveground all the while the tunnel was being dug. The deaf man had been certain they were deep enough to avoid any cave-ins, but he'd made the tunnel exceptionally strong anyway.

'I don't want anyone dropping in on us,' he had punned intentionally, and then grinned with the other men and got back to work.

The construction work aboveground, the legitimate work that went into the building of the shopping center, had really been an excellent cover for the daylight digging of the tunnel. With all that noise and confusion on the surface, no one even once imagined that some of the noise was coming from *below* the ground. During the night, of course, the men had to exercise a little more caution. But even then, they'd been protected by their phony night watchman.

The interesting part of the job, the deaf man thought, was that their construction of the tunnel had kept pace with the legitimate construction of the bank. The construction aboveground was open to all viewers. Painstakingly, the deaf man had watched while the vault was being built, had watched while the all-important wiring box for the alarm system had been imbedded in the concrete floor of the vault and then covered over with another three-foot layer of concrete. The alarm, he knew, would be of the very latest variety. But he also knew there wasn't an alarm system in the world which Rafe could not render useless provided he could get at the wiring box.

The men had proceeded to get at the wiring box. As the shell of the bank took form and shape around the impregnable vault, the tunnel drove relentlessly across the back yard and then under the vault itself, and finally into the concrete until the underside of the vault was exposed. A web of steel had been crisscrossed into the vault floor between layers of concrete. The steel was almost impregnable, the rods constructed of laminated layers of metal, the grain of one layer running contrary to the grain of the next. A common hack saw would have broken on those laminated steel rods in the first thirty seconds of sawing. And the crisscrossing web made the task of forcible entry even more difficult since it limited the work space. Set an inch apart from each other, crossed like a fisherman's net, each laminated rod of steel became a separate challenge defying entry. The steel mat was like an army of die-hard virgins opposing an under-nourished rapist. And beyond the mat, embedded in the second layer of concrete, was the wiring box for the alarm system. Assuredly, the vault was almost impreg-nable.

Well, almost is not quite.

The men had a long time to work. They used acid on the steel, drop by drop, eating away each separate rod, day by day, working slowly and surely, keeping pace with the shell of the bank as it grew higher over their heads. By the twenty-sixth of April they had cut a hole with a three-foot diameter into the mat. They had then proceeded to chip away at the concrete until they reached the wiring box. Rafe had unscrewed the bottom of the box and studied the system carefully. As he'd suspected, the system was the most modern kind, a combination of the open- and closed-circuit systems.

In an open-circuit alarm system, the cheapest kind, the alarm sounds when the current is closed. The closed-circuit system operates on a different electrical principle. There is always a weak current running through the wiring and if the wires are cut, the alarm will sound when that current is broken.

The combination system works both ways. The alarm

will sound if the current is broken, and the alarm will also sound when contact is established.

Anyone with a pair of shears can knock out the open-circuit system. All he has to do is cut the wires. The closed-contact system is a little more difficult to silence because it requires a cross-contacting of the wires. Rafe knew how to knock out both systems, and he also knew how to take care of the combination system – but that would have to wait until the evening of the thirtieth. It was the deaf man's contention that the alarm system would be tested when the money was put into the new vault. And when it was tested, he wanted it to sound off loud and clear. So the cover was screwed back onto the wiring box – the box was left exactly the way it had been found – and the men ignored it for now, hacking away at the concrete floor until they were some four inches from the inside of the vault. Four inches of concrete would hold anyone standing on it, the deaf man figured. But at the same time, four inches of concrete could be eliminated in ten minutes with the use of a power drill.

The belly of the vault was open.

When the alarm was set on the day the bank opened, no one in the world would be able to tell that the vault, for all practical purposes, had already been broken into. The belly of the vault was open.

And so was its mouth. And its mouth was waiting for the more than two million dollars which would be transferred from the Mercantile Trust Company under Dave Raskin's loft to the new bank at three o'clock tomorrow afternoon.

Tonight as the men chipped away at the concrete floor, the deaf man grinned securely. Pop was outside and waiting to turn away any curious eyes. Authority loved other authority, and a night watchman, in the eyes of the police, somehow became an automatic honorary member of the force.

'Let's play some poker later,' the deaf man said, almost cheerfully, secure in the knowledge that not a single living soul knew they were under the ground looking up at the ripped-out guts of an impregnable bank vault. Not a damn living soul can guess where we are at this moment, he thought, and he clapped Chuck on the shoulder in a sudden gesture of camaraderie.

He was wrong.

There *was* a living soul who could have made a pretty good guess as to where they were at that moment.

But he was lying flat on his back in a hospital room, and he was deep in coma.

His name was Steve Carella.

16.

IT WAS THURSDAY, the last day of April.

Not one cop working out of the 87th was happy to get up that morning. Not one cop would be any happier by the time night fell.

To begin with, no cop liked the idea of another cop getting shot. It was sort of hard luck, you know? Sort of hoodoo. It was something like walking under a ladder, or stepping on a crack in the sidewalk, or writing a book with thirteen chapters. Nobody liked it. They were superstitious, yes. But more than that, they were human. And, whereas during the course of the working day they were able to pretend that their profession was compounded mainly of pleasant interviews with interesting people, delightful phone conversations with lovely debutantes, fascinating puzzles which required stimulating brainwork, bracing legwork in and around the most exciting city in the world, fraternal camaraderie with some of the nicest colleagues to be found anywhere, and the knowledge that one was part of a spirited and glorious team dedicated to law enforcement and the protection of the citizens of these United States – whereas every cop fed himself this crap from time to time, there was the persistently throbbing, though constantly submerged, knowledge that this wonderful, exciting, spirited, bracing, fraternal job could get a guy killed if he didn't watch his step.

The squadroom was inordinately silent on that last Thursday in April.

Because coupled with the knowledge that Steve

Carella lay in coma in a hospital bed was the somewhat guilty relief usually experienced by a combat soldier when his buddy takes a sniper's bullet. The men of the 87th were sorry as hell that Steve Carella had been shot. But they were also glad it had been he and not they. The squadroom was silent with sorrow and guilt.

The hospital was silent, too.

A light drizzle had begun at 11 A.M., gray and persistent, moistening the streets but not washing them, staining the hospital windows, dissolving the panes of glass, covering the floors with the projection of the rain pattern, giant amoeba-like shapes that gnawed at the antiseptic corridors.

Teddy Carella sat on a bench in the corridor and watched the rain pattern oozing along the floor. She did not want the shifting, magnified globules of water to reach her husband's room. In her fantasy, the projected image of the darting raindrops was the image of death itself, stealthily crawling across the floor, stopping at the very edge of the window's shadow, just short of the door to Steve's room. She could visualize the drops spreading farther and farther across the corridor, devouring the floor, battering at the door, knocking it down, and then sliding across the room to envelop the bed, to engulf her husband in gelatinlike death, to smother him in shadow.

She shuddered the thought aside.

There was a tiny bird against a white sky. The bird hung motionless. There was no wind, no sound, only the bird hanging against a white sky, emptiness.

And suddenly there was the rushing sound of a great wind gathering somewhere far in the distance, far across the sky, across the huge, deserted, barren plain, gathering in volume, and suddenly the dust swarmed across the barren plain, dust lifting into the sky, and the noise of the wind grew and grew and the bird hanging motionless was swept farther upward and began to drop like a stone, falling, falling, as the wind darkened the sky, rushing, the wind heaving into the sky, overwhelming the sky until it turned to gray and then seemed to invert itself, involuting, turning to a deep black while the roar of the wind carried the bird down, down, descending yellow beak, black devouring eyes.

He stood alone on the plain, his hair whipped by the wind, his clothing flapping wildly about his body, and he raised his fists impotently to the angry descending bird, and he screamed into the wind, screamed into the wind, and his words came back into his face and he felt the beak of the bird knifing into his shoulder with fire, felt the talons ripping, tearing, felt flame lashing his body, and still he screamed into the towering rush of the black wind against his frail body, his impotent fists, screaming, screaming.

'What's he saying?' Lieutenant Byrnes asked.

'I don't know,' Hernandez answered.

'Listen. He's trying to say something.'

'Ubba,' Carella said. He twisted his head on the pillow. 'Ubba,' he mumbled.

'It's nothing,' Hernandez said. 'He's delirious.'

'Ubba,' Carella said. 'Ubba cruxtion.'

'He's trying to say something,' Byrnes insisted.

'Ubba crusha,' Carella said.

And then he screamed wordlessly.

The two men, Chuck and Pop, had started work at twelve noon. They had synchronized their watches when leaving the store, and had made plans to meet at the ferry slip at four-oh-five. A revised estimate of the time it would take to accomplish their jobs had caused them to realize they could never catch the two-fifteen boat. So, the four-oh-five it was. And, if either one of them did not appear at that time, the other was to proceed to Majesta without him.

Their jobs, actually, were not too difficult – but they were time-consuming. Each of them carried a large suitcase, and each of the suitcases carried a total of twelve bombs. Six of the bombs were explosive; six were incendiary. Pop had made all of the bombs, and he was rather proud of his handiwork. It had been a long time since he'd practiced his craft, and he was pleased to note that he hadn't lost his touch. His bombs were really quite simple and could be expected to wreak quite a bit of havoc. Naturally, neither he nor Chuck wanted to be anywhere around when the bombs went off, and so each of the bombs carried a time fuse. The explosive bombs made use of simple alarm clocks and batteries and a system of wiring set to detonate several sticks of dynamite. The incendiary bombs were slightly more complicated and for those Pop had to rig a chemical time fuse.

The deaf man had specified that he wanted the explosions and the fires to start sometime between 4 and 4:30 P.M. He wanted both explosions *and* fires to be violent, and he wanted Pop to make sure the fires would not be extinguished before 5:45 P.M. Pop had set each of the exploding machines for 4:15. The incendiary bombs were another thing again; a chemical time fuse could not be set with the same accuracy as an alarm clock unless a great deal of experimentation were done beforehand.

Pop had done a great deal of experimentation.

He knew that concentrated sulfuric acid when dropped into a mixture of potassium chlorate and powdered sugar would immediately start a raging fire. For the purposes of his time fuse, he needed something which would keep the sulfuric acid away from the mixture until such time as the fire was desired. This was no small task. He began experimenting with cork. And he discovered through a series of long tests, that cork would char when exposed to the acid, and that it would take four hours for the acid to eat through .025 inches of cork or, in other words, a slice of cork which was one fortieth of an inch thick.

Pop prepared his bombs.

He filled a shoe box with oil-soaked rags. Into the center of the box, he set a small cardboard container filled with a mixture of potassium chlorate and powdered sugar, sealed so that the mixture would not spill out. Into the top surface of the small container, he cut a hole which would accommodate the neck of a small bottle. The bottle would be filled with a 70 per cent solution of sulfuric acid, sealed with a cork cap which was one fortieth of an inch thick, and then stuck into the hole in the top of the container at twelve noon, when the men left to do their work. In approximately four hours' time, the acid would have eaten through the cork and begun to drip onto the mixture in the container. A violent fire would ensue, aided and assisted by the oil-soaked rags. In other words, the fires would begin at approximately four o'clock – *approximately* because it was difficult to cut a slice of cork exactly one fortieth of an inch thick and a variation in millimeters would, because the rate of char remained constant, start the conflagration either slightly earlier or slightly later. In any case, Pop estimated, the fires would start at *about* four o'clock, give or take a few minutes either way, and the deaf man seemed more than pleased with the estimate.

At twelve noon, Chuck and Pop stuck the bottles of sulfuric acid into the holes cut in the cardboard containers, the thin slices of cork being the only thing between the acid and the mixture. Then they sealed the shoe boxes, packed their suitcases, and trotted off to disrupt a city.

By one-thirty, when the ball game started, Chuck had set three incendiary bombs and one exploding bomb in the baseball stadium near the River Harb. He had set two of the incendiaries in the grandstand, and the third in the bleachers. The explosive had been left just inside the main entrance arch, in a trash basket there. The deaf man had figured that the game would break sometime around four-thirty. The bomb was set for four-fifteen, and he hoped its explosion would cause a bit of confusion among the departing spectators – especially since there would be three fires in the stadium by that time. To insure that the fires would still be roaring by the time the bomb exploded, he had instructed Chuck to cut the hoses of every fire extinguisher he saw anywhere in the stadium, and Chuck had done that and was now anxious to get away before anyone spotted him.

There were eight bombs left in Chuck's valise. He consulted his two remaining maps, each marked with his name in the right-hand corner, and began moving quickly toward his remaining destinations. The first of these was a motion picture theater on The Stem. He paid for a ticket at the box office, climbed instantly to the balcony, and consulted his map again. Two X's on the map indicated where he was to place the explosives, directly over the balcony's supporting columns and close to the projection booth where there was the attendant possibility of the explosion causing a fire and a stench when it hit the film. The main purpose of the blasts, of course, was to knock down the balcony, but the deaf man was not a person to turn aside residuals. In the corridor outside the balcony, Chuck glanced around hastily, and then slashed the hoses on the extinguishers. Rapidly, he left the theater. A glance at his watch told him it was two-fifteen. He would damn well have to hurry if he wanted to catch that four-oh-five boat.

He was now in possession of six remaining bombs.

The deaf man wanted three of them to be placed in Union Station: an incendiary in the baggage room, an explosive on the track of the incoming Chicago Express (due at four-ten), and another explosive on the counter of the circular information booth.

The remaining three bombs could be placed by Chuck at his discretion – provided, of course, they were all deposited at different locations on the south side of the precinct. The deaf man had suggested leaving an incendiary in a subway car, and an explosive in the open-air market on Chament Avenue, but the final decisions were being left to Chuck, dependent on time and circumstance.

'Suppose I put them where there aren't any people?' Chuck has asked.

'That would be foolish,' the deaf man said.

'I mean, look, this is supposed to be a bank heist.'

'Yes?'

'So why do we have to put these things where – where a lot of people'll get hurt?'

'Where would you like to put them? In an empty lot?'

'Well, no, but—'

'I've never heard of confusion in a vacuum,' the deaf man had replied.

'Still – dammit, suppose we get caught? You're fooling around with – with *murder* here, do you realize that? Murder!'

'So?'

'So look, I know there are guys who'd slit their own grandmother's throat for a nickel, but—'

'I'm not one of them,' the deaf man had answered coldly. 'There happens to be two and a half million dollars at stake here.' He had paused. 'Do you want out, Chuck?'

Chuck had not wanted out. Now, as he headed for Union Station, the suitcase was noticeably and happily lighter. He was itching to get the job over and done with. He didn't want to be anywhere south of the Mercantile Trust Company after four o'clock. If everything went according to the deaf man's plan, that part of the precinct would be an absolute madhouse along about then, and Chuck wanted no part of chaos.

The oil refinery was set on the River Dix, at the southern tip of the island of Isola. Pop walked up to the main gate and reached into his pocket for the identification badge the deaf man had given him. He flashed the badge casually at the guard, and the guard nodded, and Pop walked through the gate, stopped once to consult the X's on his map, and then walked directly to the tool shed behind the administration building. The tool shed, besides being stocked with the usual number of saws and hammers and screwdrivers, contained a few dozen cans of paint, turpentine, and varnish. Pop opened the door of the shed and put one of his explosive bombs in a cardboard carton of trash just inside the door. Then he closed the door and began walking toward the paymaster's shack near the first of the huge oil tanks.

By one-forty-five he had set four bombs in the refinery. He walked through the main gate, waved goodbye to the guard, hailed a cab and headed for a plant some thirty blocks distant, a plant which faced south toward the River Dix, its chimneys belching smoke to the city's sky twenty-four hours a day.

The sign across the top of that plant read EASTERN ELECTRIC.

It produced electric power for 70 per cent of the homes and businesses on the south side of the 87th Precinct.

At 3:00 P.M., they closed the doors of the old Mercantile Trust for the last time.

Mr Wesley Gannley, manager of the bank, watched with some sadness as his employees left for the new bank in the completed shopping center. Then he went back into the vault where the guards were carrying the bank's stock – two million, three hundred fifty-three thousand, four hundred twenty dollars and seventy-four cents in American currency – to the waiting armored truck outside.

Mr Gannley thought it was nice that so much money was being taken to the new bank. Usually, his bank had some eight hundred thousand dollars on hand, an amount which was swelled every Friday, payroll day, to perhaps a million and a quarter. There was a great many firms, however, which paid their employees every two weeks, and still others which had monthly bonus programs. In any case, April 30 was the end of the month, and tomorrow was a Friday, May 1, and so the bank was holding, besides its usual deposits and money on hand, an unusually large amount of payroll money, and this pleased Mr Gannley immensely. It seemed fitting that a spanking-new bank should open shop with a great deal of cold cash.

He stepped out onto the sidewalk as the bank guards transferred that cold cash to the truck. From the grime-stained window of his loft upstairs, Dave Raskin watched the transaction with mild interest, and then took a huge puff on his soggy cigar and turned back to studying the front of Margarita's smock.

By 3:30 P.M., the $2,353,420.74 was safe and snug in the new vault of the new bank in the new shopping center. Mr Gannley's employees were busily making themselves at home in their new quarters, and all seemed right with the world.

At 4:00 P.M., the deaf man began making his phone calls.

He made the calls from the telephone in the ice-cream store behind the new bank. Rafe was waiting in the drugstore across the street from the bank, watching the bank's front door. He would report back to the deaf man as soon as everyone had left the bank. In the meantime, the deaf man had his own work to do.

The typewritten list beside the telephone had one hundred names on it. The names were those of stores, offices, movie theaters, shops, restaurants, utilities, and even private citizens on the south side of the 87th Precinct. The deaf man hoped to get through at least fifty of those names before five o'clock, figuring on the basis of a minute per call, and allowing for a percentage of no-answers. Hopefully, *all* of the persons called would in turn call the police. More realistically, perhaps half of the fifty would. Pessimistically, perhaps ten would report the calls. And, figuring a rock-bottom return of 10 per cent, at least five would contact the police.

Even five was a good return for an hour's work if it compounded the confusion and made the ride to the ferry simpler.

Of the hundred names on the list, four were really in trouble. They were really in trouble because Chuck and Pop had deposited either incendiary or explosive bombs in their places of business. These four establishments would *certainly* call the police, if not immediately upon receipt of the deaf man's call, then *positively* after the bombs went off. The point of the deaf man's calls was to provide the police with a list of clues, only four of which were valid. The trouble was, the police would not know which of the clues were valid and which were not. And once reports of mayhem began filtering in, they could not in good conscience afford to ignore *any* tip.

The deaf man pulled the phone to him and dialed the first number on his list.

A woman answered the phone. 'The Culver Theater,' she said. 'Good afternoon.'

'Good afternoon,' the deaf man said pleasantly. 'There is a bomb in a shoe box somewhere in the orchestra of your theater,' and he hung up.

At 4:05 P.M., Chuck and Pop boarded the ferry to Majesta and spent the next ten minutes whispering together like school boys about the conspiracy they had just committed.

At 4:15 P.M., the first of the bombs exploded.

'Eighty-seventh Squad, Detective Hernandez. What? What did you say?' He began scribbling on his pad. 'Yes, sir. And the address, sir? When did you get this call, sir? Yes, sir, thank you. Yes, sir, right away, thank you.'

Hernandez slammed the phone back onto its cradle.

'Pete!' he yelled, and Byrnes came out of his office immediately. 'Another one! What do we do?'

'A bomb?'

'Yes.'

'A real one, or just a threat?'

'A threat. But, Pete, that last movie theater . . .'

'Yes, yes.'

'That was just a threat, too. But, dammit, two bombs really went off in the balcony. What do we do?'

'Call the Bomb Squad.'

'I did on the last three calls we got.'

'Call them again! And contact Murchison. Tell him we want any more of these bomb threats to be transferred directly to the Bomb Squad. Tell him—'

'Pete, if we get many more of these, the Bomb Squad'll be hamstrung. They'll dump the squeals right back into our laps, anyway.'

'Maybe we won't get any more. Maybe—'

The telephone rang. Hernandez picked it up instantly.

'Eighty-seventh Squad, Hernandez. Who? Where? Holy Je— *What* did you say? Have you – yes, sir, I see. Have you – yes, sir, try to calm down, will you, sir? Have you called the fire department? All right, sir, we'll get on it right away.'

He hung up. Byrnes was waiting.

'The ball park, Pete. Fires have broken out in the grandstands and bleachers. Hoses on all the extinguishers have been cut. People are running for the exits. Pete, there's gonna be a goddam riot, I can smell it.'

And at that moment, just inside the entrance arch, as people rushed in panic from the fires raging through the stadium, a bomb exploded.

The people on the south side of the precinct did not know what the hell was happening. Their first guess was that the Russians were coming, and that these wholesale explosions and fires were simply acts of sabotage preceding an invasion. Some of the more exotic-minded citizens speculated upon an invasion from Mars, some said it was all that strontium 90 in the air which was causing spontaneous combustion, some said it was all just coincidence, but everyone was frightened and everyone was on the edge of panic.

Not one of them realized that percentages were being manipulated or that a city's preventive forces, accustomed to dealing with the long run, were being pushed into dealing with the short run.

There were 186 patrolmen, 22 sergeants and 16 detectives attached to the 87th Precinct. A third of this force was off duty when the first of the bombs went off. In ten minutes' time, every cop who could be reached by telephone was called and ordered to report to the precinct at once. In addition, calls were made to the adjoining 88th and 89th Precincts which commanded a total of 370 patrolmen, 54 sergeants and 42 detectives and the strength of this force was added to that of the 87th's until a stream of men was pulled from every corner of the three precincts and rushed to the disaster-stricken south side. The ball park was causing the most trouble at the moment, because some forty thousand fans had erupted into a full-scale panic-ridden riot, and the attendant emergency police trucks, and the fire engines, and the patrol cars, and the mounted policemen, and the reporters and the sight-seeing spectators made control a near-impossibility.

At the same time, a Bomb Squad which was used to handling a fistful of bomb threats daily was suddenly swamped with bomb reports from forty different areas in the 87th Precinct. Every available man was called into action and rushed to the various trouble spots, but there simply weren't enough men to go around and they simply didn't know which trouble spots were going to erupt or when. To their credit, they did catch one incendiary in an office building before it burst into flame, but at the same time a bomb exploded on the fourteenth floor of that same building, an unfortunate circumstance since the bomb had been set in the laboratory of a chemical research company, and the attendant fire swept through three floors of the building even before the fire alarm was pulled.

The Fire Department had its own headaches. The first unit called into action was Engine 31 and Ladder 46, a unit in the heart of the south side, a unit which reportedly handled more damn fires daily than any other unit in the entire city. They connected to a hydrant on Chament Avenue and South Fourth in an attempt to control the blaze that was sweeping through the open-air market on Chament Avenue. Within a few minutes, the fire had leaped across Chament Avenue and was threatening a line of warehouses along the river. Acting Lieutenant Carl Junius in charge of the engine had a brief consultation with Lieutenant Bob Fancher of Ladder 46, and they radioed to Acting Deputy Chief George D'Oraglio who immediately ordered an alarm transmitted with orders to the responding units to expect counterorders at a moment's notice since he had already received word of a fire in a motion picture theater not twenty blocks from the market. Engine 81 and Ladder 33 arrived in a matter of minutes and were promptly redispatched to the motion picture theater, but by this time the hook and ladder company handling the ball park fire had called in for assistance, and Chief D'Oraglio suddenly realized he had his hands full and that he would need every available engine and hook and ladder company in the city to control what was shaping up as a major disaster.

The police emergency trucks with two-way radio numbered fifteen, and the emergency station wagons with two-way radio numbered ten, and all twenty-five of these were dispatched to the scenes of the fires and explosions which were disrupting traffic everywhere on the south side and which were causing all nine of the traffic precincts to throw extra men and equipment into the stricken area.

The north side of the precinct, the area between the new quarters of the Mercantile Trust Company and the waiting room of the Isola-Majesta ferry, was suddenly devoid of policemen.

Meyer Meyer and Bert Kling, cruising in an unmarked sedan, ready to prevent any crime which occurred against the harassed places of business on their list, received a sudden and urgent radio summons and were promptly off The Heckler Case. The radio dispatcher told them to proceed immediately to a subway station on Grady Road to investigate a bomb threat there.

By 4:30 P.M., six Civil Defense units were thrown into the melee, and the Police Commissioner made a hurried call to the Mayor in an attempt to summon the National Guard. The National Guard *would* eventually be called into action because what started as a simple plot to rob a bank would grow into a threat to the very city itself, a threat to equal the Chicago fire or the San Francisco earthquake, a threat which – when all was said and done – totaled billions of dollars in loss and almost razed to the ground one of the finest ports in the United States. But the wheels of bureaucracy grind exceedingly slow, and the National Guard units would not be called in until 5:40 P.M., by which time the Mercantile Trust Company's vault would be empty, by which time invasion reports had caused panic beyond anything imagined by the deaf man, by which time the river front to the south was a blazing wall of flame, by which time everyone involved knew they were in the center of utter chaos.

In the meantime, it was only 4:30 P.M., and the deaf man had completed twenty-two of his calls. Smiling, listening to the sound of sirens outside, he dialed the twenty-third number.

Mr Wesley Gannley, manager of the Mercantile Trust Company, paced the marbled floors of his new place of business, grinning at the efficiency of his employees, pleased as punch with the new building. The IBM machines were ticking away behind the counters. Music flowed from hidden wall speakers, and a mural at the far end of the building, washed with rain-dimmed light at the moment, depicted the strength of America and the wisdom of banking. The polished glass-and-steel door of the vault was open, and Gannley could see into it to the rows of safety deposit boxes and beyond that to the barred steel door, and he felt a great sense of security, he felt it was good to be alive.

Mr Gannley took his gold pocket watch from the pocket of his vest and looked at the time.

4:35 P.M.

In twenty-five minutes, they would close up shop for the day.

Tomorrow morning, May 1, everyone would return bright and early, and depositers would come through the bank's marble entrance arch and step up to the shining new tellers' windows, anxious to reap that three and a half per cent, and Mr Gannley would watch from the open door of his manager's office and begin counting the ways he would spend his Christmas bonus this year.

Yes, it was good to be alive.

He walked past Miss Finchley who was bending over a stack of canceled checks, and he was seized with an uncontrollable urge to pinch her on the buttocks.

He controlled the urge.

'How do you like the new building, Miss Finchley?' he asked.

Miss Finchley turned toward him. She was wearing a white silk blouse, and the top button had come unfastened and he could see the delicate lace of her lingerie showing where the cream-white flesh ended.

'It's beautiful, Mr Gannley,' she answered. 'Simply beautiful. It's a pleasure to work here.'

'Yes,' he said. 'It certainly is.'

He stood staring at her for a moment, wondering whether or not he should ask her to join him for a cocktail after closing. No, he thought, that would be too forward. But perhaps a lift to the station. Perhaps that might not be misinterpreted.

'Yes, Mr Gannley?' she said.

He decided against it. There was plenty of time for that. In a wonderful new building like this one, with IBM machines and music flowing from hidden speakers, and a bright, colorful mural decorating the far wall, and an impervious steel vault, there was plenty of time for everything.

Recklessly, he said, 'You'd better button your blouse, Miss Finchley.'

Her hand fluttered up to the wayward button. 'Oh, my,' she said. 'I'm practically naked, aren't I?' and she buttoned the blouse quickly without the faintest trace of a blush.

Plenty of time for everything, Wesley Gannley thought, smiling, plenty of time.

The tellers were beginning to wheel their mobile units into the vault. Every day at 4:45 P.M., the tellers performed this ritual. First they took the coin racks from the change machines on the counter and laced these racks into the top drawers of the units. The bottom drawers usually contained folding money. Today, both drawers and coin racks were empty because the bank had not done any business at its new location, and all the money had been transferred directly to the new vault. But nonetheless, it was 4:45 P.M., and so the units were wheeled into the vault and Mr Gannley looked at his watch, went to his desk, and took the key which fit into the three clocks on the inside face of the vault door. The clocks were minuscule and were marked with numerals indicating hours. Mr Gannley put his key into the first clock and set it for fifteen hours. He did the same to the other two clocks. He expected to be at work at 7:30 A.M. tomorrow morning, and he would open the vault at 7:45 A.M. It was now 4:45 P.M. – ergo, fifteen hours. If he tried to open the vault door before that time, it would not budge, even if he correctly opened the two combination locks on the front face of the door.

Mr Gannley put the key into his vest pocket and then heaved his shoulder against the heavy vault door. It was a little difficult to close because the carpeting on the floor was new and still thick and the door's friction against it provided an unusual hindrance. But he managed to shove the door closed, and then he turned the wheel which clicked the tumblers into place, and then he spun the dials of the two combination locks. He knew the alarm was automatically set the moment that vault door slammed shut. He knew it would sound at the nearest police precinct should anyone tamper with the door. He knew that the combination locks could not be opened if the time mechanism was not tripped. He further knew that, should the alarm go off accidentally, he was to call the police immediately to tell them a robbery was *not* truly in progress, the alarm had simply gone off by accident. And then, as an added precaution if he made such a call to the police, he was to call them back in two minutes to verify the accident. In short, should a robbery *really* be in progress and should the thief force Gannley into calling the police to say the alarm had been accidental, the police would know something was fishy if he didn't duplicate the call within the next two minutes.

For now, for the moment, there was one thing more to do. Wesley Gannley went to the telephone and dialed FRederick 7-8024.

'Eighty-seventh Precinct, Sergeant Murchison.'

'This is Mr Gannley at the new Mercantile Trust.'

'What is it, Mr Gannley? Somebody call *you* about a bomb, too?'

'I beg your pardon?'

'Never mind, never mind. What is it?'

'I'm about to test this alarm. I wanted you to know.'

'Oh. Okay. When are you going to trip it?'

'As soon as I hang up.'

'All right. Will you call me back?'

'I will.'

'Right.'

Mr Gannley hung up, walked to one of the alarm buttons set behind the tellers' cages, and deliberately stepped on it. The alarm went off with a terrible clanging. Immediately, Mr Gannley turned it off, and then called the police again to tell them everything was working fine. He passed the vault door and patted it lovingly. He knew the alarm was there and working, a vigilant watchdog over all that money.

He did not know that its voice was a tribute to the careful labor which had gone on below the ground for the past two months, or that it would be silenced forever within the next half-hour.

It was 5:05 P.M.

In the new drugstore across the street from the bank, Rafe sat on a stool and watched the bank doors. Twelve people had left so far, the bank guard opening the door for each person who left, and then closing it again behind them. There were three people left inside the bank,

189

including the bank guard. Come on, Rafe thought, get the hell out.

The big clock over the counter read 5:06.

Rafe sipped at his Coke and watched the bank doors. 5:07.

Come on, he thought. We have to catch a goddam ferry at five minutes after six. That gives us less than an hour. He figures we'll be able to break away that remaining concrete in ten minutes, but I figure at least fifteen. And then ten more minutes to load the money, and another ten – if we don't hit traffic – to get to the ferry slip. That's thirty-five minutes, provided everything goes all right, provided we don't get stopped for anything.

Rafe took off his gold-rimmed glasses, wiped the bridge of his nose, and then put the glasses on again.

The absolute limit, I would say, is five-forty-five. We've got to be out of that vault by five-forty-five. That gives us twenty minutes to get to the ferry slip. We should make it in twenty minutes. Provided everything goes all right.

We should make it.

Unreasonably, the bridge of Rafe's nose was soaked with sweat again. He took off his glasses, wiped away the sweat, and almost missed the bank door across the street opening. A girl in a white blouse stepped out and then shrank back from the drizzle. A portly guy in a dark suit stepped into the rain and quickly opened a big black umbrella. The girl took his arm and they went running off up the street together.

One more to go, Rafe thought.

The bridge of his nose was sweating again, but he did not take off the glasses.

Across the street, he saw the bank lights going out.

His heart lurched.

One by one, the lights behind the windows went dark.

He waited. He was getting off the stool when he saw the door opening, saw the bank guard step out and slam the door behind him. The guard turned and tried the automatically locked door. The door did not yield. Even from across the street, Rafe saw the bank guard give a satisfied nod before he started off into the rain.

The clock over the drugstore counter read 5:15.

Rafe started for the door quickly.

'Hey!'

He stopped short. An icy fist had clamped onto the base of his spine.

'Ain't you gonna pay for your Coke?' the soda jerk asked.

The deaf man was waiting at the far end of the tunnel, directly below the bank vault when he heard Rafe enter at the other end. The tunnel was dripping moisture from its walls and roof, and the deaf man felt clammy with perspiration. He did not like the smell of the earth. It was a suffocating, fetid stench which filled the nostrils and made a man feel as if he were being choked. He waited while Rafe approached.

'Well?' he asked.

'They're all out,' Rafe said.

The deaf man nodded curtly. 'There's the box,' he said, and he swung his hand flash up to illuminate the box containing the wiring for the alarm system.

Rafe crawled into the gaping hole in the corroded steel bars and reached up for the exposed alarm box. He pulled back his hands and took off his glasses. They were fogged with the tunnel's moisture. He wiped the glasses, put them back on the bridge of his nose, and then got to work.

In the fevered delirium of his black world, things seemed clearer to Steve Carella than they ever had in his life.

He sat at a nucleus of pain and confusion, and yet things were crystal clear, and the absolute clarity astonished him because it seemed his sudden perception threatened his entire concept of himself as a cop. He was staring wide-eyed at the knowledge that he and his colleagues had come up against a type of planning and execution which had rendered them virtually helpless. He had a clear and startling vision of himself and the 87th Squad as a group of half-wits stumbling around in a fog of laboratory reports, fruitless legwork, and meaningless paper work which in the end brought only partial and minuscule results.

He was certain now that John Smith had been murdered by the same deaf man who had shot and repeatedly battered Carella with the stock of a shotgun. He was reasonably certain that the same weapon had been used in both attacks. He was certain, too, that the blueprint he'd found in the Franklin Street apartment was a construction blueprint for the vault of the Mercantile Trust, and that a robbery of that vault had been planned.

Intuitively, and this was what frightened him, he knew that the murder, and his own beating, and the planned bank robbery were tied in to the case Meyer Meyer was handling, the so-called Heckler Case.

He did not question the intuition nor its clarity – but he knew damn well it scared him. Perhaps it would have frightened him less if he'd known it wasn't quite intuition. Whether he realized it or not, and despite the fact that he had never openly discussed the supposedly separate cases with Meyer, he *had* unconsciously been exposed to siftings of telephone conversations, to quick glances at reports on Meyer's desk. These never seemed to warrant a closer conversation with the other detective, but they did nonetheless form a submerged layer of knowledge which, when combined with the knowledge he now possessed, welded an undeniable and seemingly intuitive link.

But if the reasoning were correct – and it could hardly be called reasoning – if this *sense* of connection were accurate, it pointed to someone who was not gambling senselessly against the police. Instead, it presented the image of a person who was indeed leaving very little to chance, a person who was *using* the agencies of law enforcement, utilizing them as a part of his plan, making them work for him, joining them instead of fighting them, making them an integral part of a plan which had begun – how long ago?

And this is what frightened Carella.

Because he knew, detective fiction to the contrary, that the criminal mind was not a particularly brilliant one. The average thief with whom the squad dealt daily was of only average intelligence, if that, and was usually handicapped by a severe emotional disturbance which had led him into criminal activities to begin with. The average murderer was a man who killed on the spur of the moment, whether for revenge, or through instant rage, or through a combination of circumstances which led to murder as the only seemingly logical conclusion. Oh yes, there were carefully planned robberies, but these were few and far between. The average job could be cased in a few days and executed in a half-hour. And yes, there were carefully planned murders, homicides figured to the most minute detail and executed with painstaking precision – but these, too, were exceptions. And, of course, one shouldn't forget the confidence men whose stock in trade was guile and wile – but how many *new* con games were there, and how many con men were practicing the same tired routines, all known to the police for years and years?

Carella was forced to admit that the police were dealing with a criminal element which, in a very real sense, was amateurish. They qualified for professional status only in that they worked – if you will excuse the term when applied to crime – for money. And he was forced to admit further that the police opposing this vast criminal army were also attacking their job in a somewhat amateurish way, largely because nothing more demanding was called for.

Well, this deaf man, whoever he was, *was* making further demands. He was elevating crime to a professional level, and if he were not met on equally professional terms, he would succeed. The entire police force could sit around with its collective thumb up its collective ass, and the deaf man would run them ragged and carry home the bacon besides.

Which made Carella wonder about his own role as a cop and his own duties as an enforcer of the law. He was a man dedicated to the prevention of crime, or failing that, to the apprehension of the person or persons committing crime. If he totally succeeded in his job, there would be no more crime and no more criminals; and, carrying the thought to its logical conclusion, there would also be no more job. If there was no crime, there would be no need for the men involved in preventing it or detecting it.

And yet somehow this logic was illogical, and it led Carella to a further thought which was as frightening as the sudden clarity he was experiencing.

The thought sprang into his head full-blown: *If there is no crime, will there be society?*

The thought was shocking – at least to Carella it was. For society was predicated on a principle of law and order, of meaning as opposed to chaos. But if there were no crime, if there were in effect no lawbreakers, no one to oppose law and order, would there be a necessity for law? Without lawbreakers, *was* there a need for law? And without law, would there be lawbreakers?

MADAM, I'M ADAM.

Read it forwards or backwards and it says the same thing. A cute party gag, but what happens when you say, 'Crime is symbiotic with society,' and then reverse the statement so that it read, 'Society is symbiotic with crime?'

Carella lay in the blackness of his delirium, not knowing he was up against a logician and a mathematician, but intuitively reasoning in mathematical and logical terms. He knew that something more was required of him. He knew that in this vast record of day-by-day crime, this enormous never-ending account of society and the acts committed against it, something more was needed from him as a cop and as a man. He did not know what that something more was, nor indeed whether he could ever make the quantum jump from the cop and man he now was to a cop and man quite different.

Clarity suffused the darkness of his coma.

In the clarity, he knew he would live.

And he knew that someone was in the room with him, and he knew that this person must be told about the Mercantile Trust Company and the Uhrbinger Construction Company and the blueprint he had seen in the Franklin Street apartment.

And so he said, 'Merc-uh-nuh,' and he knew he had not formed the word correctly and he could not understand why because everything seemed so perfectly clear within the shell of his dark cocoon.

And so he tried the other word, and he said, 'Ubba-nuh coston,' and he knew that was wrong, and he tried again, 'Ubba-nuh . . . ubba Uhrbinger . . . Uhrbinger,' and he was sure he had said it that time, and he leaned back into the brilliant clarity and lost consciousness once more.

The person in the room with him was Teddy Carella, his wife.

But Teddy was a deaf mute, and she watched her husband's lips carefully, and she saw the word 'Uhrbinger' form on those lips, but it was not a word in her vocabulary, and so she reasoned that her husband was delirious.

She took his hand and held it in her own, and then she kissed it and put it to her cheek.

The hospital lights went out suddenly.

The bombs Pop had set at Eastern Electric were beginning to go off.

Rafe, like any good surgeon, had checked his earlier results before making his final incision. He had run a Tong Tester over the wires in the box once more, checking the wires which carried the current, nodding as they tallied with the calculations he had made the first time he looked into the box.

'Okay,' he said, apparently to the deaf man who was standing below him, but really to no one in particular, really a thinking out loud. 'Those are the ones carrying the juice, all right. I cross-contact those and cut the others, and it's clear sailing.'

'All right, then do it,' the deaf man said impatiently.

Rafe set about doing it.

He accomplished the cross-contact with speed and efficiency. Then he thrust his hand at the deaf man. 'The clippers,' he said.

The deaf man handed them up to him. 'What are you going to do?'

'Cut the other wires.'

'Are you sure you've done this right?'

'I think so.'

'Don't think!' the deaf man said sharply. 'Yes or no? Is

196

that damn alarm going to go off when you cut those wires?'

'I don't think so.'

'*Yes or no?*'

'No,' Rafe said. 'It won't go off.'

'All right,' the deaf man said. 'Cut them.'

Rafe took a deep breath and moved the clippers toward the wires. With a quick, deliberate contraction of his hand, he squeezed the handles of the clippers together and cut the wires.

The alarm did not go off.

At the house in Majesta, Chuck paced the floor nervously while Pop studied the alarm clock sitting on the dresser.

'What time is it?' Chuck asked.

'Five-thirty.'

'They should be out of the bank and on their way by now.'

'Unless something went wrong,' Pop said.

'Yeah,' Chuck answered distractedly, and he began pacing the floor again. 'Put on that radio, will you?' he said.

Pop turned it on.

'. . . raging out of control along a half-mile square of waterfront,' the announcer said. 'Every available piece of fire equipment in the city has been rushed to the disaster area in an effort to control the flames before they spread further. The rain is not helping conditions. Slippery streets seem to be working against the men and apparatus. The firemen and police are operating only from the lights of their trucks, an explosion at the Eastern Electric Company having effectively blinded seventy per cent of the area's streets, homes and businesses. Fortunately, there is still electric power in Union Station where an explosion on track twelve derailed the incoming Chicago train as a bomb went off simultaneously in the waiting room. The fire in the baggage room there was brought under control, but is still smoldering.'

The announcer paused for breath.

'In the meantime, the Mayor and the Police Commissioner are still in secret session debating whether or not to call out the National Guard in this emergency situation, and there are several big questions that remain unanswered: *What is happening? Who is responsible for this? And why?* Those are the questions in the mind of every thinking citizen as the city struggles for its very survival.'

The announcer paused again.

'Thank you, and good night,' he said.

Pop turned off the radio.

He had to admit he felt a slight measure of pride.

They came out of the vault and through the tunnel at 5:40 P.M. They made three trips back and forth between the bank vault and the basement of the store, and then they carried the cartons stuffed with money to the truck. They opened the door to the refrigerator compartment and shoved the cartons inside. Then they closed the refrigerator door, and Rafe started the truck.

'Just a minute,' the deaf man said. 'Look.'

Rafe followed his pointing hand. The sky was ablaze with color. The buildings to the south were blacked out, but the sky behind them was an angry swirl of red, orange and yellow. The flames consumed the entire sky, the very night itself. Police and fire sirens wailed in the distance to the south; now and then an explosion touched off by the roaring fire punctuated the keen of the sirens and the whisper of rain against the pavements.

The deaf man smiled, and Rafe put the truck in motion.

198

'What time is it?' Rafe asked.

'Five-fifty.'

'So we missed the five-forty-five boat.'

'That's right. And we've got fifteen minutes to make the six-oh-five. I don't think we'll have any trouble.'

'I hope not,' Rafe said.

'Do you know how much money we have in the ice box?' the deaf man asked, grinning.

'How much?'

'More than two million dollars.' The deaf man paused. 'That's a lot of money, Rafe, wouldn't you say so?'

'I would say so,' Rafe answered, preoccupied. He was watching the road and the traffic signals. They had come eight blocks and there had been no sign of a policeman. The streets looked eerie somehow. Cops were a familiar part of the landscape, but every damn cop in the precinct was probably over on the south side. Rafe had to hand it to the deaf man. Still, he didn't want to pass any lights, and he didn't want to exceed the speed limit. And, too, the streets were slippery. He'd hate like hell to crash into a lamppost with all that money in the ice box.

'What time is it?' he asked the deaf man.

'Five-fifty-six.'

Rafe kept his foot steady on the accelerator. He signaled every time they made a turn. He panicked once when he heard a siren behind them, but the squad car raced past on his left, intent on the more important matters at hand.

'They all seem to be going someplace,' the deaf man said, grinning securely.

'Yeah,' Rafe said. His heart was beating wildly in his chest. He would not have admitted it to anyone, but he was terrified. All that money. Suppose something went wrong? All that money.

'What time is it?' he asked, as he made the turn into the parking lot at the ferry slip.

'Six-oh-one,' the deaf man said.

'Where's the boat?' Rafe asked, looking out over the river.

'It'll be here,' the deaf man said. He was feeling rather good. His plan had taken into account the probability that some cops would be encountered on the drive from the bank to the ferry slip. Well, they had come within kissing distance of a squad car, and the car had gone merrily along its way, headed for the fire-stricken area. The incendiaries had worked beautifully. Perhaps he could talk the men into voting Pop a bonus. Perhaps . . .

'Where's the damn boat?' Rafe said impatiently.

'Give it time. It'll be here.'

'You sure there *is* a six-oh-five?'

'I'm sure.'

'Let me see that schedule,' Rafe said. The deaf man reached into his pocket and handed him the folder. Rafe glanced at it quickly.

'Holy Jesus!' he said.

'What's the matter?'

'It's not running,' Rafe said. 'There's a little notation beside it, a letter *E*, and that letter means it only runs on May thirtieth, July fourth and—'

'You're reading it wrong,' the deaf man said calmly. 'That letter *E* is alongside the seven-fifteen boat. There are no symbols beside the six-oh-five. I know that schedule by heart, Rafe.'

Rafe studied the schedule again. Abashed, he muttered a small, 'Oh,' and then looked out over the river again. 'Then where the hell is it?'

'It'll be here,' the deaf man assured him.

'What time is it?'

'Six-oh-four.'

In the rented house in Majesta, Chuck lighted a cigarette and leaned closer to the radio.

'There's nothing on so far,' he said. 'They don't know what the hell's happening.' He paused. 'I guess they got away.'

'Suppose they didn't?' Pop said.

'What do you mean?'

'What do we do? If they got picked up?'

'We'll hear about it on the radio. Everybody's just dying for an explanation. They'll flash it the minute they know. And we'll beat it.'

'Suppose they tell the cops where we are?'

'They won't get caught,' Chuck said.

'Suppose. And suppose they tell?'

'They wouldn't do that.'

'Wouldn't they?'

'Shut up,' Chuck said. He was silent for a moment. Then he said, 'No, they wouldn't.'

The patrolman came out of the waiting room, looked past the ice-cream truck and over the river, sucked the good drizzly air of April into his lungs, put his hands on his hips, and studied the cherry-red glow in the sky to the south. He did not realize he was an instrument of probability. He was one of those cops who, either through accident or design, had been left on his post rather than pulled southward to help in the emergency. He knew there was a big fire on the River Dix, but his beat was the thirty waterfront blocks on the River Harb, starting with the ferry waiting room and working east to the water tower on North Forty-first. He had no concept of the vastness of what was happening to the south, and he had no idea whatever that the ice-cream truck standing not ten feet away from him carried two and a half million dollars, more or less, in its ice box.

He was just a lousy patrolman who had come on duty at 3:45 P.M. and who would go off duty at 11:45 P.M., and he wasn't anticipating trouble here at the ferry slip connecting Isola to the sleepy section called Majesta. He stood with his hands on his hips for a moment longer, studying the sky. Then he casually strolled toward the ice-cream truck.

'Relax,' the deaf man said.

'He's coming over!'

'*Relax!*'

'Hi,' the patrolman said.

'Hello,' the deaf man answered pleasantly.

'I'd like an ice-cream pop,' the patrolman said.

They had managed to control the fire at the stadium, and Lieutenant Byrnes, with the help of three traffic commands, had got the traffic unsnarled and then supervised the loading of the ambulances with the badly burned and trampled victims of the deaf man's plot. Byrnes had tried, meanwhile, to keep pace with what was happening in his precinct. The reports had filtered in slowly at first, and then had come with increasing suddenness. An incendiary bomb in a paint shop, the fire and explosion touching off a row of apartment houses. A bomb left in a bus on Culver Avenue, the bomb exploding while the bus was at an intersection, bottling traffic in both directions for miles. Scare calls, panic calls, *real* calls, and in the midst of all the confusion a goddam gang rumble in the housing project on South Tenth, just what he needed; let the little bastards kill themselves.

Now, covered with sweat and grime, threading his way through the fire hoses snaked across the street, hearing the clang of ambulance gongs and the moan of sirens, seeing the red glow in the sky over the River Dix, he crossed the street and headed for a telephone because there was one call he *had* to make, one thing he *had* to know.

Hernandez followed him silently and stood outside the phone booth while Byrnes dialed.

'Rhodes Clinic,' the starched voice said.

'This is Lieutenant Byrnes. How's Carella?'

'Carella, sir?'

'Detective Carella. The policeman who was admitted with the shotgun wou—'

'Oh, yes sir. I'm sorry, sir. There's been so much confusion here. People being admitted – the fires, you know. Just a moment, sir.'

Byrnes waited.

'Sir?' the woman said.

'Yes?'

'He seems to have come through the crisis. His temperature's gone down radically, and he's resting quietly. Sir, I'm sorry, the switchboard is—'

'Go ahead, take your calls,' Byrnes said, and he hung up.

'How is he?' Hernandez asked.

'He'll be all right,' Byrnes said. He nodded. 'He'll be all right.'

'I could feel the shadow,' Hernandez said suddenly, but he did not explain his words.

'One of them specials you got advertised on the side of the truck,' the patrolman said. 'With the chopped walnuts.'

'We're all out of the walnut crunch,' the deaf man said quickly. He was not frightened, only annoyed. He could see the ferry boat approaching the slip, could see the captain on the bridge leaning out over the windshield, peering into the rain as he maneuvered the boat.

'No walnut?' the patrolman said. 'That's too bad. I had my face fixed for one.'

'Yes, that's too bad,' the deaf man said. The ferry nudged the dock pilings and moved in tight, wedging toward the dock. A deck hand leaped ashore and turned on the mechanism to lower the dock to meet the boat's deck.

'Okay, let me have a plain chocolate pop,' the patrolman said.

'We're all out of those, too,' the deaf man said.

'Well, what have you got?'

'We're empty. We were heading back for the plant.'

'In Majesta?'

'Yes, the deaf man said.

'Oh.' The patrolman shook his head again. 'Well, okay,' he said, and he started away from the truck. They were raising the gates on the ferry now, and the cars were beginning to unload. As the patrolman passed the rear of the truck, he glanced at the license plate and noticed that the plate read IS 6341, and he knew that 'IS' plates were issued to drivers in Isola and that all Majesta plates began with the letters MA. And he wondered what the probability – the word 'probability' never once entered his head because he was not a mathematician or a statistician or a logician, he was only a lousy patrolman – he wondered what the probability was of a company with its plant on Majesta having a truck bearing plates which were issued in Isola, and he continued walking because he figured *What the hell, it's possible*.

And then he thought a second probability, and he wondered when he had ever seen an ice-cream truck carrying *two* men in uniform. And he thought, *Well, that's possible, they're both going back to the plant, maybe one is giving the other a lift*. In which case, where had the second guy left *his* truck?

And, knowing nothing at all about the theory of probability, he knew only that it looked wrong, it felt wrong, and so he began thinking about ice-cream trucks in general, and he seemed to recall a teletype he'd read back at the precinct before coming on duty this afternoon, something about an ice-cream truck having been—

He turned and walked back to the cab of the truck. Rafe had just started the engine again and was ready to drive the truck onto the ferry.

'Hey,' the patrolman said.

A hurried glance passed between Rafe and the deaf man.

'Mind showing me the registration for this vehicle, Mac?' the patrolman said.

'It's in the glove compartment,' the deaf man said calmly. There was two and a half million dollars in the ice box of the truck, and he was not going to panic now. He could see fear all over Rafe's face. One of them had to be calm. He thumbed open the glove compartment and began riffling through the junk there. The patrolman waited, his hand hovering near the holstered .38 at his side.

'Now where the devil is it?' the deaf man asked. 'What's the trouble anyway, officer? We're trying to catch that ferry.'

'Yeah, well the ferry can wait, Mac,' the patrolman said. He turned to Rafe. 'Let me see your license.'

Rafe hesitated, and the deaf man knew exactly what Rafe was thinking – he was thinking his normal operator's license was not valid for the driving of a commercial vehicle, he was thinking that and knowing that if he showed the patrolman his operator's license, the patrolman would ask further questions. And yet, there was no sense in *not* producing the license. If Rafe balked at this point, that holstered .38 would be in the policeman's hand in an instant. There was nothing to do but play the percentages and hope they could talk their way out of this before the ferry pulled out because the next ferry was not until 8:45, and they sure as hell couldn't sit around here until then, there was nothing to do but bluff the hand; the stakes were certainly high enough.

'Show him your license, Rafe,' the deaf man said.

Rafe hesitated.

'Show it to him.'

Nervously, Rafe reached into his back pocket for his wallet. The deaf man glanced toward the ferry. Two sedans had boarded the boat and a few passengers had ambled aboard after them. On the bridge, the captain looked at his watch, and then reached up for the pull cord. The bellow of the foghorn split the evening air. First warning.

'Hurry up!' the deaf man said.

Rafe handed the patrolman his license. The patrolman ran his flashlight over it.

'This is an operator's license,' he said. 'You're driving a *truck*, Mac.'

'Officer, we're trying to catch that ferry,' the deaf man said.

'Yeah, well ain't that too bad?' the patrolman said, reverting to type, becoming an authoritative son of a bitch because he had them dead to rights and now he was going to play Mr District Attorney. 'Maybe I ought to take a look in your ice box, huh? How come you ain't got no ice cre—'

And the deaf man said, 'Move her, Rafe!'

Rafe stepped on the gas pedal, and the foghorn erupted from the bridge of the boat at the same moment, and the deaf man saw the gates go down on the ferry, and suddenly the boat was moving away from the dock, and the patrolman shouted 'Hey!' behind them, and then a shot echoed on the rain-streaked air, and the deaf man knew that the percentages had run out, and suddenly the patrolman fired again and Rafe screamed sharply and fell forward over the wheel and the truck swerved wildly out of control as the deaf man leaped from the cab.

His mind was churning with probabilities. Jump for the ferry? No, because I'm unarmed and the captain will take me into custody. Run for the street? No, because the patrolman will gun me down before I'm halfway across the dock, all that money, all that sweet money, predicted error, I *did* predict the error, dammit, I did take into account that fact that some policemen would undoubtedly be somewhere on our escape route, but an ice-cream pop, God, an ice-cream pop! the river is the only way, and he ran for the fence.

'Halt!' the patrolman shouted. 'Halt, or I'll fire!'

The deaf man kept running. How long can I hold my breath under water? he wondered. How far can I swim?

The patrolman fired over his head, and then he aimed at the deaf man's legs as the deaf man scrambled over the cyclone fence separating the dock from the water.

He stood poised on the top of the fence for just a moment, as if undecided, as if uncertain that the percentages were truly with him, and then suddenly he leaped into the air and away from the fence and the dock, just as the patrolman triggered off another shot. He hung silhouetted against the gray sky, and then dropped like a stone to the water below. The patrolman rushed to the fence.

Five shots, the deaf man thought. He'll have to reload. Quickly, he surfaced, took a deep, lung-filling breath, and then ducked below the surface again.

All that money, he thought. *Well – next time.*

The patrolman's hammer clicked on an empty chamber. He reloaded rapidly and then fired another burst at the water.

207

The deaf man did not resurface.

There was only a widening circle of ripples to show that he had existed at all.

17.

IT WAS SURPRISING how co-operative a thief can become when he has a bullet wound in his shoulder and he knows the jig is up. Even before they carted Rafe off to the hospital, he had given them the names of his confederates waiting in the rented house. The Majesta cops picked up Chuck and Pop in five minutes flat.

It is surprising, too, how consistent thieves are. It was one thing to be facing a rap for a bank holdup. It was quite another to be facing charges like wholesale murder, arson, riot and – man, this was the clincher – possible treason. A bright boy in the D.A.'s office looked up the Penal Law and said that these birds had committed treason against the state by virtue of having levied *war* against the people of the state. Now that was a terrifying charge, even if it didn't carry a death penalty. War against the people of the state? *War?* My God!

The three thieves named Rafe, Chuck and Pop were somehow up to their necks in something more than they had bargained for. They didn't mind spending the rest of their lives in Castleview Prison upstate, but there was a certain electrically wired chair up there in which they had no particular desire to sit. And so, in concert, they recognized that a ready-made scapegoat was at hand. Or, if not quite at hand, at least somewhere below the surface of the River Harb.

And, in concert, they consistently repeated that the man in the river was responsible for all the mayhem and all the death, that he and he alone had shot John Smith and set all those bombs, that *he* had waged the war, and that their part in this little caper was confined to the robbery of the bank, did they look like the kind of men who valued human life so cheaply? Did they look like fellows who would derail trains and set fires in baseball stadiums just for a little money? No, no, the fellow in the river was responsible for all that.

And the fellow's name?

Consistently, and in concert, they identified him solely as 'the deaf man.' More than that, they could not, or would not say.

Their consistency was admirable, to be sure.

And, admirably, they were booked and arraigned on *each* of the charges for acting in concert, and it was the opinion of the police and the District Attorney's office that all three of them had a very good chance of frying, or at the very least, spending the rest of their natural lives behind bars at Castleview Prison upstate. The probabilities were good either way, the police felt.

On May 21, Dave Raskin came up to the squadroom. He walked directly to Meyer Meyer's desk and said, 'So what do you think, Meyer?'

'I don't know,' Meyer said. 'What should I think?'

'I'm moving out of that loft.'

'What?'

'Sure. Who needs that cockamamie loft? I tell you the truth, without the bank downstairs, I got nobody to look at out the window. Before, it was a busy place. Now, nothing.'

'Well,' Meyer said, and he shrugged.

'How's the cop who got shot?'

'He'll be out of the hospital in a few weeks,' Meyer said.

'Good, good. I'm glad to hear that. Listen, if your wife needs some nice dresses, stop around, okay? I'll pick out some pretty ones for her, compliments of Dave Raskin.'

'Thank you,' Meyer said.

Raskin went back to the loft on Culver Avenue where Margarita was packing their stock preparatory to the move, flinging her unbound breasts about with renewed fervor. Raskin watched her for a few moments, pleased with what he saw. The telephone rang suddenly. Still watching Margarita's energetic acrobatics, Raskin picked up the receiver.

'Hello?' he said.

'Raskin?' the voice asked.

'Yes? Who's this?'

'Get out of that loft,' the voice said. 'Get out of that loft, you son of a bitch, or I'll kill you!'

'You!' Raskin said. 'You again!'

And suddenly he heard chuckling on the other end of the wire.

'Who's this?' he asked.

'Meyer Meyer,' the voice said, chuckling.

'You dirty bastard,' Raskin said, and then he began laughing, too. 'Oh, you had me going there for a minute. For a minute, I thought my heckler was back.' Raskin laughed uproariously. 'I got to hand it to you. You're a great comedian. Since your father died, there hasn't been such a comedian. You're just like your father! Just like him!'

Meyer Meyer, at the other end of the wire, listened, exchanged the amenities, and then hung up.

Just like my father, he thought.

Suddenly, he felt a little ill.

'What's the matter?' Miscolo said, coming in from the Clerical Office.

'I don't feel so hot,' Meyer said.

'You're just upset because a patrolman cracked a case you couldn't.'

'Maybe so,' Meyer answered.

'Cheer up,' Miscolo said. 'You want some coffee?'

'Just like my father,' Meyer said sadly.

'Huh?'

'Nothing. But a guy works all his life trying to . . .' Meyer shook his head. 'Just like my father.'

'You want the coffee or not?'

'Yeah. Yeah, I'll have the coffee. Stop heckling me!'

'Who's heckling?' Miscolo said, and he went out for the coffee.

From his desk across the squadroom, Bert Kling said, 'It'll be summer soon.'

'So?'

'So there'll be more kids in the streets, and more gang wars, and more petty crimes, and shorter tempers and—'

'Don't be so pessimistic,' Meyer said.

'Who's pessimistic? It sounds like it'll be a lovely summer. Just lovely.'

'I can hardly wait,' Meyer answered.

He pulled a typewritten list closer to the phone, and then dialed the first of a group of eyewitnesses to a burglary.

Outside the squadroom, May seemed impatient for the suffocating heat of July and August.

This is the twelfth published novel of the 87th Precinct. If I may, I would like to offer my sincere gratitude at this time to Herbert Alexander, who has worked with me on this series from the time it was conceived, and whose editorial suggestions have never failed to stimulate my imagination and enlarge my original concept. Thank you, Herb.

E.McB.

Afterword

WAY BACK WHEN — early in 1959, it must have been — I was still married to a woman whose maiden name was Anita Melnick. Her father's name was Harry Melnick, to whom this book is dedicated. He's dead now, but he got a big kick out of the book when it was first published. I hope my former wife enjoys it as much now. Memories don't come cheap, you know.

Harry used to own a women's dress shop on West 14th Street in New York City. All at once, most of the things that happen to Dave Raskin in these pages started happening to my father-in-law. Eventually, all the pranks stopped. Harry never found out who had targeted him for all the practical jokes. Nor was there a bank under his loft. But he had provided me with an idea — and the springboard for a new character.

Before I wrote *The Heckler*, eleven 87th Precinct novels had already been published. We were trying to establish a new series, you see. A rule of thumb for any new mystery series is that if you haven't hit the bestseller list after five tries, go hang up your sweatpants, Gertie.

I wrote the first three books of the series in 1956, and the next two in 1957. By my count, that came to five books — and still no bestseller. Maybe because they were still being published as paperback originals. I don't think there even *was* a paperback bestseller list back then. Progress, lads, progress!

The first book published in 1958 was also a paperback original. But with *Killer's Wedge* that same year, Simon and Schuster brought out the first of the books in hardcover. It startled the entire civilized world! I jest, Maude. It would take a long, long time before one of the Eight-Sevens hit the *New York Times* bestseller list. So much for rules of thumb about mystery series. And besides, who's counting?

Anyway, there were eleven published books by the end of 1959, when I must have delivered *The Heckler* because it was first published in hardcover sometime in 1960; I'm not now sure of the month. But I can remember an evening long before then – in 1955, to be exact, while I was still writing *Cop Hater*, the first book in the series. I was riding in a car with a friend of mine on our way to meeting his wife and my then-wife (yes, Harry Melnick's daughter, Anita), whom we were taking to dinner. I was inordinately silent, and suddenly I snapped my fingers and shouted, 'A deaf mute!' which was the equivalent back then of the word *Eureka!*

I had been pondering what kind of girlfriend would be right for Steve Carella, you see. Carella was merely one of the cops in the first book. I chose a deaf mute (I know, I know, the polically correct expression these days is 'speech and hearing impaired,' but Teddy Carella knows where she's coming from, and so do I) because I felt I could place her in desperate situations from which she had to be rescued by her stalwart police detective husband. I soon tired of these 'Mr and Mrs North' shenanigans, however. Teddy was too strong a character to need rescuing all the time.

By the time I started concocting the villain of *The Heckler*, I knew that the person Steve Carella loved most in the entire universe was his wife, Teddy Carella, who was deaf and could not speak, but whom neither he nor she herself considered 'handicapped.' It occurred to me: Hey! What if the guy who's bugging Dave Raskin is *also* deaf? I had no idea at the time that the 'deaf man' would become a recurring character – he's now been in five books – or that he would grow to become Steve Carella's nemesis, in much the same way that Moriarty was Sherlock Holmes's. I don't believe in the concept of good and evil. Evil is a theological term. But I knew that Teddy Carella was deaf and really *good*, and I figured if I could make this guy deaf and really *bad*, I would have a very nice contrast.

I think it's interesting, by the way, that most people don't waste too much sympathy on deaf persons. They'll risk their lives to help a blind man cross the street in heavy traffic, but the best a deaf person can hope to evoke is impatience. I hope the deaf man in these pages inspires a bit more than that. Fear perhaps? Perhaps even awe. It ain't easy being a villain.

It ain't easy writing about one, either.

There would be more than five deaf man novels were it not for the fact that he's brilliant, and I'm not. He must forever come up with these extraordinary schemes, you see, which are foiled not by the Keystone Kops of the Eight-Seven, but instead by accident. That's hard to do. I like to think there'll be another deaf man novel down the pike. He still owes something to a woman named Gloria, I believe, who shot him and left him tied to a bed in *Mischief*. Oh dear, one mustn't do such things to someone like the deaf man, must one?

But we shall see.

Meanwhile . . .

Harry . . . thanks again.

Without you, this book wouldn't have happened.

Ed McBain
Weston, CT
June 2002

216

SEE THEM DIE

Ed McBAIN

This is for my wife
DRAGICA
whose name in Serbian means
'Precious Darling'
Yep.

1.

Heat.

In the city, they are synonymous, they are identical, they mean one and the same thing. In the 87th Precinct, they strut the streets with a vengeance, these twin bitches who wear their bleached blond hair and their bright-red lipstick slashes, who sway on glittering rhinestone slippers, who flaunt their saffron silk. Heat and July, they are identical twins who were born to make you suffer.

The air is tangible. You can reach out to touch it. It is sticky and clinging, you can wrap it around you like a viscous overcoat. The asphalt in the gutters has turned to gum, and your heels clutch at it when you try to navigate the streets. The pavements glow with a flat off-white brilliance, contrasting with the running black of the gutter, creating an alternating pattern of shade and light that is dizzying. The sun sits low on a still sky, a sky as pale as faded dungarees. There is only a hint of blue in this sky for it has been washed out by the intensity of the sun, and there is a shimmer over everything, the shimmer of heat ready to explode in rain.

The buildings bear the heat with the solemnity of Orthodox Jews in long, black frock coats. They have known this heat. Some of them have withstood it for close to a century, and so their suffering is a silent one; they face the heat with the intolerant blankness of stoics.

Scrawled onto the pavement in white chalk are the

1

words: *JESÚS VIENE, PREPÁRENSE POR NUES-*
TRA REDENCION!

The buildings crowd the sidewalks and prepare neither for their redemption nor their perdition.

There is not much sky on this street.

There are places in the world where the sky is big, where it stretches from horizon to horizon like a gaudy blue tent, but such is not the case on this street. The sky here seems to have been wedged down over the uneven silhouette of the buildings, crammed into place because it would not fit properly, battered with a grimy fist until it tightly capped the street and contained the heat there.

The street is quiet.

It is only 8:40 in the morning, and it is Sunday.

There are unfluttering scraps of newspapers in the gutters; they share the gummy asphalt with empty tin cans and broken bottles and sticks ripped from orange crates. In the empty lot on one corner, there are the charred remains of bonfires, a torn and soiled crib mattress, the trailing white snakes of used condoms. The fire escapes are hung with the trivia of life: blankets, pillows, beer cases, potted plants, and here and there a guitar. A man sleeping on one of the fire escapes moves his arm, and it dangles down through the iron bars for a moment, swings idly, and then comes to a rest.

This is the only movement on the street.

The air is fetidly still. The heat is a self-contained, lifeless unit which does not stir and which discourages the motion of anything it embraces. It has baked itself into the brick fronts of the tenements, and the asphalt, and the pavements, and the sky. It has baked itself into these things and onto these things like orange enamel on copper.

Somewhere in the distance, the church bells toll, for

2

this is Sunday morning, but even the bells ring out on the air with a harsh flatness, a metallic unevenness that must force its way through the layers and layers of heat. Beneath that, like a rushing counterpoint, the elevated train roars past two blocks south, and then the train sound dies, and the bell sound dissipates in the sticky silence of the air, and the street is still once more.

Two people will die on this street today.

The boy's name was Zip.

He was seventeen years old and he erupted from the mouth of the tenement like a hand-grenade explosion. He came onto the stoop lightly, and then almost danced down the steps. He looked up at the waking man on the fire escape, waved nonchalantly, and then glanced up the street. He was tall and thin, good-looking in a craggy way, with a light complexion and black hair which he wore in a high crown off his forehead. He was wearing tight black slacks and high-topped combat boots and a bright silk purple jacket with his name embroidered in yellow on the left breast.

He looked at his watch.

It was 8:45, and he noted the time and then nodded, as if he had correctly estimated the exact duration of each of his movements up to this moment, as if he and the universe were meshing gears correctly. He looked up at the street again. There was an air of restless urgency about him, the air a business magnate wears when he is expecting to close a deal for the purchase of a new company. The attitude was curious on a seventeen-year-old. And yet, he looked at his watch again, a person captured by the intricacies of time, the mind of a fifty-year-old banker seemingly ensnared in the body of an adolescent.

He lighted a cigarette, took several puffs on it, and

then stamped it out under one booted foot. He looked at his watch again, stepped into the center of the street, and then started for the luncheonette on the corner. A huge sign traveled the corner of the building over the luncheonette like the marching electric letters of the Times Building in New York. These letters, however, were painted in red on a white field and they did not announce world-shattering events. They simply stated: LUIS LUNCHEONETTE. The luncheonette occupied a space in the corner of the building. When the doors were rolled back, the luncheonette became an extension of the sidewalk, open on both sides, the avenue and the street. The doors were closed now. The corrugated iron presented the impregnable look of a fortress. The boy went to the door on the street side, tried it, found it locked, and kicked it in anger.

'What are you doing there?' a voice said. 'Get away from there!'

The man who came up the street had spoken with a slight Spanish accent, a gentle accent which seemed molded exactly to his appearance. He was a stoop-shouldered man wearing a small black mustache, a man who seemed older than his fifty-odd years, who moved with an economy that somehow seemed tortured.

'Don't tell me you're finally gonna open this dump!' Zip said.

Luís Amandez walked to the huge iron door and said, 'What are you doing? Trying to break in here, hah? That what you were trying to do?'

He reached into his pocket for the key to the padlock, inserted it, took off the lock, and prepared to roll the door back into its overhead tracks.

'Don't flatter the dump,' Zip said. 'Come on, come on, get the lead out. Open the goddamn doors.'

4

'This is my place, and I'll open them as slow or as fast as I want to. You snotnoses . . .'

Zip grinned suddenly. 'Come on, man,' he said, and there was infectious warmth in his voice now. 'You got to move! You want to get any place, you got to *move*.'

Luís rolled back the first of the doors. 'I wish *you* would move,' he said. 'To California.'

'Dig the old bird,' Zip said. 'He's got humor.' And he walked into the luncheonette and directly to the wall phone near the jukebox. Luís went around to the avenue side and took the padlock off the door there, rolling the door back, allowing the sunshine to rip through the corner stone like crossfire. Zip had taken the phone from its hook, reached into his pocket for a coin, and discovered that the smallest change he had was a quarter. He slammed the receiver onto the hook and went to meet Luís as he entered the shop.

'Listen, break a quarter for me,' he said.

'What for?' Luís asked. 'For the jukebox?'

'What's all the time "What for?" Don't I buy enough in this crumby joint? I ask you for change, don't give me a Dragnet routine.'

'It's too early to play the juke,' Luís said calmly, going behind the counter and taking a white apron from a hook. 'There are still people sleeping.'

'In the first place, I don't care who's sleeping. It's time they were hustling. In the second place, I ain't gonna play the juke, I'm gonna make a phone call. And in the third and last place, you don't change this two bits for me, and one day you're liable to come in and find all your coffeepots busted.'

'You threaten me?' Luís said. 'I am a friend of the police. I tell them . . .'

'Come on, come on,' Zip said, and again the warm

5

grin flashed on his face. 'You can sue me later. Right now, give me the change, huh? Come on.'

Luís shook his head, picked up the quarter, and reached into his pocket. He made the change, and Zip picked it up and started for the telephone. He began dialing. Luís, since money matters had been brought to mind, walked to the cash register, reached into his pocket, and put in his day's starting money, laying the bills into the register drawer. He was about to break open a roll of dimes when Zip yelled, 'Hey! Hey, Cooch! Over here!'

Luís turned. The second boy was also from the neighborhood, also wearing one of the purple silk jackets, but he was younger than Zip. Luís studied him from the distance of age, and wondered if he too had sported such a ridiculously thin and boyish-looking mustache when he was sixteen. He decided that he had not. The boy was short and squat, with thick powerful hands. His complexion was dark. He spotted Zip from the middle of the street and shouted, 'Hey, Zipboy!' and then broke into a trot for the luncheonette. Luís sighed and cracked the roll of dimes on the edge of the cash drawer.

'What the hell kept you?' Zip asked. 'I was just calling your house.'

'Oh, man, don't ask,' Cooch said. He spoke, as did Zip, without a trace of an accent. Both were total products of the city and the neighborhood, as far removed from Puerto Rico as was Mongolia. Studying them, Luís felt suddenly old, suddenly foreign. He shrugged, went to his stove, and began putting up his pots of coffee.

'My people are the eeriest, you know that, man?' Cooch said. He had large brown eyes, and he used his face expressively when he spoke, like a television comic going through a famous routine. 'I think my old man must be on the Chamber of Commerce, I swear to God.'

'What's your old man got to do with your being late? I said a quarter to nine, so here it is . . .'

'He gets a letter from Puerto Rico,' Cooch went on blithely, 'and right away he flips. "Come stay with us," he writes. "Come live with us. Bring all your kids, and your grandma, and your police dog. We'll take care of you."' Cooch slapped his forehead dramatically. 'So all our goddamn barefoot cousins come flop with us. And every time another one shows up at the airport, my old man throws a party.'

'Listen, what's this got to . . .'

'He threw a party last night. Out came the goddamn guitars. We had enough strings there to start a symphony. You shoulda seen my old man. He has a couple of drinks, right away his hands head for my old lady. Like homing pigeons. Two drinks, and his hands were on her ass.'

'Look, Cooch, who cares *where* your old man's . . .'

'Judging from last night,' Cooch said reflectively, 'I should have another brother soon.'

'All right, now how come you're late?'

'I been trying to tell you. The jump didn't break up until four A.M. I could hardly crawl outa bed this morning. I still can't see too straight.' He paused. 'Where's Papá? Ain' he here yet?'

'That's what I'm wondering. You all think we're playing games here.'

'Who, me?' Cooch said, offended. 'Me? *I* think that?'

'Okay, maybe not you,' Zip said, relenting. 'The other guys.'

'Me?' Cooch persisted, astonished and hurt. 'Me? Who was it first showed you around the scene when you moved up here?'

7

'Okay, I said not you, didn't I?'

'Where'd you come from? Some crumby slum near the Calm's Point Bridge? What the hell did you know about this neighborhood? Who showed you around, huh?'

'You did, you did,' Zip said patiently.

'Yeah. So right away you hop on me. A few minutes late, and you . . .'

'*Ten* minutes late,' Zip corrected.

'All right, ten minutes, I didn't know you had a stop-watch. Man, I don't understand you sometimes, Zip. Saying I think we're playing games here. Man, if ever a guy . . .'

'I said not you! For Pete's sake, I said *not you*! I'm talking about the other studs.' He paused. 'Did you stop by for Sixto?'

'Yeah. That's another reason I'm late. You give me all these stops to . . .'

'So where is he?'

'He had to help his old lady.'

'Doing what?'

'With the baby. Listen, you think it's kicks having a baby in the house? I never seen a kid could wet her pants like Sixto's sister. Every time you turn around, that kid is pissing.'

'He was changing her pants?' Zip asked, astonished.

'He was powdering her behind the last time I seen him.'

'I'm gonna powder *his* behind when he gets here!' Zip said angrily. 'See, that's just what I mean. He thinks we're fooling around here. Then you wonder why we ain't making a name for ourselves. It's because nobody on this club's for real, that's why. Everybody expects me to do everything.'

'We got a name, Zip,' Cooch said gently.

8

'We got balls! You guys still think this is a goddamn basketball team at the Boys' Club. When you gonna grow up? You want to walk the streets in this neighborhood, or you want to hide every time there's a backfire?'

'I don't hide from nothing!'

'You think anybody on the Royal Guardians is scared of anything?' Zip asked.

'No, but the Royal Guardians got two hundred and fifty members.'

'So how do you think they got them members? By being late when there's a wash job scheduled?'

'Hey!' Cooch said suddenly.

'What's the matter?'

'Shhhh.'

A woman was coming up the street, her ample breasts bobbing with the haste of her steps. Her black hair was pulled into a bun at the back of her neck. She looked neither to the right nor the left. She walked with a purposefulness, almost a blindness, passing the boys who stood in the open street side of the luncheonette, turning the corner, and moving out of sight.

'You see who that was?' Cooch whispered.

'That lady?'

'Yeah.' Cooch nodded. 'Alfie's mother.'

'What?' He walked to the corner and stared up the avenue. But the woman was already gone.

'Alfredo Gomez's mother,' Cooch said. 'Man, was she in a hurry! Zip, you think he told her?'

'What do I care, he told her or not?'

'What I mean . . . like this is his old lady . . . like if he told her . . .'

'So he told her. How's that gonna help him?'

'You know how dames are. She might've got excited. She might've . . .'

9

'Stop crapping your pants, will you? You got nothing but small-time guts, you know that? You're just like my old man. He talks like a senator. A real wheel. Always telling me about Puerto Rico. Who cares about that damn island? I was born here, right in this city. I'm a *real* American. But he's always telling me what a big shot he was in San Juan. You know what it turns out he done there? I found out from one of my uncles. You know what he done?'

'What?'

'He fixed bicycles for a living. So that's the big wheel. Big *talk* that's all. But small-time guts.'

'I got as much guts . . .'

'Sure, so you see Alfie's mother out for a stroll, and you start shaking. You know what you're gonna be when you grow up?'

'No. What?'

'A guy who fixes bicycles.'

'Aw, come on. I . . .'

'Or a guy who shines shoes.'

'I never shined a pair of shoes in my life!' Cooch said proudly. 'I don't even shine my *own* shoes!'

'That's why you look like a slob,' Zip said, and then abruptly turned his head. Someone was approaching.

2.

THE SAILOR HAD rounded the corner as Cooch spoke. He was a tall, blond man — well, not exactly a man, and yet not a boy. He was perhaps twenty-two years old, and he had reached that mysterious boundary line which divided a man from a boy, but he was still straddling the line so that it was impossible to think of him as a boy, and yet stretching a point to consider him a man. Man or boy, he was quite drunk at the moment. He walked with the sailor's habitual roll, but the roll was somewhat frustrated by his erratic drunken weaving. His white hat was perched precariously on the back of his head, and his white uniform was spotlessly clean, reflecting the early-morning sunshine with a dazzling brilliance. He stopped on the corner, looked up at the sign over the luncheonette, mumbled something to himself, shook his head violently, and then continued up the street.

Zip stifled a laugh and nudged Cooch in the ribs.

'Ten bucks says I know what he's looking for,' Cooch said, grinning.

'Never mind what he's looking for. Go get Sixto and Papá. Tell them I'm waiting, and tell them I'm getting slightly p.o.'d. Now move.'

'Don't get excited,' Cooch said, but he moved up the street quickly, passing the drunken sailor who had headed back towards the luncheonette. The sailor was in that sort of haze where everything seems to involve a decision meriting vast concentration and deliberation. He stopped at each building, studied the numerals, shook his

11

head solemnly, and finally wound up in front of the luncheonette again, still shaking his head. He studied the sign, considered the vast symbolism in the words LUIS LUNCHEONETTE, pondered this symbolism for a while, shook his head again, and was beginning to retrace his steps down the street when Zip said, 'Help you, sailor?'

'Huh?' the sailor asked.

'You look lost,' Zip said. His manner was quite pleasant. He grinned warmly and the sailor responded to the grin immediately, the lost wanderer accepting the first friendly hand.

'Listen,' he said drunkenly, 'where's La . . . La Galli . . . La . . . Listen, I was talking to a guy inna bar downtown, you know? An' we began discussin' . . .' He stopped and studied Zip with drunkenly profound narrowness. 'Listen, how old are you?'

'Seventeen,' Zip said.

'Oh.'

The sailor tabulated this silently, his mind whirring. He nodded. 'Okay, then. I didn't wanna impair the morals of a . . . so this guy an' me, we were discussin' . . . well, I was sorta expressin' my desire for sorta climbin' into bed with a female, you know? A girl. You know?'

'So he sent you up here?'

'Yeah. No. Yeah, yeah, he did. He said there was a place up here called . . . ah . . . La Gallina.' He pronounced the word with a Western twang that brought a new smile to Zip's mouth.

'*La Gallina*, yes,' Zip said, giving it the proper Spanish pronunciation.

'Yeah,' the sailor said, nodding, 'where he said I could get anything I want. Now how about that?'

'He was right,' Zip answered.

'So here I am,' the sailor said. He paused. 'Where is it?'

'Right down the street there.'

'Thank you,' the sailor said, nodding. 'Thank you ver' much.' He started off down the street again.

'Don't mention it,' Zip said, smiling. He stared after the sailor for a few moments, and then went into the luncheonette. 'Give me a cup of coffee, Luís,' he said.

The sailor went down the street, studying each doorway as he had before. He stopped suddenly, looked at the lettering on the plate-glass window of a bar, and muttered, 'La Gallina, I'll be damned. Feller was right.' He walked directly to the front door, not expecting it to be locked, trying to open it, and then discovering that it was locked, immensely annoyed that the knob had resisted his hand. He backed away from the door and yelled, 'Hey! Hey, wake up! Wake up, goddamnit! I'm here!'

'What the hell is that?' Luís said.

'Sailor out there,' Zip said, grinning.

Luís came from behind the counter. Up the street, the sailor was still shouting at the top of his lungs.

'You!' Luís said. 'Quiet, quiet.'

The sailor turned. 'You talking to me, mate?'

'Sí, I'm talking to you, mate. Stop the racket. This is Sunday morning. People like to sleep, you know? You wake them up.'

'Well, hell, thass what I'm *trying* to do, you know.'

'Why you trying to wake them up for?'

''Cause I wanna go to bed.'

'That makes sense, all right,' Luís said, nodding patiently. 'Are you drunk?'

'Me?' the sailor said. 'Me?'

13

'Yes.'

'Hell, no.'

'You look perhaps a little drunk.'

The sailor walked to where Luís was standing, put his hands on his hips and said, 'Well, maybe I am perhaps a li'l drunk. So ain't you never been perhaps a li'l drunk?'

'I have been a little drunk,' Luís said, 'and I have been a lot drunk. Come. I'll make you a cup of coffee.'

'Whuffor?'

'What for?' Luís shrugged and walked into the luncheonette. The sailor followed him. 'Because I like sailors,' Luís said. 'I used to be a sailor myself once.'

'Did you find it, pal?' Zip interrupted.

'Yeah. It's closed.'

'I coulda told you that.'

'So why dinn you?'

'You didn't ask.'

'Oh, you're one of *those* guys,' the sailor said.

'Which guys?' Zip asked, and he stiffened suddenly on the counter stool, as if expecting an attack.

'The guys you got to ask.'

'Yeah,' Zip answered. 'I'm one of *those* guys. So what?'

Rapidly, perhaps because he sensed Zip's sudden belligerence, perhaps because he simply wanted to switch the conversation back to himself, Luís said, 'Yes, I was in the Navy from 1923 to 1927. Yes, sir.'

'Was you on a ship?' the sailor asked. If he had detected any challenge in Zip's voice, he was studiously ignoring it. Either that, or he was too drunk to have noticed.

'A man who has not been on a ship is not a sailor.' Luís looked over at the bubbling Silexes. 'The coffee is almost ready.'

'What kind of a ship?'

14

'A garbage scow,' Zip said quickly, and he grinned.

'Never mind this smart one. I was on a mine sweep.'

'What was your rate?' the sailor asked suspiciously.

'You never heard of Rear Admiral Luís Amandez?' Zip asked, mock surprise spreading over his uneven features.

'I was a steward's mate,' Luís answered with dignity. 'And you shut up, you little snotnose.'

'Wha'd he say your name was? Louise?'

'Yeah, that's right,' Zip answered, chuckling. 'This here is Aunt Louise.'

'Louise? Yeah?'

'No, Luís. Luís.'

'No, Louise,' Zip insisted.

'Are you a Mexican, Louise?' the sailor asked.

'No.' Luís shook his head. 'Puerto Rican.'

'Well, that's the same thing, ain't it?'

'Well—' Luís thought for a moment, and then shrugged resignedly. '*Sí*, the same thing.'

'What part of Mehico you from?' the sailor asked obliviously.

'The part down in the Caribbean,' Luís said dryly.

'The annex,' Zip put it. 'South. You know?'

'And whereabouts in Puerto Rico?'

'A town called Cabo Rojo, do you know it?'

'I only know Tia Juana,' the sailor said, 'and I ain't even been *there*. Closest I ever got was San Diego.'

'Here,' Luís said, pouring a cup of coffee. 'Drink this.'

'Where's mine?' Zip asked.

'I have only two hands.' He finished pouring the sailor's coffee, and then poured a cup for Zip.

'What brung you all the way here from Puerto Rico?' the sailor asked.

'Work,' Luís said. 'A man has to work, you know.'

'Where *you* from, sailor?' Zip asked.

15

'Fletcher,' the sailor said. 'That's in Colorado.'

'I never heard of it.'

'It's there, all right.'

The three fell silent.

Zip and the sailor sipped at their coffee. Luís got to work behind the counter. There seemed to be nothing more to say to each other. The three, after all, had very little in common. One had inquired about the whereabouts of the bar-quasi-whorehouse. The other had told him where it was. The third had served them both coffee. One was in his early fifties, the other was perhaps twenty-two, and the third was seventeen. One was born in Puerto Rico, the other in Fletcher, Colorado, and the third was a native of the city. Thus divided by time and space and natural inclination, there was nothing each could say to the other at the moment, and so they fell silent.

And yet, within the silence, their thoughts ran in strangely similar patterns so that, if the thoughts had been voiced, each would have instantly understood – or thought he'd understood – the other.

Luís had begun thinking about why he'd come to the mainland, about why he'd left the place of his birth. He had told the sailor he had come here to work, and yet he knew it was something more than that. It was not to work, it was to *begin*. He had lived on the island with a wife and three children, and the island – despite his love for it – had meant primarily one thing, and that thing was hunger. Constant hunger. Hunger that lingered through the cane-cutting season because you could not spend all of your earnings while the season was in swing; you had to save some for the empty days ahead. There was not much to hold and not much to save. You fished in the off season, and sometimes your haul was good –

but most of the time you were hungry. And being hungry, even knowing that everyone else around you was hungry, being hungry somehow reduced you to being nothing. There were things he would always love about the island, the innate pride and decency and hospitality of the people, the respect humans automatically showed to other humans, a respect bred of sunshine and lush tropical foliage where cruelty seemed blatantly out of place. The island seemed to draw people closer together, strengthening their bonds as humans. And yet, contradicting this was the dire economic need, so that on the one hand Luís had felt like a very important person with many friends and much love, and on the other he had felt like a hungry animal.

And so he'd left the island. He'd left the island in search of a beginning. He had worked hard for the luncheonette. It was still owned mostly by the bank, but he knew now that he would never go hungry again. And if he had lost something else, something quite dear to him, he had another sort of satisfaction, and this satisfaction was in his stomach and his bowels where perhaps a man feels it most.

The sailor sipped at his coffee and thought of Fletcher, Colorado.

He did not often think of Fletcher because he found he got sad whenever he did. He had been born in Fletcher, and he learned early the meaning of the words 'small town'. When a place is called a small town, it has nothing whatever to do with the size of the town. A giant metropolis can be a small town, and some very large cities *are* small towns in every sense of the word. Fletcher, Colorado, was just like every other small town in the United States of America. There was a schoolhouse, and a church, and a row of stores. There were

17

DRIVE — CHILDREN — SLOW signs, and SPEED LIMIT STRICTLY ENFORCED signs, and there were the teenage kids hanging out in the corner drugstore, and the Boy Scout cookouts, and the Little League, and the choir practice, and the *Saturday Evening Post* route, and in the spring the forsythias lined the highway with bright yellow and there was the bursting pink of cherry blossoms, and in the fall he would go hunting for deer with his father and his older brother, and the woods would shriek with color. In the winter, there was deep snow and skiing. The mountains surrounded the town. You could always see the mountains. Everybody in town knew everybody else in town.

He met Corrine at a church picnic when he was six years old. By the time they were eleven, everybody in town had decided that one day they would get married. When he got a swimming medal in his freshman year at high school, he gave it to Corrine. He went everywhere with Corrine and did everything with Corrine, and it became plain to him after a while that Corrine was perfectly happy to have been born and raised in a town like Fletcher, and that she would be happy to get married there, and breed kids there, and eventually to die there. And suddenly, he wondered if this was what he himself wanted.

Oh, he loved Corrine, it wasn't that. He supposed he loved her. She had very straight red hair that she wore loose around her shoulders, and she had very bright blue eyes and a nose that tilted slightly at the tip, she looked exactly like those pictures of small-town American girls he had seen on the covers of the *Saturday Evening Post* when he used to deliver the magazine. And he liked to neck with her. He liked to touch her, too, whenever she let him, which wasn't often, and he never could figure

18

out when she wanted him to and when she didn't want him to; he supposed he loved her because he respected her wishes in the matter.

And then, one day, all of a sudden, he decided he was going to join the Navy. When his parents asked him why, when Corrine asked him why, when his friends asked him why, he told them he would be drafted soon anyway, and he might just as well go into the Navy where a fellow didn't have to go on hikes or sleep in the mud. That was what he told all the people. But he knew why he was really joining the Navy. He was joining the Navy to get out of Fletcher. He was joining the Navy because Fletcher was slowly and surely suffocating him, and he could feel those mountains moving in closer and closer every day, and he knew that one day he would no longer be able to breathe, that one day he would be crushed by everything in this small town. When he left, he told himself he would never return. And so it made him sad to think about Fletcher.

Zip, drinking his coffee, studying his reflection in the mirror behind the counter, did not feel sad at all. Zip felt pretty damn good. Zip felt, at last, that things were beginning to click. They had never clicked for him in that ratty neighborhood downtown. There'd been nothing there for him but getting kicked by the older kids. Fat Ass Charlie, they used to call him. Fat Ass Charlie, and *bam*! a well-placed kick right in the middle of that fat ass. The nickname had persisted even when he began thinning into adolescence. And then they'd moved.

And suddenly, he wasn't fat-assed any more, and he wasn't even Charlie any more. He began calling himself Zip, and he began feeling that there was opportunity in this new neighborhood, the opportunity to be the person he wanted to be, and not the person everybody else thought he should be. He'd met Cooch, and Cooch had shown him the ropes and suggested that they join the biggest club in the neighborhood, the Royal Guardians.

But Zip had ideas of his own. Why become a schnook running around the fringes of the higher-ups when you could have a club of your own? And so he suggested the Latin Purples, and he planned to start it small, six, seven guys to begin with – so far there were only four. And Cooch's sister-in-law had sewn the purple jackets for them, and he wore his jacket with a great deal of pride now because the jacket meant something to him, the jacket meant that he was on his way.

If you'd asked him where he was going, he couldn't have told you.

But he knew he was on his way, and he knew that today would be the clincher, today would be the day he realized himself fully as a person.

And so the three of them sat with their separate thoughts, thoughts which were strangely similar, and when the sailor finally spoke, both Luís and Zip knew instantly what he meant.

The sailor said, 'You can lose yourself in Fletcher. You can get just plumb lost.' He shook his head. 'That's why I left. I wanted to know who I was.'

'And have you found out?' Luís asked.

'Give him time,' Zip said. 'You think a guy can make a rep in one day?'

'I'll find out, Louise,' the sailor said.

'How? With the girls from La Gallina?'

'Huh?'

'Sailor, take my advice,' Luís said. 'Go back to your ship. This neighborhood is not always a nice place.'

'Leave him alone,' Zip said. 'He wants a girl, I'll help

20

him find one.' He winked at the sailor, and then he grinned broadly.

'Don't let Sunday morning fool you,' Luís said. 'Last night, there was drinking and guitars. And this morning everyone sleeps. But sometimes . . . sailor, take my advice. Go back to your ship . . .'

'I think I'll hang around for a while.'

'Then be careful, eh? You are a stranger here. Choose your company.' He looked at Zip meaningfully. 'There are good and bad, *entiende*? You understand? Take care.'

The sailor swung around on his stool. He leaned his elbows on the countertop and drunkenly looked out over the sun-washed street.

'It looks nice and peaceful to me,' he murmured.

'Can you see through the walls, sailor?' Luís asked. 'Do you know what goes on under the skin of the buildings?'

3.

THE SKIN OF the building which housed the uniformed cops and detectives of the 87th Precinct was not lovely, nor engaged, nor had it been washed in more than half a century. It presented a characterless gray to the park across the street, a gray which seemed contradictory to the bright sunshine that filled the air. The gray stones were rough and uneven, covered with the soot and grime of the city, relieved only by the hanging green globes which announced in white numerals to the world at large that this was Precinct 87.

The low, flat steps of the front stoop led to a pair of glass-fronted doors which were open now to permit the entrance of whatever scant breeze rustled across Grover Park. The breeze, unfortunately, did not get very much further than the entrance doors. It certainly did not pass into the muster room where Sergeant Dave Murchison sat behind his high desk pulling at his undershorts and cursing the heat. A rotating electric fan sat on top of the switchboard to the left of the desk. The switchboard, at the moment, wasn't blinking with calls from the violated citizenry, thank God. Murchison wiped sweat from his brow, tugged at his undershorts, and wondered if it was any cooler upstairs.

A long wooden plaque, painted white and then overlaid with the black letters DETECTIVE DIVISION, pointed to a flight of narrow iron-runged steps which led upstairs to the bull pen. The flight of steps, gathering heat only from a small window where the steps turned back upon themselves before continuing to the second floor, was perhaps the coolest spot in the station house. Beyond the steps, a long corridor led to the detective squadroom where a battery of electric fans fought valiantly to produce some semblance of a breeze. The grilled windows at the far end of the squadroom admitted bright, golden sunlight which spread across the wooden floor like licking flames. The men in the squadroom sat in shirt sleeves at sun-drenched desks.

If there was one nice thing about being a detective, it was the fact that a gray flannel suit, a button-down shirt, and a neat black tie were not requisites of the job. Detective Steve Carella was perhaps the only detective in the squadroom on that Sunday morning in July who looked as if he might be an advertising executive. But then, Carella always looked as if he were dressed for the pages of *Esquire*. Even wearing a leather jacket and dungarees, he managed to exude the scent of careful grooming. He was a tall man whose sinewy body gave only the slightest hint of the power he possessed. Unpadded, slender with a rawboned simplicity, he seemed built to flatter whatever clothes were heaped onto his frame. This morning he was wearing a blue seersucker suit, the jacket of which was draped over the back of his chair. He had worn a bow tie to work, but had untied it the moment he entered the squadroom so that it hung loosely about his neck now, his shirt unbuttoned, his head bent over the report he was studying.

The other cops presented a slightly less sartorial appearance. Andy Parker, a cop who would have looked like a bum even when dressed for his own funeral, was wearing a pair of tan nylon slacks and a sports shirt which had surely been designed in honor of Hawaii's having achieved statehood. Hula girls swayed their hips all over Parker's shirt. Surfboarders flitted over his huge barrel chest. The colors on the shirt exploded like Roman candles. Parker, who looked unshaven even though he had shaved closely before reporting to the squadroom, pounded at a typewriter with both huge hands, using his fingers like fists. The typewriter seemed to resist each successive assault wave, a machine refusing to succumb to brute force. Parker continued to smash into it as if he were engaged in mortal combat, cursing each time the keys locked, slamming the carriage over whenever he reached the end of a line of the D.D. report, the bell clanging savagely in protest.

'No arrest,' he muttered savagely, 'but I got to type up a damn report, anyway.'

'Be glad you're alive,' Carella said, not looking up from the sheet in his hands.

'It'll take more than a punk like Pepe Miranda to put the blocks to me, pal,' Parker said. He continued smashing at the typewriter.

'You're lucky,' Carella said. 'He was feeling charitable. He had your gun, and he had everybody else's gun, and you're just damn lucky he didn't decide to kill you all.'

'He was chicken,' Parker said, looking up. 'If that was me in his place, I'd have blasted every cop in sight, and then shot a few passers-by just for the hell of it. But Miranda was chicken. He knows the jig's up, so he figured he wouldn't add anything else to what we already got on him.'

'Maybe he liked your face,' Carella said. 'Maybe he figured you were too sweet to shoot.'

'Yeah,' Parker said, and he ripped the D.D. report from the machine. He did not like Carella. He could still remember the time in March when he and Carella had mixed it up a little in the squadroom. The fight had ended abruptly because Frankie Hernandez had reminded them both that the lieutenant was in the building. But Parker didn't like unfinished business. And maybe Carella had forgotten all about the incident – though he doubted it – but Parker had not, and would not until the thing was resolved finally, one way or another. Thinking back to that March day, he thought it odd that the same men had been present in the squadroom, the three of them, and that Carella had taken offense at a chance remark made to Hernandez. Why the hell were people always so touchy? He dropped the report on his desk and walked to the water cooler.

Frankie Hernandez, the third man who'd been there on that March day, the third man in the squadroom on this day in July, was standing at one of the filing cabinets, the drawer open. He wore a short-sleeved white shirt and dark-blue trousers. A .38 police special protruded from the holster strapped to his chest. He was a wide-shouldered man with a tan complexion and straight, black hair. His eyes were brown, the eyes of a man who expected to be offended and who, as a result, was constantly prepared for the eventuality. It was not easy to be a Puerto Rican cop in a neighborhood with such a large Puerto Rican population – especially if you happened to have been born and raised in the streets of the precinct. Whatever battles Hernandez fought with his neighbors, the police, and himself were reflected in his eyes. He was not a happy man. No man dedicated to a single cause ever is.

'What do you think of your pal there?' Parker asked from the cooler.

'What pal?' Hernandez asked.

'Miranda.'

'He's no pal of mine,' Hernandez answered.

'I thought we had him cold yesterday,' Parker said, filling a paper cup and drinking from it. He wiped his lips with the back of his hand. 'Five of us walked into that apartment, and the son of a bitch pulls a gun from someplace up his sleeve and cold-cocks us. The rotten punk. He made us look like amateurs. You see the paper today? "Miranda Foils Cops." A punk getting headlines.'

'He's still no pal of mine,' Hernandez said.

'Yeah,' Parker answered. He seemed ready to say more, but he let the matter drop. 'Who was that woman up here?' he asked.

'Her name's Gomez,' Hernandez answered.

'What'd she want?'

'Her son's in some kind of trouble. She wants me to talk to him.'

'What the hell does she think you are? A priest?'

Hernandez shrugged.

'You gonna go?' Parker asked.

'As soon as I finish what I'm working on.'

'Maybe you are a priest.'

'Maybe,' Hernandez replied.

Parker walked to the coat rack in one corner of the room and took a dark-blue Panama from one of the pegs. 'I'm going outside,' he said, 'see if I can't hear something.'

'About what?' Carella asked.

'About that punk Miranda. He didn't vanish into thin air, that's for sure. So where would you go if you was him?'

26

'To Russia,' Carella replied.

'Yeah. Well, I think he came back here. Right here someplace. He sure as hell wouldn't try to find another pad in Riverhead, not after we almost collared him there. So where? Home. Home to the 87th. And if he's somewhere around here, you can bet your ass everybody in the streets knows just where. So Andy Parker goes on the earie.' He stopped at his desk, opened the top drawer, took out his service revolver and holster, and clipped the holster into his right hip pocket. 'Don't work too hard,' he said, as he went through the gate in the railing. 'Not that I think you need the advice.'

His footsteps echoed down the long corridor. Hernandez watched him as he turned to go down the flight of iron-runged steps. When he looked back into the squadroom, he saw that Carella had been watching the other man, too.

A glance passed between them. Neither said a word. Silently, they got back to work.

Azucena Gomez had been one of those fortunate people who are born beautiful and who remain beautiful no matter what tricks life decides to play on them. Her name, translated from the Spanish, meant White Lily, and she seemed to have been appropriately named because her skin was white and smooth, and her face, her body, seemed to combine all the delicate beauty and regality of that flower. The oval of her face was dominated by brown eyes which slanted to lend an exotic flair to otherwise serene features. Her nose was straight and slender, her mouth was a mouth which looked as if it could cry. She had managed, without the benefit of dieting, to maintain a body which had evoked many a street-corner whistle in her native Puerto Rico. She was forty-two years old, and she had known what it was to be a woman, still knew, and she knew the happiness and sorrow of motherhood. She was not a tall woman, perhaps the one flaw which robbed her of true beauty, but she seemed exceptionally tall as she stood by the bed and looked down at her son.

'Alfredo?' she said.

He did not answer her. He lay on the bed full length, his face buried in the pillow.

'Alfredo?'

He did not look up. He did not turn his head from the pillow. 'Mama, lee me alone,' he mumbled. 'Please.'

'You have to listen to me,' she said. 'It is important that you listen to me.'

'It don' make no difference wha' you say, Mama. I already know what I got to do.'

'You must go to the church, is that what you must do?'

'*Sí.*'

'And they will harm you.'

He sat up suddenly. He was a sixteen-year-old boy with his mother's fair complexion and wide, brown eyes. The slight fuzz of adolescence clung to his cheeks. His mouth, like his mother's seemed ready to twist into sorrow.

'I go to church every Sunday,' he said simply. 'I go today too. They cannot stop me.'

'They cannot stop you, but they will harm you. Is this what they said?'

'*Sí.*'

'Who told you this?'

'The boys.'

'Which boys?'

28

'Mama, this is not for you,' Alfredo said plaintively. 'This is somethin' . . .'

'Why? Why will they hurt you?'

Alfredo would not answer. He stared at his mother, but he remained silent.

'Why, Alfredo?'

The tears came suddenly. He felt them welling into his eyes, and he turned from her quickly so that she would not see him crying. He threw himself onto the bed again, his face buried in the pillow, his shoulders heaving as he sobbed. His mother touched his shoulder.

'Cry,' she said.

'Mama, I am asha—'

'It is good to cry. Your father used to cry sometimes. It is not a sin for a man to cry.'

'Mama, Mama, please, you don't understan' . . .'

'I understand that you are my son,' Mrs Gomez said with simple logic. 'I understand that you are good, and that those who wish to harm you are bad. It is not for the bad ones to rule the streets, Alfredo. You say you must go to eleven o'clock mass, the way you always do. You say you must go, even though they will hurt you. *This* I do *not* understand.'

He sat up again, and the words sprang from his lips like a scream.

'*I cann turkey out!*'

'You can't . . . turkey out?' she asked, puzzled.

'I cann be afray, Mama. I cann be turkey. You don' understan'. This is not somethin' you understan'. Please. Let me do what I got to do.'

His mother stood by the bed, staring at him, staring at her son as if somehow she did not know him any longer, as if somehow the infant she had held to her breast, the infant who had sucked of her milk was no

29

longer someone she knew. His face, his language, even his eyes seemed distant and strange. She studied him as if trying to force the reconstruction of an earlier bond through the power of her eyes alone.

At last she said, 'I have gone to the police.'

'What!' he shouted.

'*Sí.*'

'Why did you do that? You think the police will care abou' me? About Alfredo Gomez? The police are no good. Don' you know the police here in this neighborhood?'

'There are good police and bad police. I have gone to Frankie Hernandez.'

'He iss the same as dee ress. Mama, why did you do this? Why cann you stay out of this?'

'Frankie will help you. He is from the *barrio.*'

'But he's a cop now, a detective. He . . .'

'He grew up here in these streets. He is Spanish, and he helps his people. He will help you.'

'You shoul' not have gone,' Alfredo said, shaking his head.

'I have never been inside a police station in my life,' Mrs Gomez said. 'Today is the first time. My son is in danger, and I went for help.' She paused. 'He said he would come. I gave him the address. He said he would come to talk to you.'

'I will tell him nothing,' Alfredo said softly.

'You will tell him all that is necessary to tell him.'

'Wha' time is it?' he asked suddenly.

'You have time yet.'

'I got to dress for church.'

'Not until you talk to Frankie Hernandez. He will know what to do.'

'He will know what to do,' Alfredo said. 'Sure, he will

know what to do,' and the mockery in his voice was tinged with bitterness and inescapable sorrow.

'He will know what to do,' Mrs Gomez said confidently.

4.

THE SAILOR'S NAME was Jeff Talbot, and the rosy glow of the alcohol was beginning to wear off, and as he surveyed the street outside the luncheonette, he wondered how he could ever have said it looked like a nice neighborhood. Somehow, even the sunlight did not help the look of the street outside. It helped only in the way a powerful spotlight helps to illuminate a garbage dump. He blinked at the sunshine, and he blinked at the street outside, and he suddenly said, 'I'm sober,' and just as suddenly realized that he was.

'Good,' Luís said. 'How does the world look?'

'Miserable.' He swung his stool back toward the counter. 'I'm getting a headache. This is a pretty rotten neighborhood, ain't it?'

'It depends how you look at it,' Zip said. 'I happen to like it.'

'You do?'

'It's where I live. When I'm here, that sidewalk sings.'

'What does it sing?' Jeff asked. His head was beginning to pound. He wondered why he was talking with a stranger, wondered why he'd drunk so much the night before.

'With him,' Luís said, 'it sings Rock and Roll.'

'The old man is very hip, sailor. He knows all the proper . . .'

Zip stopped talking. He tensed suddenly on the stool, his eyes fastened to the street outside.

'What's the matter?' Jeff asked.

32

'The Law,' Zip said quietly.

The Law to which he had referred was the law as personified by Detective Andy Parker who walked up the street with a sort of slumped, indifferent swagger, a cigarette dangling from the corner of his mouth, looking for all the world like a penniless bum who had just come from sleeping one off in a doorway. His bright Hawaiian shirt was rumpled and soiled with coffee stains. He scratched his chest indolently, his eyes flicking the street as he walked.

'The only law I got to worry about is the Shore Patrol,' Jeff said, dismissing him. He shoved his empty cup across the counter. 'Can I get another cup of joe?' He grinned and then winced in pain. 'Oh, man, but that head hurts when I smile.'

Outside the luncheonette, Andy Parker waved at Luís and said, '*Qué pasa, maricón?*'

'Hello, Andy,' Luís said, smiling. 'Some coffee?'

'I can use a cup,' Parker answered. 'Hot.' He walked into the luncheonette and took the stool next to Jeff's. He studied Zip for a moment and then asked, 'When did you start catering to the punk trade, Luís?'

'I'm having a cup of coffee,' Zip answered. 'Anything wrong with that, Lieutenant?'

'I ain't a lieutenant, and don't get smart.'

'I thought you'd at least be a captain by now. After all the drunks you pulled in from Grover Park.'

'Look, kid . . .'

'This is Detective Andy Parker, sailor,' Zip said. 'He's what is known as a tough cop. Fearless. For two cents, he'd arrest his own grandmother.' He grinned almost immediately, and Jeff recognized the pattern suddenly. It was as if someone had advised the boy that a grin would take him a long way, especially a grin composed

33

of such sparkling white teeth, a grin that never failed to generate a warm response in its recipient. Even Parker, faced with the sudden dazzling brilliance of the grin, smiled.

'For two cents,' he answered, 'I'd kick your ass all over the sidewalk.' But there was no menace in his words. The threat, disarmed by the grin, was a hollow one.

'See?' Zip said, still grinning. 'I'll bet he can lick any sixteen-year-old kid on the block.'

'Go ahead,' Parker said, 'push me another inch, kid.' But again the threat was not real, the smile had stolen all its power. He turned his attention to the sailor, studied him for a moment and then said, 'What are you doing around here, sailor?'

'Same thing as the kid here,' Jeff answered. 'Having a cup of coffee.'

'Let's try it again,' Parker said tiredly. 'What are you doing around here?'

'I heard you the first time,' Jeff said.

'Then give me a straight answer.'

'Is this neighborhood off limits?'

'No, it ain't off limits, but it sure as hell . . .'

'Then leave me alone.'

Parker studied him silently for a moment. Then he said, 'Pretty salty, huh?'

'Yeah, pretty salty,' Jeff said.

'Andy, he's a little drunk,' Luís put in, spreading his hands. 'You know, go easy on . . .'

'Keep out of this, Luís,' Parker snapped.

'I'm sober now, Louise. Thanks.'

'I asked a question.'

'Oh, for God's sake,' Jeff said, 'I came to sit up with a sick grandmother.'

34

Zip burst out laughing and then immediately squelched the laughter when Parker turned a frigid glare on him. Zip shrugged. Parker turned back to the sailor.

'What's your grandmother's name?' he asked icily.

'Now you got me, officer. I always just called her plain Grandma.'

'What ship you off?'

'Why?'

'I'm asking!'

'How do I know you ain't a Russian spy?'

'You guys think you're pretty wise, don't you? Coming up here and fouling up my precinct?'

'Who's fouling up your lousy precinct? I'm drinking a cup of coffee, that's all.'

'Here, Andy, here,' Luís said, anxious to make peace. 'Here's *your* coffee. Drink it while it's still hot.'

Parker took the cup. 'You know how many sailors get rolled up here?' he persisted.

'How many?' Jeff asked.

'This sailor don't get rolled, Lieutenant,' Zip said. 'He's under my protection.'

'You couldn't protect a wooden nickel from a blind man. What'd you come looking for, sailor?'

'I told you,' Jeff said, annoyed now. 'Grandma.'

'Tail?'

'Why? You peddling it on the side?'

'Sailor, don't get . . .'

'You mean to tell me I could actually find some in this nice, sweet, clean precinct you're so afraid I'm going to foul up?'

'Sailor, I'm talking to you like a friend. Get the hell out of here. Luís, am I giving him bum advice?'

35

Luís shrugged. 'I told him the same thing, Andy!'

'Sure,' Parker said, nodding. 'Look, Luís lives here. He knows this place like the back of his hand. Did you tell him about this neighborhood, Luís?'

'I told him, I told him.'

'About what you run into around here? The guys like Pepe Miranda?'

'*Sí*, ah, there's a one,' Luís said.

'What's the matter with Pepe?' Zip asked. 'He made you guys look like a bunch of monkeys yesterday.' He grinned suddenly. 'How many cops did he ambush? Four? Five? Man, he made you look sick.' He turned to Jeff. 'They walked into the apartment, and in ten seconds he had their guns and was on his merry way. They're lucky he didn't shoot them, just for kicks.'

'Big hero, huh?' Parker said. 'He eludes the law, so you make him . . .'

'I ain't making him nothing. It only seems to me that you big detective masterminds should have got him by now, that's all. Don't you think so?'

'We'll get him,' Parker said. 'Especially if he came back to this neighborhood.'

'*Did* he come back?' Zip asked, leaning forward.

'Maybe,' Parker said.

'No kidding?'

Parker shrugged.

'Here? No kidding?'

'You wouldn't happen to know where, would you?'

'Me? Why, Lieutenant, I would tell you instantly if I knew. But, unfortunately, I do not follow the movements of the underworld.'

'Luís?' Parker said, turning to the counter suddenly, as if hoping to catch Luís off guard.

36

'This is the first I'm hearing, Andy. Why did he come back here? He didn't cause enough trouble here?'

'Who's Pepe Miranda?' Jeff asked.

'Pepe Miranda is a thirty-five-year-old punk. Am I right, Luís?'

'He's only a punk 'cause you can't nab him,' Zip said.

'No, no, Andy is right,' Luís said. 'Miranda's no good. Pghhh, he's rotten.'

'Luís and I get along fine,' Parker said. 'We understand each other. He's been around here as long as I have, and he never so much as spit on the sidewalk.' Parker grinned. 'He knows I'd drag him down the station house if he did, huh, Luís?'

'Oh, sure, sure,' Luís said, riding with the gag.

'Why don't you drag Miranda down the station house, Lieutenant?' Zip asked sweetly.

'Don't think we won't! And cut the lieutenant crap! He's been riding for a fall for a long time now. When a kid has a j.d. card before he's fourteen . . .'

'A what?' Jeff asked.

'A juvenile delinquency record. At fourteen. So what can you expect? He's no different now than when he started that street gang years ago. The Golden Spaniards. Remember them, Luís? This was even before street gangs were normal around here.'

'He was ahead of his time,' Zip said, grinning.

'Ahead of his time, my ass.'

'No good,' Luís said, pulling a face. 'I remember. Snotnoses. Like today. No different.'

'Except today is the atomic age,' Parker said, 'so they carry guns instead of knives. Miranda killed a kid in 1942, sailor, when he was seventeen. Slit the kid from ear to ear.'

'The kid probably deserved it,' Zip said.

37

'His lawyer got him off with manslaughter,' Parker said.

'He should have got the chair,' Luís put in. 'They should have burned him.'

'They sent him upstate, to Castleview, and he spent just enough time there to get out of fighting in World War II. When he was paroled, he came back here. Heroin was the big thing then. Miranda started pushing it.'

'Poisoning children! Argh, what makes men do this!'

'Nobody starts on horse unless he wants to, dad,' Zip said. 'Don't go blaming Miranda.'

'Okay by you if we blame him for all the people he's killed in this goddamn city?'

'You can't prove he killed anybody.'

'That's what you think. There's a lady dying in General Hospital right now, and she identified a photo of Miranda as the guy who beat her up and took her purse.'

'Miranda mugging? Don't snow me, cop.'

'Miranda mugging, yes! Not such a goddamn big shot any more, is he? No more high-pay torpedo jobs now that the heat's on. Only little ladies to beat up. Believe me, when we get that bastard we're gonna throw away the key on him.'

'Sure, *when* you get him.'

'We'll get him. He's here someplace, that's for sure. Once we find out where, goodbye Miranda. One less hero in the neighborhood.' He took a long draw at his coffee, finishing it. Putting down the cup, he said, 'That was good coffee, Luís. Luís makes the best damn cup of coffee in the city.'

'Sure, sure.'

'He thinks I'm kidding him. Even if I didn't like you,

Luís, I'd still come here to drink your coffee, you know that?'

'It's good having a cop for a steady customer. It keeps trouble away.'

'And there's plenty of that around here,' Parker said.

'Well, you don't die from being bored around here,' Luís said, grinning.

'It's a hell of a lot different from the island, ain't it?'

'Oh, yes, yes.'

'I was down there for a week once, had to bring back this punk who skipped the city after holding up a jewelry store on South Fourth. That's the life, all right. Lay in the sun all day long, suck sugar cane, go fishing. And at night . . .' He winked at Luís. 'There's no holding down the Puerto Rican men at night, eh, Luís?'

'Andy, for a man who's a man . . . the nights are the same any place, no?'

'Oh, brother, watch out for this guy!' Parker said, laughing. 'He's got three kids already, and I think he's gunning for number four.'

'At my age?' Luís said, laughing with him. 'No, no, it would take a miracle.'

'Or a boarder,' Parker said. 'Keep your eye on the boarder, Luís.' He put his hand on Jeff's shoulder. 'There are more boarders in this neighborhood than you can shake a stick at. We got areas called "hot bed" areas, where guys rent out apartments on an eight-hour basis, three sleeping shifts, would you believe it?'

'We don't have any boarders,' Luís said, still laughing. 'Teresa is safe.'

Parker sighed and pulled a handkerchief from his pocket. He wiped his face with it and then said, 'Well, back to crime prevention, huh? Sailor, I'd forget that sick grandmother if I was you. Get out of here. This neighborhood ain't for clean-cut kids.'

'Who's clean-cut?'

'You're liable to be, if you don't take my advice. From ear to ear, you're liable to be.'

'I'll chance it.'

'Sure, chance it. Famous last words. I hope you're wearing your dog tags. We'll want to know where to send the body.'

'Send it to his grandma,' Zip said, grinning. 'She's expecting him.'

'Kid, you're lucky I'm in a good mood today,' Parker said. He turned back to Luís. 'Hey, *pinga?*'

'*Sí, cabrón,*' Luís answered, and both men grinned as if pleased by their intimate use of profanity in addressing each other.

'If you hear anything about Miranda, don't forget me, huh?'

'I won't,' Luís answered.

'Good. *Adiós.*'

He walked away from the luncheonette, blinking his eyes against the sunshine. He wondered why it was that he could have such a good relationship with Luís Amandez and such a bad one with Frankie Hernandez. Weren't both men Puerto Ricans? Of course they were. But Luís was different. Luís was willing to accept certain things about his own people, whereas Frankie was a son of a bitch who was just deaf and dumb on the subject. How could you hope to discuss anything intelligently with a guy who had a chip on his shoulder? Where was the give and take in a relationship like that? There just wasn't any. Now with Luís, Parker enjoyed a give and take.

That's why it was so good. Why couldn't Hernandez be that way, too?

Parker sighed heavily.

It takes all kinds, he told himself. It takes all kinds.

5.

ZIP CONTINUED GRINNING until Parker had turned
the corner and walked off up the avenue. Then the grin
dropped from his mouth.

'You'd stool on Pepe for that rotten cop?' he asked
Luís.

'Pepe Miranda is no brother of mine,' Luís answered.

'A stoolie is a stoolie,' Zip said. He swung around and
walked to the jukebox. He studied the selections for a
moment, inserted his coin, chose one, and then stepped
behind the box and turned up the volume so that a
mambo fairly blasted into the luncheonette.

'Lower that, lower that,' Luís said.

'Shhh, man,' Zip said, grinning. 'I can't hear the
music.'

'I said lower that,' Luís shouted, and he came around
the counter, walked to the juke, and was reaching around
to the back when Zip stepped into his way, laughing.
The music screeched into the shop, trumpets bellowing,
bongo drums pounding their steady beat. At the counter,
Jeff's headache responded to the assault wave of sound.
He turned toward the juke. The old man was still trying
to reach the volume control. Zip, laughing, danced
before him, blocking his path, stepping out of it, teasing
the old man closer, blocking him again. The grin did not
leave his face, but there seemed to be no humor in his
laughing defense of the volume control. The old man
lunged, and Zip stepped aside finally and danced into the
street like a boxer moving away from the ropes. Luís

located the volume control and turned it all the way down.

From the street, Zip said, 'Not too low, you old bastard. That's still my loot in there.'

Luís stamped angrily to the cash register. He rang up NO SALE, took a dime from the cash drawer and threw it on the counter. 'Here!' he shouted. 'Take your money and go!'

Zip threw back his head and laughed, a loud mocking laugh which – like his earlier smile – was totally devoid of humor. 'Keep it, dad,' he said. 'It probably took you all week to make.'

'Puncture my eardrums!' Luís muttered. 'On a Sunday morning! No decency, no decency!'

But the music, despite Luís' preference for comparative silence, seemed to have awakened the neighborhood all at once. The street had been as still and empty as a country road before the record started, and now it suddenly teemed with humanity. In the distance, the church bells had begun tolling again and, in response to the bells, the people of the neighborhood were coming out of the tenements, drifting down the steps leisurely because this was first call, and there was still time before the Mass would begin. The record spun to an end, but the church bells persisted, and the street was alive with color now, color which seemed appropriate to the heat of July, color so vivid, so tropical, that it assailed the eyeballs. Two young girls in the brightest pink came out of a tenement and walked arm in arm down the street toward the church. An old man in a brown silk suit, wearing a bright green tie, came from another tenement and began in the same direction. A woman carrying a red parasol to shield her from the sun walked with the dignity of a queen, trailing a boy in a short-trousered suit by her side. The people nodded at each other, and smiled, and exchanged a few words. This was Sunday morning. This was the day of rest.

From the other end of the street, rushing against the tide of humanity that swelled with a single mind toward the church at the far end of the block, Cooch appeared with two other boys. Zip saw them instantly, and went to join them.

'What the hell kept you so long?' he asked.

'We had to wait for Sixto,' Cooch said.

'What the hell are you, Sixto? A man or a baby sitter?'

Sixto looked as if he were about to blush. He was a thin boy of sixteen with eyes that seemed ready to flinch at so much as an unkind word. He spoke English with a Spanish accent which was sometimes marked and sometimes mild. His voice was very soft, and he used it reticently, as if he were not ever certain that anyone wanted to hear what he had to say.

'I ha' to help my mother,' he told Zip.

The other boy with Cooch was a six-footer with a face so dark that all personality somehow became lost in the overall impression of blackness. His features were a mixture of Negroid and Caucasian, a mixture so loosely concocted that even here there was an impression of vagueness, of vacuity. The boy was sixteen years old. He moved slowly, and he thought slowly. His mind a blank, his face a blank, he presented a somewhat creaking portrait to his contemporaries, and so they had named him Papá, as befitted a sixteen-year-old who seemed to be seventy.

'When my fodder go on a trip,' he said, 'I hep my mudder. He tell me to hep her.' He spoke with a Spanish accent so marked that sometimes his words were unintelligible. At these moments, he would revert back

44

to his native tongue, and this too added to the concept of a young boy who was old, a young boy who clung to the old language and the old slow-moving ways of a land he had deeply loved.

'That's different,' Zip said. 'When he's away, you're the man of the house. I'm not talking about a man's work.'

Proudly, Papá said, 'My fodder's a merchan' marine.'

'Who the hell are you snowing?' Zip asked. 'He's a waiter.'

'On a boat! Tha' makes him a merchan' marine.'

'That makes him a waiter! Listen, we've wasted enough time already. Let's lay this out. We're gonna have to move if we want to catch that eleven o'clock Mass.' He turned suddenly to Sixto who had been staring blankly at the street. 'You with us, Sixto?'

'Wah? Oh, yes. I'm . . . I'm with you, Zip.'

'You looked like you was on the moon.'

'I wass thinkin' . . . well, you know. This Alfredo kid, he not sush a bad guy.'

'He's getting washed and that's it,' Zip said. 'I don't even want to hear talk about it.' He paused. 'What the hell are you looking at, would you please mind telling me?'

'The organ-grinder,' Sixto said.

The organ-grinder had rounded the corner and stopped just outside the luncheonette. His parrot had bright-green feathers. The parrot perched on the instrument, accepted coins in his beak, gave them to his master, and then reached down to select a fortune slip from the rack of slips on top of the hand organ. A crowd immediately gathered around the organ-grinder and his trained bird. The crowd was a Sunday churchgoing crowd, bedecked in bright summer colors. The girls

45

shrieked each time they read a fortune. The old men and the old ladies grinned knowingly. Jeff walked out of the luncheonette and handed the parrot a nickel. The parrot reached into the rack, *peck*, a narrow white slip appeared in his beak. Jeff took the slip and began reading it. The girls squealed in delight. There was an innocence surrounding the organ-grinder, the mechanical music he produced was countered by the skill of the bird and the faith of the crowd. For this was Sunday morning, and this was a time to believe in fortunes, a time to believe that the future would be good. And so they crowded the man and his bird, crowded around the sailor who read his fortune from the card and grinned, laughed again in delight as the parrot dipped his beak for another fortune. There was innocence here, and it shimmered on the summer air like truth.

Not ten feet from the organ-grinder, not ten feet from the crowd in their gay Sunday clothes, Zip stood in a whispering circle with three other boys who wore purple silk jackets. The backs of the jackets were lettered with the words THE LATIN PURPLES. The words were cut from yellow felt and stitched to the purple silk. The Latin Purples, The Latin Purples, The Latin Purples, The Latin Purples, four jacket backs and four young men who huddled close together and spoke in low whispers while the organ-grinder filled the air with the music of innocence and truth.

'I . . . I wass thinkin',' Sixto said, 'maybe we shoul' jus', you know, maybe warn him.'

'For messing with one of the debs?' Cooch whispered, astonished.

'So, he dinn really do nothin', Cooch. He jus' only say hello to her. Thass not so bad.'

'He made a grab,' Cooch said with finality.

46

'Thass not what she say. I ask her. She say he ony jus' say hello to her.'

'What right did you have to go asking her questions?' Zip wanted to know. 'Whose girl is she? Yours or mine?' Sixto remained silent. 'Well?'

'Well, Zip,' Sixto said, after long deliberation, 'I tink . . . well, I don' tink she knows. I mean, I don' tink she got no understanding with you.'

'I don't need no understanding with a chick. I'm telling you she's my girl, and that's good enough.'

'But *she* don' tink so!'

'I don't care what she thinks.'

'Anyway,' Sixto said, 'no matter whose girl she is, if Alfie don' do nothin' to her, why we got to *shoot* him?'

The boys were silent for a moment, as if mention of the word, as if translation of their plan into sound, into a word which immediately delivered the image of a pistol, had shocked them into silence.

In a very low voice, Zip asked, 'You going turkey?' Sixto did not answer. 'I thought you was a down cat, Sixto. I thought you had heart.'

'I *do* got heart.'

'He gah heart, Zeep,' Papá said, defending Sixto.

'Then why's he backing out? How'd you like it if this was your girl, Sixto? How'd you like it if Alfie went messing around with your girl?'

'But he *dinn* mess with her. He ony say hello. So wha's so bad about dat?'

'You in this club?' Zip asked.

'Sure.'

'Why?'

'I . . . I don' know. You got to belong to . . .' Sixto shrugged. 'I don' know.'

'If you're in this club, if you wear that purple jacket,

47

you do what I say. Okay. I say the Latin Purples are washing Alfredo Gomez right after eleven o'clock Mass. You want to turkey out, go ahead.' He paused meaningfully. 'All I know is that Alfie give China a rough time. China's my girl whether she knows it or not, you dig? China's my girl, and that means Alfie got himself trouble.'

Cooch nodded. 'Big trouble.'

'And that don't mean a burn. I don't want him burned. I want him *washed*! You can turkey out, Sixto, go ahead. Only you better watch your step around here afterwards, that's all I'm telling you.'

'I jus' thought . . . oh, I jus' thought . . . well, Zip, cann we *talk* to him?'

'Oh, come on, for Christ's sake!' Zip said angrily.

'Cann we jus' tell him to stop . . . to stop talking to her no more? Cann we do dat? Why we have to . . . to *kill* him?'

There was another long silence, for another word had been spoken, and this word was stronger than the first. And this word meant exactly what it said, this word meant kill, to take someone's life, kill, to murder. This was not a euphemism, a handy substitute like 'wash.' This was kill. And the word hung between them, the sentence hung between them on the still July air. 'Why we have to . . . to *kill* him?'

'Because I say so,' Zip said softly.

'It be diff'ren if he really was . . .'

'What else you going to do, huh? Get pushed around?' Zip asked. 'Man, ain't you sick of all the time getting pushed around?'

'I dinn say that. I said . . .'

'Everybody in the neighborhood knows he made a pass at China!' Zip said plaintively. 'Am I supposed to . . . ?'

'He *dinn* make no pass! He ony say hello!'

'Am I supposed to go over and have a chat with him? *How are you, Alfie old boy, how you been? I understand you was feeling up China the other day, was it good?* Am I supposed to hold his goddamn hand, Sixto?'

'No, but . . .'

'Don't you want these other clubs to notice us? Don't you want them to know we got self-respect?'

'Sure, but . . .'

'So we going to let a creep like Alfie go around screwing our debs?'

Sixto shook his head. 'Zip, Zip, he dinn even . . .'

'Okay, listen to me,' Zip said. 'After we pull this today, we're in. You understand that? We wash this creep, and there ain't nobody in this neighborhood who don't know the Latin Purples from then on in. They'll know we don't get pushed around by *anybody*! Every damn kid on this block'll want to be in the club after today. We're gonna be . . . something! *Something!*' He paused to catch his breath. His eyes were glowing. 'Am I right, Cooch?'

'Sure,' Cooch answered.

'Okay, Alfie's going to eleven o'clock Mass, like he always does. Mass'll break around eleven-forty, a quarter to twelve. I want to get him on the steps as he's coming out.'

'On dee— !'

'*On the steps!* All four of us blast together, and nobody stops until Alfie's down. You better shoot straight 'cause there'll be a lot of innocent people around.'

'Zip, on dee church steps?' Sixto said. His face was twisted in pain. '*Ave Maria*, cann we . . . ?'

'On the steps, I said! Where everybody'll see him die. We've got four pieces. I'm using the .45 because I want to blow that creep's head off.'

The organ-grinder stopped his music. The street seemed suddenly silent.

'There's two .38s and the Luger,' Zip whispered. 'Take whatever you want.'

'The Luger,' Cooch said.

'You got it. Sixto, you and Papá'll use the .38s. The pieces are up at my pad. We get them first, and then round up a couple of gun bearers.' He paused for a moment. 'Second thought, you better stay here, Sixto. Keep an eye on Alfie's house. Right around the corner. The first building.'

'Okay,' Sixto said blankly.

'Make sure he don't leave. If he does, follow him. If you ain't here when we get back, we'll start looking for you.'

'Okay.'

'What?'

'I said okay.'

'Okay,' Zip repeated. 'Come on.' He put his arm around Cooch as they began walking toward his building. Papá shuffling along beside them. 'You excited, Cooch?' he asked.

'Huh? Oh, yeah, I guess. A little.'

'Man, I'm excited. This day is beginning to tick, you know what I mean? Things are moving!'

'Yeah, that's true,' Cooch said.

'Some Sundays, you can sit on that front stoop and go nuts. Especially like now in the summer. But today is different. Today, there's like a million things to do, ain't there? What I'm trying to say, Cooch, this makes me feel good. This action, you know? Man, it makes me feel real good!'

Cooch grinned as the three boys entered the tenement. 'It ain't gonna make Alfie feel so good,' he said.

Sixto stood on the corner outside the luncheonette, watching Alfredo's building, nervously biting his lower lip.

Inside the luncheonette, Jeff handed his fortune slip to Luís and said, 'How do you like that?'

'Be patient and of firm resolve,' Luís read, 'and you will achieve all your ends.'

'Yeah,' Jeff said. 'What time does La Gallina open?'

'I had hoped you would forget La Gallina.'

'Well, since I'm already up here . . .' Jeff shrugged and let the sentence trail. 'What time does it open?'

'This is Sunday,' Luís said, 'and La Gallina is a bar – among other things. It does not open until noon.'

'Then I've got plenty of time yet.'

'If you'd take my advice . . .'

'*Hey! Hey you!*' the voice bellowed, and they both turned simultaneously to face the street. Andy Parker seemed to have materialized from nowhere. He approached Sixto, who stood on the corner, and shouted '*You! You there!*'

Sixto, frightened, began to inch away from him. 'Me?' he asked. 'Me?'

'What are you doing?' Parker asked, coming up close to him.

'Nothin'. I wass ony jus' standin' . . .'

'Against the wall!'

'Huh?'

Parker seized his jacket front and slammed him up against the supporting post at the corner of the luncheonette. 'I said against the wall!'

'I . . . I dinn do nothin',' Sixto said. 'I wass only jus' . . .'

'Bend over!'

51

Sixto stared at him blankly, uncomprehendingly.

'Bend over, goddamnit!' Parker shouted.

Sixto still did not understand. Furiously, because he felt his command was being openly flouted, Parker chopped a fast right to Sixto's gut, doubling him over. He spun him around then so that he faced the corner post, his hands clutching his stomach, his head bent.

'Put your hands against the wall, palms flat, goddamnit, do what I tell you!' Parker shouted.

Sixto, doubled over with pain, made an abortive attempt to stretch out his arms, clutched his stomach again, and then shoved his arms out convulsively when Parker hit him in the ribs. He extended his hands and placed them, trembling, against the corner post. Quickly, Parker frisked him. He did an intent and thorough job, so thorough that he did not notice Frankie Hernandez who walked up the street and stopped just short of the luncheonette.

'Turn around!' Parker shouted. 'Now empty your pockets! Everything on the sidewalk! Hurry up!'

Hernandez walked to where they were standing. 'Leave him alone, Andy,' he said. He turned to Sixto. 'Take off, kid.'

Sixto hesitated, frightened, looking first to one detective and then the other.

'Get out of here, go ahead! Beat it!'

Sixto hesitated a moment longer, and then broke into a sprint around the corner, racing up the avenue.

'Thanks, Frankie,' Parker said sarcastically.

'There's nothing in the penal code that makes it a crime for a kid to be minding his own business, Andy.'

'Who's saying anything?' Parker said. He paused. 'But suppose that nice innocent kid was holding a deck of heroin?'

52

'He wasn't holding anything. He's no junkie, and you know it. He comes from a good family.'

'Oh, is that right? Junkies don't come from good families, huh? Suppose he *was* holding, Frankie? Just suppose?'

'The only thing he's holding right now is contempt for the cop who shook him down.'

'Seems to me you should be interested in looking up the people who are doing something wrong,' Jeff said from the luncheonette.

'We do, sailor,' Parker answered. 'Day and night. That kid belongs to a street gang, don't he? You saw his club jacket, didn't you? Do you expect me to take crap from every hoodlum on the street?'

'That kid probably has little enough self-respect as it is,' Hernandez said. 'So you come along and . . .'

'All right, all right, cut it out with the kid, will you? Boy, you'd think I worked him over with a rubber hose.' He paused. 'Where you headed?'

'To see the Gomez woman,' Hernandez said.

'She was quite a little trick, that Gomez woman. Pushing fifty, maybe, but still got it all in the right places. You sure this is a business call, Frankie?'

'I'm sure,' Hernandez said.

'Well, just so long as you're sure. Was there any word on Miranda back at the squad?'

'Not when I left, no.'

'You know,' Luís said thoughtfully, 'I think maybe Frankie's right. I don't mean to tell you how to do your job, Andy. Don't think that. But this boy could be hurt by such treatment. What I mean . . . well . . . on the island, it was not this way.'

'Juvenile gangs ain't a problem in Puerto Rico,' Parker said flatly.

'No, of course not, but that's not what I meant. There just seemed to be . . . I don't know . . . more respect there.'

'For what? For siestas?' Parker asked, and he burst out laughing.

'Well, now you're making it a joke,' Luís said, embarrassed.

'Me? Why should I joke about your homeland?'

'It was just . . . you know . . . we were poor and hungry, true. But there was always the plaza in the center of town, and the pink church, and the poinsettias, and the mango trees. And you could go to the plaza and talk to your friends. And you were a person, and people knew your name. It was important, Andy. You knew who you were.'

'Who were *you*, Luís?' Parker said, chuckling. 'The governor?'

'Ah, he makes it a joke,' Luís said good-naturedly. '*You* know what I mean, don't you, Frankie?'

'Yes. I know what you mean.'

'Sometimes here, you feel lost. And without identity, there can be no dignity, no respect.'

'I know just what you mean, Louise,' Jeff said. 'It's like what I was telling you about Fletcher. How you can just get swallowed up in a pile of people and forget who and what you are.'

'*Sí, sí*. The island had respect for people, and for life . . . and respect for death, too. Life is cheap here, and death is cheaper. On the island . . .' He paused, as if giving himself time for the memory to grow, to blossom in his mind. 'On the island,' he said, 'in the towns, when there is a funeral, the casket bearers walk in the center of the main street, and the mourners follow behind the casket.'

'I know this,' Hernandez said softly. 'My father used to talk about this.'

'About the little girls dressed in white, carrying their flowers in the sunshine?' Luís said. 'The town all dusty and quiet and still.'

'Yes,' Hernandez said. 'About that.'

'And the shopkeepers stand in their doorways, and when the casket goes by, they close the doors. They are showing respect for the dead man. They are saying, "I will not conduct business while you pass by, my friend."'

'Argh, bullshit,' Parker said. 'That ain't respect. They're just scared of death. I'll tell you something, Luís. I don't know what it's like on that island of yours, but here – right *here* – the only ones who get respect are the live ones – the hoodlums like Pepe Miranda.'

Luís shook his head quickly and emphatically. 'No,' he said.

'No, huh? Take my word for it.'

'I'm going,' Hernandez said. 'You argue it out between you.'

'Who's arguing?' Parker said. 'We're having a discussion.'

'Okay, so discuss it,' Hernandez said, and he walked out of the luncheonette and around the corner.

Jeff swung around on his stool and stared up the street. Behind him, he could hear the detective and Luís arguing – well, discussing – but he was not interested in what they were saying. He kept staring at the closed door of La Gallina, wondering when the bar would open. He really didn't know whether he actually felt like spending the day in bed with a woman or not, but he couldn't think of much else to do with his time. And he *had* come all the way uptown, and he hated to think of the trip as a total loss. So he kept staring at the closed door, almost willing it to open and – quite miraculously – it opened.

6.

THE GIRL WHO stepped out of the bar was no more than nineteen years old, a slender girl with the curved body of a woman thrusting against the sweater and skirt she wore. Her hair was black, and her eyes were dark. She took a key from her purse and was leaning over to lock the door when Jeff got off his stool and ran up the street.

'Hi,' he said.

The girl whirled, surprised. Her eyes opened wide, the brownest eyes Jeff had ever seen in his entire life.

'Oh!' she said, and her lips rounded over the single word, and slowly the shock gave way to puzzlement, and she stared at him curiously, waiting for him to speak.

'I've been waiting for you all morning,' Jeff said. 'Were you in there all along?'

'Yes?' she said, delivering the word as a question, as if she expected further explanation from him and was waiting for it. He continued to watch her. A slow realization was coming to him. He was beginning to recognize the fact that this was possibly the most beautiful girl he'd ever met, and her beauty left him somewhat tongue-tied. The girl waited. Jeff remained speechless. Finally, she tucked the key into her purse, gave a small feminine shrug, and began walking away. Jeff stepped around her quickly, directly into her path.

'Hey, where are you going?' he said.

'Home.'

'Why? I only just found you.'

'I have to get dressed,' the girl said.

'You look dressed fine to me,' he said, and his eyes traveled the length of her body, pausing on the soft swell of her breasts beneath the light blue sweater, the abrupt curve of her hips against the black skirt.

'I have to get dressed,' the girl repeated blankly, seemingly embarrassed by his scrutiny.

'Well, that can wait, can't it?' he asked.

The girl seemed very puzzled. 'What do you want?' she said.

'Well . . . uh . . . don't *you* know?'

'No?' the girl said, and again she raised her voice at the end of the word so that it sounded like a question.

'Well . . . I was talking to a fellow last night. It was really very early this morning. Downtown. In a bar.'

'Yes?'

'And he said I should come up here.'

'What for?'

'He said I'd find you here,' Jeff said.

He looked at her, and he thought, Well, he didn't exactly say I would find you here, because no one ever expects to find something like you, no one ever really expects to come across something like you ever in his life.

'He didn't say that,' the girl said.

'Yes. Yes, he did.'

'What was his name? The man who told you about me?'

'I don't remember,' Jeff paused. 'I was drunk.'

'Are you drunk now?'

He smiled tentatively. 'Sober as a judge.'

'And this fellow told you about *me*? He said you would find *me*?

'Well . . . not exactly. I mean, I didn't expect anyone as . . . as pretty as you. But he said—'

'What *did* he say, exactly?'

58

'He said I should go uptown . . .'

'Yes?'

'And I should look for a place called La Gallina.'

'La Ga— oh.' She paused and looked at him more closely. 'I see. Yes. Now I understand.'

'Good. I got to admit, you're really something. I mean a guy just doesn't expect . . . I mean, I'm not trying to say anything against what you do, or anything like that . . . but . . . well, you know, it's just unusual, that's all. To find one as pretty as you.'

'Thank you,' the girl said. She smiled. 'I think you've made a mistake.'

'This *is* La Gallina, isn't it?' Jeff asked, looking at the gilt lettering on the plate-glass windows again.

'Oh, yes. This is La Gallina.'

'And you did come out of there, didn't you?'

'Yes, I certainly did.'

There was a strange twinkle in her brown eyes. He looked at her suspiciously and realized she was trying to suppress a laugh.

'You *do* work in there?' he asked. 'Don't you?'

'I do.'

'Well, what's so funny?' he said, beginning to get slightly annoyed.

The girl would not allow the laugh to escape her mouth. 'Nothing,' she said. 'Nothing.'

'Well, then, all right,' he said.

'All right,' she answered.

They stood staring at each other, Jeff trying to figure out what was so goddamned funny, and the girl trying her best not to laugh.

'Well?' he said at last.

'Well what?'

'Well, let's go to bed.'

59

'You and me?'

'Well, sure, you and me. Who did you think I meant?'

The girl shook her head. 'No. I don't think so.'

She started to move away from him, and he caught her arm, stopping her.

'Why not?'

'Well . . .' Again, she held back a laugh. She thought for a moment, and then said, 'I guess I don't like sailors.'

'That's no attitude,' Jeff said, grinning. 'Some of my best friends are sailors.'

'No,' the girl said, shaking her head. 'No. Sorry. No sailors.' She saw the disappointment on his face and quickly added, 'Besides, I'm too high.'

'High?'

'Yes, my price. My . . . uh . . . my fee?' She made it sound as if she were asking him what the correct word should be.

'Well, how high is high?' Jeff asked, beginning to bargain.

'A lot.' The girl considered the question gravely. 'More than you earn in a week.'

'How much is that?'

'Very, very high,' she said.

'Well, how much? Can't you tell me? Boy, you sure act strange for a . . .'

'I told you,' the girl said. 'Very very very high.' She seemed at a loss for words. She struggled with her thoughts and then desperately said, 'What's the highest you ever paid?'

'Twenty. But that was on the Coast. On the Coast . . .'

'I'm much higher than that,' she said quickly, seemingly relieved.

'Forty?'

'Higher.'

'A hundred?' he asked, appalled.

'Goodness,' the girl said, her eyes twinkling again. 'Do I look like a common streetwalker?'

'Well, no, no,' he said hastily, 'you don't. But a hundred dollars, God, I . . .'

'I didn't say a hundred. I said higher.'

'I haven't even got twenty,' he said despondently. 'You see, I was in a poker game and . . .'

'Well, there are other girls,' she said curtly. 'Goodbye.'

She turned on her heel and began walking up the street. Jeff watched her and then, galvanized into sudden action, he yelled, 'Hey! Wait!' and ran after her.

'What is it?' she asked.

'Listen, can't we talk this over?'

'Why?'

'Well, I . . . I think you're pretty.'

'Thank you.'

'I mean it. I'm not just saying it so you'll . . .' He paused. 'I mean it.'

'Why don't you go home, sailor?' she said kindly, her face suddenly turning so tender that he wanted to kiss her right then and there in the street, even though you weren't supposed to kiss girls like this, still he wanted—

'Home?' he said. 'Hell, I live in Colorado. Listen, can't we talk this over?'

'Sailor—'

'Jeff.'

'Jeff, all right, Jeff, I'm not what you think. I'm not what the fellow sent you uptown for.'

'Huh?'

'I cook for La Gallina and some of the other bars. They have steam tables. I prepare the food for them.'

'You pre— oh.' He paused. 'So you were in there . . .'

'Getting things ready for when they open,' the girl said, nodding.

'Oh.' He paused again. 'And all that business about price . . .'

'I was fooling you.'

'Oh. Well, I'm sorry.'

'That's all right. I'm sorry I fooled you.'

'Oh, that's all right.' He studied her soberly. 'You're still very pretty.'

'Thank you.'

'Do you . . . do you have to run off?'

'I have to get dressed. I'm going to church.'

'I'll go with you,' he said quickly.

'Are you Catholic?'

'Presbyterian. I'll go with you anyway. I've gone to all kinds of religious services in the Navy. I'm something of an expert. You see, I do it to get out of work parties. Whenever I'm on a work party and they announce like, "All people of the Jewish faith, prepare to leave the ship for religious services," I all of a sudden become a person of the Jewish faith. I'm just sorry there aren't less work parties and more religions.'

The girl shook her head. 'I would feel funny.'

'Are you religious? Is that it?'

'I suppose so. Yes.'

'Well, I mean, the church won't fall down or anything if I walk into it. Believe me. I've been inside Catholic churches before. It's a nice service.' He nodded, thinking over the various services he had been to.

'I would still feel funny,' the girl said. She looked at him in indecision, and then made a slight movement of departure.

'Look,' he said. 'Look . . . don't run off.'

'Why not?'

'I don't know.'

'You'll be busy,' she said. 'La Gallina opens at noon.'

'Well, that . . . you know, it's not that important.'

'Isn't it?'

'No, it isn't,' he said firmly. 'Look, won't you . . . won't you stay with me?'

The girl looked at her watch. 'I have to go,' she said. 'I want to catch the eleven o'clock Mass.'

'Will you meet me after church?'

'Why should I?'

'I want you to. Don't you want to?'

The girl hesitated. Then she said, 'Yes, I do.'

'Then why don't you?'

'Are you on a ship?'

'Yes. Look, will you . . .'

'What kind?'

'A destroyer.'

'Is it big?'

'Pretty big. Will you meet me?'

'Why do you want to meet me? Haven't you got a girl back home?'

'I used to, but not any more. Have . . . have you got a . . . a boy?'

'No.'

'Good. That's good.' He smiled.

'Yes,' she said, and she returned the smile.

'Will you . . . will you meet me?'

'If I do . . . would we go someplace outside the neighborhood?'

'If you like.'

'Where will we go?'

'I don't know. I don't know this city too well.'

'But we will leave the neighborhood?'

'Yes. You see, if we were back in Colorado, I'd take you up in the mountains. We'd pack a picnic basket and go up in the mountains. I'd drive you in my car. I've got a '37 Ford.'

'What color is it?'

'Yellow. I painted it myself.'

'I knew it was yellow,' she said.

'Did you? How'd you know?'

'Yellow or red. Those are the two colors I thought.'

'Hey, you know I *was* going to paint it red but Jenken's – that's the hardware store back home – was all out. So I took yellow.'

'Do you live in a very small town?'

'Fletcher? Well, it's not *so* small, you understand.'

'Do you have apartment buildings?'

'Oh, no.'

'Why did you leave home?'

'I wanted to see the world,' he said glibly, and then he knew immediately that glibness was not for this girl. With this girl you played it straight or you didn't play it at all. 'I was going to get drafted,' he said, 'so I figured I'd rather be in the Navy. So I enlisted.' He shrugged.

'And the world? Have you seen it?'

'A little of it.'

'Have you been to Puerto Rico?'

'No. Have you?'

'No. It's supposed to be beautiful there. I was born here. I've never been outside this city.' She paused. 'Oh, yes, I once went to a wedding in Pennsylvania.'

'You'd like my town,' he said. 'You really would.'

'Yes, I know I would.'

They fell silent. She stared up at him, and he felt terribly unsure of himself all at once, unsure and far

64

younger than he actually was. In a very small voice, he said, 'Meet me after church. Please.'

'If I met you, we could go to the park,' she said. 'There are no mountains, but we could take a picnic basket. There are trees there.'

'Any place you say. Only . . . you know . . . I've only got about eighteen bucks. We can go as far as that'll take us.' He grinned tentatively. 'Okay?'

The girl nodded. 'Okay.'

'Gee, that's— You'll meet me?'

'Yes.'

'Look, I'll . . . I'll meet you right here. Right on this spot. I won't budge from this spot until you come back.'

'No, not here. When La Gallina opens, the girls'll congregate here, on the sidewalk. Not here.'

'The luncheonette then, okay? On the corner.'

'Luís? All right, fine.'

'What time?'

'Mass'll be over at about a quarter to twelve. I'll make the lunch now and—'

'Hey, you don't have to—'

'I want to.'

'Well . . . okay.'

'And I'll stop home for it before I come. Twelve o'clock? Would that be all right?'

'Fine. Hey, listen, I'm sorry I mistook you for . . .'

'That's all right. Twelve?'

'Twelve,' he said.

'All right.' She stared at him for a moment and then said, 'Wait for me.'

'Yes, I will.'

She turned and began walking up the street, walking quickly, not looking back, almost as if she knew his eyes

65

were on her, almost as if she were waiting for him to call after her. When he did call, she whirled immediately.

'Hey!'

'Yes?'

'Hurry! Please hurry, would you?'

'Yes,' she said. She gave a small wave, turned, and began walking again.

'Hey!' he called.

'Yes?'

'I don't even know your name!'

'What?'

'Your name,' he shouted. 'What's your name?'

'Oh,' the girl said, and she giggled.

'Well, what is it?'

'China!' she called back, and then she ran up the street.

7.

HEAT IS A strange thing.

Like love, it can drive men to opposite extremes. Like love, it can be a persistently nagging thing, relentless, unwilling to budge, until one day it explodes in wild passion. 'I hit him with the hatchet because it was hot.' That is an explanation, a reason, and an excuse. It was hot. Everything is contained in those three words. It was hot, and so I was not responsible for my actions, I only knew that it was hot, that I was suffocating all day long, that I could hardly breathe, there was no air, it was hot, and he said to me, 'This coffee is too strong,' and so I hit him with the hatchet. It was hot, you see.

A shrug.

You understand. It was hot.

And, like love, the heat can generate a different kind of feeling, a feeling which – had the slick paper magazines not defiled the word – could be described as togetherness, a knowledge that human beings on this day, on this insufferably hot day, are at least sharing one thing in common. The heat becomes a bond as strong as reinforced concrete. Do you hate the color of my skin? That is interesting, but God it is hot, God we are sweating together. Do you lech for my wife? That is unforgivable, but let's go have a beer together to escape this damned heat, and later we can work it out.

Heat, like love, is no good unless you can talk about it. The adulterer seeks a confidante, the lecher boasts of his conquests in the pool hall, the sixteen-year-old cheerleader spends hours on the telephone describing a football player's kiss – you have to talk about love.

Lieutenant Peter Byrnes came out of his office wanting to talk about the heat. He was a compact man with graying hair and steel-blue eyes. He liked to believe that he sweated more than men who were less chunky than he. He liked to believe that the heat had been designed in hell especially for him, sent earthward to plague him. He didn't quite understand why he'd been singled out for such torture, but he did know that he suffered more when it was hot than any man had a right to suffer.

The squadroom was silent. Steve Carella, his shirt sleeves rolled up, was sitting at his desk, reading an FBI report on a suspected burglar. Hot sunlight covered the top of his desk like molasses. Byrnes walked to the grilled window and stared out at the street. The cars, the people, all seemed to have been captured in transparent plastic, suspended in time and space, unmoving. Byrnes sighed.

'Hot,' he said.

'Mmm,' Carella answered.

'Where is everybody?'

'Parker's on the prowl, Hernandez is answering a squeal, and Kling . . .' Carella shrugged. 'He's on a plant, isn't he?'

'That drugstore thing?'

'I think so.'

'Yeah,' Byrnes said, remembering. 'The guy who's passing phony cocaine prescriptions.' He shook his head. 'He won't turn up. Not in this heat.'

'Maybe not,' Carella said.

'I always choose the wrong time for my vacation,' Byrnes said. 'Harriet and I spend months figuring it out. I'm the senior officer around here, so I get first choice. So what happens? I always miss the good weather by a month. It's so hot you can't even think, and then it's time for my vacation, and it starts raining, or it turns gray, or we suddenly get a snowstorm from Canada. It never fails. Every year.' He paused for a moment. 'Well, every year except one. We went to the Vineyard once. We had good weather.' He nodded, remembering.

'Vacations are rough anyway,' Carella said.

'Yeah? How so?'

'I don't know. It generally takes me two weeks to unwind, and the minute I start relaxing, it's time to come back to work.'

'You going away this year?'

'I don't think so. The kids are too small.'

'How old are they, anyway?' Byrnes asked.

'They were a year old in June.'

'Boy, time flies,' Byrnes said, and fell silent. He thought about the passage of time, thought about his own son, thought how much Carella seemed like a son to him, thought how his squadroom seemed like a family business, a candy store or a grocery store, thought how good it was to have Carella working behind the counter with him.

'Well, talking about the heat never helped it any,' Byrnes said, and he sighed again.

'Some day, they're going to invent . . .' Carella started, and the telephone rang. He picked up the receiver. 'Eighty-seventh Squad,' he said. 'Detective Carella.'

The voice on the other end said, 'I know where Pepe Miranda iss.'

They saw Sixto as he came out of the drugstore. His face looked flushed. It seemed as if he were about to cry. He kept blinking his eyes like a person fighting to hold back tears.

'What's the matter?' Zip asked. He studied Sixto impersonally, not as if he were truly concerned, not as if he really wanted to know what the matter was, but asking the disguised question, 'How will your present state affect *me*?'

'Nothin',' Sixto said.

'You look like somebody hit you with a ball bat.'

'No.'

'What were you doing in the drugstore?'

'Havin' a Coke. I wass thirsty.'

'I thought I told you to keep an eye on Alfie's pad.'

'I could see his buildin' from where I wass sittin',' Sixto said.

'We gah dee guns,' Papá said, grinning.

'Come on,' Zip told them both. 'Cooch is rounding up some kids. We got to meet him near the luncheonette.'

They walked down the avenue together, Zip in the middle flanked by Sixto and Papá. He felt rather good with the boys on either side of him. He walked with his shoulders back and his head erect, setting the pace, knowing they would keep up with him, and feeling very friendly towards the boys as he walked, feeling a bond with them which he could not have described accurately if he'd tried. There was no logic to the bond because he admitted to himself that he didn't even particularly like either Sixto or Papá. One was a mama's boy and the other was a half-wit. And yet he could not deny the emotional satisfaction of walking down the avenue with these two by his side, like a general with his trusted aides. The bond, he knew, would become stronger once they had washed Alfredo Gomez. The word crossed his mind, washed, and he was instantly face to face with the other word, the stronger word. Kill. He did not flinch from it. Kill. He repeated the word in his mind. Kill. We will kill Alfredo Gomez. Kill.

By the time they reached the luncheonette, the word had no more meaning to him than the word 'wash'. Cooch was there, waiting for them. Two small boys were with him. Parker, the bull, had taken off, but the sailor was still inside the luncheonette, probably waiting for La Gallina to open, waiting for a Spanish girl. The idea pleased Zip at first. He felt a fierce pride in the knowledge that the sailor had come uptown to seek the passion only a Spanish girl could give him. And then the pride turned sour, and he thought darkly that the sailor had no right to be here, no right to be emptying himself into Spanish girls, the way sewers empty into the river. He frowned and cast a black scowl at the sailor's back, and then walked quickly to where Cooch stood with the younger boys.

The first of the boys was wearing dungarees and a white, sweat-stained T-shirt. His nose was running, and he constantly wiped at it with the back of his hand, the mucus streaked there like a healed burn. He was eight years old.

The other boy was nine. He wore khaki shorts and a short-sleeved blue sports shirt. An Army sergeant's stripes had been sewn to the left sleeve of the shirt. He moved his feet constantly, as if trying to erase chalk from the sidewalk.

'These the kids?' Zip asked Cooch.

'Yeah,' Cooch said.

Zip looked at the one with the snotty nose. 'What's your name, kid?'

'Chico.'

'And yours?' he said to the other boy.

'Estaban,' the boy answered, his feet erasing invisible chalk.

'Did Cooch explain the picture to you?'

'*Sí*,' Chico said.

'You and Estaban, one on each side of the church steps. You keep the pieces under your shirts until we get on the scene. Then you give them to us and hang around until we blast. We give you back the pieces when it's all over, and you cut out. You got that?'

'*Sí, yo comprendo*,' Chico said.

'*Sí, sí*,' Estaban echoed, his feet moving nervously. He seemed undecided as to whether he should break into a dance or begin stamping the sidewalk in anger. Nervously, his feet continued moving.

Zip looked at his watch. 'Okay, the church bells should begin ringing any minute now. That'll be first call for the eleven o'clock Mass. You kids cut out as soon as you hear them bells. We'll drift up toward the corner around eleven-thirty. You be ready for us, you hear me?'

'Zip, when we grow up, me an' Estaban,' Chico said, 'we coul' go gang-bustin' wi' you?'

Zip grinned and touched the boy's hair. 'Sure, when you grow up. Right now, you have them pieces ready for us when we need them.'

'I know how to shoot, Zip,' Chico said. 'I know how to shoot good.'

Zip laughed aloud. 'Not this trip, Chico. You got time yet before you begin . . .'

The church bells rang suddenly, abruptly, and then were silent. Whoever was pulling on the cord had made an abortive start, perhaps the cord had slipped from his hands, perhaps he'd had a sudden cramp in his fingers. The heavy solemn bonnnnng of metal upon metal sounded, reverberated, and then died. The boys stood in silence, straining for the peal of the bells. And then the bells started again, ringing out on the still July air, calling the flock to Mass, reaching into the streets and into the open windows, summoning the congregation, summoning Alfredo Gomez to whatever waited for him on the church steps.

'That's it,' Zip said tightly. He reached beneath his jacket and, one by one, began pulling the weapons from where they were tucked into his belt. Jeff, in the luncheonette, turned at the sound of the church bells, thinking of China, a smile on his face. He saw the first weapon pass from Zip's hand to Chico's snot-smeared fist, and he blinked as the other weapons changed hands, watched as the two youngsters tucked them into their waistbands, four guns in all, and then pulled their shirts down over them.

'Okay, go,' Zip said.

The two boys grinned, nodded, and then ran off up the street. A frown had come onto Jeff's forehead. He swung his stool around and picked up his cup of coffee. The church bells had stopped now. An old man rushed from the mouth of a tenement, paused on the stoop while he pulled on his suit jacket, and then ran spryly up the street.

'Nice quiet Sunday,' Luís said to Jeff, smiling.

Jeff nodded and said nothing. The four boys in the purple silk jackets had moved to a position near the jukebox. The street had gone silent again. It seemed to be a street of many moods and many temperaments, changing in the space of seconds like a vaudeville performer who snaps a wig into place and becomes a clown, discards the wig, puts on a black mustache and becomes Adolf Hitler. Now, the street in its sunbath seemed like a golden corridor leading to the high over-head arch of the elevated structure two blocks away, the sky a dazzling yellow-white beyond. Quiet, burning with light, the street was mute, the street waited. The boys lounged near the jukebox, their hands in their pockets. Occasionally they glanced in the direction of the church. Their eyes were squinted against the reflected sunlight.

The girl turned the corner from the avenue and entered the street like a circus train. She was wearing a bright-red jacket, a bright-yellow silk skirt, purple spiked-heel shoes with ankle straps. Her hair was a mass of thick black, sticking out from her head in near-burlesque of a Bushman. She was carrying a bright-blue carpetbag, and she walked with a suggestive swagger, the yellow skirt tightening over plump, jiggling buttocks, huge breasts jutting from the V-necked opening of the red jacket. She seemed to be wearing nothing under her outer clothing, and she didn't give a damn who realized it. Her buttocks begged to be pinched, her breasts beneath the white rayon blouse and the red jacket pointed sharp nipples like compass needles indicating north. Her walk did nothing to hide the pulchritude. This was what she owned, and if she preferred to exhibit her possessions, that was her business.

But despite the suggestive swagger, despite the bobbing breasts and the fluid grinding motion of buttock against buttock, despite an apparent attitude of indifference, the girl seemed frightened and somehow hesitant. She stared up at the buildings, ogling the city, overwhelmed by the size, somewhat confused and a little lost.

The whistles that came from Zip and Cooch did not help her at all. She suddenly clutched at the small red jacket in an attempt to close it over her thrusting breasts. The boys whistled again, and Jeff turned to watch the girl, fascinated by the tautness of the yellow skirt and the bobble of her backside. The girl began walking faster, just as lost, just as confused, and the whistles followed her up the street until she was out of sight.

Zip began laughing.

And then his laughter stopped when he realized the sailor was laughing too.

'What was *that*?' Jeff asked.

'Argh, a Marine Tiger,' Luís said.

'A what?'

'Marine Tiger. Fresh from the island, her first day here probably. Marine Tiger. That was the name of one of the first boats to take Puerto Rican immigrants to the mainland.'

'Boy, that was really something,' Jeff said.

'Did you see that hair?' Luís waved his hands around his head in demonstration. 'And now she'll ride the subway, and everyone will think all Puerto Ricans are like her.' He shook his head. 'I need more soup out here,' he said vaguely and went into the back of the shop.

'I wouldn't have minded dumping her on her back, huh, sailor?' Zip said.

'Well, she's not exactly my type,' Jeff said. He turned back to the counter. He did not like talking to this boy, and he did not wish to encourage a friendship which, now that he was sober and now that he had met China, seemed hardly necessary.

'Not your type, huh?' Zip said. 'What's the matter? You don't like Spanish girls?'

'I didn't say that.'

Zip lighted a cigarette and blew out a stream of smoke. He considered his next words carefully. He did not know why, but the sailor was beginning to annoy him immensely. At one and the same time, he wanted the sailor to desire a Spanish girl, and yet wanted him to have nothing to do with a Spanish girl. The conflict disturbed him. He frowned as he began speaking.

'I've got a few minutes to kill. You still interested in a girl, I can fix you up with something real nice.'

'I'm not interested,' Jeff said.

'No? The frown got deeper. 'Why not? You got something against Puerto Rican girls?'

'No. I'm just not interested any more.'

'What'd you come up here for? A girl, right?'

'That's right,' Jeff said.

His answer angered Zip. 'So why won't you let me get you one?'

'I told you. I'm not interested any more.'

'Then why are you hanging around here?'

'That's my business,' Jeff said curtly.

'If you ain't interested any more, why don't you get out of the neighborhood?'

'You ask a lot of questions,' Jeff said.

'Yeah, that's right. What about it?'

'Suppose you answer one,' Jeff said.

'I don't have to an—'

'Why'd you pass out those guns?'

Zip's eyes opened wide. 'What?'

'You handed an arsenal to those two kids. Who do you plan on shooting?'

They sat side by side on adjacent stools, Jeff's fists bunched on the counter, Zip's eyes narrowing as the sailor's words penetrated. The other boys, with the exception of Sixto, had moved away from the jukebox, and advanced towards their leader.

'You got big eyes, Grandma,' Zip said, as he suddenly struck Jeff full in the face with his closed fist. Jeff, surprised by the blow, tried to maintain his balance on the stool, realized intuitively that it would be a mistake

76

to fall, a mistake to be on the ground. He clutched for the countertop, but the imbalance was complete and his hand slid over the Formica top as he went over and back, his foot hooked into the stool's rung, the asphalt tile floor coming up to meet his back. He caught the force of the fall with his shoulder blades, snapping his head so that it wouldn't collide with the floor. He was struggling to get his foot free of the rung when the first kick exploded against the side of his head.

He brought up his hands instinctively, trying to free his foot, squirming to get his foot loose from this ridiculously foolish position, and the second kick caught him in the rib cage, and he felt all the breath in his body escape from his mouth in a grunt, and then another kick caught the side of his neck, and now the kicks were coming with methodical precision and his foot was still hooked into that goddamn rung, a boot connected with his right eye and he felt shocking, stabbing pain and then the warmth of blood and he thought I'm going to be kicked to death on the floor of this goddamn luncheonette and then he heard Luís shouting, 'What are you doing? Bastards, what are you doing?' And above that, or beyond it, around it, circling it, filling the air, the high penetrating wail of a police siren.

8.

HERNANDEZ HAD SEEN this apartment before, had been inside it. Not this one, exactly, but countless others like it in buildings of the precinct. This could have been the very apartment he had lived in as a boy.

The front door opened into the kitchen. There was the usual police lock; the first plate screwed to the door, the second plate embedded in the floor, and the unbending steel bar which, when wedged into its triangular place between the two, made forcible entry impossible. A window was at the far end of the kitchen. It opened on the interior shaftway of the tenement. There was linoleum on the kitchen floor, a spatter pattern. It had been scrubbed clean but left unwaxed. It had worn through in patches near the door, the icebox, and the stove. A white enamel-topped table was on the wall opposite the stove. A picture of Jesus in supplication was above the table. The walls were painted a pale green, but the grime of countless meals in preparation had worn itself into the walls so that the green seemed darker, bile-like. The paint, too, was beginning to flake off in several places on the walls and on the ceiling. A toaster was on the table. A plastic shield covered it. The room seemed shoddy but clean. It was a room he remembered well.

On winter days, when he was a boy, he would sit on the floor by the stove, playing with his soldiers on the clean worn linoleum. His mother had miraculously managed to cook her meals with him underfoot. The smells of *arroz con pollo* would fill the kitchen, and it was cozy by the stove where he endowed each of his metal men with a personality and an identity. There was warmth in the kitchen of the Hernandez home, warmth from the stove and the smell of cooking food, warmth in the gentle voice of his mother as she went about her work, warmth in the monologues the boy Frankie addressed to the metal men surrounding him.

There was no warmth in the Gomez kitchen on that day in July, no warmth but the suffocating heat of summer. Outside, they could hear the wail of the siren. Mrs Gomez went to the window and closed it. The sound withdrew.

'Always fires,' she said. 'Always the sirens. Never a day without a fire.' She shook her head. 'And it's worse in the winter.'

'Where's the boy?' Hernandez asked.

'In the bedroom. Frankie, please go easy with him. This thing he is in, it is great trouble. But . . . he is hard to know.'

'I'll go easy,' Hernandez said.

She led him through the apartment, into the 'parlor' furnished with a three-piece living-room suite, a television set, a floor lamp, the fixture in the ceiling boasting three light bulbs of different colors. When he was a boy, he had done his homework in the parlor, stretched out on the floor. There had been no television in those days. In those days, the 'William Tell Overture' had announced the arrival of the Lone Ranger. In those days, there was Omar the Mystic, and The Witch's Tale, and Renfrew of the Mounted, and, of course, on Sundays – the Shadow. He had grown up with the idea that Lamont Cranston was the most glorious name in the entire world. He now laughed whenever anyone mentioned it and yet, despite his sophisticated laughter, the name still touched a core of envy and awe somewhere deep within him. Lamont Cranston – the Shadow. Memories of a boy, the howl of a wolf and then the words, 'Rennnnnnn-frew offffffff the Mounnnnnnn-ted,' Dick Tracy every afternoon at – five was it? – five-fifteen? – milk on the kitchen table and chocolate-covered graham crackers, the memories of a boy. And now, the same living-room, called a 'parlor' as it was in Puerto Rico, the same colored lights in the ceiling fixture, the same peeling paint, the same long tred through a railroad flat, a man entering a bedroom which could have been the twin of the one he'd slept in as a boy, and a man coming face to face with a boy of sixteen, and seeing in that face pain and trouble, trouble in the eyes and the mouth, and Hernandez the man suddenly wondering where Hernandez the boy had gone. And wondering what had been lost somewhere along the way.

'This is Frankie Hernandez,' Mrs Gomez said.

The boy regarded him without hostility. But there was determination in his eyes, a stubborn commitment to reveal nothing. Hernandez had seen this look before. He had seen it in the squadroom and it had been worn by hardened criminals and by docile housewives; it was the same look, it never varied. It was a look which plainly stated, 'You are the Law, and anything I tell you will be held against me.'

'Hello, Alfredo,' Hernandez said.

'Hello,' the boy answered warily.

'Your mother's worried about you.'

'She hass nothin' to worry abou'.'

'Well, she seemed to think so. Came all the way over to the police station because she thought so. What about it, Alfredo?'

Alfredo sighed deeply. 'I'm goin' to church, Mr Hernandez,' he said. 'I got nothin' to tell you.'

80

'Your mother thinks you've got plenty to tell me.'

'My mother doesn't know. She don' know this neighborhood.'

'*I* know this neighborhood, Alfredo,' Hernandez said flatly, and their eyes met, and in the boy's eyes was a recalculation now, a quick estimate of Hernandez's knowledge of the streets, an appraisal of the extent to which he was a neighborhood boy, and the extent to which he was a cop like all the rest. 'Now what's all this about?' Hernandez asked.

Alfredo made his decision in a single moment. The decision changed nothing. Hernandez could not help him, Hernandez was the Law, there was nothing he could tell him. 'It ain't abou' nothin',' he said.

'Your mother said somebody's going to kill you, is that right?'

Alfredo did not answer.

'Answer me!' Hernandez said, and he seized the boy by the shoulders and forced the contact, forced eyes to meet eyes levelly and honestly. 'Answer me!'

Alfredo remained mute, his eyes probing Hernandez's. And then he nodded.

'Who?' Hernandez asked.

'The . . . the boys,' Alfredo answered. His shoulders ached where Hernandez gripped him. His eyes remained locked with the detective's.

'Why?'

'No reason,' Alfredo said.

'Is there a girl involved in this?'

'*Sí.*'

Hernandez released his grip tiredly. This was an old story, and he had heard it many times before. 'What'd you do to the girl?' he asked.

'Nothin'.'

81

'Come on.'

'Nothin'.'

The room went silent again. Hernandez stared at the boy. Patiently, he asked, 'Then why do they want to kill you?'

'To show they big shots, thass all,' Alfredo said. 'They tink iss big to kill.' He paused. He was talking more freely now, but he still wondered how far he could trust Hernandez. In a very low voice, he said, 'She ain' even his girl. China ain' nobody's girl.'

'You must have done something to the girl!' Hernandez said angrily.

'Nothin'! I swear! I swear on my mudder's eyes. Nothin'! I ony say hello to her. She a nice girl, smilin' an' everything, she smile at everybody. So I say hello. Iss somethin' wrong with dat? On the islan', you could say hello to girls, nobody bodder you. So now I am come here the city, an' now I cann say hello.'

'How long have you been in this city?' Hernandez asked.

The boy shrugged and turned to his mother. 'Mama?'

'He's a year now,' she said. 'We took the girl over first. His sister. Alfredo we left with his grandmother in San Juan. A year ago, we could afford to bring him here, too.'

'Where's the girl now? Your daughter?'

'She belongs to the Girl Scouts. Today, they went on a picnic. Honeyside Beach, you know that?'

'Yes,' Hernandez said. 'You like this city, Alfredo?'

'Sure. I come from La Perla, thass where my gran'mudder lives. La Perla, thass a big *fanguito* in San Juan. A slom, you know? Shacks.'

'I know La Perla.'

'It means The Pearl, but thass jus' a joke, you know? It's not sush a pearl. Here iss better. Not so poor, you know? There, it iss all dirty an' mud, an' iss poor all the time. Here iss better.' He paused. 'But what can you do here?'

'You can do a lot here, Alfredo.'

'Yeah? You go outside the neighborhood, they call you "spic." It's my fault I cann speak English so good? How I'm spose to learn? There's only one teacher in all my high school who speaks Spanish!'

'Others have learned English, Alfredo.'

'Sure, I know. I'm tryin', ain' I? I do pretty good, don't I?'

'You do fine.'

'Still . . .'

'Still what?'

'Am I . . . am I spose to join a gang or somethin'?'

'Do you belong to a gang now. Alfredo?'

'No, I don' belong no gang. In Puerto Rico, we don' have this bullshit, these gangs like here. In Puerto Rico, you can say hello to girls, you can hang aroun' like whoever you want, you know? An' there's none of these dope. The kids here take dope. So I don' wann take dope, an' I don' wann belong to no gang. I ony wann to go my own way, nobody should bodder me.'

'So how'd you get into this mess?' Hernandez asked.

'I say hello! I swear to God, all I say is hello! So Zip, he . . .' Alfredo cut himself short.

'Who?' Hernandez said quickly.

Alfredo was silent for several seconds. Then, as if finally committing himself, he said, 'Okay. Zip. He sees me an' he says I bodderin' his girl. He says I don' go to church or they wash me.'

'You ever been in trouble with this Zip before?'

'Once or twice. Like he try to shake me down at school, you know? We go the same school.'

83

'What school is that?'

'A trade school. I'm learn a job.'

'What kind of job?'

'Automotive. But thass not what I wann to be.'

'What do you want to be?'

'I wann study radio. So when I wass in junior high school, I go the adviser, you know? I say, "I wann study radio." She tell me I should be an automotive. She says iss better for a Spanish kid. She says iss better opportunity. But I still wann study radio.'

'Why don't you tell this to someone at your school?'

'Oh, I don' know. Who's to listen? Sometimes I feel . . . I don' know . . . like as if bein' here I'm jus' . . . not a real human bein', you know? Like I feel . . . secondhand.'

Hernandez nodded. 'What happened with this Zip? When he tried to shake you down?'

'Oh, I give him my lunch money,' Alfredo said. 'It wass ony a quarter. I dinn want bad blood with him.'

'And that was the extent of it? And you haven't had any trouble with him since that time?'

'Never. Like he's ony new aroun' here, you know? Maybe he lives here fi', six months. He come from somewhere downtown, you know? So I don' bodder with him, I ony want to go my own way, thass all. I don' like this . . . I mean . . . look, they go aroun' stomping people . . . they have these street bops . . . what I got to fight for? For what? I'm here this city now, so here should be better, not *worse* than Puerto Rico. So why I got to bodder with kids like Zip? He thinks to be big is to kill.' Alfredo paused and then stared solemnly at Hernandez. 'To be big is to *live*, no?' he asked.

'Yes, Alfredo.'

84

'Sure. But he's leader of the Latin Purples. So I don' belong no gang, no Royal Guardians, no Spanish Dukes, nothin'. So who's to protec' me?'

'*I'm* to protect you, Alfredo.'

'You? What can you do? You tink they afraid of cops? If I don' show in the street, they call me turkey, they say I afraid of them. So den everybody laugh at me. So den how can I walk the street? If I be turkey, how can I walk the street?'

'It's not turkey to want to live, Alfredo. Every man wants to live.'

'I tell you the truth, I'm tired,' Alfredo said. 'I'm tired of walkin' alone. You walk alone, they all pick on you. But I'm spose to join a gang? I'm spose to go aroun' shootin' people? What for I want to shoot people?'

'Don't leave the apartment today, Alfredo,' Hernandez said. 'You'll be safe here. I'll see to that.'

'And tomorrow?' Alfredo asked. 'What about tomorrow?'

'We'll see. Maybe this'll all be cleared up by tomorrow.'

'Will tomorrow be any better?' Alfredo asked. 'Tomorrow I'm still here. I'm always here in this neighborhood.' He began to weep suddenly and gently. 'Always,' he said. 'Always here. Always.'

There were four squad cars in the street outside when Hernandez got downstairs. They formed a loose cordon about the bar called La Gallina, and Hernandez immediately wondered if a Vice Squad raid was in progress. The street was filled with people who seemed to gather immediately at the sign of any excitement, who stood speculating in small knots outside the barrier formed by the squad cars on either end of the bar. Hernandez pushed his way through the crowd, saw that Parker was standing and talking to Lieutenant Byrnes and Steve Carella, who stood leaning against a fender of one of the squad cars. His first thought was *Who's minding the store?* and he realized instantly that this was no vice raid, that something big must have happened. Quickly, he walked to where the other detectives were standing.

'When do we start, Lieutenant?' Parker asked. There was a glow in Parker's eyes. He reminded Hernandez of a Marine who had been in his outfit. The guy's name had been Ray Walters, and he had joined the company on the day before the Iwo Jima landings. He hated the Japanese, and he couldn't wait for the landings to begin. He was the first man out of the landing barge, his eyes glowing, a tight grim smile on his mouth. The smile was still there when the Jap bullet took him between the eyes.

'We're getting cars on the next block,' Byrnes said, 'so we'll have radio contact with the men there. We'll start as soon as they're ready. This isn't going to be a picnic. He said we wouldn't take him alive.'

'Are we sure it's him?' Parker asked.

'Who knows? We got a telephone tip. If it *is* him, we can't take any chances.'

A woman came out of the tenement doorway to the left of La Gallina. She was carrying a baby in one arm and a bird cage in the other. A blue parakeet fluttered wildly about the cage. The woman came off the stoop, glancing over her shoulder to the windows above La Gallina. She seemed to sense that she was a star performer stepping into the spotlight and that an impatient audience was waiting for the one line she had to deliver, a line which would suddenly solve and resolve doubts and uncertainties which would have been mounting ever since the curtain rose. She stopped in the middle of the street, faced the crowd that milled restlessly beyond the squad cars and, in her loudest voice, shouted, 'Ees Pepe! Ees Pepe Miranda up there!' and then she extended the bird cage, pointing with it to the first-floor windows while the bird fluttered and screamed against the brass bars.

'Come on, lady,' a patrolman said, 'before you stop a bullet.'

The woman rushed into the crowd where the whisper had already gone up, a confirming whisper passed from mouth to mouth, accompanied by a knowledgeable shaking and nodding of heads, 'Pepe Miranda, Pepe Miranda, Pepe Miranda.'

'Is that what this is?' Hernandez asked Byrnes.

'It looks that way, Frankie,' Byrnes said.

'Who called in the tip?'

'Don't know,' Carella said. 'He gave the info and then hung up.'

'I'm going to see what the hell's happening with those other cars,' Byrnes said. He walked around to the other side of the squad car, sat with his legs out on the street, and picked up the hand mike. 'This is Lieutenant Byrnes,' he said. 'We're about ready to roll here. Are those other cars in position yet?'

'So we finally cornered your *landsman*,' Parker said, grinning. 'And we're gonna kill him. I'm personally gonna see to that.'

'He's no *landsman* of mine,' Hernandez said.

'Of course not,' Parker answered. 'That's just a way of speaking. All I meant was you're both Puerto Ricans.'

'Sure.'

'Hell, you know me better than that. I don't care if a guy's Puerto Rican or even Chinese.'

'Sure.'

Parker looked around suddenly. 'Boy, look at these kids, will ya? They think Miranda's a god.'

'He's only a god to the ones who don't know any better,' Carella said, looking at the kids who had joined the crowd around the squad cars. The kids ranged in age from toddlers to adolescents. Some of them tried to climb onto the squad cars, but the patrolmen swiped at them with their night sticks. None of the kids seemed certain as to what sort of behavior was expected of them. Some laughed, and some stood solemnly staring at the first-floor windows of the building. Some seemed on the verge of tears. It was curious to watch their faces and to study their fidgeting. Each of them knew that this was an occurrence of unusual interest, and each of them was quite naturally excited by it. But they had seen many things, these children, and their reactions to all of these things had always been mixed. They had seen sudden blood, and every fiber in their bodies had urged them to scream at the sight of a man leaking his life onto the pavement, but fear had coalesced in their throats and erupted into the laughter of bravado. For these children, the emotions had become confused, with vague boundary lines separating one from the other. Fear was a twin to courage; tears and laughter were interchangeable.

'He's gonna be a *dead* god soon, that's for sure,' Parker said. 'He's gonna pay for every damn heartache he ever gave this city.'

Carella, watching the children, said simply, 'The city gave him a few too, Andy.'

'Sure,' Parker agreed. 'It's the neighborhood. A kid grows up here, what the hell do you expect? Miranda was cutting up people before he knew how to walk.'

'Maybe nobody ever took the trouble to teach him to walk,' Hernandez said.

'Hey, you ain't getting sore at *me*, are you?' Parker asked, his eyes opening wide. 'I thought he was no *landsman* of yours.'

'He isn't. He's a punk. He's going to die. That doesn't make it all his fault.'

'I can understand how you feel,' Parker said. 'There's a blood tie that . . .'

'There's no blood tie between me and . . .'

'I didn't mean a real blood tie, for God's sake. I know he's not your relative or anything. But, you know, you're both Spanish. That sort of makes you brothers, you know what I mean?'

'No. What the hell *do* you mean, Parker?'

'Aw, forget it. If you're gonna get sore, there's no sense talking. You're the touchiest guy I know, Frankie. I mean it. You oughta get over that. It don't help you none, believe me.' He smiled at Hernandez and put his arm around his shoulder. 'All I was saying, in a manner of speaking, is that I'm gonna kill your brother up there. I'm gonna put a dozen bullets in his goddamn skull and watch him bleed all over the sidewalk.'

Hernandez shook the arm free. 'You know something, Parker.'

'What?'

'He's more *your* brother than he is mine.'

A half-dozen patrolmen had begun erecting barricades across the street. The people crowded the barricades. The kids began sitting on them, spilling over onto the side where the policemen and the squad cars waited for the word from the next street. Byrnes came out of the squad car and yelled, 'All right, everybody *back*! *Step back*! Back of the barricade! Let's *go*!' He walked rapidly to Hernandez, pulling a handkerchief from his back pocket and wiping at his sweating face. 'Frankie, do me a favor, will you?' he said. 'Make with some Spanish. These people are gonna get shot up if they don't respect that barricade. Get them to move back, will you?'

'Sure,' Hernandez said. He moved up to the wooden horses with their supporting crossbars, the stenciled POLICE DEPARTMENT letters shrieking against the white paint. '*Bueno!*' he shouted. '*Todos retroceder, Detrás de la barricada! Todos retroceder!*'

The crowd began moving back from the barricade. On the edge of the crowd, Zip grabbed Cooch's arm and said, 'You hear that? You hear what that bull said? There's gonna be shooting!'

'With Miranda up there, there's gotta be shooting,' Cooch said, his eyes wide.

'Who's Miranda?' Papá asked.

'Don't you know nothing, you dumb tiger?' Cooch said, shoving at him. 'Miranda's the greatest thing ever happened to this neighborhood.' He turned to Zip. 'How you like this jerk? Don't know Miranda.'

Zip shook his head, his eyes searching the first-floor windows for a sign of life. He could see nothing.

'When he lived around here,' Cooch said to Papá, 'this neighborhood really jumped, I kid you not.'

'Even in my old neighborhood we knew about him,' Zip said, his eyes never leaving the first-floor windows. 'He was down there once, you know. I seen him. He was driving a big yellow Caddy.'

'No crap?' Cooch said.

'Sure, I seen it. And he had this blonde with him. Man, you could see she was gassed completely out of her skull, just being with him. This was before things got so hot for him. Man, he was swinging then, swinging.'

'A Caddy, huh?' Cooch said. 'That's for me. Give me the wheel, man. I'll know just what to do with it.'

'You should see the way this guy walks, Cooch,' Zip said. He stepped away from the barricade and did a quick imitation. 'This real cool glide, you know? Like he owns the world. That's the way to walk. Pepe walked with his head up. He ain't afraid of nothing or nobody!'

'Look at the way he got out of that Riverhead apartment!' Cooch said. 'A dozen cops, and they couldn't touch him.'

'Nobody can touch him,' Zip said.

'Man, when he lived here, Zip, you shoulda been here, I mean it. A nice guy, you know? I mean, you think him being a big shot an' all, like he'd think us kids was dirt. But he was always nice to us, I swear. Used to hand out nickels, like that, you know? And stories? Man, the stories he used to tell us. You know, real straight-from-the-shoulder stuff. Not like the crap you get from your people.'

'Man, I read you,' Zip said. 'If my old man gives me his pitch about the island one more time, I'm gonna lose control. Who gives a damn about customs on the island, huh? Who cares about the *hospitality* there, or the *sunshine* there, or the way the people close the doors when a stiff goes by, huh? This is *here*, man! This is where people are *living*!'

'You can bet Pepe knows how to live.'

'Ohhh, brother, does he? This cat knows *the* story, dad! Hey, hey, look at that!'

'What?' Cooch said.

'Over there.'

Two patrolmen were entering the tenement. They moved cautiously and with their revolvers drawn.

'It's about to start,' Zip said, straining to see over the heads of the people in front of him. 'We gotta get something to stand on, Cooch. We won't be able to see nothing this way.'

'What about our other business?' Cooch asked.

Zip glanced cursorily over his shoulder, looking into the luncheonette where Jeff sat at the counter. 'The sailor? Forget him. We scared him half to death.'

'I mean Alfie,' Cooch whispered.

For a moment, Zip seemed to have forgotten something that had kept him awake most of the night, something that had accompanied him as he'd got out of bed this morning, roaring in his mind as he dressed. For a moment, Zip seemed to make no association with the name 'Alfie' and puzzlement showed plainly on his face. And then, as if being called away from something which was extremely pleasant and entertaining to take care of some simple task which was at best boring, he said, 'Well, what about him?'

'We got a date, remember?'

'Of course I remember,' Zip said angrily. 'But how we gonna get to the church? The block's shut off. Besides, the kids with the pieces are on the other side of the street.'

'Iss better this way, Zip,' Sixto said. 'We let heem . . .'

'Oh, shut up, will ya, Sixto?' Zip snapped. 'Man, where'd we scrounge up this yo-yo?'

Papá burst out laughing. 'You a yo-yo, Sixto,' he said.

Cooch looked thoughtful for a moment. Then he said, 'Zip, I can cut around the avenue and reach the kids that way. I can get those pieces for us.'

Like a business magnate who cannot be bothered by a petty administrative detail, Zip answered, 'Yeah, good. Go ahead, get them. Bring them back here.' His eyes wandered up to the first-floor window again. 'Man, I wonder how many pieces Miranda has in that pad with him.'

'They say he took guns from all them cops in the . . .'

'Oh, man, this is gonna be the unholiest! Jee-sus, is he gonna give it to them bastards! Go ahead, Cooch. Go get the pieces. Come on Sixto!'

'Where we going?'

'Get something to stand on. There's always a million boxes in that empty lot on . . .'

The shots exploded from inside the building, a short volley with the echoing roll of distant thunder. The crowd went instantly silent. The silence hung over the street, and then was shattered instantly when a woman in the crowd screamed. An instant chorus went up after the scream, filling the street. A wisp of smoke drifted from the mouth of the building. The smoke hung on the air for an instant, silencing the crowd again, as if they had been a crowd in St Peter's Square waiting for the smoke to rise from the Sistine Chapel, announcing the new pope, and now that they had seen the smoke, they still did not know who the pope was, and so they fell silent, and they waited.

From inside the building, a voice shouted, 'Lieutenant! Lieutenant!'

9.

THE POLICEMEN ON the rooftops and on the fire escapes, dangling from open windows perched behind parapets, seemed like a band of monkeys who had climbed into an intricate zoo gymnasium and now didn't know what to do with themselves. To say that Pepe Miranda was completely surrounded would certainly have been the understatement of the century. There were two tenements facing La Gallina, within the rather narrow confines of the cordon. These two tenements bristled with cops of every size, shape and rank – and each of these stalwart defenders of the peace was carrying a loaded and drawn revolver. An additional armory which seemed sizable and formidable enough to have stormed the gates of Stalingrad included such choice delicacies of destruction as rifles with affixed telescopic sights, submachine guns, regulation hand grenades, gas masks, tear-gas pellets, and even a flame thrower or two.

Nor did the siege confine itself to the two buildings facing La Gallina. The police had moved into the adjoining block as well, entering apartments which faced the back windows of the apartment in which Miranda, like an animal driven into a hole, was trapped. Clean white wash fluttered on the back-yard lines. Policemen leaned out of open windows, pistols drawn, peering between the fluttering underpants and brassieres. There were policemen facing the front of the apartment and policemen covering the back of it, and policemen on the roof of the building itself, ready to descend upon Miranda from above.

The adjoining rooftops were covered with the citizenry of the city. Like a bunch of hicks who had come to see a circus daredevil dive eight hundred feet into a thimbleful of water, the people of the neighborhood were anxious to see whether or not Miranda could make the dive without splattering his brains out on the sawdust. To many of these people, Miranda was simply the rebel and the underdog. Consciously or not, they were rooting for him. They wanted him to stand up to this formidable army of men in blue, blast his way out of that goddamn apartment, tip his hat, throw a kiss to the ladies, and ride off into the sunset. Perhaps all of them knew how it would really end. Perhaps they all knew that a single man, no matter how mighty, could not withstand such forces arrayed against him. But many of them nurtured the secret hope that for once, just for once, the rebel would win, the revolutionary would defeat the incumbent dynasty, the anarchist would throw his bomb and escape.

For many others, there was an undeniable cultural tie between themselves and the man in the apartment. The tie was a curious one in that they all knew Miranda was a criminal. In all probability, none of them would have welcomed Miranda into their homes. He was a dangerous man, an unreliable man, a thief and a murderer. But he was Spanish. And, in much the same way that they took pride in the work of Pablo Picasso, they took a strangely curious pride in the fact that Miranda was causing so much excitement. In their minds, there was a very thin line between fame and infamy. Miranda, whatever he had done, was a celebrity. And he was a celebrity whom most of his audience knew on a first-name basis.

For the others who watched, there was only curiosity. A man was trapped in an apartment. The other men wanted to get him out of that apartment. This was a baseball game. There were no good guys or bad guys, only two teams which were trying to win.

At the moment, Miranda's team seemed to have scored the first run. The cry of 'Lieutenant! Lieutenant!' which had come from the hallway of the tenement was followed almost immediately by the sight of the man who'd shouted the words. He was a police sergeant, and he had a patrolman's arm draped over his shoulder as he dragged him into the street. The patrolman had been shot. The blood on his blue shirt was plainly visible even to the people who crowded the edges of the rooftops. The sergeant carried the man out and put him on the ground beside the radio motor patrol car. The cop inside the car immediately picked up the hand microphone and requested an ambulance. The crowd watched all this with the eyes of prophets who are noting an interesting development, but who are aware that the final outcome will have little or nothing to do with this minor incident. Miranda had shot one of the cops. That was interesting. But the fireworks were yet to come. Patiently, they awaited the fireworks. It is a rare year that has two Independence Day celebrations.

Standing alongside the wounded patrolman, sweating profusely, Lieutenant Byrnes asked, 'How bad is it, Sergeant?'

'His shoulder, sir,' the sergeant said. He paused, catching his breath. He was a big beefy man with graying hair. His uniform was a little too tight for him, but he didn't want to buy a new one because he expected to retire next year. When a man pays for his own working clothes, he's apt to consider replacements carefully. 'Sir, you shoulda heard Miranda,' he said, wedging the words in between his gasps for breath. 'We was just making sure all the tenants was out of the building, sir. He began cursing in Spanish and shooting through his door. He must have fired about six shots. Two of them clipped Cassidy.'

Byrnes stared at the man lying in the street. 'Well, we're getting an ambulance, Sergeant. Stay with him, will you? Do whatever you can to make him comfortable.'

'Excuse me,' a man on the other side of the barricade said. He was a tall, thin man with penetrating blue eyes. He wore a tan tropical suit and a blue straw Panama. 'Did I understand the sergeant to say . . . ?'

'Who the hell are you?' Byrnes asked.

'I'm a reporter. I work for the city's largest afternoon tabloid. I couldn't help overhearing . . .'

'I know your paper,' Byrnes said flatly.

'Did I understand the sergeant to say . . .'

'I'm busy, mister,' Byrnes replied, and he went around to the other side of the squad car and picked up the hand mike.

'Nice guy, your *landsman*,' Parker said to Hernandez. 'Couple of inches lower, and Cassidy'd be dead.'

'I didn't do the shooting,' Hernandez said. 'Miranda did.'

'So who's blaming you? Listen, every race has its crumbs, ain't that so?'

'Knock if off, Parker.'

'Ain't nobody blaming *all* the Puerto Ricans for a foul ball like Miranda. Look at yourself, for God's sake. Didn't you come from this neighborhood? So look at you now. A detective third grade. It took guts to do what you did. Hell, think of all your own people you had to arrest.'

'I do my job, Parker.'

'No question about it. You're a good cop, Hernandez. And it sure don't hurt to talk Spanish in a precinct like this one, does it?' He began chuckling. 'Listen, who cares if you're taking unfair advantage of the rest of us poor slobs? You keep on the way you're going, and some day you'll be commissioner. Then your father can hang another picture in his candy store.'

'Why do you needle me, Parker?'

'Who? Me? I needle you?'

'Why?'

'I don't needle nobody,' Parker said innocently. 'I'm just like you, pal. I do my job.'

'And what's your job?'

'My job is keeping the streets clean. I'm a street cleaner with a gun. That's a cop's job, ain't it?'

'That's not *all* of a cop's job.'

'No? Maybe you think I should go around holding junkies' hands, huh? I used to be that way, Hernandez. I used to be the kind of cop who felt sorry for people. Used to break my heart to tag a car even.'

'I'll bet it did.'

'You don't have to believe me. Ask any of the old-timers at the station. But I learned my lesson, all right. I learned my lesson.'

'How?' Hernandez asked.

'Never mind,' Parker answered, and he turned away.

He had been turning away for a long time now, for fourteen years, to be exact. He had been turning away from his duty as a cop, and from his duty as a man, but he excused his negligence by telling himself that he had once been the kind of cop who'd felt sorry for people, and that he'd learned his lesson since. There was a slight inaccuracy to his rationale. Andy Parker was not the kind

98

of man who had ever felt sorry for anybody in his life. It was simply not in his make-up to exude sympathy for his fellow humans. What he probably meant was that one time he felt a closer identification with the people of the precinct than he did now.

And, to give the devil his due, Parker *had* once approached this somewhat elusive task of law and order with a distinctly different viewpoint. When he was a patrolman – though it never broke his heart to tag a car – he was inclined to be lenient with petty offenders, letting them off with a whack of his billet and a warning. There was, he had concluded, enough real crime going on in this precinct without persecuting decent people for minor infractions. He learned in those days that the law was open to interpretation long before it reached the law courts. He learned that the lowest arbitrator in the city's judicial system was a man who wore no legal robes at all; he was the patrolman on the beat. And so he handed down a dozen decisions each day, and his decisions definitely leaned toward giving the petty offender a break. At the same time, he felt he was tough and uncompromising with the out-and-out thief. He considered himself a good cop.

One day, the good cop who was Andy Parker was walking his beat when the proprietor of a dry goods store called him over. The man was holding the wrist of a young kid who had allegedly stolen a bolt of silk from the sidewalk stand. Parker questioned the owner, and Parker questioned the kid, and then he donned his judicial robes and said, 'Well, we don't want to cause this kid any trouble, do we? Now, can't we just forget about all this?' The proprietor of the store was loath to forget about all this because the kid had allegedly passed the bolt of silk to an accomplice who had made his escape with the merchandise. But Parker kept administering his sidewalk practice, and finally everyone seemed satisfied to let the entire matter drop.

That evening, after he had changed to his street clothes, Parker went for a beer in a neighborhood bar. He had the beer, and he had a shot, and then he had another beer and another shot, and he was feeling like a pretty nice guy by the time he left the bar, and that was the last time in his life he ever felt like a pretty nice guy.

He was ambushed on his way to the subway by three men who didn't allow him the opportunity to draw his revolver. He was ambushed and beaten within an inch of his life. He lay on the sidewalk in a pool of his own blood, and when he regained consciousness he wondered *why* he'd been beaten or *who* had done the beating, and he drew what seemed to be the only logical conclusion. He figured that he had been beaten by friends of the shopowner because he'd let the kid get away with the theft of the silk.

He never did find out who had administered the beating on that lonely autumn night.

Perhaps it had been friends of the shopowner. Actually, it could have been any one of a hundred people who disliked Parker even in those days of amiability. Actually, it didn't matter who'd beat him up.

He learned several things.

The first thing he learned was that it wasn't nice to receive a beating. In the movies, a beating is usually a battle. The person getting the lumps is a fighting devil who manages to pick off a dozen of his assailants before he is finally subdued. Then he gets up, shakes the dizziness out of his head, wipes a trickle of blood from his lip, dusts off his clothes, and narrows his eyes, leaving the audience to speculate on just what that narrowing of eyes meant. In real life, a beating is very rarely administered with fists. The men who worked over Parker on that night in autumn were all as big as he was, and they were armed with sawed-off broom handles, and they really beat the piss out of him. They kept beating him long after he was unconscious, they beat him within an inch of his life, and the cliché happened to fit the situation well because they damn near beat him to death, and he may have been a lot closer than an inch to leaving the land of the quick. He had not liked that experience at all. So the first thing he learned was that he would never again, ever, as long as he walked the earth, be on the receiving end of a beating. Ever. He learned this the way a young boy learns his catechism. I will never again take a beating. I will never again take a beating.

And the way to be certain you will never take a beating is to hit first and ask questions later. It's handy to own a policeman's badge at such times. It makes apologies to innocent people easier afterward.

The second thing that Parker learned was that he was being entirely too easy and naïve in his approach to police work. From that day on, Parker would give a summons to anyone who so much as spat on the sidewalk. In fact, and curiously, from that day on Parker brought in more drunks, vagrants and innocuous offenders than any other cop working in the precinct. In his own eyes, Parker had stopped being a nice guy. He was a mean, tough son of a bitch, and he knew it. And if you didn't happen to like him, that was just too bad. Parker had a life to lead, and he knew how to lead it.

I will never again take a beating, he told himself.

I will never again take a beating.

In the luncheonette on the corner, Jeff Talbot held the

wet handkerchief to the cut on the side of his face, wiping away the blood. Some of the blood had spilled onto the collar of his jumper, and he was already looking ahead to the scrub job he would have to do on it to get out the stain. Luís, behind the counter, was more concerned with the sailor's condition than with the excitement in the street outside. He watched the sailor anxiously, almost like a father.

'You all right?' he asked.

'I'm all right,' Jeff replied. 'What's that kid supposed to be?'

'Zip?'

'Is that his name? Yeah. Him.'

'I don't know.'

'I mean, what the hell, who was giving him any trouble? I was minding my own business.'

'His business is minding other people's business. He'll wind up no good. Like Miranda up there.'

'What I'm trying to get at . . . well, what's he looking for trouble for? Is he hotheaded or something?'

Luís shrugged. 'No more than most.'

'Spanish people are supposed to be hotheaded, ain't they?'

'Some are, some aren't,' Luís said, shrugging again.

'We ain't got a single Spanish person in all Fletcher, you know that?' Jeff said, a touch of surprise in his voice. 'I never even *seen* a Spanish person until today, how do you like that?'

'I never saw anybody from Fletcher until today,' Luís answered.

'What I'm trying to figure out . . .' Jeff paused, studied the blood-smeared handkerchief, and then looked up at Luís. 'Well, *you* seem all right.'

'All right?'

'I mean . . . you ain't like him.' Jeff paused. 'That Miranda's Spanish too, ain't he?'

'*Sí.*'

Jeff said nothing. He nodded, and then seemed to fall into silent thought.

'If you figure that way, sailor, you will be making a big mistake.'

'What way?'

'You know what way. That's the easy way to figure.'

'This is pretty personal with me, Louise,' Jeff said. 'I *got* to know. I ain't doing this just for the fun of it. It's . . . it's important to me.'

'Why is it so important to you?'

'Because, well . . .' He looked at the clock on the wall, and he wondered if China would keep her date with him. And then he wondered if he still wanted to see her. He frowned and said, 'It's just important to me, that's all.'

10.

EVERYONE SEEMED READY for whatever might lie ahead.

The police in the streets and on the rooftops and in the back yard were ready. The people watching the show were ready. Zip and Sixto had obtained a large packing crate from the lot on the corner and had set it up just beyond the barricade; *they* were ready. And even Lieutenant Byrnes seemed ready now. He apparently had learned that his forces were deployed exactly the way he wanted them. He held a large, battery-powered megaphone, and he stepped out from behind the squad car, put the cumbersome apparatus to his mouth, blew into it several times to test the volume, and then said, '*Miranda? Pepe Miranda? Can you hear me?*'

His voice echoed on the silent street. The people waited for Miranda's reply, but none came.

'*Can you hear me?*' Byrnes said again, his voice booming out of the speaker. Again, there was silence. In the silence, the crowd seemed to catch its breath together, so that something like a sigh escaped their collective lips. '*All right, I know you can hear me, so listen to what I'm saying. We've got this street and the next street blocked. There are policemen with guns in every window and on every rooftop facing that apartment, front and rear. You're trapped, Miranda. You hear that?*'

Zip and Sixto clambered up onto the crate and peered over the heads of the crowd. 'This is *our* box, you dig me?' Zip said. 'Only for the Latin Purples. I don't want nobody else climbing on it.'

'*How about it, Miranda?*' Byrnes said. '*You coming out, or do we have to come in after you?*'

'Why don't he answer?' Zip said impatiently. He turned to the first-floor windows, cupped his hands to his mouth, and shouted, 'Answer him, Pepe!'

'*If there's shooting around here,*' Byrnes said into the megaphone, '*some of these people in the street might get hurt. Now how about it, are you coming out?*'

There was another long silence. Byrnes waited.

'*Okay,*' he started, '*if you . . .*' and the voice came suddenly from one of the first-floor windows. There was no body attached to the voice, no one visible in any of the windows. The voice seemed to materialize from nowhere, a shouted voice which rang into the street, cutting off the lieutenant's words.

'Who did I shoot?'

'It's Pepe!' Zip shouted, and the cry spread through the crowd like lava rushing down a mountainside, 'It's Pepe, Pepe, it's Pepe, it's Pepe, Pepe, Pepe.'

'*You shot one of our patrolmen,*' Byrnes said.

'Did I kill him?' Miranda shouted from the apartment, still invisible, his voice floating down into the street.

'*No.*'

'You're lying to me. I killed him.'

'*You hit him in the shoulder. Are you coming out?*'

'Did I kill him? Is he dead?'

'Let them come after you, Pepe!' Zip shouted.

'*Miranda, we don't want to play games here. If you're coming out . . .*'

A new sound erupted, drowning out the words that came from the megaphone, filling the air with its familiar wail.

'What's that?' Miranda shouted.

105

'It's an ambulance. What do you say, Miranda?'

'He shouldn't have tried nothing with me,' Miranda said. 'He could have got killed. I could have killed him.'

'But you didn't. So what do you say? Yes or no? You coming out?'

'No!' Miranda shouted, suddenly and viciously. 'You think you got some cheap punk up here? This is Pepe Miranda!' His voice rose. 'You hear me? You want me, you come in here and get me!'

'That's telling them, Pepe!' Zip yelled, and he poked Sixto in the ribs, and suddenly the street was alive with cheers of encouragement.

'Yea, Pepe!'

'Bravo, Pepe!'

'Tell 'em, tell 'em!'

'Quiet!' Byrnes roared. 'Everybody quiet!' Patrolmen moved quickly into the crowd, and the people in the street fell suddenly silent. But the rooftops still rang with cheers for the trapped killer in the apartment. Byrnes waited for the sound to die out. He put the megaphone to his mouth and said, 'All right, Miranda. No more talk. We're coming in.'

'Then stop talking and come get me, you yellow bastards!' Miranda shouted, and suddenly the shade on one of the windows snapped up, and there he was, Pepe Miranda the killer, a short, wiry man standing in his undershirt, his lips pulled back into a snarl, a three days' growth of beard on his face, a gun in each hand. He pulled back his head, and then snapped it forward with a short jerking motion, spitting into the street. And then he began firing blindly, both guns blazing as if he were trying to prove he was the marshal of a tough Western town.

Byrnes waved at the rooftops, and an ear-splitting

volley shattered Sunday like a piece of crystal. He scooted for cover behind the squad car while the guns roared down from the rooftops. In the crowd, women were screaming and men were ducking behind each other for cover. Byrnes waved his hand again. The volley stopped, Miranda was no longer at the window.

He gathered Carella, Parker and Hernandez around him. 'Okay,' he said, 'we're moving in. This time Miranda bit off too big a piece.' He paused and looked at the faces of the men around him. 'Has Captain Frick arrived yet, Steve?'

'Yes. I saw him a little while ago.'

'Let's find him. I want this to be right.'

Frederick Block was on his way home when he suddenly found himself in the middle of a traffic jam. Block hated traffic jams, and he especially hated them on weekends. He had gone to his office downtown to pick up a carton of eyelets which a factory in Riverhead needed instantly. He had made the delivery himself – 'When you deal with Block Industries, you get service,' he had told his client – and had then taken the shortest route he knew from Riverhead to the Calm's Point Bridge, and that route happened to take him through the heart of Isola and the 87th Precinct. And now he was in the middle of a traffic jam, on a Sunday, sweating inside his automobile when he should have been at the beach. Block was a fat man. Not one of those fat men who try to kid themselves by applying euphemistic terms like 'stout' or 'chubby' to their obesity. He was fat. F-A-T. And being fat, he sweated a great deal. And being a person who sweated – fat men, Block knew, never *perspired* – he did not appreciate being locked in a parked car in the middle of Isola on a day like today.

He bore the heat with tolerant malice for as long as he could. Then he got out of the car and tried to find out just what the hell was causing the tie-up. As far as he could see, there had been no accident. It always annoyed the hell out of Block when there was an accident. In the first place, careful drivers didn't get into accidents. And in the second and more important place, even if the wrecked car itself didn't block the road, traffic always slowed down to a snail's pace because every passing motorist wanted to study the extent of the damage.

Today, there had been no accident. And yet traffic was tied up on the avenue in both directions. Now why? Block wondered. With the instincts of an old bloodhound, he followed the crowd. They all seemed to be heading in the same direction, and he assumed the prime attraction was in that direction. Waddling along, mopping his brow with a big white handkerchief, cursing mildly under his breath, Block made his way up the avenue, and stopped at the luncheonette on the corner. A sailor was sitting at the counter. Block sidled up to him and said, 'What's going on, mate?' He had never been in the navy, but he was a born salesman who adapted his speech to fit any and all occasions. 'Why can't I get my car through here? What's going on?'

The sailor did not answer. The sailor kept dabbing at his face with a wadded handkerchief. Block didn't see the blood on the handkerchief, so he assumed the sailor was hot and wiping away sweat. He sympathized with the sailor and turned to the man behind the counter.

'Can you tell me what's going on?' he asked.

'The traffic's tied up,' Luís said.

'You're telling *me* it's tied up?' Block said, and he began chuckling, his layers of fat jiggling. 'Say, what kind of answer is that? It's tied up downtown and uptown and probably crosstown, too. What's going on? A parade?'

'There's a gunman in the apartment up there,' the sailor said suddenly.

'A what?' Block wiped his brow. 'A gunman, did you say?'

'Pepe Miranda,' Luís put in, nodding.

'I never heard of him. What'd he do, rob a bank?' Block said, and he began chuckling, the fat jiggling all over him again. He didn't look at all like Santa Claus.

'You live in this city?' Luís asked.

'Sure, I live in this city. Not around here, though. I live in Calm's Point. What is this Miranda, a celebrity?'

'He's a killer,' the sailor said quietly.

'Yeah?' Block opened his eyes wide in appreciation. 'Yeah? A killer?'

'That's what he is,' Jeff said.

'They going up there to get him?' Block said.

'That's what it looks like. You better go back to your car, mister. There might be shooting around here.'

'No, no,' Block said, very interested now. 'I want to watch this. I want to see him die.'

He shoved his way through the crowd, using his huge stomach like a battering ram.

'Louise,' Jeff said, 'what time is it?'

'I don't know. Eleven-thirty, something like that. Why?'

'I'm . . . I'm supposed to meet a girl here. At noon.'

'Sailor, why don't you take your own advice? Get out of here before you run into more trouble. Take a walk over to the park, eh? When the girl comes, I'll tell her you're waiting there for her. What's her name?'

'China. That's a funny name, ain't it?'

'Not for a Spanish girl. Only in Spanish, it's pronounced Chee-na.' Luís shrugged. 'A lot of the girls today, they give it the English sound. Or maybe people do it for them, and then they decide it's easier that way.' He paused. 'Go. Go to the park. I'll tell her where you are.'

'I thought she was a whore when I first met her, Louise. That's a damn rotten way to start off, isn't it?'

'Well, I know many men who have married prostitutes,' Luís said. 'They make good wives.'

'Oh, she ain't!' Jeff said, almost shouting the words in his haste. 'I didn't mean to give you that impression. I mean, you can see that, once you know her. She's got this . . . this real sweet face, you know?'

Luís smiled. '*Sí.*'

'Yeah, like a little girl, you know?' He grinned at Luís and then quickly said, 'Not that she doesn't look womanly. I mean, she certainly has all the . . . the . . . things a . . . woman has.'

'I have never seen an ironing board among Puerto Rican women,' Luís said.

'Huh?'

Luís curved his hand through the air, pantomiming a woman with uncommonly pronounced curves.

'Oh, yes,' Jeff said. 'Sure. But she doesn't look sloppy, you understand that, don't you? I mean, she's not one of these . . .' He used his hands to indicate a woman whose upper portions were mountainous. Both men nodded in solemn agreement on the proper size of a bosom. 'She talks nice, too,' Jeff said. 'I like a girl with a good voice and . . . and eyes that look at you. When she talks, I mean. She looks at you. That's good. It makes you feel like . . . like you're important.'

'*Sí,* a man must feel that he is important.'

'That's what I didn't like about Fletcher, Louise. I just

felt like anybody else there. It's funny but, well, meeting her I feel like – I don't know – I feel like *me*! That's pretty stupid, ain't it? I mean, like who the hell else would I feel like? And I hardly even know her. I mean, she's just another girl, isn't she?'

'Sure,' Luís agreed, 'she's just another girl. You can find girls anywhere.'

'Well, now she's not exactly *just* another girl,' Jeff said hastily. 'She's prettier than most, you know.'

'Pretty girls are easy to find, sailor. The world is full of pretty girls. And for every man in the world, there is one girl who is pretty.'

'Sure, sure. But she's, well, I guess you could call her beautiful. I guess you really could, Louise.' He paused. 'Do you . . . do you think she'll come?'

'I don't know,' Luís said. 'Perhaps.'

'I hope so. Gee, Louise, I hope so.'

From Zip's vantage place on the packing crate, he saw her at once, working her way through the crowd. He waved to her instantly, and then shouted, 'Elena! Hey, Elena, over here!' He poked Sixto and said, 'Hey, Sixto, it's Elena.'

Softly, Sixto said, 'I thought China wass your girl.'

'Variety, huh?' Zip said, grinning. 'Hey, Elena!'

The girl waved back. She was sixteen years old, an attractive girl with dark hair and dark eyes, wearing a skirt and blouse. The girl with her, slightly shorter than she, was wearing black tapered slacks and a boy's white shirt. 'Hello, Zip,' Elena called, and then said to her friend, 'Juana, it's Zip and the boys.'

Flatly, Juana said, 'He's a terrifying creep.'

'He's not so bad,' Elena said. 'Come on.'

They walked over to the crate. Zip offered his hand to Elena and pulled her up beside him, Papá studied the

111

chivalrous gesture, and then repeated it, offering his hand to Juana who took it with the disdain of a countess accepting aid from a doorman.

'You ever see anything like this, Elena?' Zip asked excitedly. 'He shot one of them.'

'Who shot one of them?' Elena asked.

'Pepe Miranda!' Papá said.

'Who?'

'Pepe Miranda,' Zip said. 'He's got a whole arsenal in that apartment with him. The cops can't figure how to get him out. Man you shoulda seen him. He come right up to the window and spit at the bastards!'

'Who's this?' Juana asked, turning her attention to Zip.

Papá, as if repeating a lesson he had learned, a lesson he *had* indeed learned earlier from Cooch, said, 'He the grays thin' ever happen this neighborhood.'

'Yeah?' Juana said aloofly. 'I never heard of him.'

'So *that's* what this is all about,' Elena said. 'We were walking over on the next block and everybody was heading here like somebody hit the numbers for a million dollars.'

'There ain't no numbers on Sunday,' Juana said distantly. She was not a very pretty girl, but she had learned somewhere that her eyes were very attractive and had further learned how to use make-up on them. Her eyes were the focal point of her face, as green as jade and, combined with her jet-black hair, they created an instant impression of desirability which overshadowed the true facts of her plainness.

'You came through the next block?' Zip asked Elena.

'Sure. Why not?'

'No reason.' He paused. 'That's Royal Guardian territory.'

'So what?'

'Nothing. Nothing.'

'Royal Guardians or not,' Elena said, 'this is a free country.'

'We walk where we want to,' Juana added.

'That's because you're a chick. It ain't so easy when you're a guy,' Zip said.

'Why not?' Juana asked.

'Because it ain't, that's all. You can't go messing in another club's territory.'

'That's nuts. Haven't you got anything better to do than play war? That's kid stuff.'

'There's nothing kid stuff about it,' Zip said. 'You just don't know.'

'I know plenty,' Juana said. 'You haven't got anything better to do, that's all. That's why you've got these territories and these street bops and . . .'

'I got plenty to do,' Zip said. 'We always got plenty to do, ain't we, Sixto?'

'Sure, he's got plenty to do,' Elena said. 'He's got China to chase after.'

'Hey, listen,' Zip said, grinning. 'How about a hug, Elena?'

'If you had things to do,' Juana persisted, 'you wouldn't get involved in this childish nonsense. What you are is an acting-out neurotic.'

'A *what*?' Zip said.

'An acting-out neurotic,' Juana said professorially.

'How come you're so smart, huh? Where'd you get your medical degree, huh?'

'I read an article in the newspapers,' Juana said smugly.

'Dig the big reader!' Zip said, and he burst out laughing. Dismissing her, he turned to Elena. 'Hey, come on, no hug for me?'

'Go hug China,' Elena said coldly.

'Come on, come on,' Zip said, still grinning. But his grin seemed to have no effect on Elena. Deliberately she turned to Sixto.

'Who's your cute friend?' she asked archly.

'Huh?' Zip said.

'What're you?' she asked Sixto. 'The strong silent type?'

'Me?' Sixto asked, bewildered by her sudden attention.

'What's your name?' she asked, moving closer to him, smiling the way she had once seen Jane Russell smile in a movie.

'Sixto,' he answered.

'The article said you're insecure,' Juana said to Zip.

'Don't give me any bull you read in the newspapers,' he said, turning on her angrily, miffed by Elena's behavior. 'I don't believe nothing I read.'

'You probably don't even know *how* to read,' Juana said.

The thing that was happening on the packing crate was rather odd. Because despite Juana's protests that Zip was a terrifying creep, an acting-out neurotic, and insecure to boot, her conversational efforts had all been directed at him. And even though her approach took the form of an attack, it was clear that she was bidding for Zip's attention and no one else's. Elena, meanwhile, was doing exactly the same thing, even though she seemed to be addressing Sixto. A none-too-subtle tug of war was taking place on that crate. Whatever Zip's flaws, he was obviously recognized by the girls as the most desirable of the three boys. And, thanks to either his indifference or his stupidity, he hadn't the faintest idea of what was happening.

'So how come you're so quiet?' Elena said to Sixto. 'Aren't you excited about your friend Pepe Miranda?'

'He's no' my frien',' Sixto said. 'Pepe's no damn good!'

The girl caught the accent. She looked at Sixto for a moment and then said, 'Hey, what are you? A tiger or something?'

'I no tiger.'

'You sound like one. Can't you speak English?'

Papá had been thinking over Sixto's comment, and had finally fathomed the meaning of it. 'What you minn, he's no good?' he asked now. 'Hey, Zeep! Sixto, he say Pepe's no good.'

Zip turned from Juana. 'What? Did you say that?'

'I dinn say nothin',' Sixto said.

And now Elena, anxious to recapture Zip's attention, quickly leaped in. 'That's what he said, Zip. That's what the Marine Tiger said, all right.'

'I no tiger. I speak English good!'

'He speaks a well English,' Zip said, chuckling.

'He said Pepe's no good,' Elena repeated.

'Is that what you said?' Zip asked, and he shoved out at Sixto. 'Is that what you said, huh?' and he shoved again. 'Huh?' and again he shoved, pushing Sixto closer to the edge of the crate. 'Is that what you said, Sixto?' and he pushed hard this time, sending Sixto over the edge of the crate, reeling backward into the gutter. Zip burst out laughing. Papá and Elena joined him. Juana seemed undecided for a moment, as if her natural instinct was to climb down and help Sixto to his feet. The indecision passed. She tittered nervously, and then burst into laughter with the rest of them. Zip put his arm around Elena.

'What's wrong with you, anyway?' he asked.

'Nothing.'

'So how come the big freeze?'

'What's with you and China?'

'That?'

'That.'

'Nothing.' He shrugged.

'The word says you're after Alfie.'

'Well, like he's got it coming, you know?'

'Why? Because of something with China?'

'What're you worried about China for, huh?'

'*Is* there going to be trouble?'

'With Alfie?'

'Yes,' Elena said.

'Naw, no trouble,' Zip answered. 'Don't worry, huh?'

'Have you got a thing on with China?'

'Me?' Zip began laughing again. 'Hey, you're jealous, ain't you? I'll be damned.'

'She's old enough to be your mother,' Elena said sullenly. 'She must be nineteen, maybe even twenty.'

'That don't make her old, only experienced. What's the matter, honey, huh?' he said sweetly. 'You jealous, baby, huh?'

'No.'

'You worried about poor little Alfie?'

'I don't care what you do to Alfie. Just answer me one question.'

'Sure, what's that?'

'You got eyes for China or not?'

'Like, you know, doll, your interest gasses me, but don't start strong-arming me. I'll bust you right in the mouth, you know?'

Juana turned to him suddenly. 'It takes a big man, don't it, to hit a girl?'

'Oh, get lost, zombie,' he said to her. He wrapped his arms around Elena. 'Come on, where's my hug?'

'Zip, cut it out,' she said. 'There's people watching.'

'So let them, who cares?' He took one arm from

116

Elena and pointed into the crowd. 'Hey! Hey you! Fat boy!'

Frederick Block, who had shoved his way up to the barricade, looked up at Zip.

'You watching us, Fat Boy?'

Block turned away with a look of extreme disgust on his face. Zip burst out laughing.

'See, honey?' he said. 'Nobody watching us.' He pulled her closer to him. 'Mmmm, you are the softest girl.'

'I shouldn't let you,' Elena said. 'Not after this China thing.'

'Somebody's got to protect little China, no?' His hands roamed her body. He touched her breast, and she pulled away from him quickly, embarrassed, but he drew her close again, and she stood unprotesting in the circle of his arms. Zip stroked her back gently.

'You going to hurt Alfie Gomez?' Juana asked.

'Drop dead,' Zip told her.

'Big man,' Juana said. 'Everybody in this neighborhood's a big man. It's just you're insecure, that's all.'

'Man, she sprouts that crap like as if she grows it in her mouth,' Zip said. 'I got news for you, zombie. I *am* a big man, now how about that? The Latin Purples ain't afraid of nothing or nobody!'

'Whoever heard of the Latin Purples outside of you and your mother?' Juana asked. 'If one of those Royal Guardians came down the street right now, you'd pass out cold.'

'I ain't afraid of no Royal Guardians,' Zip said angrily. 'I ain't afraid of *nobody*!' He searched his mind for a clincher to his argument, and then blurted, 'Why, one of my boys is out right now, rounding up a couple of pieces!'

'If one of them goes off accidentally, you'll run a mile.'

'You better tell your pal to shut up, Elena,' Zip warned.

'Juana, stop picking on . . .'

'A gun is a psychological symbol,' Juana said. 'You only want one because you're afraid.'

'I ain't afraid to rap you right in the mouth,' Zip said.

'Big man,' Juana repeated, but she shut up.

Zip looked out over the crowd. 'They're coming back,' he said. 'The bulls are coming back.'

11.

THE PLAN WAS a simple one, but Lieutenant Byrnes had discovered in his years of police work that most feasible and practical plans *were* simple.

The plan was one of deception, a plan which would utilize every man's innate susceptibility to the expected, and then knock him flat by suddenly producing the unexpected. The plan, of course, undertook to presume what Miranda would consider 'expected'. But it seemed a reasonable guess to suppose that Miranda expected the cops to get him out of that apartment, and that one certain way to accomplish this was to bust into the joint. If a rush were made across the street, a rush which carried all the earmarks of a frontal attack, Miranda would brace himself for an assault on his front door. Actually, the assault would come from elsewhere. Such was the un-original and simple nature of the deception. Broken down into simple terms, the police plan could have been stated thusly: *Hit him where he ain't.*

'Have you got it straight?' Byrnes asked his men.

'I want the fire escape,' Parker said.

'We'll see about that.'

'I want to be the one who gets him,' Parker said. 'I want to blow his head off.'

'Sometimes, Parker, you turn my goddamn stomach,' Byrnes said.

'What?'

'Nothing.'

'Well, what do you want to say something like that for?'

119

'Skip it,' Byrnes said. 'Do you understand the plan?'

'I understand it,' Parker said sullenly.

'Frankie?'

'I've got it.'

'Steve?'

'Run through it once more, would you, Pete?'

'Okay, this is it in a nutshell. I'm going to tell Miranda we're coming in after him. A pile of us'll rush the stoop when the shooting starts. Miranda – I hope – will think we're going to force the apartment door from the hallway. But one of us will break away from the rest and flatten himself against the side of the building.'

'Me,' Parker said.

'Whoever it is, he'll pull down the ladder of the fire escape and climb up to the first floor. He may be able to get Miranda from the window. Otherwise, he'll have to enter the apartment and have it out there. It's tricky, but I'd rather risk one man than a dozen.'

'Let's get started,' Parker said.

'In a minute. I need a volunteer for that fire escape job.'

'You've already got your volunteer, Lieutenant,' Parker said.

'You've got *two*,' Hernandez said.

'Keep out of this, Frankie. This is my baby.'

'Why should it be?'

'Because I want it.'

'I'll decide who . . .' Byrnes started.

'Lieutenant, you'd be crazy to send up a guy who's . . .' Parker cut himself short.

'Who's *what*?' Hernandez said.

'Okay! Who's got a personal stake in this, okay?'

'Personal? What the hell are you talking about?'

'You grew up with Miranda!'

'What difference does that make? We want him out of that apartment, don't we?'

'We want him *dead*,' Parker said. 'He's a punk. He should have been killed a long time ago. He's the biggest stink in these streets.'

'What the hell do you know about the stink here, Parker? Did you . . .'

'I seen plenty of it. I been in this precinct for . . .'

'Did you grow up with the stink in your nostrils, day and night? Did you live with it every day of your life?'

'You're telling me about this precinct? I know it like my own mother. There's nothing you can tell me about . . .'

'No, nothing! To you, this precinct is one big violation, one big crime being committed every hour on the hour. And you're scared of the place! You're scared out of your wits!'

'Scared? Who the hell . . .'

'Well to me it's *people*! And they deserve a goddamn break! They want to get that son of a bitch as much as you do!'

'They want him to hold off the whole damn city!' Parker shouted. 'You know that! You know it's true!'

'They only want a Puerto Rican to win for a change. Okay, if I go up there, a Puerto Rican wins.'

'If I go up . . .'

'If you go up, you purge yourself. You think killing him is gonna help you, Parker? You think that's the answer?'

'I don't know what the hell you're talking about.'

'If you go up there, you accomplish nothing. Not for yourself, and not for the city. You'll be making Miranda a hero. I'm telling you that right now. You kill him, and this neighborhood has a martyr. The kids'll

121

be playing *Pepe Miranda and the Cops* for the next six weeks.'

'The hell with the kids. You think I'm interested in . . . ?'

'Who's gonna show them, Parker? You want a hundred more Mirandas ten years from now?'

'*You* gonna show them?' Parker asked sarcastically.

'If I kill him,' Hernandez said flatly, 'the neighborhood gets nothing but a dead punk.'

'You've got him, Frankie,' Byrnes said.

'Thank you.'

'Get to the car, Parker. Radio the men on the next block to open up. I want to draw his fire away from these windows.'

'You're sending Hernandez up there?'

'Yes. Any complaints?'

'Damn right I've got a—'

'Take it to the mayor!' Byrnes snapped, and he turned his back and walked toward the patrolman who was holding the megaphone. Parker stared after him, spat viciously into the gutter, and then walked around to the other side of the squad car.

A reporter behind the barricade caught at Hernandez's sleeve. 'Hey, are you in charge here?' he asked.

'No.'

'Well, who is? Can't we get some men in there for pictures?'

'The police department'll send out pictures,' Hernandez said. He pushed past the reporter and walked to the luncheonette. 'Look at these kids,' he said to Luís. 'Sucking violence from the same tits Miranda used.' He shook his head. 'He's waiting up there to die, Luís, you know that? He's waiting up there for us to kill him.'

Luís nodded.

'And you know something? I think he *wants* to die. I think he *wants* to end it, once and for all.'

The two girls who came around the avenue and stopped at the mouth of the street were apparently more interested in beginning something than in ending it. They were both tall brunettes. One was wearing a tight, bright-red silk dress. The other wore the identical dress in yellow. The dresses were designed to exhibit and reveal; they were incapable of keeping a secret. Every nuance of flesh beneath the skintight silk, every subtle hint of muscle or bone, every flowing curve, every dimple, every pucker, insistently shrieked its existence to the most casual observer. The girls were not the bashful type. They moved with a fluidity of breast, hip, thigh and leg that aided the dresses in their task of nonconcealment. They were, in fact, so much the Hollywood concept of what a whore should look like that at first glance they seemed to be imitations. If there was one quality which every prostitute in the 87th Precinct shared, it was the ability to look like anything *but* a street walker. In most instances, the precinct whore was the best-dressed girl on the streets. Her careful grooming, more than any other attribute, was usually the one clue to her occupation.

These two were either new at the trade, or else they'd canceled their subscriptions to *Vogue* magazine. In any case, they walked directly to the barricade and stopped there. The girl in the red dress touched the arm of the nearest patrolman who turned, ready to start yelling, and then looked as if a movie queen had wandered into his bedroom by mistake.

'Excuse me, officer,' she said in a tiny little voice, 'but can't we get through here? We work right across the street.'

'Where?' the patrolman asked.

'At La Gallina.'

'What the hell do you do *there*?'

The girl in the red dress seemed at a loss for words. She turned to her companion. The other girl smiled at the patrolman sweetly and said, 'We're in . . . ah . . . public relations.'

'Well, I'm sorry, girls,' the patrolman said. 'My orders are to let nobody through this barricade unless he's a cop or a fireman. Now you two girls ain't cops or firemen, are you?' He grinned politely, thinking how clever he was being, and making a note to repeat his comment to the boys in the locker room when he checked in later.

'No, indeed,' the one in the red dress said.

They moved away from the barricade.

'What now, Marge?' the one in the yellow dress asked.

Marge shrugged. 'Let's hang around. It looks like a lively crowd. There may be something in it for us, Marie.'

Marie looked skeptical. Together, walking with a hip-swiveling, crazy-socketing, ball-bearing, thigh-thrusting, leg-strutting motion that turned every head on the block, they began appraising the potential customers watching the siege. Marie raised an eyebrow at Marge, and Marge glanced in the direction she indicated.

They were both looking at Frederick Block, the fat man.

12.

THERE ARE TIMES when it must be nice to have a Cinemascope camera and stereophonic sound. There are times when it must be great to have a wide screen stretching across the front of the world, with things happening on every corner of that screen, with the eye gathering in all these things like a net sweeping the ocean floor. It isn't enough to say this and this were happening here, that and that were happening there. A city street is not a tiny canvas; a city street is not a page in a book. It is a tumultuous thing teeming with life, and you can't hope to capture life in a sentence or a brush stroke. The things that happened on that street, on that particular day in July, happened almost simultaneously, separate and distinct from each other, but nonetheless almost at the same time, so that there was a feeling of continuous motion, of one event overlapping and flowing into the next. The wide screen stretched the length of a city block. The life on that street stretched to the very edges of time.

Cooch stood on the steps of the building next door to the church.

China came down a flight of stairs and into bright sunshine.

A man selling ices entered the street at the opposite end.

Marge and Marie, the two prostitutes, approached Frederick Block.

Jeff Talbot looked at the wall clock and left the luncheonette.

Two boys wearing bright-gold jackets turned into the block.

The cops of the 87th rushed the doorway to the left of La Gallina.

These are the things that happened, minute over-lapping minute, time lost and time replaced by the tireless eye of space. These are the things that happened . . .

Cooch stood on the steps of the building next door to the church. He had been standing there for ten minutes now, watching the people pour down the church steps and into the bright confused sunshine of the street. There were not many people left inside the church now. He looked at his wrist watch, and then studied the few stragglers again. He was certain that Alfredo Gomez had not left the apartment to attend mass this morning. But he would wait a few moments more, just to make sure.

Against his belly he could fell the hard, cold metal of the pistols he had retrieved from Chico and Estaban. The weapons made him feel very strong and very powerful. Too, he considered this independent reconnaissance an act of foresight worthy of a general. He would wait until everyone had come out of the church, and then he would go back to Zip with the guns *and* with a report on Alfie's whereabouts. This was acting above and beyond the call of duty. Zip would be pleased. And whereas it would not be as dramatic to catch Alfie in his house instead of on the church steps, Cooch didn't much care. The important thing was to wash the little bastard. That was the important thing.

Cooch had been thinking about it all week long, ever since Zip first got the idea. There were times when Cooch couldn't sit still, just thinking about it. There were two stimulating and contradictory feelings which rushed through Cooch's mind and body whenever he considered what they were about to do. The first of these was the very concept of killing. This excited him. He had fantasized the squeezing of a trigger many times, had imagined Alfie tumbling down the church steps, had wondered what it would feel like to know that he had killed another human being. He had convinced himself that Alfie deserved killing. He had, after all, messed with China.

This was the second idea, and this was as exciting as the first. A hundred or more times in the past week, Cooch had imagined Alfie messing with China. He wondered just what Alfie had done to her, and his imagination created new images each time. Alfie gently stroking China's full breast. Alfie unbuttoning China's blouse. Alfie thrusting both hands beneath China's skirt. Alfie . . .

The images continued to stimulate him. And they were images clouded with guilt. Lying alone in his bed at night, he would think of Alfie and China, and then he would roll over into his pillow and think *The son of a bitch has to die for that*.

Of that he was certain.

Alfredo Gomez had to die.

Standing on the steps of the tenement, he watched the last few stragglers leaving the church, and he thought again of Alfie and China, and he bit his lip and then thought of shooting the little bastard.

China came down a flight of stairs and into the bright sunshine.

The tenement hallway had been dark, and she blinked now against the sudden brilliance, knowing she still had at least five minutes before she was to meet the sailor, not wanting to get there too early or seem too anxious, and yet almost unable to control the forward motion of her feet as they took her onto the stoop. Jeff was his name. Jeff, Jeff, Jeff, her mind echoed, and her heart beat with the idea of the rendezvous, and she found herself gripping the shopping bag in her hand more tightly. She had wrapped chicken in wax paper, had put up some eggs to boil before going to church, had later packed the hard-boiled eggs, and salt, and fruit, and a thermos of iced coffee, all of which were in the shopping bag now. She wondered if he liked chick—

'Hello, China.'

She blinked and then shielded her eyes from the overhead sun.

'Oh, hello, Cooch,' she answered, and she smiled and began to walk around him, but he stepped into her path.

'I was just thinking about you,' Cooch said.

'Oh?' China glanced at her watch. 'Cooch, I haven't got time to talk to you right now. I have to . . .'

'About what we're going to do for you today.'

'What? I don't under—'

'Alfie?' Cooch said, smiling.

'Alfie?' She paused, puzzled. 'Alfredo, do you mean? Alfredo Gomez?'

'Uh-huh,' Cooch said, nodding.

'What about him?' She looked at her watch. She would have to hurry. With all that police trouble up the street, she would have to cut around the avenue and that didn't leave much time to . . .

'We're gonna get him,' Cooch said. 'For what he done to you.'

'What?' she asked.

'Alfie,' he repeated.

'Yes, but what . . . what did you say?' She studied his

128

face. She was certain she had heard him correctly, and yet his words hadn't seemed to make any sense.

'For what he done to you,' Cooch said.

'What do you mean?'

'You know.'

'No. I don't know.'

He had taken a step closer to her, and she had backed away from him slightly. Blocking her path to the steps, he moved closer now, so that she was forced to take another step backward, almost into the darkened hallway of the building.

'You know what he done, China,' Cooch said.

She looked at his face. His face looked very strange. He was a very young boy with a ridiculously silly mustache over his upper lip, and she had always thought . . . but now he . . . he . . . looked different somehow.

'I have a gun,' he said suddenly.

'A—'

'A gun, China.'

'What . . . what . . .' She was forced to back away from him again, into the hallway this time. He stood silhouetted in the doorway of the building, the bright sunshine behind him. His hand moved. For a moment, she didn't know what he was doing. And then she saw the dull glint of metal.

'It's a Luger,' Cooch said.

'Wh-what are you going to do with that, Cooch?'

'Kill Alfie,' he answered.

'Kill . . . ? Why? What for?'

'For what he done to you?'

'He didn't do anything to me!' China said.

'You know what he done, China.' He held the gun up close to her face. 'You know what he done.'

She was truly frightened now. She did not want to

retreat further into the hallway, but he kept moving closer and closer to her, and there was no place to go but back. For a crazy moment, she wanted to turn and run up the steps to her apartment. And then it was too late. He had stepped between her and the steps and was moving toward her again so that, in backing away from him, she stumbled toward the garbage cans stacked under the steps on the ground floor.

'Cooch, I . . . I have to go,' she said. 'I don't know what you're talking about. Alfie didn't do anything to me. If you're angry at him because you think . . .'

'*This* is what he done, China,' Cooch said, and his hand reached out for her.

She felt his fingers tighten on her breast, and she screamed, pulling away from him. His fingers clung. She thought her blouse would tear. Blindly, she brought up the shopping bag, swinging it at him, screaming, and then shoving her way past him into the bright sunlight again, rushing down the steps, still screaming, into the crowd.

A man selling ices entered the street at the opposite end.

'*Pidaguas!*' he called. '*Pidaguas!* Come buy some *pidaguas.*'

Zip, standing on the crate, turned to watch the man who pushed through the crowd with his cart. 'Hey, you want some ices?' he asked Elena.

'You got any loot?'

'Sure,' Zip answered. 'What flavor you want?'

'Lemon,' Elena said.

'I'll have a lemon, too,' Juana said.

'Oh, now she knows me,' Zip said, leaping down from the crate. 'Now it's buying time, she knows me. Okay. I'm the last of the red-hot spenders. Everybody gets ices!'

From the crate, Papá said, 'Me, too, Zeep?'

'You, too, Papá! Everybody! Everybody gets *pidaguas* today! Hey, Mac, slow down! Don't you want no business?'

He went over to the cart and placed his order. He seemed happy as hell. He paid no attention at all to the detectives who stood not six feet from him.

'Where are your men, Andy?' Byrnes asked.

'Coming, sir.'

Byrnes turned to Hernandez who stood staring up at the first floor of the tenement. 'You scared, Frankie?'

'A little,' Hernandez answered.

'I don't blame you.' He paused. 'This is the damnedest thing ever, isn't it? The last one I remember like this was back in 1931 when this guy Nelson O'Brien was holed up in an apartment on the North Side. I was a patrolman at the time. He held off a hundred and fifty cops for two hours that day. We were chopping holes in the roof and dropping tear gas down on him, but the bastard wouldn't give up. We wounded him three times, but he was still standing when we went into the apartment to collar him. Standing and cursing – but out of amo. He'd hidden both his guns in his socks, hoping to use them later for an escape. A real prize, he was.'

Byrnes paused and stared at Hernandez. 'I didn't feel so hot that day, Frankie.'

'Why not?'

'The guy in the apartment was Nelson O'Brien.' He paused again. 'I'm Irish.'

'Yes, sir,' Hernandez said.

'But I'll tell you something, Frankie. The guys like Nelson O'Brien don't stop me from marching in the St Paddy's day parade every year. You understand me?'

'I understand you.'

'Good.' Byrnes hesitated. 'Take care of yourself on that goddamn fire escape,' he said. 'I wouldn't want to lose a good cop.'

'Yes, sir,' Hernandez said.

Byrnes extended his hand. 'Good luck, Frankie.'

'Thank you.' Byrnes turned to walk back to the squad car. 'Pete?' Hernandez called. Byrnes faced him. 'Thank you,' Hernandez said again.

Marge and Marie, the two prostitutes, approached Frederick Block. Block was pulling his handkerchief out of his back pocket, preparatory to mopping his face with it, when his elbow struck something very soft. He turned casually. The something very soft was covered with bright-red silk.

'Hello,' Marge said.

'Well, hello,' Block answered. 'Quite a show, isn't it?'

'If you like this kind of jazz,' Marie said.

'Well, it's pretty exciting,' Block said. He studied the low-cut front of Marie's dress. Damn, if this girl didn't have the . . .

'There are plenty things more exciting than watching a cheap gunman get shot,' Marie said.

'Like what?' Block asked, beginning to get the impression that this girl wasn't even wearing a brassiere.

'Can't you think of anything?' Marie said.

'Well . . . I can think of a few,' Block said.

'Whatever you can think of,' Marie said, 'we can manage.'

Block studied the girls a moment longer. He mopped his face. Then, with a practiced eye, and a whispered voice, he asked, 'How much?'

'For one of us or both?' Marie asked.

'Both? Well, I hadn't . . .'

'Think about it.'

'I am.'

'Think fast,' Marge said.

'We like to work together,' Marie said.

'The Bobbsey Twins down on the Farm,' Marge said.

'We know things they don't even know in Paris yet,' Marie said.

'We know things ain't even been invented yet,' Marge said.

'How much?' Block asked again.

'Fifty for the afternoon, including the stretcher bearers.'

'The what?'

'The stretcher bearers. To carry you out when it's over.'

Block chuckled. 'How much without them?'

'Twenty-five for me alone. My name's Marie. It's a bargain, believe me.'

'I'll think about it,' Block said.

'Come on, come on,' Marie prompted.

'Can't you just wait a minute?'

'Love don't wait a minute, mister,' Marie said.

'Not in July it don't,' Marge added.

'Twenty-five's too high,' Block said.

'Make it twenty, sport. A double sawbuck, what do you say?'

'You're on.'

'Or vice versa,' Marie said dryly. She turned to her friend. 'Well, I'm set. Now what are *you* gonna do with all that love busting inside you, huh, Marge?'

Jeff Talbot looked at the wall clock and left the luncheonette.

It was fifteen minutes past twelve.

133

She wasn't coming. He'd been a jerk to think she'd keep the date. He went out into the street, thankful that he had worn his whites today. God what a hot day, why hadn't she kept the date, why in hell hadn't she kept the date? He wanted to hit somebody. He just for the hell of it felt like hitting somebody. You meet a girl like that maybe once in— Oh, the hell with it. Angrily, he stamped back into the luncheonette.

'I'm shoving off, Louise,' he said.

'What?' Luís answered.

'She didn't show. I'm leaving.'

'Good,' Luís said nodding. 'You will be better off out of this neighborhood. There are other girls, sailor.'

'Yeah, that's for sure,' Jeff said.

He walked out of the luncheonette again. It was a damn shame, he thought, because . . . well . . . he'd almost found it. He'd almost, in the space of what was it, ten, fifteen minutes? In that short a time, he'd almost found it, but of course he should have known. Nothing good comes easy. And yet, it had seemed so right, it had just seemed . . . seemed right, where . . . where eyes meet and . . . and without touching . . . without saying very much . . .

The hell with it!

As he left the luncheonette, the first people he saw were Frederick Block and the two prostitutes.

Marge winked at him.

Jeff squared his hat and walked directly to the trio.

'Well, well, well,' he said.

'Feel like a party, sailor?' Marge asked.

He hesitated for just a moment, his eyes roaming the street. Then he said, 'Yes, goddamnit, I feel *just* like a party!' and he grabbed Marge's elbow, and the four of them turned the corner and went off up the avenue.

Two boys wearing bright-gold jackets turned into the block.

They stood with their hands on their hips for a moment. Both wore sunglasses, both wore their dark hair in high crowns. The bigger of the two, and the older – a boy of about twenty who stood a little over six feet tall – wore a silver identification bracelet on his right wrist. His name was Tommy. The other boy, nineteen and short by modern standards, was called Li'l Killer. His real name was Phil. He had never killed anyone in his life, but the name made him sound like a guy who'd cut out your liver for the price of an ice-cream soda. The tall one, Tommy, nodded at Phil and they walked directly towards the crate where Papá and the two girls stood craning their necks.

'Hey, kid,' Tommy said.

Papá turned. 'You talk to me?'

'Off the box,' Tommy said flatly.

'Huh?' Papá said. 'Wha'?'

'You heard him,' Phil said. 'Off the box. We want a view.'

Papá looked down to where Sixto stood near the side of the crate.

'Sixto, go call . . .' he started, and Phil shoved out at Sixto before he could move.

'Stay put, sonny,' he said.

'Don't hurt him, Li'l Killer,' Tommy said. He chuckled. 'Just cripple him.'

'Listen, why do you want trouble for?' Elena said, looking past them to where Zip stood at the ices cart near the corner.

'Who wants trouble?' Tommy asked gently. 'Li'l

Killer and me, we asked your friend very politely to get the hell off that box, that's all. That ain't no trouble.'

'That ain't no trouble at all,' Phil said.

In that instant, Lieutenant Byrnes waved his arm at the rooftops, and the police opened fire. The firing was a precise, methodical operation designed to keep Miranda away from the front windows. At the same time, the distant echo of guns could be heard in the back yard, and over that, like a triangle player in a hundred-piece orchestra, the sound of shattering glass. Miranda appeared at the front windows for just an instant, looked into the street, saw what he was supposed to see, and ducked back into the apartment.

The cops of the 87th rushed the doorway to the left of La Gallina.

Miranda saw them the second before he ducked his head. Lieutenant Byrnes led the charge, shooting up at the windows as he ran. Behind him were Steve Carella and Andy Parker and half a dozen patrolmen, all with guns in their hands. Frankie Hernandez brought up the rear. One by one, the cops entered the tenement. Hernandez seemed to be following them and then, suddenly, at the last moment, he swerved to the right of the doorway and flattened himself against the front of the building.

At the same time, Captain Frick – who commanded the uniformed cops of the 87th – brought the megaphone to his mouth and shouted, *'We're coming in, Miranda! We're going to knock that front door right off its hinges.'*

There was no answer from within the apartment.

'We're coming in, Miranda! We're coming up those steps right now!' Frick shouted, and he hoped Miranda would buy it.

In the hallway, Byrnes, Carella, and Parker crouched

on the steps. They could hear the gunfire outside, could hear shouts from the cops, screams from the crowd, the sound of glass breaking and wood splintering, the high whistle of slugs that caromed and ricocheted.

Outside, Frankie Hernandez stealthily moved past the glass front of La Gallina, working his way toward the fire escape.

The crowd was suddenly hushed.

The only sound on the street now was the explosion of the revolvers on the rooftops and in the windows facing Miranda's apartment.

She came around the corner hurriedly.

There were tears on her face, and her blouse had pulled free from her skirt, and she thought she could still feel the imprint of Cooch's fingers where he had touched her. It was twenty minutes past twelve, and she hoped against hope that Jeff would still be there, hoped he had at least the faith to realize . . . to realize *what*? Tears streaking her face, she rushed into the luncheonette.

He was not there.

She looked at the empty stools, and then she turned to Luís and she said, 'Luís, there was a sailor . . .' and Luís nodded instantly.

'He left.'

'I . . . I couldn't get away and then . . . the crowds in the street . . .'

'He left,' Luís said again.

She turned from him quickly and went into the street again. She could hear the pistol shots, thunder on a sunny day. 'China, hey, China!' She wished it would really rain, she wished the skies would open and – 'China, hey, don't you hear me?' – rain would come down to wash the streets, wash all the . . .

'Hey! *China!*'

She looked up suddenly. 'What? Oh – oh, hello.'

Zip was standing by the ices cart, grinning.

'Hey, how are you, China?'

'Fine,' she said. 'I'm fine, thank you.'

'You want some ices?'

'No. No, thank you, Zip.'

He studied her. 'What's the matter?'

'Nothing.'

'You look like you was crying. Was somebody bothering you?'

She shook her head. 'No, no.'

'If anybody bothers you, you just let me know,' he said. 'I'll take care of them the way I'm gonna take care of Alfie.'

'You leave Alfie alone!' she said sharply and suddenly, her eyes flashing.

'Huh?'

'Why do you want to hurt him? You have no right to hurt him!'

'Hell, I ain't afraid of *him*!' Zip said.

'Nobody said you were.'

'It's just, he's got this coming, that's all.'

'You know he didn't do anything, Zip. You *know* that.'

'He done plenty! I'm gonna bust him wide open. I'm gonna . . .'

She began crying suddenly and fitfully. 'Why do you *talk* that way?' she shouted. 'Why do you have to sound so tough? Aren't you ever yourself? Can't you be *yourself*?'

Surprised by her sudden passion, he stared at her, speechless.

'What are you trying to show?' she asked, the tears

138

running down her face. 'What are you trying to do? Make it worse here than it really is? What's wrong with you? What the hell is *wrong* with you?'

He stared at her, confused. He reached out to touch her, not knowing that the tears were something which had been building inside her from the moment Cooch attacked her, building on the wild run from the tenement to the luncheonette, building against the desperate hope that the sailor would still be there, kept in check by sheer will power, and now overflowing; he did not know these things, he only knew that she was crying. And in the face of such female vulnerability, in the face of anguish such as he had never known or seen, Zip pulled back his hand, unable to touch her in that moment, unable to establish a contact which seemed in that moment too intimate, too revealing.

'Hey . . . hey, listen,' he said, 'don't cry. What do you want to cry for?'

'Promise me you won't do anything to Alfie,' she said. 'Promise me.'

'Listen . . . hey, you don't have to cry.'

'Promise me.'

'China . . . everybody knows what I said I was gonna do. Like I told them—' He hesitated. 'I told them you was my girl.'

'You shouldn't have said that.'

'I know. I mean, even *I* know you ain't my girl. Listen, can't you stop crying? You want my handkerchief?'

'No,' China said, sobbing. 'I'm not crying.'

'Here, take it,' he said, handing her the handkerchief. 'I hardly used it yet.'

She took the handkerchief and blew her nose.

'You want some ices?' Zip asked lamely.

'No. Zip, you won't hurt him, will you? He did nothing to me, believe me. He's a nice boy.'

Zip did not answer.

'You'll be doing something very wrong if you hurt him.'

'You ain't sore at me, are you?' His voice dropped. 'Like because I said you was my girl?'

'No. I'm not sore.'

'I won't say it no more,' he said gently. He shrugged. 'I don't even know why I said it.' He thought for a moment. 'Except maybe because you're so nice, you know?'

'Thank you,' she answered, and she smiled weakly. She handed him the handkerchief. 'I got it all wet.'

'Oh, that's okay, that's okay.' He shrugged. 'You feel a little better now?'

'A little.'

'You really shouldn't cry, China. It's a sin to cry unless like something serious happens, you know? Like unless you lost somebody or something.'

'I *did* lose somebody, Zip.' Her eyes clouded for an instant, and then she shook her head. 'You promised? About Alfredo?'

'Well, I didn't exactly . . .'

'I wouldn't want you to get into trouble,' she said.

He stared at her as if she had uttered the words in Russian. His brow furrowed. He kept staring at her. The concept seemed new to him. Nor could he understand her concern. It wasn't as if she was struck on him or anything, he knew lots of girls who were, but China wasn't. So what was it? Why should she give a damn about him one way or other? And yet, he knew she wasn't lying. Standing with her, he knew that she was as much concerned for his safety as she was for Alfie's.

'I got to think about it,' he said.

'Yes, think about it. Please.' She touched his hand briefly, and started off toward the corner.

He watched her go, a frown on his face.

'*Pidaguas*,' the man at the cart said.

Zip nodded. The man had put the five cups of ices into a cardboard container. Zip paid him, and then picked up the container with both hands. He kept frowning, and then the frown disappeared, and his face broke into a grin as he turned back toward the packing crate.

Frankie Hernandez had reached the hanging ladder of the fire escape.

Be careful with those bullets, he thought. *If you dumb bastards put them any lower, you'll hit me. And that would be the end of this little caper.*

Bracing himself, the gun in his holster now, he leaped up for the hanging ladder, missed, and dropped silently to the pavement. He flattened himself against the building and looked up. The volley from the rooftops was effectively keeping Miranda away from the windows. He moved out, jumped for the ladder again, caught it with one hand, reached up with the second hand, and then, hand over hand, began climbing. The ladder began to drop as he climbed, inching on squeaking, rusted iron hinges, drowned out by the roar of the guns from across the street. He drew his .38, hefted it in his hand, and began climbing the remaining rungs to the fire escape.

The people in the street watched him silently.

The guns showered destruction against the front of the building.

Zip was still smiling when he reached the crate, still thinking of what China had said. Somehow, he felt curiously relieved, as if . . . as if something very heavy had been taken off his mind. And then he heard the voice.

'Well, now, ain't this nice? One of the darling Latin Purples bought ices for us!'

He looked up sharply. He recognized the gold jacket instantly, and the words 'Royal Guardian' flashed into his mind, and he told himself not to be afraid, but he felt a tight knot of fear beginning in his stomach.

'H-hello, Tommy,' he said.

'Hello, Zip,' Tommy answered. 'You're just in time. Get your boy off the box.'

'Get . . . but . . .' He paused, nibbling his lip. The carton of ices in his hands felt suddenly very heavy. 'But it's . . . it's *my* box,' he said. 'I brought this all the way over from the . . .'

'It belongs to whoever's using it,' Tommy said. 'And we want to use it.'

'Aw look, Tommy,' Zip said, 'what do you want bad blood for, huh? Can't we . . . ?'

Tommy reached up suddenly, twisting his face into Papá's trouser leg, pulling him off balance, and dumping him into the street. Zip, his hands full of ices, his mind whirring with the new thoughts China had put there, stood by helplessly, wondering what to do now, wondering why . . .

'Blow,' Phil said to him.

'Aw, come on, Phil, can't we . . . ?'

'Li'l Killer,' Phil corrected.

'Sure, can't we . . . ?'

'*Blow!*' Phil said firmly.

He shoved out at Zip suddenly. Tommy, trained for the maneuver, stuck out his foot. Zip tripped, staggered backward, the cups of ices leaving his hands and spattering over the street. He jumped to his feet instantly, his hand darting for his pocket. Nothing was in his mind right now but salvation. If China had said anything to him, he'd now forgotten it. All he knew was that he was being threatened by two Royal Guardians, that he was outnumbered and vulnerable. As his hand closed on the switch knife in his pocket, he thought only *I got to get out of this*.

'Don't pull the blade, Zip,' Tommy said gently.

Zip's eyes moved quickly to Tommy, saw that his hand was already in his pocket. They flicked to Phil who was ready to charge in on his flank. Undecided, he faced them. Elena, on the crate, began to laugh nervously. Tommy grinned and then picked up the laugh, and then Phil joined him, and their laughter was triumphant and, hearing the laughter, Zip began to tremble. He wanted to fight them, he wanted to destroy them, wanted to pull the blade and rip into them, show them who he was, show them who they were laughing at. But fear crawled in his belly like black worms, and he felt his fingers loosening their grip on the knife. In impotent rage, his eyes brimming with tears he did not wish to show, he whirled suddenly and kicked at one of the ices cups in the street.

And then he saw Hernandez on the fire escape.

Flat against the side of the building, edging silently past the first shattered window, and then the next, his gun in his hand, Hernandez hesitated for a moment, and then crouched beside the third window.

He brought up his revolver.

Zip understood what was happening in an instant.

Burning with shame and indignation, wanting to explode, wanting to show these rotten bastards they couldn't kick him around, wanting to shout, to rip, to gouge, to release the shame that growled inside him, wanting to show that he was Zip, Zip, ZIP!, he looked up at the first-floor windows and suddenly, without knowing why, he cupped his hands to his mouth.

'*Pepe!*' he bellowed. '*The fire escape!*'

13.

WHEN HERNANDEZ HEARD the yell, he thought at first that his ears were deceiving him. His immediate reaction was to turn his head toward the street. And then he realized that Miranda, in the apartment, had whirled at the sound of the shouted words. And then he recognized the look in Miranda's eyes, and Hernandez tightened his finger on the trigger of the .38, and then he heard the explosions inside the apartment and then he was spinning backward and falling. He had been crouched outside the window, so he fell no more than three feet to the iron floor of the fire escape, but it seemed to him that he was falling through space for a very long time, and it seemed to him that he hit the iron slats with the force of a meteor slamming into the earth.

There were two bullets in his chest.

He had never been shot before, not when he'd been a Marine participating in the Iwo Jima landings, and not since he'd joined the police force. He had seen wounded men, a *lot* of wounded men, when he'd been in the service, but somehow he had detached the wound itself from the event which had caused the wound. He had been raised on the kid games of Cops and Robbers, Cowboys and Indians, *bang!* I got you! *bang!* you're dead! and there had always been something glamorous to the idea of getting shot. Even when he had seen the open gaping wounds, the notion of glamour had persisted.

He knew now that the notion was false, and he

wondered which con man had ever sold him such a silly bill of goods. When the bullets slammed into his chest, he felt nothing at first but impact. He had been punched before, punched with hard driving fists that had knocked the wind out of him, and he knew what it felt like to be hit. He had once been struck with a hammer swung by a delirious building superintendent, catching the blow on his shoulder, feeling the sharp sudden pain of metal against flesh. But he had never been shot, and he knew now that when a man got shot he didn't daintily clutch his chest and say, 'Uggggh!' and then do a fancy movie-extra dive. He knew that the force of a bullet was like the force of a steam locomotive, and he knew that when you got hit with a bullet, you got knocked off your feet. It was as simple as that. Maybe *everyone* didn't get knocked off his feet when he was shot, but the bullets that struck Hernandez spun him around from his crouch and then knocked him flat to the fire escape.

He felt only impact and shock at first, and then the cold sensation of falling through space, will-less, unable to control himself, simply falling, falling, and then colliding with metal, powerless to stick out his arms to cushion the fall.

And then he was on fire.

The fire engulfed him. It started with the two gaping holes in his back where the bullets had left his body, and then ran straight through his body like burning tunnels to the two smaller holes at the points of entry, and then suddenly flared up to consume his entire chest, and then his shoulders, and then his throat and his face, a roaring fire. He found it hard to breathe, he sucked in air through his parted lips, and he dimly realized that one of the bullets must have gone through a lung, and then blood bubbled out of his mouth, and he thought it was saliva until he saw its bright-red splash on the cuff of his shirt, and then he panicked.

Gasping for breath, his body on fire, pain lancing through him, he felt the panic rush into his head and settle behind his eyes like a pair of thumbs pressing outward. More blood bubbled from his mouth.

Giddily, he wondered if he were going to die.

The thumbs kept pressing against the backs of his eyes, spreading darkness which came in waves and retreated. He could hear shouting in the street below. He wondered if they'd collared whoever had done the yelling.

He wanted to puke.

He felt the nausea start deep in his stomach, tasted the vomit in his throat, and then the fire escape was spinning, the sky was spinning, the world was spinning, and he choked on his own blood and crashed into unconsciousness.

The boys had vanished like Arabian horse thieves.

Zip had begun running the moment he'd shouted the warning to Miranda, shoving his way through the crowd, dashing around the corner. Papá and Sixto, as soon as they realized what had happened, followed him. All three were gone before Byrnes, Carella, and Parker rushed from the doorway of the tenement.

Byrnes turned his head toward the fire escape instantly. 'Frankie!' he yelled. 'Frankie!' There was no answer.

'What happened?' Parker asked, struggling to catch his breath. 'Is he dead?'

'I don't know. He's just lying up there. We got to get him down.' He stared suddenly at the sidewalk beneath the fire escape. 'What the hell is . . . Jesus! Jesus Christ!'

147

'What is it?' Carella asked.

'That's blood!' Byrnes said, something like awe in his voice. 'That's *blood* dripping down!'

The men watched the steady patter of drops to the pavement. The drops fell silently, as straight as arrows, one after the other, spattering to the pavement in an ever-widening stain.

'We got to get him off there,' Byrnes said.

'It was a kid who yelled the warning to Miranda,' one of the patrolmen said.

'Leave it to the kids,' Byrnes said, shaking his head. 'Sometimes I think the kids in this precinct are more damn trouble than all the professional thieves put together.'

'It ain't them,' Parker said, watching the dripping blood in fascination. 'It's the parents. They come here without even knowing how to speak the language. What the hell can you expect?'

'My old man had a brogue you could cut with a knife,' Byrnes said. 'What's that got to do with . . .'

'What'd you say, Lieutenant?' a reporter behind the barricade asked. 'About the kids?'

'Nothing for publication.'

'You think the kids today will grow up to be like Pepe Miranda?'

'No. That's not what I think.'

'What *do* you think, Lieutenant?'

'I think we've got a bleeding man on that fire escape, a man who may be dying. I think I want to get him off there while there's still a chance for him, and I think you'd better get off my back before I restrict the area to all reporters.'

'Don't get touchy,' the reporter said. 'I've got to peg this story on *something*.'

'On something? What the hell do you want? A Barnum and Bailey circus? Peg it on Miranda, peg it on Frankie Hernandez who may be up there dead, for all I know!'

'Life is cheap, Lieutenant,' the reporter said.

'Is it? Then peg your story on your asshole! And leave me alone!' Angrily, Byrnes strode off toward the squad car.

'Boy,' the reporter said, raising his eyebrows. 'He's sure got a low boiling point, hasn't he?'

'He's been working in this precinct for a long time now,' Parker said. 'This ain't exactly the garden spot of the universe.'

'I'm only trying to get some ideas about Miranda, that's all,' the reporter said. 'What the hell, nobody's job is easy.'

'You want some ideas on Miranda?' Parker asked. 'Then look around you. Miranda's only the end product. You don't have to be in that apartment with him to know what he's like. Just look around you, pal. You'll see Miranda in every stage of his development.' Parker nodded sagely. 'Just take a look,' and then he followed Byrnes to the patrol car.

Tommy and Li'l Killer saw Cooch the moment he came around the corner.

'Hey, Tommy,' Phil said. 'There's one of them.'

'One of who?'

'The Latin Purples. Man, if the cops spot that jacket . . .'

'Call him over,' Tommy said.

'What for?'

'To tip him off. You want the cops to get him?'

'Who cares they get him or not? He's a jerk.'

'Jerk or no, I don't like the cops to score. Call him over.'

Phil shrugged. 'Hey! Hey, kid! Hey, you!'

Cooch, who had been searching the crowd for Zip and the boys, stopped dead in his tracks, recognizing the gold jackets at once, hesitating.

'Come here,' Phil said.

Cooch approached the crate warily. 'You talking to me?'

'Yeah. Hey, what's your name again?'

'Me?'

'Yeah, who do you think? I forget your name. What is it again.'

'Cooch.'

'Sure. Cooch. That's right.' Phil nodded. 'Cooch, this is Tommy Ordiz, he's war counselor for the Royal Guardians. He's maybe got a tip for you.'

'What kind of tip?' Cooch asked suspiciously.

'On the fourth at Hialeah,' Phil said, and he burst out laughing.

'Don't clown around,' Tommy warned. 'You want this tip, Cooch?'

'Who's clowning?' Phil said. 'Rrrrrrracing fans . . .'

'Knock it off!'

'I was just . . .'

'*Knock it off!*'

Phil fell silent. He put his hands in his pockets and glowered at Tommy.

'You want the tip, Cooch?' Tommy asked again.

'Depends on what kind.'

'A good tip. I'm being nice to you.' He paused. 'Get rid of that purple jacket.'

Cooch was silent for a moment. Then he said, 'Who says?'

150

'I'm giving you good advice. Ditch the jacket.'

'Why?' Cooch said narrowly. 'So you can say you busted a Latin Purple?'

'Huh?'

'You heard me.'

'Oh, man, don't be a worse meatball than you are,' Tommy said. 'I got better things to do than . . .'

'Screw him,' Phil said. 'Let him find out for himself.'

'You don't get no trophy from me, pal,' Cooch said.

'Look,' Tommy started, patiently trying to explain, 'if you keep wearing that jacket . . .'

'The jacket stays on! No goddamn Royal Guardian tells me what to wear.'

'See?' Phil said. 'What'd I tell you? Let the creep find out for . . .'

'No, wait a minute, Phil,' Tommy said. Something hard and cold had crept into his voice and into his eyes. He studied Cooch minutely, and then said, 'You ought to watch your mouth, boy, you know?'

'I don't have to watch nothing,' Cooch said. He did not know whether or not he was afraid. Actually, he did not feel afraid. Not with four guns tucked into the waistband of his trousers. But at the same time, he knew that something was pushing him into sounding two members of the toughest gang in the neighborhood. He could only assume the force propelling him was fear. And yet, he did not feel afraid.

Tommy climbed down off the packing crate. 'You got a *real* loose mouth, boy,' he said. 'You ought to watch the way it spills over.'

'You take care of your own mouth,' Cooch said.

'You're really looking for it, ain't you, boy? Your day ain't gonna be complete until we break your arm, is it?'

'You finished making big noises?' Cooch asked. 'I'm in a hurry.'

Tommy stepped into his path. 'Stay put, boy.'

'Tommy,' Phil warned, 'there's a million bulls all over the . . .'

'Shut up!' Tommy said tightly, without turning his attention from Cooch. 'I give you a chance to take off that jacket nice and polite, now didn't I, Cooch? For your own good, I asked you. Okay. Now you're gonna take it off because I'm *telling* you to take it off. Now how about that?'

'How about it?' Cooch answered.

'You take it off, or I cut it off your back!'

'Sure. Try it.'

'You're the kind I like,' Tommy said, taking a step forward, his hand reaching into his pocket. 'You're the kind of spunky little bastard I . . .'

'Hold it!' Cooch whispered. 'Hold it right there, man! I got four pieces under this jacket, and I swear to God I'll use every friggin' one of them!'

Tommy stopped suddenly, eyeing Cooch, wondering if this were just a bluff. It did not seem to be. Cooch's eyes were steady, his mouth tight.

'So come on, hero,' he said confidently.

'Let it go, Tommy,' Phil said worriedly, his eyes flicking to the cops swarming over the street.

Tommy studied Cooch an instant longer, and then backed away. 'We got a big man with a piece here, Phil,' he said. 'You're real big with them pieces, huh, Cooch? Well, I got some more advice for you. Friendly advice. Don't never go walking about without a piece from now on, you hear? Because, buddy, you are going to need one. You are really going to need one.'

'Thanks, you yellow bastard,' Cooch said, grinning,

and then he turned on his heel and ran off toward the corner.

'Cooch, huh?' Tommy said, smoldering. He nodded. 'Okay, Cooch. We're gonna see about you, Cooch.'

'A nut!' Phil said, shaking his head. 'We try to help him, and he turns on us.' He shook his head again. 'It just don't pay to be nice to nobody.' He looked up at the girls. 'You chicks gonna stand on that box all day long?'

'What else is there to do?' Elena asked.

'Let's go up to my pad,' Phil said. 'My people are out. We roll back the rug in the parlor, and we have a little jump, what do you say?'

'I don't know,' Elena said. 'Juana?'

'I don't know. What do you think?'

'It's too hot to dance,' Elena said.

'Okay, so let's go get a beer,' Phil said. 'What the hell's the sense in hanging around here? Don't you know what's gonna happen?'

'No. What's gonna happen?'

'Eventually, they're gonna shoot Pepe,' Phil said simply. 'What do you think? He's gonna get away?'

'He might,' Elena said.

'Impossible.'

'Why is it so impossible?'

'Because there's got to be a moral,' Phil said. 'The Bad Guy never wins. Crime don't pay. Otherwise the Breen Office don't let it through.' He burst out laughing. 'Hey, Tommy, you dig that? The Breen Office . . .'

'Yeah, I caught it,' Tommy said. 'The son of a bitch! I was trying to help him, can you imagine that?'

'Come on, girls,' Phil said. 'Let's cut out, huh?'

'Juana?' Elena said.

'Okay,' Juana said.

'Great,' Phil said, helping them off the crate. 'Believe

153

me, you'd be wasting your time hanging around here. Ain't nothing gonna happen to Pepe but he's gonna get killed.'

If the police had been as confidently sure of the outcome as was Phil, they would not have bothered to arm themselves with tear-gas pellets this time at the bat. For whatever Phil might have thought about the inevitability of Hollywood-type gangland movies, Pepe Miranda *had* broken out of an apartment the day before, and today he had shot a patrolman and a detective, and the possibility existed that he might shoot a few more detectives – or even another lowly patrolman or two – before the festivities were over. And, granting this possibility, there was the further possibility that he could and might break out of this apartment today, foiling the police, the Breen Office, and brothers Warner, and even Anthony Boucher.

In any case, this time the cops were playing it safe. One of their patrolmen had been carted away in an ambulance, and one of their detectives lay spilling his blood, drop by drop, to the sidewalk below, and those seemed like enough casualties for one day.

So they lined up across the street like Hessians on a Massachusetts field in 1777, and they put their tear-gas guns to their shoulders, and they awaited the order which would release a new volley of bullets against the windows across the street, driving Miranda back so that they could plop their triple tracer shells into the apartment. There was nothing as sad as a crying thief, and all those valiant men in blue would watch Miranda with aching hearts as he burst into tears, but that was the way the little tear-gas pellet bounced.

Lieutenant Byrnes waved his arm at the rooftops, and

the volley began. There was no glass left to shatter, and even the window frames were so badly splintered that the new cascade of bullets seemed to seek out instinctively the relatively untouched brick surrounding the windows. Big chunks of red brick showered onto the fire escape and the pavement below. Hernandez, lying as still as stone, was covered with red dust.

'Okay,' Byrnes said to the men in the street, 'get it going. Aim for the windows and get as many in there as you can!'

The men started firing. The triple tracer shells arced in lazy spirals toward the window. From inside the apartment, Miranda let out a roar like a wounded animal. There was a hiss, and then a cloud of smoke, and then more hisslike explosions and suddenly tear gas was pouring from the open windows. The pellets raced about the apartment like decapitated rats, designed to wriggle and squirm so that they could not be picked up and returned to the street. The scent of apple blossoms drifted into the street, a mild scent wafted over the heads of the crowd. Miranda was cursing a blue streak now, shouting and roaring. He appeared at the windows once, and was driven back by a Thompson gun which all but ripped away half the side of the building.

And then, suddenly, in the street, there was a pop and a hiss, and the scent of apple blossoms was unimaginably strong, and Andy Parker reeled backward from one of the patrolmen and shouted, 'You stupid idiot! You goddamn stupid idiot!'

14.

WELL, YOU CAN'T blame people for accidents. People have accidents all the time, and cops are only people, and if a gun misfires, it misfires, and that's that. And if a tear-gas pellet which is supposed to go zooming up through the air suddenly plops onto the asphalt and explodes there, those are just the breaks. Maybe Parker shouldn't have been standing so close to the patrolman firing the pellet. But accidents *will* happen, and Parker *was* standing close to the gun when it misfired, and close to the pellet when it exploded, so that he got the first mushrooming whiff of tear gas before the pellet went dizzily skipping into the crowd. Tear gas ain't Chanel Number 5. Especially when it goes off practically in your face. His eyes began to burn instantly. Blindly, he reached for his handkerchief, cursing the patrolman, and compounding the felony by rubbing the chemical deeper into his smarting eyes.

Bawling like a baby, he staggered toward the lunch-eonette, the handkerchief to his face. Behind him he could hear the shrieking of the crowd as the pellet traced a crazy path among them. People began coughing and shouting. Byrnes was yelling orders at patrolmen. All Parker knew was that his face and his eyes were burning.

'Luís!' he shouted. 'Luís!'

He groped his way to the counter, the handkerchief to his face.

'Luís, where are you?'

There was no answer. Parker took the handkerchief

away from his face. He tried to see past the tears in his eyes, but he saw only blurred shapes, dazzling, shimmering tears of streaked light.

'Luís!' he shouted. 'Get me some water! I can't see.' He was beginning to panic. Why didn't Luís answer him? Why wouldn't Luís help him? 'Luís! *Where are you?* Help me! Get me some water! *Luís! Luís!*'

Luís came running from the back of the shop, his eyes wide with concern. '*Qué pasa?*' he said. '*Qué pasa?*'

And Parker shouted. 'Where are you, you stupid spic!'

The words stopped Luís as effectively as bullets. They slammed into his ears and ricocheted in his mind and then paralyzed him. He stood with his arms at his sides, staring at Parker.

'Luís?'

'*Sí.*'

'For Christ's sake, get me some water. Please get me some water.'

'*Sí,*' Luís said. '*Sí.*' Dazed, he moved away from the counter.

'Hurry!'

In the street outside, the firing had stopped. Great billows of gas poured from the shattered windows of the apartment, hovered on the windless air. People were covering their faces with handkerchiefs and cursing at the police for unleashing this blight. Luís brought a bowl of water to the counter. Parker groped for it blindly, touched the rim with his hand, and then dipped into it. Luís watched him silently. Parker washed his eyes and his skin, sighing, repeating the motion over and over again. And finally he dried himself with the handkerchief and lifted his face. Luís was still staring at him.

'*Qué pasa, maricón?*' Parker asked, grinning, using a Spanish obscenity.

'Nothing,' Luís said. He shook his head wearily. 'Nothing.'

'What's the matter, huh?' Parker asked, still grinning. 'What's the matter, eh, *cabrón*?' Another obscenity, but there was no answering smile from Luís.

'*De nada*,' Luís said. 'Nothing.'

'You sore at me? 'Cause I was yelling at you? Is that it? Man, I felt like my eyes were on fire. You sure were a lifesaver.'

'*Sí*, I was a lifesaver,' Luís said blankly.

Parker felt suddenly uneasy. 'Hey, come on,' he said. 'You going to let a little yelling come between friends?'

After a long while, Luís said, 'No, Andy, I would not let a little yelling come between friends.'

Outside, Lieutenant Byrnes lifted the megaphone to his lips. '*Miranda? Can you hear me?*'

'What do you want, you son of a bitch?' Miranda shouted, coughing.

'*This is it, Miranda. Are you ready to come out? Or do we shoot our way in?*'

There was a long silence. Parker moved quickly out of the luncheonette. Luís was still staring at him as he left.

'What the hell is he doing?' Parker asked Carella. 'Why don't we move in right now? I'll bet he can hardly see in there.'

'Pete doesn't want any more shooting unless it's absolutely necessary,' Carella answered.

'Why give that punk a break? We can go in there and mop him up in two seconds.'

'Suppose he starts shooting into the street again?'

'So what?'

'You want these people to get hurt?'

'All I want is Miranda.'

'And after Miranda, then what?' Carella asked.

'What do you mean?'

'When does your private crusade stop?'

'What the hell are you . . . ?'

'When are you going to forget that beating you took, Parker?'

'What beating? What . . . ?'

'You know what I'm talking about!'

'All right. I'm never going to forget it,' Parker shouted. 'Okay? Never. It taught me a lesson, buddy, and only a sap would . . .'

'What lesson, Parker?'

'It taught me you can't trust anybody in this lousy precinct, that's what it . . .'

'And it also taught you to be afraid,' Carella sad.

'What?'

'You heard me. Afraid.'

'Look, mister, you'd just better stop right now, while you're winning. I still ain't forgotten the time you . . .'

'When are you going to make a *real* arrest, Parker? When are you going to stop pulling in junkies and drunks? When are you going to tackle the real trouble-makers?'

'I do my job!' Parker shouted. 'I keep the streets clean!'

'By picking up the wrong garbage!'

'It's *all* garbage here!'

'And you're afraid of it! You're afraid to take another beating!'

'You son of a bitch, I warned you to . . .'

'*I'm waiting, Miranda!*' Byrnes shouted, and both men turned their attention to the lieutenant. Carella's fists were bunched. Parker glowered at him, and then walked to where Byrnes was standing.

159

'*How about it, Miranda? Give it up! You haven't got a chance!*'

'What chance do I have if I come out? That old lady died, didn't she?'

'*What old lady?*'

'The one I mugged,' Miranda said. He went into a fit of coughing which lasted for several moments. Then his voice came from the apartment again. 'Tell the truth, cop.'

'*That woman's still alive, Miranda.*'

'I shouldn't have hit her,' Miranda said. His voice faded. 'I needed money. I had to . . .' He paused for a long time. 'She's dead, ain't she?'

'*She's alive, I told you.*'

'You're lying to me. You'll never get me out of here, cop. You think I'm coming out to face a murder rap?'

'*The woman's alive. If you force us to come in after you, you haven't got a chance.*'

'I got news for you, cop. I never *did* have one.'

'*Okay, so make it easy on yourself now.*'

'For what? In payment for all the crap I've taken from cops since I was old enough to walk?'

'*You dished out a bit yourself, Miranda. Let's cut the talking. Yes or no? Do you come out with your hands up, or do we blast you out?*'

'You want me, come and earn your salary.'

'*Okay, you're calling it. There's just no talking to you, is there? Okay, we're coming in.*'

'Hey . . . hey, cop!'

'*What is it?*'

'Listen, I . . . I want a priest.'

'*A what?*'

'A priest. I . . . I wanna talk to a priest.'

'*Will you come out if we get you one?*'

'Send him up here. I gotta talk to him.'

'*Why? Are you hit?*'

'No, I ain't hit. Goddamnit, do I need a federal warrant to get a priest? Can't I get anything in this friggin' city without having to beg for it?'

'*Just a minute, Miranda.*' Byrnes put down the megaphone. 'What do you think, Steve?'

'It's a trick,' Carella said.

'Sure,' Parker said. 'He don't want no priest. All he wants is a shield.'

'I know,' Byrnes said.

Carella stared at him. 'Are you thinking what I'm thinking, Pete?'

'Yes,' Byrnes said. He put the speaker to his mouth. '*Miranda?*'

'Yeah?'

'*I'm getting a priest for you.*'

There was something in Zip's eyes which had not been there before. Sixto studied his face and tried to figure out what it was. Zip looked as if he might begin crying at any moment. His face was red, and his lips were tight, and his eyes seemed to blink too often, as if he were struggling to hold back tears. But at the same time, there was a strength to the rigid thrust of his back, an impatience to the way he clenched and unclenched his fists.

The boys were standing on the avenue opposite Alfredo's building. None of them wore the purple jackets now. Without the jackets, they seemed like four high-school kids discussing girls or baseball or swimming. But, of course, they were discussing murder.

'What do you think, Cooch? Is he up there or not?'

'I don't know,' Cooch said, looking across at the building. 'One thing for sure, he didn't go to church.'

'Why we deetch dee jackets, hey?' Papá asked. 'I lak dee purple jacket.'

'The jackets are hot,' Zip said impatiently. 'Can't you keep your mind on what we're doing here?'

'But I lak dee jacket. I don't see why . . .'

'You think this is the right time, Zip?' Cooch interrupted. 'The streets are crawling with bulls.'

'It's *exactly* the right time. Every cop in the city's got his hands full with Pepe. We can move in on Alfie and get him before they even know what happened.'

'What's dee sense havin' a jacket if you cann wear it, huh?' Papá persisted.

Zip whirled on him angrily. For a moment, it seemed as if he would strike him. 'You want to end up on Bailey's Island?' he shouted.

'Where's dat?'

'In the middle of the River Dix! It's a prison. You wear the jacket, and that's where you'll wind up.'

'Wha' did I do, huh?' Papá asked. 'Why I cann wear dee jacket? Why they put me in jail if I wear dee jacket?'

'Oh, man, try to explain anything to this moron! Why the hell don't you go back where you came from?' Zip said angrily. 'Go to Puerto Rico, will ya? Do me a favor.'

'If I b'long dee Latin Purples,' Papá said logically, unfazed, 'I shoul' wear dee jacket. Den ever'body knows who I am. Thass what you say, Zeep. So now I cann wear dee jacket. Why not?'

'Don't try to figure it out, Papá,' Zip said. 'Just take my word for it. Right now, we got Alfie to worry about.'

'Cann we let it wait, Zip?' Sixto said. 'Wha's the hurry? Maybe tomorrow . . .'

Zip's eyes flashed, and again he looked as if he were about to cry, and yet he seemed strong and determined at the same time. 'Now!' he said. 'Today! I'm sick of waiting for tomorrow! I'm gonna be somebody *today*!'

'You don' have to kill Alfie to be somebody,' Sixto said.

'What's the sense talking to a tiger? You're like a goddamn foreigner. Look we ain't debating this no more. It's decided already.'

'But who decided?' Sixto asked.

'*I* decided.'

'Then why don' *you* go shoot him?'

The words came out of his mouth before he realized he was going to say them. They produced an instant silence. Zip clenched his fists and then unclenched them.

'What's your story, Sixto?' he said softly.

Sixto took a deep breath. 'I don' think we should shoot him.'

'You don't, huh?'

'No.'

'Well, I think we should. And that's that.'

'That's what . . .'

'That's *what*?' Zip said, his fists working. 'Go ahead, finish it.'

'Tha's what Pepe Miranda would do,' Sixto blurted. 'Tha's not what my fodder would do. My fodder woul'n shoot nobody.'

'So what the hell is your father? A big shot? He works in a factory, for Pete's sake!'

'What's wrong wi' workin' in a factory?'

'You want to be a factory worker, go ahead. I don't wanna work in no damn factory!'

'What you *wanna* do?' Sixto asked, and again there was a silence. He was certain that Zip would begin crying this time. This time the tears seemed on the verge of eruption. 'You wanna go aroun' killing people

163

all the time? Is that what you wanna do?' Sixto persisted.

'Look . . .'

'You tink it's so smart to kill somebody? My people never kill nobody, not here, not on the islan'. So what's so special abou' . . .'

'You're looking for trouble,' Zip said quietly.

'We kill Alfie . . . wha's the sense? What does that make us?'

'You're looking for trouble,' Zip repeated.

'You tink 'cause we beat up somebody, 'cause we . . .'

'Shut up!'

'. . . act like tough guys . . .'

Zip slapped him suddenly and viciously. Sixto's head snapped back. He was shocked for a moment, and the blow had hurt him. But he stared at Zip coldly, and then wiped his hand across his mouth.

'All right?' Zip asked.

Sixto did not answer. Cooch watched his face, a slight smirk beginning on his mouth. Papá seemed confused, as if he did not know whether to smile or frown.

'All right?' Zip asked again. Again, there was no answer. 'All right,' he said nodding. 'Let's map this out.'

Cooch grinned. He was glad this nasty disciplinary business was out of the way. He was glad they were moving into action again. 'What's the first step, Zip?'

'First, we gotta find out if Alfie's still in the apartment. Papá, you and Sixto'll take care of that. Go up in the hallway and listen outside the door. If he's in there, you'll hear him. Then you come back and report to me.'

'How do we get him out, Zip?' Cooch asked.

'All we got to do is get him in the hallway.'

'But how?'

'I don't know.' He paused, thinking. 'Ain't he got no

buddies? Like Papá could call him out, makin' believe he was a buddy.'

Cooch shook his head. 'Alfie's a lone wolf.'

'There must be somebody he trusts, somebody he'd come out in the hallway to talk . . . hey!' He snapped his fingers. His face was suddenly alive. If ever he'd looked about to cry, he did not look that way now. 'Sure,' he said. 'We say we want to be friends, see? That's the story we give. And the go-between believes it, and tells that to Alfie. When Alfie comes out in the hallway, *bam!*'

'Yeah, but who, Zip? Who's gonna be the go-between? Who we gonna get that Alfie would trust?'

Zip grinned from ear to ear.

'China,' he said.

15.

IN THE HALLWAY of the building in which Alfredo Gomez lived, Sixto suddenly knew what had to be done. Perhaps he had known it all along, perhaps he had known ever since he'd gone into the drugstore, known without admitting it to himself. But he knew now that one could not stand committed by refusing to commit oneself. And he knew now that more than the mere presence of police on the street was necessary to prevent the senseless murder of Alfredo Gomez. He recognized that he must choose a side and choose it now, and that once he had made his choice he would have to defend it. He was very young to be finding himself at such a crossroad. Too young, perhaps, to be making a choice which would influence another's life as well as his own. But the crossroad was there, and he faced it, and he made his choice unheroically. He made his choice the way most choices are made, made it through a combination of character and conviction. For Sixto, no other choice would have been possible. The choice was as much a part of him as his hands.

'Papá,' he whispered.

'Wha's dee matter?' Papá said.

'Sit down. I wann to talk to you.'

The boys sat on the steps leading to the first floor. It was dark in the hallway, and quiet. Most of the building's tenants were out in the street watching the siege. But even though he knew he would not be overheard, Sixto whispered. And because whispering is contagious,

Papá whispered, too. Side by side in the darkened hallway, the boys talked.

'Wha's dee matter?' Papá asked again.

'Papá . . . this . . . this is all wrong.'

'Wha's all wronn?'

'What we going to do. To Alfie.'

'Zeep say . . .'

'Papá, please. Listen to me. Please.'

'I lis'nin', Sixto.'

'Iss wrong to kill Alfie, Papá.'

'Wronn? But Zeep say . . .'

'Iss wrong! Papá, look . . . look, you like it here? You like this city?'

'*Sí.*'

'We come here . . . is nice here . . . is better. We don' want to be like that Pepe Miranda up there!'

Papá hesitated for a moment, confused. Then he said, 'Pepe Miranda's the grays thin' ever happen this neighborhood.'

'No, Papá. No. He brings shame to us.'

Papá shook his head. Gently, like a father about to explain something to a favored child, he covered Sixto's hand with his own. Then, with little patting motions characteristic of the slow movement which had earned him his nickname, he said, 'No, no *you* wronn, Sixto. He the grays thin' ever happen aroún' here.'

'Papá, he *kills* people!' Sixto said, pulling back his hand.

'*Sí.* He's brave.'

'Papá, that's not . . .'

'He's a brave man,' Papá insisted. 'He hole off all dee cops, an' he . . .'

'He's not brave! He's no good! He don' care for you or me, ony for himself. He iss bad, an' he brings disgrace to us.'

'No, Sixto,' Papá said slowly. '*No es verdad. De ningún modo . . .*'

'Don' speak Spanish!' Sixto said. 'We here now, we speak English.' He paused. 'Papá, you understan' what I'm saying?'

'*Sí, yo comprendo. Pero . . .*'

'Don' speak Spanish!'

'Why I cann speak Spanish?' Papá asked, puzzled.

'Papá, listen to me,' Sixto said desperately. 'We not gonna kill Alfie.'

'Sure, we gon' kill him,' Papá said, nodding.

'No. No, we not. We kill him, then we doin' wrong. Like Zip. Like Pepe.'

'Zeep bought me *pidaguas*, Sixto,' Papá said.

'Papá, he iss bad.'

'Zeep? Bad?'

'Yes, yes.'

'An' Pepe?'

'Yes, him too.'

'No,' Papá said. He shook his head. 'Zeep say he iss good.'

Sixto was trembling. He did not want to play his trump, and yet he saw that Papá was still unconvinced, saw that more was needed.

'Papá, you think I am good?'

'*Sí.*'

'Would I do something bad, Papá?'

'No. I don' think so.'

'Papá . . .'

He sucked in a deep breath.

'Papá . . . the one who called the police . . . the one who told them were Pepe wass . . . it was me. I called them.'

The hallway was silent. He felt at once that he had

168

made a terrible mistake, that he had revealed something which should have remained secret. Papá studied him with blank eyes.

'*You* tole on Pepe?' he asked incredulously.

'Yes.'

'How you know where he wass?'

'I saw him yesterday. I recognize his picture from the paper. All day, I wonder about it. Then I think . . . I think it's best to tell.'

'But . . . but tha's bein' . . . a *rat*, Sixto.'

'No.'

'But you tole on Pepe!'

'Yes.'

'Why? Why you do this?'

'Because he iss bad.'

Papá was silent for a long time. Then he scratched his head and said, 'If Pepe iss bad, why does Zeep say . . . ?'

'Zip only wants to be big. He thinks it makes him big to boss. But it's ony big when you let everybody live his own life. Papá, listen. Please. Please listen.' He suddenly felt like crying. He clutched Papá's arm fiercely and said, 'Papá, we go this way now, we never stop, you hear?'

'I hear. *Sí, sí.*'

'We go this way now, we get like Zip, and then we wind up like Pepe. We bring more shame to the *barrio*. We hurt ourselves.'

'*Sí, sí, comprendo.*'

'*Papá, quien adna al revés anda el camino dos veces.* If we take the wrong road, we make the journey twice.'

'But . . . Zeep iss *bad*?'

'Yes, yes.'

Struggling with this new idea, Papá said, 'But he bought me *pidaguas*,' and then fell silent. His brow was furrowed, his eyes puzzled. After a long time, he said, 'An' Pepe iss bad too?'

'Yes.'

'Sixto . . . iss you alone who thinks like this? Or ever'body?'

'Everybody, Papá. Everybody in the streets.'

'I . . . Sixto . . . I wanna be lak ever'body in thees city. But Zeep say . . .'

'Papá, we are only strong if we do the right thing.'

Again Papá was silent, thinking. He shrugged and turned to Sixto.

'I . . . I don' wann to be dee bad guy, Sixto.'

'No.'

'I wann to be dee goo' guy.'

'Sí, sí.'

He shrugged again. 'I don' know how to say in English.'

'You are with me, Papá.'

Papá beamed. 'Sí, I am wi' you, Sixto.' He continued smiling. 'Sixto?' He paused. 'We dee goo' guys, Sixto?'

'Yes, Papá,' Sixto said very softly. 'We the good guys.'

The other good guys came up the street.

There were two of them. One was a detective lieutenant named Peter Byrnes. The other was a priest named Steve Carella.

Carella felt rather foolish. He had felt foolish in the rectory of the church while arguing with Father Donovan who had, perhaps rightfully, insisted that the policemen were planning something which would make a mockery of a man's faith in God.

'This man doesn't have a faith in God,' Byrnes had said. 'He wants a priest up there for one reason and one reason alone. He wants to use him as a shield to get out of that apartment.'

'How do you know that?'

'I know it,' Byrnes said. 'Take my word for it. The last time Pepe Miranda was inside a church was the day he was baptized.'

'He may wish to make his peace.'

'Father, I respect your attitude, believe me. But I think I know a little more about this man than you do. Now can you either let me borrow one of your black things, whatever you call them . . .'

'Cassock.'

'Yes, your cassock, or else we'll have to root around someplace else and find one. That'll take time, and Miranda may shoot somebody else during that time. Now, it's up to you.'

'And suppose his request for a priest is legitimate?' Father Donovan asked.

'Then I'll come straight down from the apartment, and I'll come straight here, and I'll give you back your hassock . . .'

'Cassock.'

'Cassock, and you can go up and see him yourself. Is that fair?'

'It sounds fair.' Father Donovan had studied Byrnes. 'My garment would never fit you, Lieutenant.'

'I'll squeeze into it.'

Father Donovan shook his head. 'No. You've got at least thirty pounds on me. The garment is cut tight to begin with.'

'Father, we're in an awful hurry. Could we please . . .'

'Besides,' Carella said, 'you can't go up there, Pete.'

'Why not?'

171

'You've been our talk-man so far. If somebody else starts using the megaphone, Miranda'll get suspicious. You've got to stay in the street and keep talking to him.'

'I'm going up,' Byrnes said. 'I wouldn't ask any of my men to take a chance like . . .'

'The cassock doesn't fit you,' Carella said.

'The hell with the . . . pardon me, Father.'

'And Miranda would smell a rat,' Carella said.

'I don't care what he . . .'

'So I'd better go up. Father Donovan and I are about the same size.'

'Steve, you can't . . .'

'That's settled,' Carella said.

'Steve . . .'

'What?'

'I . . . nothing.' He paused. 'He's a killer.'

'I know.'

'And it was *my* idea to . . .'

'It was *our* idea. We got it at the same time, Pete. Remember?'

'If you get shot, you damn fool . . .'

'I've been shot before,' Carella said.

The men stared at each other.

'All right,' Byrnes said, sighing, 'where's the cassock, Father?'

Now, walking down the street, Carella still felt foolish. For if Pepe Miranda had not been inside a church since the day of his baptism, Carella hadn't been inside one – not to pray, at least – since shortly after his confirmation. That was a long, long time ago. Parading down the street now in a priest's long black apparel, feeling the cold hard snout of a .38 against his belly beneath the black cloth, trying to look pious as hell, he

172

felt only foolish. A set of prayer beads was entwined around his right hand. He quickly shifted them to his left, so that his right would be free for a quick draw if it came to that.

'What's the plan?' he asked Byrnes.

'I'll tell Miranda we've got his priest. He'll probably check from the window. Then you go up.'

'Then want?'

'If he wants to confess or something, let him confess. Watch for your chance, and slug him if he turns his back.'

'But you told Father Donovan . . .'

'Yeah, I lied in church,' Byrnes said. 'Actually, Miranda isn't going to make any confession, Steve. He's going to grab you the minute you walk into that apartment, and he's going to use you as a shield when he walks out.'

'What do I do? Wait for my chance and then . . .'

'You do nothing. Let him lead you out. I'll have men on either side of the doorway. The minute he steps into the street, you'd better duck.' Byrnes paused. 'I'd feel a lot happier if I were doing this myself, Steve.'

'Why?' Carella grinned. 'Because I might get killed? My goodness, what a thing to be worrying about.'

'You're not worried about it, huh?'

'Didn't you hear that reporter, Pete?'

'What do you mean?'

'Life is cheap,' Carella answered.

They had come up to the squad car now. Byrnes reached into it for the megaphone. 'You set, Steve?'

'As set as I'll ever be.'

'Steve, we're going to begin blasting the minute he clears the front stoop. The shots will be coming from behind him, but I can't guarantee that all these bums learned anything at the police academy. When you clear the stoop, make a dive for the sidewalk.'

'Okay.'

'Good luck.'

'Thanks.' Carella paused. 'Suppose he just wants to pray a little?'

Byrnes shrugged. 'You've got a set of prayer beads. Use them.' He paused. 'Good luck,' he said again.

'Let's get it moving,' Carella said, 'before I chicken out.'

Byrnes picked up the megaphone and blew into it. '*Miranda?*' he called. There was no answer. '*Miranda?*' Still no answer.

'Maybe he slit his own throat,' Carella whispered.

'*Miranda, this is Lieutenant Byrnes. Can you hear me?*'

'I hear you. What is it?'

'*We've got your priest.*'

'Where is he? Get him out in the middle of the street. I want to see him.'

Carella nodded at Byrnes, and then took a deep breath. Slowly, he walked to the center of the street.

'*You can't see him if you don't look,*' Byrnes said.

There was a long silence. Suddenly, Miranda's head popped up above the window sill. He looked into the street for no longer than ten seconds, and then dropped from sight again. Even in that short a time, Byrnes and Carella saw that his eyes were puffed and his face was streaked.

'All right,' Miranda shouted. 'Send him up.'

'*Not so fast, Miranda,*' Byrnes said, thinking, I've got to make this look good. He knows we wouldn't send up a priest unless he makes some concession. He knows we're considering the idea that this may be a trap. He knows we're not stupid.

'What is it now?' Miranda said.

'*The priest stays right where he is unless I get some promises from you*,' Byrnes said.

'Here we go,' Miranda answered, and the people in the street began chuckling.

'*Yes, here we go, Miranda. I'm not sending up a man you can use as a shield to get out of that apartment.*'

'What kind of a louse do you think I am?'

'*Do I have to answer that one?*' Byrnes said, and again the crowd chuckled. This was beginning to get good. None of that grim stuff any more. Just a plain old battle of wits, like a good television routine.

'All right, cop, what do you want from me?'

'*Number one: we're sending up an unarmed man who insists he wants to see you alone as a representative of God. I want you to respect that, Miranda.*' God forgive me, Byrnes thought.

'All right, all right.'

'*Number two: I want you to talk to him. About coming out of there. I don't know why you want to see him, and I don't care. But I want your promise that you'll talk to him about coming out.*'

'Is that all?'

'*Do I have your promise?*'

'What makes you think I'll keep any promise I make?'

'*This is a man of God, Miranda.*'

'Okay, okay, I promise.'

'*Did you hear him, Father?*' Byrnes asked Carella.

'I heard him,' Carella answered.

'*You can enter the building any time you like.*'

Carella nodded, sucked in another deep breath, walked directly to the front stoop of the tenement, and entered the hallway.

Byrnes put down the megaphone, looked at his watch, and then told Captain Frick he wanted four of the best marksmen he could find. Then he began praying.

16.

IF YOU'RE GOD, you've got all these little things to take care of, you see. Oh, not the business of getting the sun to rise on time, or the stars to come out. And not riding herd on the seasons so that they arrive when they're supposed to, not things like that. Those are the big things, and the big things almost take care of themselves. It's those damn *little* things that get so bothersome. And if you're God, you can't just ignore them, you know. You can, of course, move in mysterious ways your wonders to perform. This means that you can leave a few loose ends here and there and nobody will question them because you are, after all, God. Maybe you've got a bigger design in mind which will not become apparent to us poor slobs until maybe decades from now. Or centuries. So who are we to question? Being God, you are perfectly entitled to occasional sloppiness.

Or maybe these things aren't even in your control, who knows? Maybe you just sort of set the universe every day, the way somebody sets a clock, and then let it run on its own, fast or slow, however it wants to, without touching it again until it's run down and needs another winding. Maybe that's the way you operate, and nobody's going to question that either, God, you can bet your life on that, God.

Only sometimes, no offense meant, you ought to work a thing out and not just let it happen, you know? Like take that Puerto Rican girl and that sailor, take them for example. Now, being God, you could fix them up real fine, couldn't you? Like, for example, Zip and Cooch could find her, you see, and Zip is dragging her down the street towards Alfie's pad when *wham!* who should appear? The sailor! How's that, huh? He didn't go off with the whore Marge, you see. He only started to, but then he changed his mind. And here he is back on the street, face to face with China. He looks at her, and she looks at him, and their eyes lock, and slowly they walk across that street to each other, and tolerance and understanding flash in the sailor's eyes, *I love you, China*, coupled with a little bit of honest lust, *I love you, Jeff, wham* they clinch, and we fade out on Zip who shrugs his shoulders and says, 'Oh well, what the hell, easy come, easy go.'

How's that, God?

That's great.

But that isn't the way it happened.

The street was impossible. The crowd was anxious for the kill now, anxious for the die to be cast either way. They didn't much give a damn at this moment whether or not Miranda would kill the priest and the police lieutenant and the commissioner and the mayor and the governor and even the president. They didn't care whether or not a cop on one of the rooftops would fire a lucky shot and catch Miranda *splank* between the eyeballs. They only wanted it to be over and done with, either way. And so the crowd was restless, and a little mean, and hot, and uncomfortable. It was a crowd which was beginning to resent this tie game which had run into fourteen innings. The tenth inning had been a treat and the eleventh a distinct bonus and the twelfth a lovely dividend, but the thirteenth brought on thoughts of other things to be done. Watching a game was great fun – but life was real and life was earnest, and life was going on *outside* that ball park.

So the crowd resisted the shoving of Zip and Cooch, and occasionally the crowd shoved back at the two boys and cursed a bit, and did everything possible to make the task of locating China unimaginably difficult.

In fifteen minutes' time, Zip and Cooch gave up the search.

It was just as well that they had, because China wasn't in the neighborhood any longer. China had gone over to the park where she had sat by the lake and watched the people in the rowboats. That's where China was. She cried a little, yes. In the park, by the lake, watching the rowboats.

The sailor? Did he wander back to the street? Did he amble over to the park?

The sailor went to bed with a prostitute named Marge. Marge was a practiced whore, and she pleased the sailor immensely. The sailor paid her fifteen dollars, which was nearly every cent he had. Then he walked to the subway, got on a train, went downtown to where his ship was docked, started up the gangway, saluted the ensign on the fantail, saluted the officer of the deck, went to the rear compartment, took off his whites, put on a pair of dungarees and a chambray shirt, climbed into his sack, and went to sleep until the loud-speaker amidships announced, 'Chow down.' He ate a good dinner, saw a movie on the boat deck that evening, went to bed about eleven o'clock, and sailed for San Diego the next morning. He never saw the Puerto Rican girl named China again in his life. He probably went back to Fletcher, Colorado, eventually. Maybe she flashed into his mind every now and then – like once every twelve years. Maybe he remembered her dimly and wondered what had become of her. Maybe, married to Corrine and running an insurance business, he sporadically thought of China in an idealized way, the most beautiful girl in the world, exotic, that day in a strange city, far away, I wonder what became of her, I wonder.

She sat in the park and wept a bit and watched the rowboats.

You are God, and you can do it any way you want to. You can even get them married the next day before his ship sails. Anything you want to do. All the possibilities are there. And you're God, and there isn't anyone who's going to slap your wrist, no matter how you do it.

But God, man, that is the way it happened.

Steve Carella knocked on the door. There were bullet holes in the door, and Carella remembered that Pepe Miranda had shot a patrolman through that door, and he suddenly wanted his .38 in his hand.

Now, easy, he told himself. Now just take it easy, and don't panic. We are going to play this Miranda's way because there are a lot of people out there on the street, and we don't want them to be getting shot. So be cool. Your hand is shaking, and you are itching to pull that .38 so that you'll have something more than a set of prayer beads in your fist when that door opens, but be cool, Steve-o, be cool and . . .

The door opened.

A .45 automatic was the first thing Carella saw. The door opened just a crack, and there was the .45, its big ugly snout pointing into the hallway. Carella's mouth felt very dry.

'I'm . . . Father Donovan,' he said to the automatic.

The door opened wider. Carella's eyes panned up from the .45, the hand holding it, the thin wrist, the black hair curling on the arm, the narrow shoulders, the sweat-stained undershirt, the sudden puff of black hair in the hollow of the throat, the wings of the man's collarbones, his thin neck, and high cheekbones, brown eyes, puffed lids, a balding head, and desperation. Add a man up, add the parts, form a total picture, and the total is desperation. It was there in Miranda's eyes and in his mouth and even in the way he held the .45, his head tilted to one side, his shoulder sort of leaning into the gun, the gun close to his body as if it were something he cherished, a tie to reality.

'Come in a minute,' Miranda said.

Carella stepped into the apartment. The place was a shambles. The furniture, the floors, everything in the room bore the ravaging marks of gunfire. It was in-conceivable to think that a human being had been in this bullet-pocked room and managed to escape getting shot.

'Looks like they dropped an atom bomb in here, don't it?' Miranda said.

'Yes,' Carella answered.

'You're not scared, are you? They won't shoot with you in here, it's all right.'

Carella nodded. He was not scared. It was only . . . he felt odd all at once. He did not feel like a cop. Miranda was not treating him as if he were a cop. Miranda was behaving as if he were truly a priest, a person he could talk to, relax with. He wanted to say, 'I'm not what you think, Miranda! Don't show yourself to me!' but the words would not come.

'Boy, this has been murder,' Miranda said. 'Look, I didn't ask you up here to confess to you or nothing. I think we ought to get that straight.'

'Then why did you ask me to come up?'

'Well . . .' Miranda shrugged. He seemed like a young kid in that moment, a young kid who is about to tell a priest that he took off a girl's underpants on the roof. Carella kept staring at him. Miranda held the .45 in his hand loosely, expecting no trouble from this man he thought was a priest, embarrassed because he was about to reveal something dishonorable to him. 'I'll put it to you straight, Father,' he said. 'I got to get out of this apartment.'

'Yes?'

'So . . . so you're going to take me out.'

'I am?'

Miranda nodded. 'I know that's pretty crumby. But I got to get out of here.'

'Where do you go from here, Pepe?'

'I don't know.' Miranda shook his head. 'You know, Father, you reach the point where . . . where there ain't many places left to go.' He laughed nervously. 'Where . . .' He laughed again. 'I don't know. I don't know where I'll go once I get out of here.'

'There're a lot of cops out there, Pepe.'

'Yeah, I know.' He sighed. 'Man, this kind of stuff . . . I *hate* this kind of Public Enemy Number One stuff, you dig? I just hate it. Oh man, it's like . . . like something is expected of me, you know what I mean? I've *got* to be the bad guy. I don't know if it makes any sense to you, Father.'

'I'm not sure it does,' Carella answered, puzzled.

'Well, like . . . like there are sides. I'm the bad guy.' He shrugged. 'I've *always* been the bad guy. Ever since I was a kid. So I'm still the bad guy. They expect me to be the bad guy. The people, I mean. It's like . . . I don't know if I can explain this. It's like sometimes I don't know who is the real Pepe Miranda, and who is the guy

I . . . the *pictures* of the guy, you follow? The various *pictures* of the guy.'

'I don't know what you mean,' Carella said.

'The *pictures*,' Miranda repeated. 'Like the cops have a picture of me.' He chuckled. 'It's got a number right across the face of it.' He chuckled again. 'And the people in the street got another picture of me. And the kids got a picture. And *you* got a picture. But they're all different pictures, and none of them are really me, Pepe Miranda.'

'Then who is?' Carella asked.

'I don't know.'

'You've killed people, Pepe.'

'Yeah.' He paused. 'I know.' He shrugged, but it was not a shrug of indifference, not a shrug which said, 'So I killed people, so what?' If it had been that, Carella would have instantly felt like a cop again. But it was not that. It was simply a shrug which said, 'I know I've killed people, but I don't know why,' and so Carella still felt like a man who had come up here to *talk* to Miranda, not to harm him.

'Well, anyway,' Miranda said, 'I've got to get out of here.'

'Because the people in the street expect it?' Carella asked.

'No. No, I don't think that's . . .'

'Then why?'

'Well . . .' Miranda sighed heavily. 'I ain't got a chance, Father,' he said simply.

'Then give up.'

'Why? Go to jail? Maybe the electric chair if that woman dies? Don't you see? I got nothing to lose.'

He recognized in an instant that Miranda was absolutely right. Moreover, if Carella were in his position, in this apartment, surrounded by policemen, facing either a lifelong jail sentence or death in the electric chair, he would undoubtedly react in exactly the way that Miranda was reacting. He would try to get out of that apartment by fair means or foul. He would try to escape.

'Well . . .' he said, and he fell silent.

The two men faced each other.

'You see what I mean, Father?'

'Well . . .'

Miranda shrugged. The apartment was silent.

'So . . . so I got to use you as a shield, Father. They won't shoot if I come out with you in front of me.'

'Suppose they refuse to recognize . . .'

'Oh, they won't. They won't try nothing. I'll tell them I'll shoot you if they try anything.'

'And if they *should* try anything? *Will* you shoot me, Pepe?'

Pepe Miranda frowned.

'*Will* you, Pepe?'

After a long while he said, 'I got to get out of this apartment, Father. *I got to get out of here!*'

There were two patrolmen on either side of the stoop. Captain Frick had chosen them from his ranks, had chosen four of his best shots, and then they had gone to Lieutenant Byrnes for their instructions. Their instructions were simple. Shoot to kill.

And so they waited on either side of the doorway now, four marksmen with their pistols drawn, waiting for something to happen.

From the first-floor windows of the tenement, Miranda's voice came.

'Lieutenant!'

'*Yes?*'

'This is Miranda! I've got the priest. I'm coming out.'

'*What do you mean, Miranda? You're giving up?*'

'Giving up, my ass! The priest is coming out with me. If you've got any cops in the hallway, you'd better get them out now. You hear me?'

'It's gonna work,' Parker whispered to Byrnes.

'*There are no policemen in the hallway, Miranda.*'

'There better not be. I want a clear path when I come out. This priest is staying with me all the way. Anybody so much as looks cockeyed at me, the priest gets it.'

'*I thought you made a promise, Miranda.*'

'Don't make me laugh! I'm coming out.'

Byrnes put down the megaphone and quickly drew his revolver. He turned slightly, so that his body hid the revolver which hung in his hand alongside his right thigh. Parker drew his gun, too, and then looked around for a good spot from which to fire. Behind the squad car? No, no. There! There was a place! The packing crate over there. He pushed his way through the crowd and climbed onto the crate. He checked the chambers of his .38, wiped his upper lip, and then faced the doorway. The street was very silent now. Upstairs, inside the building, they could hear a door slamming.

'Any cops in the hallway?' Miranda shouted. 'Any cops here?'

There was no answer. Standing, watching the doorway, watching the patrolmen flanking the stoop, Byrnes thought, *All he has to do is turn his head. He'll see the patrolmen, and he'll put a bullet in Steve's back. That's all he has to do.* Patiently, Byrnes held his breath.

'I got the priest!' Miranda shouted from the hallway. 'Don't try nothing, you hear?'

The crowd had turned toward the doorway to the building. They could see nothing beyond the door. The hallway was dark, and the bright sunshine did not reach beyond the flat top step of the stoop.

'Clear a path!' Miranda shouted. 'Clear a path, or I'll shoot into the crowd! I don't care who gets hurt!'

The crowd could see a pair of figures in the hallway now, dimly. The priest was almost invisible because of his black cassock, but Miranda could be seen fairly clearly, a short thin man in a white undershirt. They hesitated in the vestibule, and Miranda peered past Carella's shoulder and into the street.

Zip pushed his way through the crowd with Cooch. The street was terribly silent, and he wanted to know why. What the hell was happening? He was angry because they'd been unable to locate China, angry because he wanted this Alfredo Gomez thing to end now, angry because things seemed to be going wrong, and he wanted them to go right. But, in spite of his anger, he was curious. The silence intrigued him. He pushed up to the barricade just as Carella and Miranda came onto the front stoop.

Miranda's eyes flicked the street. He was partially covered by the priest, so that a shot from across the street could not be risked. That left only . . .

And Miranda turned to look to the left of the stoop.

Carella was ready. He'd been waiting for the movement ever since they'd left the apartment. He'd been wondering where he would look if he were Miranda, and he'd realized that nobody could shoot from the other side of the street, and so any trap would have to be set on this side of the street, any shots would have to come from behind.

So Carella knew that Miranda knew, and he'd been waiting for the sideward movement of Miranda's head because he had further reasoned that Miranda would begin shooting the second he saw the cops on either side of the stoop.

Zip saw the cops the same moment Miranda did. It was too late to shout a warning.

Carella felt Miranda's head and eyes flickering to the left.

Go! he told himself.

He went.

No one said a word. Miranda turned toward Carella in the same instant that Carella threw himself headlong down the flight of steps.

And then the shooting started.

17.

'PEPE!' ZIP YELLED. 'Pepe!' But he was too late.

The crossfire was true crossfire. Miranda whirled to the left, and the bullets suddenly smashed into him from the right side of the stoop, spinning him around. He slammed into the railing and fired a shot at the patrol-man who seemed closest to him, and then suddenly there were shots on his left, and he realized he was caught in a deadly crossfire, and he ran off the stoop toward where Carella lay sprawled at the foot of the steps. Byrnes began firing from the other side of the street, and Parker began firing from the crate, and then it seemed that every cop on that block had been waiting for just this moment because the street suddenly reverberated with ear-shattering sound as the bullets caromed into the gutter.

He seemed to be bleeding from a dozen places.

The white undershirt seemed to sprout blood like poppies in an instant. His own gun kept bucking in his hand, but there was blood dripping from his face and into his eyes, and he just fired blindly and sort of groped out toward the crowd as if he were reaching for salvation and didn't know whose face held it.

Parker came down off the crate, his service revolver trembling in his hand. The cops on the rooftops stopped firing all at once, and the men behind Miranda stopped firing as he stumbled blindly across the street, moving toward Parker who was similarly drawn toward him. It was almost as if someone had placed two magnetic figures on a long table. They moved toward each other inexorably, Miranda blinded by blood, and Parker drawn into that street by something he would never understand.

Miranda's gun clicked empty, and he looked at Parker in supplication, blood dripping into his eyes and bubbling out of his mouth, the mouth open, the hands limp now, the head twisted to one side like a Christ who had climbed down from the cross.

'Give me a break,' Miranda whispered.

And Parker fired.

His shot took Miranda in the throat at close range, nearly ripping away the back of his neck. A fresh blossom of blood erupted, exposing Miranda's windpipe as he staggered forward again. His voice bubbled from his torn throat, a whispered voice that sounded as if it were coming from one of those trick underwater recording chambers, a voice directed only to Parker, a voice that sought out Parker on that spinning red street.

'Can't you . . . can't you give me a break?' And again Parker fired. And this time, he kept his finger on the trigger, tightening the pressure each time a slug roared from the barrel of the gun, watching the slugs rip into Miranda, watching Miranda topple into the gutter lifelessly, and then standing over him and pumping bullets into his body until his gun was empty, and then grabbing a gun from the patrolman standing next to him and beginning to fire at the dead Miranda.

'That's enough,' Carella shouted.

Zip pushed past the barricade and flung himself at Parker's back. Parker brushed him off like a pesky fly, swinging his huge shoulders, knocking Zip to the pavement.

'Leave him alone!' Zip shouted. 'Leave him alone!'

But Parker was hearing nothing. He fired the

patrolman's gun at Miranda's head, and then he fired again, and he was preparing to fire a third time when Carella grabbed his arms and pulled him away from the body.

'Somebody get up there to Frankie!' Lieutenant Byrnes shouted. 'On the double!'

Two patrolmen rushed into the tenement. Byrnes walked over to Miranda and stared down at him.

'Is he dead?' a reporter called.

Byrnes nodded. There was no triumph in his voice. 'He's dead.'

'They killed him,' Zip said to Cooch. 'They killed him. The bastards killed him.' He clutched Cooch frantically. 'Where's Sixto? Where's Papá? We're gonna get him now, you hear me, Cooch? They killed Pepe, Cooch. You understand that? They killed him!' His eyes were wild. A thin layer of sweat covered his entire face.

'What about China?' Cooch asked. 'You said we needed China to . . .'

'The hell with China! Alfie's gonna get his, you hear?'

A patrolman appeared on the fire escape. The street went quiet. He walked to where Frankie Hernandez lay still and silent, and he knelt down, and Byrnes waited. The patrolman stood up.

'Lieutenant?'

'Yes?'

'Frankie.' The patrolman paused. 'He's dead, sir.'

Byrnes nodded. He nodded again. And then he realized the patrolman was waiting for instructions and, still nodding, he said, 'Bring him down. Off there. Off the fire escape. Would you . . . would you bring him down, please?'

The reporters had pushed past the barricade now, and

they surrounded the body of the dead Miranda. Flash bulbs popped on the street, challenging the sunshine.

'Where's Sixto and Papá?' Zip asked. 'Didn't I say to meet me here?'

'Look, Zip, calm down. Try to . . .'

'Don't tell me what to do!' Zip shouted, shaking Cooch's hand loose. 'I know what I'm . . .' and he stopped talking.

Sixto and Papá had turned the corner, but it was not *their* appearance which had caused the sudden widening of Zip's eyes. He stared at the two boys and then he stared at their companion, and he balled his fists, because the person with them was Alfredo Gomez.

'Wha— ?' he started, and in that instant two patrolmen came from the doorway of the tenement, carrying the body of Frankie Hernandez on a stretcher. The people in the crowd began murmuring his name as the body went past. Handkerchiefs appeared, and women sniffled into them. The men in the crowd were taking off their hats and holding them to their chests.

'It's Frankie,' Luís said. 'Close the doors! For respect! For respect!' He reached up for the overhead door of the luncheonette and pulled it down. On the avenue side of the shop another man pulled down the door there, so that the shop faced the street blindly – *We will not conduct business while you pass by, my friend* – as the patrolmen carried the body of Hernandez toward the ambulance.

'Can we get a few more pictures of Miranda, Lieutenant?' one of the reporters asked.

'Take all the pictures you want,' Byrnes said. 'He's in no hurry. Not any more.'

Luís rolled back the doors. The shop was open again.

'What happens now, Lieutenant?' the reporter asked.

Byrnes sighed heavily. 'We pile him in the meat wagon, and we cart him off. I get my men off the streets. Try to unsnarl the traffic. And then take up a collection for a good cop. I don't know. What happens next?' He turned to Carella. 'Steve?'

'Yeah?'

'Who's gonna tell Frankie's father? Who's gonna go into that candy store around the corner, where he's got Frankie's picture pasted to the mirror, who's gonna go in there and tell him Frankie is dead?'

'I'll do it if you like, Pete.'

'No,' Byrnes said, sighing and shaking his head. 'It's my job.'

'We really nailed him, didn't we?' Parker said, striding over. 'We really nailed the son of a—'

'Shut up, Parker!' Byrnes snapped.

'Wh— ?'

'Shut your goddamn mouth!'

'Wh-what the hell is wrong *now*?' Parker asked, his face taking on a hurt and astonished look.

Sixto, Papá, and Alfredo stood near the luncheonette. Zip walked to them quickly.

'What is this, Sixto?' he asked.

'What do you think it is, Zip?'

'I don't like guessing games. What are you up to?'

'I tell you, Zip,' Sixto said simply. 'If you wann to kill Alfredo, you got to kill us all.'

'What the hell are you talking about, you meatball?'

'I say it pretty plain, Zip.'

'You know me an' Cooch are heeled? You know we can blast you all over the sidewalk?'

'*Sí*, we know,' Sixto said. 'Go ahead. Blast us all ov' the sidewalk.'

'What do you . . . ?' Zip stopped and looked into

Sixto's eyes. Slightly unnerved, he said, 'What do you —
mean?'

'Be careful, Zip,' Cooch said quickly. 'They got something up their sleeves. I can see it. They're too . . .
they're too sure of themselves.'

'Sixto's got them buffaloed,' Zip said quickly. He
turned his attention to Papá. 'You're on the wrong side,
Papá. You stick with Sixto, and it's like siding with the
ones who killed Pepe. You'd be . . .'

'Pepe brings disgrace to the *barrio*,' Papá said.

'All right, that's enough pictures,' Byrnes shouted.
'Let's get him out of here, huh?'

Two patrolmen reached down and rolled Miranda onto
a stretcher. Another patrolman threw a blanket over
him. Gingerly, they stepped around the pool of blood
in the gutter and began moving toward the luncheonette.

'The doors!' Zip shouted. 'Close the doors for him!'

But no one moved toward the doors. Instead, the
people in the street watched the body as it passed by,
and slowly, one by one, they turned their backs to it, so
that the body, as the cops carried it toward the luncheonette, was presented with a solid wall of denial.

'The doors!' Zip shouted again. 'We should close the
doors!'

But no one moved. One by one, they denied the body
of Miranda, and then — silently, so silently — they began
moving off the street. What had been a milling, shouting mob not ten minutes ago was suddenly a dispersing
group of whispering people, and then not even a group
any more, simply a few stragglers, people in twos and
threes; and then the street barricades were carted away,
and the squad cars revved their engines, and the street
seemed to settle down into its Sunday niche again, quiet,

peaceful. It almost seemed as if nothing had happened on that street that day.

Zip stood before the opened doors and watched the body of Miranda shoved into the ambulance, and then he whirled toward Sixto and shouted, 'You think you're gonna get away with this?'

'Move aside, Zip,' Sixto said calmly. 'We wann to get through now.'

'You won't be able to walk the street no more!' Zip shouted. 'You think you . . .'

'We'll see,' Sixto said, and the three boys stepped away from the luncheonette, and walked past Zip and Cooch who did not move to stop them.

'You're making a mistake!' Zip yelled after them. 'You're making a *big mistake*!' But he did not run after them, and he did not try to stop them. 'Why didn't you help me, Cooch?' he said suddenly, angrily. 'For Christ's sake, we just let them walk *away*, for Christ's sake!'

'They're . . . they're too strong, Zip,' Cooch said in a whisper.

'We're the ones with the guns!' Zip protested.

'Yeah, but . . . they . . . they were strong,' Cooch said, and his voice fell.

'Aw—' Zip made a meaningless little gesture with his right hand. 'Aw—' He stared off down the street. The squad cards had pulled away now. Patrolmen were still lingering on the block, but most of the police were gone. The street stretched ahead in sticky blackness washed with hot sunshine. On the avenue, the traffic had started up again. 'Jesus, what a . . . what a miserable day this turned out to be,' Zip said, and he looked at Cooch with troubled eyes.

'Yeah,' Cooch said softly.

Zip looked back at the street, and then he sighed

heavily. 'Well . . . what do you want to do the . . . the rest of the afternoon, Cooch?'

'I don't know,' Cooch said.

'Ain't you . . . ain't you got no ideas?'

'We could go to the flicks, I guess.'

'Yeah,' Zip said emptily.

'Or play some stickball, maybe.'

'Yeah.'

'Maybe go for a swim at the pool.'

'Yeah. Yeah, maybe we could do that.' He turned his head suddenly and jerkily because he did not want Cooch to see the tears that had sprung into his eyes. Nor did he know why he was crying. It was just that, all at once, in the heart of one of the biggest cities in the world, Zip had felt all alone, utterly alone, and the enormity of the city and the inconsequence of himself had – had suddenly frightened him.

'I guess – I guess we'll find something,' he said, and he thrust his hands into his pockets, and the two boys walked up the sun-drenched street, their heads bent.

Andy Parker passed them on his way to the luncheonette. He glanced at them, shrugged, and went in to say hello to his friend Luís.

'You still sore at me, Luís?' he asked, as if this had been troubling him all along, as if it were important for him to know that Luís was not angry.

'No, Andy,' Luís said.

'Everybody's sore at me,' Parker said blankly. He paused. 'Why's everybody sore at me?' He paused again. 'I do my job.' He looked up at Luís. 'I'm sorry I yelled at you, Luís.'

'It doesn't matter.'

'Well, I'm sorry.'

He stared at Luís. And because Luís was a human

195

being, and because apologies are never sincere unless they are tested, unless someone hurls into the face of 'I'm sorry,' the unforgiving reply, 'who cares whether you're sorry or not? Go drop dead in a corner!' and gets one or two further responses. Gets, 'In any case, I really am sorry,' or gets, 'Well if that's the way you feel, go to hell!' and knows by these further responses whether the apology was real to begin with, being human, Luís tested the apology.

'You should have thought of that before you spoke,' he said, and his eyes narrowed, and he waited for Parker's answer.

Parker nodded. 'I should have,' Parker agreed. 'I'm sorry.'

The men stared at each other. There was nothing further to say for now. Perhaps there was nothing further to say *ever*.

'Well, I . . . I better get back to the squad,' Parker said.

'*Sí*.'

Parker waved, seemed to become embarrassed in the middle of the gesture, and let his hand drop. Slowly, he shuffled off up the street.

A reporter walked into the luncheonette and took a stool. 'Well, everything quiet again, huh?' he said. 'Let me have a cup of coffee, huh?'

'*Sí*, everything quiet,' Luís answered.

'Just like the island, huh?' the reporter said.

Instantly, Luís answered, 'No, not just like the island,' and then he paused, and then he looked at the reporter, and then he said, 'But maybe not so bad anyway, eh? Maybe not so bad.'

Down the street, the church bells began tolling.

Books by Ed McBain

☐ **Alice in Jeopardy** £6.99
978-0-7528-5791-6

☐ **The Pusher** £6.99
978-0-7528-5793-0

☐ **The Con Man** £6.99
978-0-7528-5794-7

☐ **'Til Death** £6.99
978-0-7528-5795-4

☐ **King's Ransom** £6.99
978-0-7528-5796-1

☐ **Give the Boys a Great Big Hand** £6.99
978-0-7528-5979-8

☐ **The Heckler** £6.99
978-0-7528-6378-8

☐ **See Them Die** £6.99
978-0-7528-6379-5

☐ **Lady, Lady I Did It** £6.99
978-0-7528-6410-5

The Pusher

Two a.m. in the bitter cold of winter: the young Hispanic man's body is found in a tenement basement. The rope around his neck suggests a clear case of suicide – until the autopsy reveals he'd overdosed on heroin.

He was a pusher, and now a thousand questions press down on the detectives of the 87th Precinct.

Who set up the phony hanging? Whose fingerprints were on the syringe found at the scene? Who was making threatening phone calls, attempting to implicate Lieutenant Byrnes' teenage son? Somebody is pushing the 87th Precinct hard, and Detective Steve Carella and Lieutenant Pete Byrnes have to push back harder – before a frightening and deadly chain tightens its grip.

Like Love

A young girl jumps to her death. A salesman gets blown apart. Two semi-naked bodies are found dead on a bed with all the hallmarks of a love pact . . .

Spring really was here for the 87th Precinct.

Steve Carella and Cotton Hawes thought the double suicide stank of homicide, but they just couldn't get a break. Fortunately Hawes has something else going on in his life at the moment – something like love.

Give The Boys a Great Big Hand

The mystery man wore black, and he was a real cut-up king. Why else was he leaving blood-red severed hands all over the city? Was he an everyday maniac with a meat cleaver, or did he have a special grudge against the 87th Precinct?

Steve Carella and Cotton Hawes went along with the grudge theory, because the black-cloaked killer didn't leave any clues to go on – the grisly hands even had the fingertips sliced off. And how do you nail a murderer when you can't identity or unearth most of his victims?

That's what the boys of the 87th Precinct have to do: find a killer before he carves up any more corpseless hands.

King's Ransom

Wealthy Douglas King has received a ransom demand. But it isn't his own son who has been kidnapped, it's his chauffeur's. If he pays up, it could ruin the biggest deal he ever made in his life, and throw away his future. But is the alternative to sacrifice a child's life?

Detective Steve Carella and the rest of the 87th Precinct can only keep trying to nab the kidnappers and hope that Doug King decides to give them the payoff. But if King doesn't play ball, they'll have a cold-blooded murder on their hands . . .

Cop Hater

When Detective Reardon is found dead, motive is a big question mark. But when his partner becomes victim number two, it looks like open-and-shut grudge killings. That is, until the third detective is murdered.

With one meagre clue, Detective Steve Carella begins his grim search for the killer, a search that takes him into the city's underworld to a notorious brothel, to the apartment of a beautiful and dangerous widow and, finally, to a .45 automatic aimed straight at his head . . .

The Mugger

The mugger was special. He preyed only on women. He waited in the darkness, coming from behind to snatch their purses. He punched his victims, told them not to scream and, as the women reeled with pain and fear, he bowed and said 'Clifford thanks you, madam.'

The cops in the 87th precinct are not amused. Especially when he puts one victim in hospital – and the next one in the morgue. The dead girl was pretty, and only seventeen. And patrolman Bert Kling has a personal reason to go after her murderer. A reason that becomes a burning obsession and an easy way for a cop to get killed . . .

The Empty Hours

She was young, wealthy – and dead. Strangled to death in a slum apartment. All they had to go on was her name and some cancelled cheques. As Steve Carella said, 'Those cheques are the diary of her life. We'll find the answer there.' But how was he to know that they would reveal something much stranger than murder?

On Passover the rabbi bled to death. Someone had brutally stabbed him and painted a J on the synagogue wall. Everyone knew who the killer was – it had to be Finch, the Jew-hater. Or did it . . . ?

The snow was pure white except where Cotton Hawes stared down at the bright red pool of blood spreading away from the dead girl's body. Hawes was supposed to be on a skiing holiday, but he couldn't just stand by and watch the local cops make a mess of the case. He had to catch the ski-slope slayer before he killed again.

Lady, Lady I Did It

October on the 87th Precinct. Indian Summer. Telephones ring lazily in the police squad room. Tired cops slump at their desks, measuring their hours with cups of coffee.

Then it happened. A multiple murder in a downtown bookshop. Four people are dead, and one of them is Detective Bert Kling's fiancée. The summer was over.

There's no time for tears – and Kling was the first to admit it. There are clues to find, leads to follow, people to see. And Kling was going to get the sonofabitch who murdered the only person in the world he cared for. For him, it would be a long, cold winter . . .

Alice in Jeopardy

Alice thought she had lost everything when her husband's yacht was found empty and adrift. He had slipped out to sail under the stars and is never going to come back. A year on, Alice and her two children are still struggling to come to terms with their new life – but troubles are only just beginning . . .

One sunny day, Alice's children don't come home. The police are caught up in interdepartmental battles and Alice, now very much alone in the world, believes that the only way to save her children is to find them herself. But as the questions multiply, the answers seem more elusive than ever.

'Til Death

The groom in question is Tommy Giordano – and he's about to marry Steve Carella's sister, Angela. So the wedding party suddenly becomes a deadly game of hide-and-seek for Steve and the boys of the 87th Precinct.

Tommy is 'it' and Steve has only a few hours to find a killer and prevent Tommy from being tagged out for good.

But how do you find a murderer with hundreds of wedding guests to choose from? Is it Tommy's best man, who would collect everything the groom owns if the killer finds his mark? Or Ben Darcy, who is still madly in love with the bride and would do anything to get her back? Or what about the crazy ex-GI who swore he'd get revenge against Tommy?

Carella has to work fast, or someone is going to make Angela a widow on her wedding day . . .

The Con Man

A trickster taking money from an old woman for his own private charity. A cheater fleecing the businessmen of their thousands with the oldest gimmick in town. A lady-killer after the ladies' dollars with just a little bit of love . . .

The guys of the 87th Precinct thought they knew every trick in the book – so why are there bodies still washing up on the shore?

The Con Man: handsome, charming – and deadly.

All Orion/Phoenix titles are available at your local bookshop or from the following address:

Mail Order Department
Littlehampton Book Services
FREEPOST BR535
Worthing, West Sussex, BN13 3BR
telephone 01903 828503, *facsimile* 01903 828802
e-mail MailOrders@lbsltd.co.uk
(Please ensure that you include full postal address details)

Payment can be made either by credit/debit card (Visa, Mastercard, Access and Switch accepted) or by sending a £ Sterling cheque or postal order made payable to *Littlehampton Book Services*.
DO NOT SEND CASH OR CURRENCY.

Please add the following to cover postage and packing

UK and BFPO:
£1.50 for the first book, and 50p for each additional book to a maximum of £3.50

Overseas and Eire:
£2.50 for the first book plus £1.00 for the second book and 50p for each additional book ordered

---

BLOCK CAPITALS PLEASE

name of cardholder ....

address of cardholder ....

....

....

postcode ....

delivery address
(if different from cardholder)

....

....

....

postcode ....

☐ I enclose my remittance for £ ....

☐ please debit my Mastercard/Visa/Access/Switch (delete as appropriate)

card number ☐☐☐☐☐☐☐☐☐☐☐☐☐☐☐☐☐☐

expiry date ☐☐☐☐   Switch issue no. ☐☐

signature ....

prices and availability are subject to change without notice